Dedalus Original

BORDER LINES

Ros Franey's first novel *Cry Baby* was published by Dedalus in 1987 and reprinted in 2023 as part of the Dedalus Retro list.

She has worked as a journalist and producer of television documentaries and has written non-fiction as well as fiction. A revised and updated edition of her book about the Guildford bombing case and the IRA, *Time Bomb*, written with Grant McKee, was published in 2024.

Border Lines is her third novel.

Ros Franey

BORDER LINES

Dedalus

Supported using public funding by
**ARTS COUNCIL
ENGLAND**

Published in the UK by Dedalus Limited
24-26, St Judith's Lane, Sawtry, Cambs, PE28 5XE
info@dedalusbooks.com
www.dedalusbooks.com

ISBN printed book 978 1 915568 73 1
ISBN ebook 978 1 915568 76 2

Dedalus is distributed in the USA & Canada by SCB Distributors
15608 South New Century Drive, Gardena, CA 90248
info@scbdistributors.com www.scbdistributors.com

Dedalus is distributed in Australia by Peribo Pty Ltd
58, Beaumont Road, Mount Kuring-gai, N.S.W. 2080
info@peribo.com.au www.peribo.com.au

First published by Dedalus in 2025
Border Lines copyright © Ros Franey 2025

The right of Ros Franey to be identified as the author of this work has been
asserted by her in accordance with the Copyright, Designs and Patents Act,
1988.

Printed and bound in the UK by Clays Elcograf S.p.A.
Typeset by Marie Lane

To Elinor and Maya

who heard the start of this story
— and encouraged me to finish it —
when we walked in the west of Ireland
one January, long ago.

CHAPTER 1

Autumn 1997

On the morning Daniel Booth's life was to change forever, he made toast, fed the cat and set out for Whitehall, just as he did every day of the working week.

The document arrived in his morning mail. He knew it must be a mistake, yet his colleague Vernon Potts said mistakes were as impossible as a cash dispenser paying out the wrong amount of money. Daniel had noticed that although Vernon was new to the department, he was very certain of everything.

'Computers don't make mistakes,' Vernon assured him. 'The only thing to go wrong with computers is the human beings that program them.' Daniel rummaged through the jumble of news releases, periodicals, information briefings on his desk and found the brown internal envelope: BOOTH,

D, 105, his room number, handwritten. The error was human. A quick glance told him the document was about Northern Ireland: no surprises there. What was the British Army getting up to now? He started to read. It was in the form of a memo, most of it taken up with a list of places, numbers beside them. A few of the places he had never heard of but others were familiar, and not in a good way. Something about the document didn't feel right: this was definitely not for him. Stuffing it back into its envelope, he took it to his boss, Tiffin, and pointed out the error.

'I'm not cleared for this. It must be for one of the others.'

Major Tiffin was the senior information officer. 'Damn cretins downstairs. Did you read it?'

'No, Major.' If the minister could lie to Parliament, he told himself, Daniel could lie to Willy Tiffin.

'Good man. Done the right thing. Let's see…' He reached for the internal directory then, taking a new envelope from a stack beside him, wrote the correct address. 'Thank you, Daniel. Bad mistake. Pop it back in the post, there's a good chap. I've got to shoot off now.' And he bustled out of the room.

Where was Tiffin sending it? The room number scrawled on the new envelope was an inversion of their own: 501, the executive floor. This document must be top secret. Daniel was about to slip it inside when his eye caught the paragraph at the end of the list. He froze. Within half a minute, he had read the whole thing, one hand steadying himself on the corner of his metal desk. *Oh my God*, he breathed. Who knew about this stuff? He read it again: it was surely untrue, yet here it was. He couldn't just let this pass.

The office was deserted and, for once, quiet. Fluorescent lights in the high ceiling illuminated the tattered poster of the Red Devils at Harpenden Air Show. Daniel stood up. In the grimy glass masking the inner well that served the room with fresh air, he saw his mirrored face, the smudges of eyes beneath the hair his mother had called fair but was probably just mousy; a man who at thirty-five felt young, but sensed time slipping quietly away. He thought of the Official Secrets Act he had signed. Is this what it was for: obedience to a set of lies? Clear-headed, he knew he was about to behave badly; and that it was the only decent thing to do.

Carefully folding the top corners to conceal the memo's reference numbers, he walked over to the photocopier and punched in his code. The start button flashed green. Daniel placed the sheet face down on the glass screen and pressed the button. The obsolete copier gave an intestinal rumble but no clean copy slid from its tightly strained jaws; instead, the flashing of three small orange lights and a message with a hint of menace: CLEAR JAM IN AREA 1 OR. Vernon's internal phone rang. Sweat started from Daniel's armpits. He reached across to Vernon's desk and jerked the receiver off its hook. 'Press Office.'

'Oh, hello. Is that the press office?'

'Speaking.'

'Oh, hello. Consignments Section B12 here. I wonder if you can help?'

'I'm afraid the officer you need isn't here at the moment. Can you call back in half an hour?'

'I'm sure you'll do. I'm enquiring about copies of Form M11[b]/B ordered by your section last Thursday…'

Daniel could hear footsteps coming down the corridor. He felt as if arteries were about to explode through his chest. 'Would you hold the line a moment?' he asked.

Vernon swung through the door, the turn-ups of his slightly-too-short grey flannel trousers flapping at his ankles. Daniel's phone rang. 'Christ,' said Vernon.

'This one's for you!' Daniel waved the receiver at him.

Vernon, ignoring him, picked up Daniel's phone instead. 'MOD Press office. Sure. I'll get him for you. *Daily Mail*,' he said to Daniel. 'Challenger 2. You look awful,' he added. Daniel's stomach turned over. They swapped telephones. As he listened to the man from the *Mail*, Daniel's eyes ground into Vernon's back.

'Nothing to do with me, I'm afraid,' Vernon was saying to the woman from Consignments.

'Can you repeat that?' asked Daniel, his mind on the incriminating document stuck inside the machine.

'Call after lunch and speak to Miss Hare,' Vernon instructed in a no-nonsense voice. He put down the receiver and strode towards the photocopier.

'I'll have to phone you back,' Daniel told the man from the *Mail*. He put his hand over the mouthpiece. 'It's broken!' he called to Vernon.

'Bugger,' said Vernon.

Daniel took the number of the man from the *Mail*, rang off and darted over to the copier.

'I've got to distribute the submissions on the AS-90 by three,' Vernon grumbled.

'Bloody madhouse,' Daniel agreed. 'Phones going all over the place. Can't get anything done. And I've got to go to the dentist this afternoon.' He nudged Vernon out of the way. 'CLEAR JAM IN AREA 1 OR...' a second message appeared: '...REFILL CARTRIDGE'. Daniel started to fiddle with the release catch on the paper tray. To his relief it was empty. He refilled it, reset the copier and pressed the button. This time the copied memo peeled into the out-tray. Vernon had lost interest. Daniel carried both papers back to his desk. 'It's all right now,' he said casually.

He slipped the original into the internal envelope Tiffin had addressed earlier and folded the copy into a blank envelope, sealed it and put it in his briefcase. Vernon had seen nothing. Then he opened the file on Challenger and dialled the number of the man from the *Mail*. Bloody tanks. It was definitely time to move on.

*

Perdita Burn stepped out of the restaurant and turned up towards Oxford Circus. Sushi. She felt for the toothbrush in her pocket, mindful of the hygienist. She had fifteen minutes to get to Welbeck Street.

She'd hoped the walk would restore her spirits, but the more she thought about what had just happened, the more unnerved she felt. It wasn't supposed to have been a work meeting. She'd been surprised when Nick had arrived with his briefcase and a young man Perdita had never seen before.

'This is terrific,' said Nick, beaming at Perdita. 'Must be—what? Eighteen months, at least. Perdita saw him notice the absence of her wedding ring. 'You look great,' he told her. She smiled back at him. Nick was her mentor: the man who had given her chances, trusted her judgement on risky occasions. It was for him her best films had been produced. Over the years they had become friends as well as colleagues. So why was this stranger to share their lunch? Perdita turned to Nick's companion expectantly.

'Oh, this is Jeremy,' Nick announced. 'I thought it would be good for him to come and meet the guru.'

Perdita felt neatly dated. She took in Jeremy's expensive haircut, his designer jeans.

Nick was saying, 'Meet the woman who brought us some of our greatest successes, Jeremy. I hope you two can form as good a relationship for the future... As I expect you've read,' he told Perdita, 'Jeremy is our new head boy.'

'Congratulations, Jeremy!' Perdita said. She wondered what this meant.

'You didn't see the piece in *Broadcast?*'

Perdita shook her head. 'I always forget to read *Broadcast,*' she admitted.

Nick's eyes narrowed. 'Unwise, Perdita. You need to keep up with it, otherwise you might miss the news of your own assassination!' If she hadn't read *Broadcast,* he continued, she might not know about the changes.

Perdita's last two films had been for a different channel and she was suddenly on her guard. As soon as the waitress had guided them to a table, Nick in his laconic way informed her that there was to be *restructuring* in Factual. He'd still be around, of course, but Jeremy would be doing the commissioning.

As they talked, Perdita sipped at something she suspected to be seaweed tea and watched Nick carefully. He was looking tired, she noticed, and suddenly felt protective towards him. Had he persuaded himself that his promotion, if that's what it was, would be as interesting as the money? Or had he been given no choice? She realised he was sticking his neck out to introduce her to the new man, and was touched. New men preferred new brooms. Jeremy looked bored.

Despite its menu the restaurant was workaday, no-nonsense. It was not a place you took people for atmosphere.

'Sorry it's not Zulu.' Nick grinned at Jeremy. Jeremy shrugged. Perdita knew Zulu. She had once taken her daughter Daisy there on demand. It was full of people like Jeremy. Perdita knew Nick knew Zulu wouldn't do for Perdita, because Perdita was too old. 'Zulu is so noisy,' said Nick.

As lunch continued, it became clear she was on trial, to be judged by her new ideas. Nick might at least have warned her!

'…Why Afghanistan?' Jeremy was asking. 'So *eighties*, isn't it?'

Perdita turned to him, startled. 'Under the Taliban,' she began, 'women are now being excluded from *hospitals*: just think what that actually means. There's a doctor in Kabul who runs a secret mother-and-baby clinic from her house. She's agreed to let us film—' She broke off. Jeremy was shaking his head.

'It's *niche*, Perdita.'

She blinked. 'It's half the population of the country!'

'…and it's subtitles,' he finished.

Pointless to argue, but Perdita felt a small explosion of rage. 'The doctor trained in Bristol,' she told him evenly. 'Her English is perfect.'

Nick leaned the elbows of his suede jacket on either side of the sushi and said, 'I'm afraid people aren't interested in those things, Perdita. But look at the outpourings last month over Princess Di's death! We should all take lessons from that. A landmark in history wrapped in a story that viewers can engage with.'

Perdita was uneasy. 'Not exactly my territory, is it, all that?'

'Of course not. But what about the response to Helstone B: that got them going, didn't it? Everyone can relate to workers and their kids living under the threat of nuclear contamination. You exploded Britain's bomb!'

For the first time since they had sat down, Perdita sensed the return of Jeremy's attention. 'What do you want?' she asked cautiously. 'If I'd come with more of that, you'd have told me the world's moved on.'

'It set the agenda for an important debate about risk and the price of progress,' Nick assured her.

Jeremy put in, 'We want the same *appointment-to-view* applied to an issue for today.'

This wasn't exactly radical: there must be a catch. 'So...' she ventured, 'we could look at refugees arriving here. The British government are sending back asylum seekers, splitting families, breaking international law, right on our doorstep.'

'Well, that'll really get the advertisers going,' Jeremy said.

Nick frowned at him. There was a silence.

Perdita decided she needed to behave herself. 'Okay, so what's this year's "landmark"?' She paused. 'How about Ireland? The peace?'

Jeremy and Nick exchanged glances. 'Indeed,' said

Jeremy. 'Ireland at the crossroads.'

She nodded. This was more interesting.

'End of the Troubles: hands across the border,' he went on. 'The fusion of two cultures. Two great industries with fractured ideologies: Irish tweed and Ulster linen.'

'I'm sorry?'

'Think of it as a metaphor,' Nick suggested. 'Unity? Unification?'

'Why?'

They both spoke at once. 'WGBH—' Jeremy began.

'Cashmere was a huge success,' said Nick. 'Multi-layered, you see.'

'Fabulous shots.'

'Hang on.' Perdita held up a restraining hand. 'You've made a film in Kashmir, then?'

'Not *separatists*. Of course not,' said Jeremy impatiently.

Nick explained, 'Wool.'

'Wool?'

'The Cashmere wool story. This would be a sort of companion piece.' He couldn't quite meet her eye as he said it.

'We'd have complete editorial freedom, of course,' Jeremy interrupted. 'Co-producers would be nowhere near it.'

'So that's not *niche* then?' She threw them a mischievous look.

Jeremy snapped, 'We can't continue to make your kind of films, you know: worthy, open-ended investigations that don't earn their keep and—let's face it—viewers won't come to.'

Perdita, furious, shot back, 'And the Princess Diana connection is…?'

Nick intervened gently, '*Heritage*, Perdita.'

She was still glaring at Jeremy. 'Why me, anyway? If my films are so boring, what's all that stuff about Helstone?'

'You, because we want a grown-up on the subject,' Nick said.

'Oh yes. *Appointment-to-view.*' She felt wretched at taking it out on Nick because she knew it was not his fault. He was trying to help her—perhaps it was the last time he would have the power—to ease her passage into this tame new world. Maybe that's why he was getting out.

Jeremy drawled, 'It's not a regional commission, you know. Edit right here in Soho. But, hey, if you're not interested, I've plenty of other people on my list who are... Actually. Directors the Americans already know.' He didn't look at Nick as he said this. Perdita understood she would not have been on his list at all.

'This is the millennium, Perdita,' Nick explained, and the set of his shoulders confirmed her worst suspicions. '*Digital*. And co-production is *it*.'

Turning into Welbeck Street, Perdita tried to shake off her despondency. Of course, she had known this was coming—everyone knew. But to receive news of one's own assassination, as Nick might put it, over lunch, was a shock. Were pointless films like this to be her future, then? As she climbed the stairs to the surgery, she realised she hadn't told them whether she would do it.

The small waiting room was empty when she entered, apart from a youngish man sitting in the corner, reading. Perdita breathed deeply. She was a little late. She laid her jacket over the arm of the sofa, propped her briefcase beside it and picked up a copy of *London Portrait*. The shag-pile carpet was looking pretty dated, she noticed; they would change it soon. Most of the patients were private these days though not, she decided, this man here: he somehow didn't seem the sort, with his serious-looking book and preoccupied air. Perdita took in these things automatically, but was too distracted to dwell on them. She turned the pages of the magazine and tried to forget about lunch.

Daniel was sitting in the waiting room thinking about Sarah Tisdall. His first instinct had been to post the memo to *The Guardian*, but their behaviour over the young civil servant who had leaked a document about cruise missiles, deterred him. The newspaper had revealed the source of the documents and Tisdall went to prison—and that was fourteen years ago, before the removal of the public interest defence in Section 2 of the Act.[1] Daniel clasped his briefcase tightly underneath the book on his knee. It felt as if the document inside were pulsing with plutonium.

When the waiting-room door opened, he hoped it would be the nurse to summon him, but instead he saw a slim woman with reddish hair who must have been another patient. She had wide grey eyes that made her look young, though she was probably older than him. As soon as he caught sight of her, he knew with a jolt he had seen her before. Daniel looked swiftly down at his book. He had met her only once apart from

---

1 This is the Official Secrets Act 1989. Section 2 removed the 'public interest' defence from the earlier Act of 1911—i.e. you could no longer defend yourself in court by claiming that contravening the Act was justifiable in the public interest.

watching her on television—oh, it must have been at least two years ago, when he was at the Electricity Office. He couldn't remember her name—something odd—but he clearly recalled the meeting at which they had tried to persuade her to make changes to her film. She had refused, of course, and it had given them a headache in the press office when the uncut documentary was eventually shown, but he was glad the truth was out. The injunction, and the lifting of it, had made her quite a celebrity, if you counted a ten-minute rule debate in Parliament; interviews on Channel 4 News and Newsnight. Helstone B: it had dominated their lives for a while. How weird that of all people, of all days, he should meet her now.

The door opened again. This time it was the nurse. 'Perdita Burn?' *Yes, that was it!*

She threw aside her magazine. 'Thanks,' she said. For a moment, she hesitated over the coat and briefcase. Then she walked to the door.

Now the room was empty. Daniel's heart slammed backwards and forwards against his ribs. He had intended to take the document home, sleep on it, think through what he was doing. Where was Alex when you needed some sound advice? They had always relied on each other for that. Should he pass the document on—if so, to whom?—or tear it up, forget about it?

Perdita's briefcase leaned against the arm of the sofa where she had left it. Seize the moment: that's what Alex would say. His hands were shaking so much he could scarcely close the book he was reading. The envelope. Should he write on it and, if so, what? 'Ms P. Burn'? Too premeditated. 'To Whom It May Concern'? Handwriting experts might trace him. Nothing, then. The briefcase would be locked. No, it had buckles. His fingers were sausages. The nurse would return; catch him. Courage. Calm. The bag was seven feet away. Do it now... well, *now*, then. Undo. Slip inside. Three seconds. In ten seconds, he could be sitting back here again.

Daniel returned to his seat, twitching. This was treason. He had done it. Crossed over. Pushed the rock off the edge. It was already falling. He must stop it. Can't stop it. *Can*. Take the envelope back again. Burn it as soon as he got home. Ten seconds and he could be safe—

'Mr Booth? The dentist will see you now.'

Daniel jumped. 'Oh, yes,' he said. He stood up.

The nurse smiled. 'He's very sorry to have kept you waiting.'

CHAPTER 2

It was Perdita's day for seeing Hugh. This was a throwback to the mediation that had followed the breakdown of their marriage, a *forum*—the mediator's word—for discussing Daisy, their nineteen-year-old daughter.

Daisy pretended to disapprove. 'Why put yourself through it, Mum? It makes no difference to *me*. And you always come home in a bad mood.'

'I don't see him for you, my love. I see him for me.'

'Why?'

'Because.' Because at some level she needed to explore the sense of failure that still, after four years, pervaded her; to understand the feelings they had once had for each other; to reassure herself that things were happier now.

Reading her thoughts, Daisy said, 'You're better off without him, Mum. You'd still be tiptoeing round his horrible

20

tempers. Just think how screwed up I'd be if you'd stayed together.'

'You're supposed to be screwed-up because we didn't.'

'Oh yeah?' Daisy crossed her eyes and waggled her fingers in the air.

'You've suppressed it. I'm suspicious.' Perdita was laughing.

'Damaged, either way.' Daisy stuffed her purse into the pocket of her denim jacket. 'Does this skirt make me look fat?' And without waiting for an answer, 'You ought to go to Henne's. Brilliant long frocks. Your sort of thing.'

'I thought you wanted me in skirts above the knee?'

'Oh, I've completely given up on that.' She kissed her mother. 'I'll be back—not late. Promise not to talk about me.' And she was gone.

Perdita had omitted to tell Daisy that she was meeting Hugh tonight at what he insisted on calling 'his club'. If anything could be guaranteed to generate further scorn, it was that. Perdita sighed. Hugh was far less self-important with his daughter than he was with her. Daisy simply wouldn't let him get away with it. Perdita, who didn't suffer fools in the outside world, admitted that at one level she was still in awe of Hugh. Perdita had heard Daisy say, 'Dad, *Pur-leez*,' and he would grin sheepishly, run his fingers through his hair muttering, 'Child's got no respect,' and change the subject.

Waiting at the draughty porter's lodge for Hugh to come and collect her, Perdita's thoughts returned to the document that had mysteriously appeared in her briefcase three days earlier. Her bewilderment was swiftly overtaken by disbelief, and then by alarm, as she read it. Sketchy as it was, her knowledge of Ireland and its interminable peace process was sufficient to convince her that if this memo were genuine, highly unorthodox tactics were being used by the British government; tactics that, made public, would blow the shaky peace apart. Aside from the shock of its arrival, Perdita had been preoccupied with the question of whether to tell Hugh about it. She badly needed an expert opinion. Where had the document come from? How secret was it? Was it real, or a fake? And, above all, why *her* and what should she do? This was Hugh's province. Could she trust him? Each time she asked that question, it remained unanswered. Now it was time to decide and she simply didn't know.

'Darling. Sorry, darling. Have you been waiting an age?' He kissed her briefly on the cheek. He was wearing, she noted, the most alarming tie. Daisy had said nothing about a new girlfriend, had she? Perdita found the tie oddly cheering.

They climbed the enormous staircase to dinner, Hugh informing her—not for the first time—that its extra handrail had been installed for Talleyrand who, as the disabled French ambassador, had been a regular visitor in the 1830s. A man who switched sides, Perdita reflected to herself: perhaps that's why he appealed to Hugh. This amusing thought was interrupted by Hugh abruptly changing the subject with, 'So your chaps are in trouble again, I see,' and her spirits wilted. This was a reference to an old spat between them, central to the breakdown of their marriage and, in the end, it came down to politics.

Hugh was the Port Talbot steelworker's son who left school at sixteen to work on the local paper; learned his craft the hard way in the days of the great investigations. He was a newspaperman of the old school who had defected effortlessly to the new. When Perdita met him, he had been a name to conjure with: she had been very young and very beguiled. At twenty-three he had introduced her to the writing of Wallraff and Tom Wolfe. At twenty-five she had borne him their child. For a while the imbalance suited both of them. She could date the seeds of doubt to his promotion. While numbers of his colleagues preferred to slip away and find other jobs after the newspaper group changed hands, Hugh had seized his destiny. His disdain for the kind of television documentaries on which she had begun to work became more elaborate as their careers diverged. 'Her chaps,' Perdita comforted herself, were these days often more ethical than Hugh's own.

She waited for him to ask about Daisy but he didn't, preferring, over the potted shrimps, to tell her in detail about a trip he had made in the summer to what he still called the Far East, as one of the journalists following the new Prime Minister around. Perdita wondered if he had always been as pompous as this.

A waiter brought a bottle of the Club claret. 'Would you like to taste it, sir?'

'Of course I'd like to taste it,' Hugh said. He did so. 'Yes, okay.' Then to Perdita, not bothering to lower his voice, 'See what I mean? They haven't got a clue here.' The waiter frowned as he poured the wine. Perdita smiled her thanks to him. 'You want to go to Singapore,' Hugh told her. 'That's the place for first-class service.'

Perdita decided it wasn't worth reminding her ex-husband that she had lived in Malaysia as a child, so she simply agreed that, yes, service there was excellent—and changed the subject.

'Did Daisy tell you she's been working in a solicitor's office for the last few weeks of the holidays?' she asked him.

Hugh looked pleased. 'Good girl,' he said. 'About time!'

'She doesn't get paid for it,' Perdita explained hurriedly. 'It's work experience.'

'What's the point of getting a job if she's not paid?'

'That's the system. I thought you'd approve.'

'When's she going to start earning her own money? And how long am I supposed to go on supporting her? Little madam,' he added affectionately.

The wine was at last beginning to have a mellowing effect on both of them. A dessert trolley clinked past their table, cut glass and sponge cake. Perdita gazed around at the dark-suited diners, candle flames reflecting back at them from vast spotted mirrors hanging on the walls, while their voices set a low echo murmuring down from the ceiling high above. This scene, she imagined, had probably changed little since the 1930s. The club still reeked of intrigue, which fascinated her. How many secrets had been confided here? Hugh would not betray her. He would offer practical advice. He might not respect their marriage vows, but if she told him a professional secret strictly off the record, he would surely honour that. The desire to confide in him began to rise unstoppably to her mouth. 'Hugh, I want to ask you something.' She paused and took a sip of wine for courage.

'Ah!' His eyes lit up for the first time that evening. But they were not looking at her. Perdita felt a presence behind her. Unusually for him, Hugh rose to his feet.

'So sorry to intrude,' came a voice that clearly wasn't.

'Not at all, Sir,' said Hugh, beaming. 'I was told you

24

might drop in. I was hoping to catch a word with you.' Perdita forced herself to smile up at the lean figure that had now stopped beside their table: he had wavy, greying hair and the expression of a man confident of being listened-to. She guessed he must be a politician but she didn't recognise him. Hugh did not introduce them.

'Are you here for a while?' The man raised his eyebrows.

'Sure. Whenever,' said Hugh. 'It won't take too long.'

'How about coffee in, say—' he glanced at his watch. 'Can you make it in fifteen minutes?'

They were only halfway through their main course. Perdita looked down at her cooling plate. This was so familiar.

'No problem,' Hugh told him.

The man moved on. Perdita scowled.

'Clive Blakemore,' explained Hugh. 'Busy man.'

'Evidently,' said Perdita.

'Got his hands full. We're doing a profile next week. Delicate stuff. He's having a hard time.'

'So that's why you wanted me to meet you here.' She heard an edge to her voice that she didn't like, but what the hell. 'Never let it be said Hugh Williams spent too much time with his family,' she teased.

'Sorry I didn't introduce you,' said Hugh, misunderstanding. 'Bit awkward. Don't know what to call you these days. "This is my ex-wife," sounds rather crass.'

'Not really. They're all screwing their research assistants, aren't they?'

'Not Blakemore. Married rather late, actually. Younger wife. Small kids. You ought to watch yourself, darling. You're starting to sound crabby.'

It was nine forty-five when Perdita reached home; thanks to Clive Blakemore she had left earlier than expected, her secret unspoken. A long hot bath seemed suddenly to be a priority. She stood in the bathroom with the bottle of bath oil in her hand, wondering at her jangled nerves, then fetched the radio, climbed into the bath and lay immobile in the heat till *The World Tonight* news was over.

Meetings with Hugh still produced in her a rage she couldn't express. Perdita shivered and slid further down into the water. Five minutes later, wrapped in a towel, she pottered next door into her study, leaving a trail of footprints on the carpet behind her. She took down a small blue book, *Vacher's Parliamentary Companion.* A committee clerk friend passed on duplicates; this was the latest edition and listed the new cabinet. Section Three: Chief Officers of State. Who *was* this man who had messed up her evening? She knew the name but couldn't place him. Was he a Parliamentary Under Secretary, or something? Not exactly. She caught her breath. Clive Blakemore, MP. Of course he's having a hard time: he's one of the new junior ministers in the Northern Ireland Office, working to the Secretary of State. This document of hers: he might very well *know*. Thank God she hadn't told Hugh.

Suddenly in the hall, the doorbell rang.

It was half-past ten. Damp and vulnerable, still wrapped in her towel, Perdita stood by the Entryphone. The doorbell rang a second time. Perhaps Daisy had forgotten her keys.

'Yes?'

'Mrs Burn?'

'Who is it?'

'I'm sorry to call so late. I came earlier, but you were out.'

'What do you want?'

'We met, well we didn't actually meet, but—' the intercom crackled.

'What?'

'We share the same dentist: 34 Welbeck Street.'

Perdita froze. 'Who are you?' she asked at last. 'You're not supposed to be here.'

'I have to talk to you.'

'Why?'

'Mrs Burn, please. Isn't this your job?' There was urgency in the distorted voice. He was right, of course. Here was the one person who could enlighten her. Perdita hesitated. It could be the police. It could be anyone. It was madness to admit strange men to one's home at night, but this would be her only chance to meet the sender of the document... and Daisy would be home soon. She pressed the downstairs buzzer and hurried back into her bedroom to throw on jeans and a sweater. Then, as footsteps came upstairs, she opened the flat door on the chain. When she saw it was the diffident youngish man half-remembered from the dentist's, she slipped the chain and opened the door wider.

Without speaking, he entered the hall. He looked chilled through, as if he'd been hanging around in the cold for hours. They examined each other for a moment in what she felt was mutual dismay. Perdita had a confused impression of a stripy scarf and the face of an embarrassed angel in an English church.

'I'm so sorry to alarm you,' he apologised.

'Who are you?' she asked again sternly, trying to keep the

nerves out of her voice.

'I'm sorry. Daniel Booth. Ministry of Defence.' He held out his hand. *Are we conspirators?* she wondered, as she took it.

She led him into the sitting room, running a hand through her damp hair. 'You'd better have a drink,' she said, in an effort to impose normality on a situation she found totally unnerving. 'There's nothing except wine—unless you want a cup of tea.'

'What are you having?'

'I'm shaking. I need a drink.'

'So am I,' he said. 'Yes please.'

She took his coat and went to open a bottle. 'How did you find me?' she asked, returning with two glasses.

Daniel sat down on the sofa, briefcase beside him. 'Mr Hudson's been my dentist for years. Your name was in the appointment book; your address on the, you know, Rolodex thing.' He made a vague circular movement with his hand, pleased with his sleuthing. 'I didn't check it out till yesterday. I've had a difficult week. I didn't know what to do.'

'The reluctant traitor,' Perdita said. It was meant to be a joke but it seemed to re-awaken his anxieties; the look on his face was suddenly haunted. 'Forget it,' she added hurriedly. 'That is, I'm sure most traitors are reluctant. Anyone who acts out of conscience must be all too well aware of the danger.'

Daniel was staring into his glass. 'I was always brought up to be honest, you see.' The look of embarrassment returned. 'Sounds old-fashioned, doesn't it?'

'I hope not,' she murmured, and waited for him to continue.

'You sign the Official Secrets Act. It's a serious thing. Chaps like me, we get totally institutionalised, you know.' He cast her a self-mocking glance and dropped his eyes to the glass again. 'You really don't think you'll ever do a thing like this.'

She was expecting further self-criticism, but when he looked up at her his eyes were twinkling. 'It's been coming on for months, you know,' he confided. 'This sense that the job I do, the whole place, is completely bonkers.'

His expression was so guileless she couldn't help warming to him. 'Why did you do it?' she asked, intrigued.

He thought for a moment. 'Two tenets: honesty and doing your duty. Which do you think is the stronger?'

'I'd hope they'd be indivisible,' she said, smiling.

Daniel shook his head. 'That's where you're wrong. It's why I'm in this mess. What happens when it's a *dishonest* duty? The bastards never tell you that!'

She said nothing, and he went on, 'To start with, it was easy. What I read in the document was so unthinkable that I couldn't give a damn about signing some stupid Act. Now—' he sighed. They were both silent for a few moments.

Then he asked, 'Have you shown it to anyone?'

'Not yet.'

A look of relief crossed his face. 'I came here to get it back,' he said simply.

'Why?'

'Does it matter?'

'Of course it matters.'

'Cold feet. Allegiance to the crown. In that order.'

Perdita smiled. She might have felt the same.

'If you want to know,' Daniel went on, 'I'm scared witless.'

'So am I,' said Perdita.

'You? Why?'

'Because I've read it. Why d'you think? If this is what governments do in our name, I don't trust *anything* any more.' She watched the effect of her words on him. 'Which is why I'm not going to give it back,' she finished quietly.

'What do you mean? You've got to! Perhaps I didn't make myself clear. *I've decided not to leak it after all.*'

'*Un*leak it?' She started to giggle.

'Why not? It's my document!' he argued.

She raised an eyebrow.

'All right, then. It's my head on the block. You can't force me to be a martyr!'

He was right, of course. She could give it to him now. Say it never happened; so much easier. For a full moment she was tempted to hand it over.

'But... you did it for a reason,' she said gently. 'I don't know who you are or what you do, but when you read this memo you felt so strongly that the public have a right to know what's going on, you risked your moral welfare and your career in the civil service to pass it to me. Yes?'

Daniel nodded.

'Okay, then. So let's discuss how we proceed.'

'*We* don't do anything,' Daniel protested. 'If you won't give it back, it's down to you. You're the investigative journalist!'

Perdita laughed. 'That's more like it. So. Some questions. I haven't done anything with the document yet because I wondered if I'm being set up.' She watched as this sank in, but he blinked at her in apparently genuine surprise. 'First, I'm not a public figure,' she explained. 'How did you know who I was? Second, you meet me by chance at the dentist. In this world how many things happen by chance? Third, I imagine if it's genuine this is a very restricted document. I want to know why someone with access to such material wants to leak it to the media.'

'I got it by mistake,' Daniel interjected.

'Okay. By mistake. But whose? Why should I think this document is genuine?'

'Look,' said Daniel. 'Isn't it enough that I've changed my mind? If you don't like it, give it back to me. I didn't lie awake for hours, you know, planning on who to pick from my vast acquaintance of hacks. You're not so special! The document happened. I took my chance. I had to pass it on quickly. I bumped into you in the waiting room. It seemed the right thing at that moment to entrust it to you!'

'Okay…' She took this in. 'But how did you know who I was?'

'Helstone B,' he answered promptly.

'Ah. You saw me on *Newsnight?* You've got a good memory.'

'Not just then. We sort of met. DTI[2]—when you came for that meeting? I was sitting at the back.'

'I see,' said Perdita slowly. She remembered a room somewhere in Westminster dominated by a polished oval table; three civil servants ranged around it, facing her and her executive producer; more stationed in chairs against the wall behind. It was starting to fit.

---

2 Department of Trade and Industry. For other abbreviations and translations, see Glossary (pages 373-4).

'I thought you did it out of decency, Helstone,' Daniel went on. 'We all knew the safety procedures were inadequate. There was nothing we could do. You gave us a terrible time in the press office, but I was delighted.'

'Second mystery. You're a press officer, then. I should have thought you had your own contacts.'

'My contacts are the defence correspondents.' He rolled his eyes. 'I thought that what my document needed was some objectivity.'

There was silence for a moment. Perdita said, 'So do you still want it back, or may I refill your glass?' Before he could answer, she reached for the bottle. Then, remembering her encounter from earlier in the evening, she said, 'Tell me something. Do you know anything about Clive Blakemore?'

Daniel frowned. 'How do you mean?'

'The minister. Apparently he's under a lot of pressure from Sinn Féin.'

'Oh, that. Not so much Sinn Féin, is it? More the Unionists.' She noticed Daniel spoke with authority, but immediately qualified it with, 'Of course, it's not my Ministry.'

'No, of course not.' She returned to the matter in hand. 'So, who did this document come from?'

'I don't know, do I?' he said. 'It's not *me*, all this. It's all very well for you smart bloody journalists. You aren't schooled in secrecy the way we are. You don't understand the importance because you don't have to face the consequences of what happens next.'

Perdita said, 'Daniel, I don't want to give it back because—well, it's a bloody good story. And I can't give it back because—' she sighed. 'I don't know. We're living in odd

times for my job. I suppose I'm stubborn and old-fashioned—
like you, perhaps?' She shot him a brief smile. 'So I don't want
to walk away from it, and I don't think you want me to.'

She waited. When he raised his eyes, his face was a
picture of indecision.

'I can't believe it's genuine,' she mused. 'But, if it is, the
peace will go sky-high. Of course, it isn't the sort of thing that
could be used on its own. It would need a lot more research.'

Daniel found this reassuring: she didn't intend to publish
immediately, then. 'But I don't think I can be any more help,
Mrs Burn,' he told her. 'I don't know anything else.'

Perdita ignored this. 'Have you got five minutes?' she
asked suddenly. 'And please don't call me Mrs Burn. Stay
there.' She left the room before he could object, returning
a minute later with the document. 'Now. Tell me what this
means to you?'

Daniel reluctantly took the memo from her outstretched
fingers. Was she handing it to him to test him, he wondered?
To see if he would give it back?

'This one: Keady 15.10. What's that?'

'I couldn't make it out,' he said slowly. 'I thought at first
they were code numbers or times, but this one, here, makes
it fairly clear they're dates: Lisburn 07.10. I think that must
be last year: two car bombs at the British Army HQ. You can
imagine the problems that gave us!'

She could well imagine it. 'Yes. And then there's the
next one, just last month: Markethill 16.9. That was the very
day after Sinn Féin joined the talks. They've both done the
peace process a lot of harm. Yet if this astonishing document
is genuine, the security services, the government, had prior

knowledge—perhaps even played a hand... I can't believe it. I'm sorry, I can't.'

'Actually,' Daniel said, 'I'm pretty sure the Provisionals denied that one. It's said to be one of the breakaway groups. Gerry Adams was all over the place, insisting the ceasefire's intact.'

'I simply can't believe the British would sabotage their own peace!' Perdita repeated. 'And what about the final date? I couldn't find a reference to Keady on October 15th of any year, could you?'

Daniel shook his head. 'I looked it up. Keady's a small town near the South Armagh border. There have been a number of bombings around there over the years. It must be one of those. After all—' he shrugged. 'Don't they call it bandit country? I guess they go unreported half the time. You're right. It needs more work.'

'Whether it's true or not,' Perdita said, 'someone must want to screw up the talks, particularly now Sinn Féin are on board. But what's this got to do with me?' She reached out and touched his wrist to soften what she was going to say next. 'And if I'm not being set up, Daniel, perhaps *you* are.'

Daniel withdrew his hand. 'That's ridiculous!' he muttered, but Perdita caught a flicker of something in his eyes that she couldn't place.

'I don't believe the document is real,' she said. 'If this is true, we're living in madness, a mad state. Forget your code of silence. Forget my job. We have to expose it. But if the memo is a forgery, why send it? There *are* no chances. Not like this, there aren't. You didn't receive it by accident. Either you are trying to trap me, which only you can know?'—she left the question hanging in the air for a moment—'…or someone wants *you* in trouble, Daniel. You can't just put this behind you.'

Daniel stared at her in bewilderment, but he was listening closely.

'It's not my subject,' Perdita went on. 'I invited you in tonight partly out of curiosity. Couldn't believe anyone would take me seriously enough to want to frame me. But partly because, having read it, I felt I had no choice. And now I've talked to you—' she broke off. How could she explain that she felt he was an innocent in dangerous waters? 'I believe what you say,' she continued. 'I believe in why you've done it. I want to help you.'

Daniel had no doubt she was sincere. He felt numb. 'I don't understand,' he said. 'Why should anyone want to get at *me?*'

'Will you trust me?' she asked.

He gazed at her. She had turned his world upside down. He gave her a rueful smile. 'What else can I do?' he said.

CHAPTER 3

The clerk at Reception was deeply concerned. 'There's still no message, Ms Burn. I'm terribly sorry.' If she could have conjured a message out of the telephone she would have done it.

'Bother,' said Perdita.

'People are so rude, aren't they?' the young desk clerk sympathised. 'They promise to phone back and they never do. Still,' her face broke into a mischievous smile. 'It'd only be work, now, wouldn't it? Nothing really serious.'

Perdita laughed. But it was becoming serious. She had been trying for more than two days and still no word from Sinn Féin. She must leave Dublin shortly for the North. She turned away from the desk, past the peg-board announcing today's functions, and ducked back into the conference suite under the huge banner: *Tweed Awareness Week*. Against life-sized blow-up photographs of apple-cheeked men sitting at looms against a backdrop of the mountains of Donegal, patrons shuffled from stall to stall fingering textiles and talking earnestly of weight and density, warp and weft.

*

'You will do it!' Jeremy had not been able to conceal his surprise at Perdita's decision.

'Yeah, sure.' Perdita didn't want to sound over-enthusiastic.

'Well, I think you'll enjoy this more than you imagine,' Jeremy said. 'Fascinating time to be in Ireland,' he added. 'They say the whole place is booming these days.'

*

Jeremy would not have realised, of course, that her research into tweed would take her to the offices of Sinn Féin, where signs of the new affluence were sketchy. The makeshift security cameras were evidently working, but otherwise none of the funds raised by senior republicans on their tours of Australia and North America seemed to have filtered back to the once-gracious house in Parnell Square. Perdita noted the chunks of plaster lying in an unswept avalanche at a bend on the wide stone stairs; the chill and the dark of it and the frayed carpet tiles at the top, almost obliterated by yellowing stacks of the republican newspaper *An Phoblacht*, which confirmed she had reached the publicity department.

'I've come to see Fionnuala James,' Perdita said to the

blonde young woman at the desk behind the newspapers. 'Perdita Burn. I'm afraid I'm a little late.'

The blonde young woman examined her for a moment and then opened a large desk diary. She turned the page to the correct date. The page was blank. After scrutinising it with care, the young woman said, 'Fionnuala isn't here just now.'

'I'll wait, shall I?' asked Perdita. The young woman looked uncertain. Then she called into an inner office, 'Eddie!'

A young man appeared. He was wearing track-suit pants and a t-shirt inscribed *Collusion Kills*. He stared first at Perdita, then at the blonde young woman, who explained, 'She's come to see Fionnuala.'

'Fionnuala isn't here.'

'I had an appointment for midday,' said Perdita.

'Where are you from?'

'I'm a TV producer. ITV?' she added, uncertain whether this would help. She handed them a business card on which she had written the number of her Dublin hotel. They both ignored it.

'But where *from?*'

'Oh. England. London.'

Eddie scratched his head. 'She's away.'

'Away?'

'She'll not be back.'

They all considered this. Perdita had an idea. 'Friel sent me.'

'Martin Friel? RTÉ?' Eddie's face brightened.

'That's right.'

'How is Friel?'

'He's fine. He has two babies. Twin boys.'

'Friel? That's grand.'

'He's based in London now.'

'We had some serious nights with Friel,' Eddie recalled.

'I used to work with him,' Perdita said. 'He contacted Fionnuala for me.'

'Ah. Well.'

'She's away,' said the blonde young woman, closing the desk diary. Perdita began to feel dispirited. 'When will she be back?' she asked.

Eddie regarded her as if weighing something up. 'To-morrow,' he replied after a moment. 'Aye, she'll see you tomorrow. Tell Marty I was asking for him. Twins. Jesus!' And he turned back into the main office.

Perdita was left with the blonde woman. 'What time shall I come tomorrow?' she asked.

'It's hard to say.'

'Ten o'clock?'

'Oh no.'

'So give me a time.'

'Will I get her to phone you?'

'I'd rather say a definite time now. I have to leave Dublin tomorrow afternoon.' This was not strictly true, but the deadline was borne of experience.

'Sure, she'll phone.'

'Can I leave her a note?'

'I'll tell her. No problem.'

'It's very urgent.'

'Sure. I'll say Martin Friel's friend.'

And that had been that. Perdita had called regularly throughout the following morning. Yes, Fionnuala was back. Sure, she had the message. She was in a meeting just now... The meeting was over but she was on the other line. No, it would not be possible to hold because there were no further lines into the office. Fionnuala would call her right back. Nothing.

Perdita found herself gazing into the eyes of a large wooden sheep with a real fleece. The sheep looked sympathetic. The conference crowds were starting to thin and Perdita longed to leave too. Her throat ached from talking to weavers, dyers, sheep breeders and market researchers against the airless buzz of conversation. In normal circumstances it would all have been straightforward enough, but failure in Parnell Square ate into her. Suddenly, two voices penetrated her absent mind.

'For the last time, I am not wearing that!'

'One of our most popular designs, Sir.'

'Will you get away! It's like two sick sheep have thrown up in a bog.'

Perdita turned and found herself smiling up at the good-looking man with unusually pale blue eyes who had spoken these words.

He instantly appealed for her help. 'Would you look at this now? Grotesque, isn't it! He tells me it's one of their most successful designs.'

'We sell miles of it every year,' said the salesman, who found the whole thing hugely amusing. 'To Americans mostly.'

'Well, there you have it!' cried the blue-eyed man. 'But we shouldn't be pandering to bad American taste.'

'I thought everyone had to do that,' said Perdita.

'Not a bit of it,' he responded. 'Americans have to take

us as they find us. Good American taste is better than ours, of course. We have built a proud trade on quality and British good taste. Americans love it—at least, East Coast Americans do.'

Perdita regarded him. '*Irish* good taste?' she suggested with a smile.

'No, Ma'am. I'm not in the tweed business. Ulster linen. British taste. Don't teach your grandfather to suck eggs. You'd better come and have a cup of tea.'

He turned and led the way out of the conference hall and back into the hotel foyer where it was quieter. Perdita followed meekly. Whoever he was, he was good for research. The only free seats were positioned on the far side of a large flower arrangement. Without consulting her, the man threw an order for tea to a passing barman and sat down.

'Ian Frazer,' he said, introducing himself. 'How do you do?'

'Mr Frazer!' cried Perdita, appraising him with new interest. 'I'm on my way to see you in Belfast. We have an appointment for Thursday. I'm Perdita Burn from London.'

'Well, so you are,' he said, displaying no surprise. 'You see? I've saved you a trip to the North.'

'Well no, in fact there are a number of other—'

'And how do you find the Celtic Tiger?'

'It's beautiful,' Perdita said.

'It's rich,' he corrected. 'And it's a miracle, considering the poverty and apathy of this country in the recent past. I would advise you, however, to give the suburbs a miss.' Perdita thought of the house in Parnell Square and said nothing. 'But then,' he qualified himself, 'there are no miracles. Listen to me talking as if I were already a united Irishman!' He paused, as if waiting for her to comment but Perdita had no comment to make. 'No miracles. Only grants. Lovely grants from the European Union.' He smiled.

'Well, and you have the peace dividend,' Perdita reminded him.

'Indeed,' said Frazer. 'So we have.'

Perdita's spirits were lifting. Ian Frazer was one of the North's most powerful industrialists, his name synonymous with everything energetic and optimistic about the expanding economy of Northern Ireland. She had not known what to expect, but certainly not someone as approachable as this. If she could persuade him to be one of the major contributors to her film, perhaps the project would not turn out to be as bland as she had feared.

'Ms Burn!' The young receptionist came hurrying up. 'Oh, Ms Burn, there's me paging the conference room and you sitting here right under my own nose. I couldn't see you for the flowers!'

'Hello,' said Perdita. 'What's up?'

'Jesus, would you ever forgive me? I told her there was no reply and she's just rung off.'

'Who?'

'That Mrs Fionnuala James you were desperate to hear from? She just called you!'

'Ah.' In the split second that Perdita cursed the open charm of the Irish, she caught the tightening of muscles in Ian Frazer's face.

'Will you not phone straight back?' the young woman persisted. 'She's only just this moment gone.'

'Thanks. In a while, yes. Please don't worry about it,' Perdita said. The desk clerk retreated, looking puzzled. Ian Frazer was examining Perdita closely. Fortunately, at that moment the waiter brought tea.

'What exactly is your film about?' he asked when the waiter had gone. The tone was affable enough but the humour had left him. Perdita gave him the standard line she had rattled off several times that day. He appeared to be listening; asked questions. Perdita relaxed. Perhaps the name Fionnuala James meant nothing to him, after all. She felt too tired to hold in advance the meeting with him scheduled for later in the week. Anxious to recapture the informality of their first encounter, she asked him his impressions of Tweed Awareness Week.

They were both laughing at his account of a visit to a mill near Kilkenny when he asked abruptly, 'And what's the Sinn Féin line on Tweed? Do they plan any… publicity stunts?'

'Oh—' She had been preparing her answer. 'That call.' She waved her hand towards the reception desk. 'It's unconnected. An errand for a colleague back home.'

'Really?'

'Getting through to them. You know. When you have an English voice?' She shrugged. She was not doing this well. 'It's like an imperial court. Impenetrable.'

'It must be important, then, for Mrs James to call you back.'

'Yes.'

'My dear Mrs Burn. Perdita. I can see Mrs James is of far more interest to you than I am. Please don't let me detain you.'

'No. I mean, she isn't. She can wait.'

'She won't wait. Mrs James waits for no one. Certainly

not for someone with an English accent—unless, of course, she is leaving a bomb under their car. Your colleague did tell you about her background, I hope?'

'I—I know that a long time ago she was wanted—'

'Let's not pussyfoot around. She was a terrorist. She has never been brought to justice. It may seem romantic from your side of the water; less so from ours.'

Perdita suddenly felt exhausted. 'Mrs James is the publicity officer for Sinn Féin. Sinn Féin is a legal organisation and I have an errand for her office on behalf of a colleague in London. I have not met her. I'm grateful for your views, but I am not concerned with her past. Now, Mr Frazer, will you please have some more tea!'

Ian Frazer threw back his head and laughed. 'Oh, you English. You think it's so simple. Two religions, one nation, no border, no problem. You wait. It isn't over yet. Forget your tea. Make your phone call. I'm off.' He pushed his chair back and then hesitated, as if weighing something in his mind. 'Here—' He pulled out a pocketbook, made a note, tore out the page and handed it to her as he stood up. 'If you're going to talk to republicans, at least talk to the right republicans. Mention my name. I don't know what your game is, but these are the people you really want to see. I know—' he held up a hand to stall the astonished question on Perdita's lips. 'You're thinking what's a dyed-in-the-wool old Unionist doing with people like this? Well, the first lesson you have to learn about Ireland, Mrs Burn, is that nothing is as clear-cut as it seems.'

Perdita was in fact wondering, although she would not dream of asking him, why he should divulge such contacts to a perfect stranger.

Again, Frazer was a jump ahead of her. 'And make no mistake,' he continued. 'My motive is naked self-interest. I'm a businessman, after all. Watch yourself, now!' And he was gone, pushing an Irish five-pound note into the waiter's hand as he crossed the foyer.

Perdita sat for a few moments frowning at the empty seat before her. Then she poured herself a second cup of tea and drank it rapidly. The waiter approached to clear the tray. Perdita went slowly up to her room and dialled the number for Sinn Féin. It was half-past four. The telephone rang and rang. She could imagine it echoing down the stone stairs. Of course, they were all volunteers. Their office hours were short. And tomorrow she really must leave. Damn. She began to sort files and to throw away the newspapers and publicity brochures she had accumulated from her three-day stay. How many times, in how many hotel rooms over the years had she performed this automatic ritual? Passing the television, she absently punched the power button. On RTÉ 1, the news. But this was too early for the news.

'...*RUC from surrounding police barracks began a minute examination of the scene. Although it is not thought to be large, the bomb was placed in the staff canteen and timed to inflict maximum injury. Despite a partial relaxation of security since the ceasefire, insiders claim terrorists would have had the greatest difficulty in penetrating the building. According to new measures of cross-border cooperation, a Garda unit from Castleblayney has been dispatched to Keady to take part in the search. No terrorist organisation has so far claimed responsibility...*'

It isn't over yet. Weren't they the words of Ian Frazer? Perdita felt sick. From the innermost compartment of her bag, concealed in a box of Tampax, she unfolded the photocopy she had brought with her of Daniel Booth's memo. The date: 15th October. What fools she and Daniel had been. This was no tale of pre-ceasefire collusion. No wonder her trawl of the cuttings had failed to turn up one of the incidents on the list: it had yet to occur. Here it was: 'Keady 15.10'. The date was today. Damn Fionnuala. Damn the IRA. Had they no control over the dissidents? Surely, now they had experienced it, everyone understood the value of peace. Perdita switched off the TV and threw herself on the bed, thinking furiously. Her first impulse was to call Daniel, but she knew she must not do that. This new development made his position infinitely more dangerous. There was no one to telephone, no one to help her. No one but the impassive young people in Parnell Square, or... she remembered the piece of paper given to her by Ian Frazer. Slowly, Perdita collected her thoughts into a plan. First, she showered and changed into jeans. Then slipping from the room with Daniel's memo in her handbag she went down to reception, deserted now that the conference had closed for the day.

'Hello there,' she said, catching the eye of the same young desk clerk.

'Hello, Ms Burn. What can I do for you?'

'I wonder,' said Perdita. 'Would you let me photocopy something?'

Back in her room, Perdita sat down to write to Fionnuala James. She did not attach the photocopy but, after some thought, wrote that she was in possession of a memo with important information about the Keady bombing that predated the bomb itself. Then she put on her coat and scarf and set off across the bridge and down O'Connell Street, where a mild wind blew rain into her hair. There was no letterbox at the house in Parnell Square. Security, of course: Perdita had expected this. Stooping, she removed her glove to feel along the bottom of the door; hopefully the warped, untended building would not have draught excluders. The envelope slid easily beneath. Retracing her steps, she found her way to Bewley's Cafe in Grafton Street, its yellowish gloom disgorging the diners of early evening. It was one of Perdita's maxims never to act on an empty stomach. Ordering bacon, potato cakes, wheaten bread and a thick white mug of coffee, she settled in a corner, unfolded her road map and planned her journey. Her first appointment in Belfast, a hundred miles away, was scheduled for the following afternoon. From her purse she took Ian Frazer's scrap of paper. A name, Brian Doherty; a place, Cullabeg; and a telephone number. Who was this? Who indeed was Frazer? He didn't strike her as one of those insecure men she sometimes met in her job who found it necessary to brag about their low-life connections. Cullabeg, when she eventually found it on the map, was a border village in South Armagh. The comforting warmth of Bewley's tugged at her. Reluctantly, she drained her coffee and left.

Near the National Bank of Ireland, she found a telephone box. On the point of feeding her BT credit card into the slot, Perdita thought better of it and pushed an Irish pound coin into the machine instead. She would have to become more security conscious, she told herself. The number on Ian Frazer's paper was unobtainable.

'Sure you'll be having difficulty,' the operator told her when she called to enquire. 'That there's an international number.' He gave her the code.

'It's Ireland.'

'The North of Ireland,' the operator corrected her. 'Perhaps not for much longer.'

'Sounds crazy,' said Perdita.

'It is crazy. It's been crazy for centuries.'

'So are you pleased, then, if the border goes?' She tried to remember if she had ever discussed politics with an English telephone operator and thought not.

'Can't say I'm bothered if it's there or not,' said the operator. 'To be honest, I haven't thought about it. The calls will be a whole lot cheaper, that's for sure.'

'Thanks, anyway.'

'You're welcome.'

Perdita dialled the number with its British prefix.

The voice was unmistakably North. 'Yes?'

'Is it possible to speak to Brian Doherty, please?' Perdita winced at the sound of her English accent.

'Who wants him?'

'Ian Frazer suggested I call. He doesn't know me.'

'Wait 'til I find out.' The receiver was put down noisily. There followed a long silence. At one point a door in the distance opened and closed, a brief sound of voices, then nothing. The pips went. Perdita fed the rest of her change into the slot. Then the receiver was snatched up.

'Yes.'

'Brian Doherty?'

'Not at home.'

'Will he be there later?'

'You're from Ian Frazer?'

'He gave me this number, yes.'

'You must know, then, it's not a good night.'

'Oh, I see.'

'No, you obviously don't,' said the voice. 'What d'you want with him?'

'Ian Frazer suggested I should see him.'

'You'd better come, then. Ten o'clock.' The line went dead. Perdita realised she had no address.

For the second call she used her BT card: Daisy would be home by now for her reading week.

'*Hello... Please leave your number and we'll get back to you...*' Her own voice sounded irritatingly calm.

'Daisy! Are you there? I need to talk to you, love.'

The calm voice died mid-sentence. 'Hi, Mum,' said Daisy.

'Screening calls!' Perdita mocked.

'They're all boring. They're for you.'

'Really? Who are they?'

'Work, I think. That Jeremy person. He sounds a bundle of laughs. Why d'you always have to work with those sort of *snappy* people? Oh, there's this other man, though. Really keen. You didn't tell me you had a man pursuing you. He sounds desperate.'

'Some hope. Who is he?'

'Daniel. Rather serious. You're not going out with a serious person called Daniel, are you, Mum?'

'I think not, my love.'

'Who is he, then?' Daisy asked.

'Someone at work. If he phones again, will you tell him I'll be back on Friday night? Listen, darling, I'm leaving Dublin now—' Was it better to lay a trail in case something went wrong, or should she keep quiet about where she was going? Oh, for goodness' sake, this was Ireland, not the Congo! 'I'm going to Belfast. I'll be at the Europa tomorrow night. But tonight I'll probably stay over on the way. Maybe Crossmaglen. Would you do me a favour and phone me tomorrow evening? I left the number on that list in the kitchen for you.'

'Sure,' said Daisy. 'Are you okay?'

'Yes, of course.'

'So why am I to phone you?'

'Oh, you know the stupid prices they charge from hotels like that.'

'You should get the office to give you a mobile phone,' Daisy said. 'Dad's got one.'

'We're not all as posh as Dad. Still the Dark Ages for most of us. So will you do that, please, darling?'

There was a short silence. 'It's near where that bomb's just gone off, isn't it?' said Daisy.

Good girl, Perdita thought. 'Sorry?' she said aloud.

'Crossmaglen.'

'Is it? I don't know.'

'You know it is, Mum. Take care.'

'Daisy, the film is about Ulster linen.'

'Okay,' Daisy said. 'Just don't do anything dumb.'

'I promise,' Perdita assured her.

It was seven-thirty as she left Dublin and headed North up the N1. Once past the airport, the road narrowed. She was distracted by a succession of signposts: Swords, Slane, Bog of the Ring. Feeling around on the seat beside her she found one of the tapes she had bought the previous day from the Irish music section at the HMV shop; like so many things in Ireland, familiar, and yet on closer inspection not familiar at all. This was not Perdita's music, yet tonight, in this place, it exercised an uneasy fascination. She turned up the volume.

> *The time has come to part, my love,*
> *I must go away.*
> *I leave you now my darling girl*
> *No longer can I stay.*[3]

To the casual listener, it sounded like a tender ballad. But this was no love song. Its soft-spoken lyrics were about the violent death of hunger strike, written about men who were seen as martyrs.

> *My heart like yours is breaking*
> *Together we'll prove strong.*
> *The road I take will show the world*
> *The suffering that goes on.*

Perdita switched off the tape. What was she getting herself into? Each side in this conflict perplexed her equally. What the hell, really, was the meaning of Daniel's memo? For the first time since leaving Dublin she considered the idiocy of what she was going to do.

---

3 *Time Has Come,* written and performed by Christy Moore and Dónal Lunny, 1983.

Nine o'clock. She must be getting close. She had turned off the highway onto a road marked brown on her map that appeared to climb north and west leading straight to Cullabeg. In the fitful moonlight she glimpsed a landscape of hills and rocks and silence. The beauty of it, sensed rather than seen, took her wholly by surprise. She had imagined this bandit country to be bleak and spoiled. Instead, it was all romance and intrigue. Perdita wanted to giggle: no wonder people thought they saw leprechauns. But the further she travelled, she began to realise that the beauty was also impenetrable; she had stumbled into a magic land where maps had no significance. For now she was truly lost. The road had narrowed to a single lane that gave out in a bunch of capillary tracks, impossible to follow. Perdita threw the map aside, cursing, foxed by signs to places that weren't supposed to be anywhere near, or that seemed to lead her back in the direction she had come. One of them pointed to Keady, but Keady wasn't where she wanted to go.

Around the next bend, she found herself on the shore of a wide lough fringed with reeds. The road ran along the edge, but a path of moonlight led straight across its surface to an island of black trees. For a few moments, Perdita was seized with the impulse to take that path and drive straight out into the depths. Tall shadows loomed at her as the headlights swept past them. She thought she felt a tugging at the steering wheel and gripped it furiously, fingers slithering with sweat. What was happening to her? She wrenched her gaze back from the beautiful lough and forced herself to drive steadily. At the far end, the track plunged into a forest. Perdita accelerated away from the treacherous water, on and on, until she reached a crossroads where once again the lane forked. Here she stopped and opened the window.

A rush of clean wind scented with pine needles filled her head. She breathed in deeply, interlocking her fingers in her lap to stop them from shaking. Nothing had happened back there, she told herself fiercely. She got out of the car to check the tyres, but no, it wasn't a puncture pulling her off the road: the tyres were fine. For a few minutes, she sat staring out into the night. It was, of course, insane to keep the appointment. The moon re-emerged from behind clouds and lit up a steep hillside on the summit of which loomed the asymmetrical rectangles of a watchtower, alarmingly close. Further away across a valley she saw a second, its tower capped like a phallus, and from this second tower, blown in waves, the thud of rotor blades. As she watched, a helicopter rose slowly behind the watchtower, dipped back over the hill and reappeared, louder, closer, swooping low towards her before veering away to the north. This must be the border.

Perdita closed the window, restarted the engine and drove off slowly down the right-hand fork. She would make straight for town, find a pub with a room and start afresh in the morning. To her relief, the walls and hedges of a village came into view around the next corner, and at last a sign. Now she would be able to locate herself on the map once more. She slowed down to read it. *Cullabeg*. Frayed by her experience (or whatever it was) out there by the lough, she felt every nerve in her body tighten. It was a quarter to ten. Perdita drew up beyond the sign and reached for her map, uncertain what to do. The foolhardiness of the whole expedition hit her again, forcefully. And yet… Doherty came from an impeccable source. A man of Ian Frazer's standing would not involve himself with terrorists. Perdita was conscious of a streak in her that avoided potentially difficult situations. And that, she told herself, was what—at the very worst—this might turn out to be: difficult but not dangerous. *Do it*, she urged her reluctant self. Behind her, flashed the lights of another car. She hurriedly moved into gear, but the driver was already beside her, leaning towards her window. She opened it cautiously.

'You okay there?' he asked. It was the same easy friendliness that had touched her several times in Dublin.

Perdita took a deep breath, hesitating to ask. 'I'm trying to find Mr Brian Doherty,' she said at last. 'I suppose you wouldn't—'

'No problem. Drive through the village here. Turn first left after the ending of it. Two hundred yards, you come to a track on your right, through the wood there. Dohertys live up the track. You can't miss it.' He waved his hand and was gone, pulling past her in a rasp of wet gravel.

Obediently, Perdita followed his instructions. The track through the woods was boggy from the rain. Should she leave the car and walk, she wondered? But at that moment the path opened out into a clearing where sawdust and bark chips made the ground firmer. A car, a broken-down estate, was parked there already. Perdita pulled off the track, switched off the engine and reached into her bag for her little Maglite torch. Through the trees she could just make out the lights of a house. A path led towards it from one end of the clearing. Perdita locked the car, switched on the torch and followed it.

After fifty yards the trees thinned. The house was set on a low slope surrounded by an untended rock garden, its porch door propped open by the undercarriage of an old pram.

Curiously for a chilly night, the inner door was also ajar. Perdita could make out a section of a deep-set hall, lit by a single plastic-shaded light. Raised voices came from a room on the left. She knocked tentatively and after a few moments a second time, louder. No answer. They had not heard her above their argument. Perdita's fingertips touched the door. It gave silently. Was it madness, she wondered, that prompted her to enter? Well, she had not driven all this way to be put off by a tiff. Next moment she was standing in the hall. A mirror on the far wall reflected her own face, blurred with apprehension. The door behind which the voices angrily ebbed and flowed stood closed, forbidding. After a few moments, straining to gauge the nature of the dispute and whether she should stay or leave, she moved to the room next to it; an open door, darkness within.

The shadows from the hall illuminated a dining room, but there was a further source of light: in the wall dividing the two rooms, the open doors of a serving hatch revealed, as through a miniature proscenium, a section of the drama. First, Perdita saw a plump neck above a donkey jacket. As she edged around the bulky table, the open rectangle was next filled by a black leather jacket, a navy jersey beneath and an arm, flexed, tense. The voices rose, grew cacophonous. She heard one of the men speak for the first time in a tone of imprecation that made Perdita's blood run cold. The arm in her frame shifted slightly; beyond the voices, a metallic *clack*. Drawing closer for a wider view, Perdita now saw that the arm was braced against the weight of a pistol, its barrel pointing offstage right. The voices had changed pitch. The tones of the man being threatened were pleading, keening almost. Perdita instinctively stepped aside to blot out the reality of what was about to happen, but in so doing knocked into a chair that grated on the floorboards. This time they seemed to hear. A shout of warning; a man's screech; boots scuffing the bare boards; the thud of the gun; the slump of a body, like a stuffed grain sack falling. Perdita dropped in terror to the floor as the dining-room door shuddered open and boots marched into view from where she now crouched beneath the table.

'Is there more of them?' shouted a voice from within.

'Fuckin' light-switch—' The owner of the boots was slapping the walls around the lintel. A light blazed on. Perdita locked her arms over her head and held her breath. Splatters of blood on the toe-caps of the boots transfixed her. Surely, she would be discovered. But with a grunt and the jag of leather, the man turned away and stamped out. Exposed now, for the light still glared, Perdita's one thought was escape. The boots had taken the stairs two at a time; she could hear them crashing overhead. In the room next door there was a frenzy of activity; it sounded as if the body was being dragged and dropped. How many killers were there, she wondered? Could she make for the front-door undetected while they were thus engaged? Then one of the men in the next room spoke.

'Cover it well. We don't want this botched.' So there were three of them, at least.

Her ear caught the slop of liquid in a metal container, the glug, the tell-tale reek. Without further thought for the wisdom of exposing herself, she scrambled under cover of the table as close to the door as she could get and launched out into the hall. Not pausing to ascertain whether they could see her, she dived through the outer porch, jamming her shins on the pram wheels, and stumbled into the garden as, with a whoosh, the murder room caught fire, lighting up the trees on the far side of the clearing. Perdita ran, knowing she must be visible if anyone were bothering to look, and that they could not be far behind. She had covered the ground to the edge of the clearing and was pounding headlong down the path through the trees, which creaked around her, when behind her came a roar as the entire house erupted in flames. Their reflection on its windows lit up her car, parked ahead. Groping in her pocket as she ran, her right hand closed on the key. She flung herself round to the driver's door, trembling fingers jabbing with the key-shaft at the shadowed place where the lock should be. Damn strange cars! Which way up? Which way round? She could hear the men now coming behind her, a shouted command as they crossed the clearing. Heaving the car door open she hurled herself into the driver's seat. But they were near. Had they seen her? Did they realise she was a witness? Against the wall of flame she saw three figures ducking and running down the track. No time to even attempt an escape. Perdita threw herself sideways over the gear stick. At the sight of the parked Nissan the men pulled up short.

'What the fuck?'

'Go. Leave it!'

'Can't fuckin' leave it!'

'Just *go*,' the second voice commanded. 'I'll do it. Get out. Now.'

Thank God there was no interior light. Perdita heard feet approaching; the slam of bodies into the unlocked estate on the far side of the clearing; the kick of the surprisingly healthy engine and the bumping roll as their car left at speed. Then silence. Had they all gone? She waited, scarcely breathing. After a few moments, she shifted her head to try and glimpse the window on the passenger side. Beyond the clearing the house blazed, flames lighting shadows that danced before her eyes. But one shadow wasn't moving. Against the window, hard, dark, immobile, the metal faintly scritch-scratching the glass, Perdita found herself staring down the barrel of a gun.

CHAPTER 4

In a corner of the lobby of Berners Hotel, quiet now as it was nine o'clock in the evening, Milton Lithgow drew on a Players Navy Cut and leered at his companion.

'Very conspiratorial, Hugh. Isn't this the place for spies and floozies?'

Hugh Williams laughed a fraction louder than the joke warranted. 'Sorry to disappoint you, Milton. I'm neither.'

'Is that so?'

This time they both laughed. 'What are you having?' Hugh asked as the waiter approached. 'Scotch. Am I right?'

'Right enough there, my friend. Macallan, if you will. Is your scurrilous broadsheet paying for this?'

'You bet,' Hugh said.

Lithgow spoke directly to the waiter. 'Make that the eighteen-year-old, then. A large one. Information doesn't come cheap,' he added to Hugh.

'I'm sorry, sir,' replied the waiter. 'We don't carry the eighteen.'

'What is there, then?' Hugh demanded.

'The twelve-year-old, sir.'

Hugh raised his eyebrows at Lithgow, who shrugged. 'The twelve will have to do,' said Hugh to the waiter. 'Not good enough, is it?'

'We have a large selection of single-malt whiskies, sir.'

'I'm not interested,' Hugh said. 'Go away.'

The two best things about Milton Lithgow MP, and the reasons Hugh had sought his views on the new minister in the Northern Ireland Office, were, first, that he represented his party around the conference table at Stormont and was therefore one of the few to have seen Blakemore in action; and second, more pertinently, that he was a huge gossip, particularly if the Macallan were of a sufficient age to win his approval. This in part explained Hugh's rudeness to the waiter, who now returned with their drinks.

As Lithgow discoursed on the new government in general and Clive Blakemore in particular, Hugh marvelled at the capacity of politicians, particularly of the minor parties, for solipsism. To hear Lithgow talk, you would imagine that his particular Unionists held the House of Commons in thrall, evolving strategies, dictating terms, ascribing to their personal skill and charisma an unrelated series of events that swung round to backfire on any senior figure who crossed them. Yet when he goes to bed at night, Hugh told himself, he must know his days are numbered.

'...one shouldn't underestimate the extent to which the

self-righteousness of these Marxists covers a multitude, oh I assure you a *multitude* of sins,' Lithgow was saying. His cheeks trembled slightly as he fixed his beady eyes on Hugh.

'Is our man self-righteous?' Hugh asked. Blakemore had not struck him as such during their chat the previous week: keen, yes; very, very ambitious, but not self-righteous exactly. Hugh would have attributed that particular quality more to the Unionists themselves.

He began to wonder if he was wasting his time, but Lithgow was getting into his stride. 'Have you ever asked yourself,' he intoned, 'how these upstarts of the left passed their youth while they waited for power?'

'Blakemore was a lawyer, wasn't he? Quite suitable really.'

'And where do lefty lawyers cut their teeth?'

'I dunno,' said Hugh. He thought to himself that he had been a young 'lefty' journalist once; Clive Blakemore's brand of socialism was probably not carved out on the picket line.

'Look at it this way, then,' Lithgow continued. 'What do we know about Blakemore's background?'

'Father in the colonial service. Oundle. Saw the political light at LSE. Late developer.'

'No, no, no. His private life.'

'Much younger wife. Two children, four and eighteen-months.'

Lithgow was watching him intently. 'Go on.' He took a noisy swig of whisky and rolled it around his mouth.

A dull excitement began to throb deep within Hugh. 'He didn't marry till he was forty-three. Before that—girls? Unusual habits?'

Lithgow shook his head, swallowed and reached two pudgy fingers into an inside pocket. He handed Hugh a faded colour photograph. Hugh peered at it. It was circa 1977, flares and shaggy hair, four self-conscious-looking young men and one woman carrying large, pink, cut-out triangles clustered under a banner at a march: 'Lawyers for Gay Rights'. None of them was recognisable as Clive Blakemore. 'Second from the left,' said Lithgow.

'Well, well.' Hugh looked again. 'I'll take your word for it,' he said at last. He handed back the photograph. 'I didn't know the term "gay" was coined as long ago as that,' he said casually. Where was Lithgow coming from? Unionists, he reflected, were on rather thin ice where homosexuality was concerned.

Lithgow was now in full flow. 'Of course, he's just a new boy among many other new boys, but in Blakemore's case it's a little trickier. It's Ireland, of course: the peace process at a very delicate stage, and all that. And he's more in the spotlight, more exposed, than most new boys—working to a Secretary of State who is not in the best of health herself.' He took a swallow of whisky and pulled a meaningful face at Hugh over his glass.

Hugh had heard rumours about the ill-health of Blakemore's boss, the Secretary of State for Northern Ireland. He grunted assent.

'And of course,' Lithgow was saying, 'like all socialists, Blakemore is *terribly* in favour of the peace.' One shoulder twitched in disapproval. 'No intellect for the complexities. No grasp of the real issues at all.'

Hugh was about to observe that presumably we were all in

favour of the peace these days, but seeing the look of disdain on Lithgow's face, said merely, 'All the same, I suppose there's nothing that constitutes a security risk, is there?'

Milton Lithgow gazed at Hugh thoughtfully and picked a flake of tobacco from his fleshy tongue. The best was yet to come. 'Not,' he began, 'in the normal course of events…'

*

With every pothole of the forest track, the pistol bumped Perdita's left ear. It was infinitely more frightening than she had imagined anything could be.

'What if it goes off?' she breathed.

'You'll be dead,' replied her captor.

A moment later, she said, 'I'm not going anywhere. I'm in your hands, gun or no gun.'

'Shut the fuck up, will ya?'

They drove in silence. It was not the track by which she had come, but another that crossed it. The burning house was well behind them. Eventually they hit a lane and turned right. The pistol was steadier now. The moon had disappeared. It seemed to Perdita they drove for miles, she obeying his directions in silence. Darkness enclosed them. Nailed to a telegraph post on one dizzy bend, the headlights swept over a street sign, a familiar British triangle, but the red edges of this one framed a hooded figure with an Armalite and underneath, *Caution. Sniper at Work*. Was he taking her somewhere to kill her? The trees thickened and crowded in on the narrow road.

'Can you not go faster?' he demanded.

Perdita drove steadily up a hill to a point where the forest thinned out into heathland, and there she stopped. Nothing, she told herself, could be worse than this. Staring out through the windscreen, her head unnaturally still for the firearm at her temple, she said, 'I can't drive faster because I'm terrified… the gun… I've done nothing to you.' She was shuddering uncontrollably.

'You've seen my face.'

'I haven't,' she cried. 'I could never recognise you. I don't know who you are. All I know is that you've stuck a gun at my head.' She was gambling on the hope they had not seen her run from the house.

'You Brits are all the same. You all want to wheedle your way out of trouble. You talk so nice and reasonable. Then at the first opportunity you'd go bleating to the security forces. You've seen my face. That's enough.'

'I've told you, I haven't. Anyway, don't you normally wear a mask, or something?'

'What I *nawmally* do,'—he mimicked her English vowels—'What I normally do is none of your friggin' business!'

Perdita had the renewed sense that any false move would get her face blown off. Without a word, she started the car and drove on down the road. Suddenly the distant drone of a helicopter broke the silence. As the noise grew louder, to her infinite relief her captor lowered the pistol. The helicopter passed overhead and flew on.

'Were you seen?' he asked.

'Seen? When?' Her voice still shook.

'On your way to… where we met you.'

Perdita remembered the driver who had given her

directions.

'Okay, we'll have to ditch the car,' her captor said.

Perdita didn't like this 'we'. 'Couldn't you just get out?' she suggested timorously.

He didn't bother to reply. The road had straightened and broadened somewhat. They began to see other vehicles. Buildings appeared. The man looked at his watch. Suddenly, around a corner, they came upon two land rovers slewed across their path; men with camouflage gear and black face paint on either side of them; the glint of automatic weapons from the rear of the nearside vehicle; an RUC officer in a flat green cap with a flashlight. Perdita felt her captor tense beside her. She slowed down. Here was her chance: it was a roadblock.

A soldier approached. Perdita took a deep breath. She opened the window.

'Evening, Ma'am.' She heard a flat East Midlands twang. She wanted to throw her arms round the soldier's neck and hug him. The RUC officer had moved over to the front of the car to look at the registration plate. 'Can I ask where you're going this evening?' enquired the soldier.

'We're driving to Belfast,' Perdita said, hoping this would be a ludicrously improbable answer. Apparently it was not. The man beside her leaned forward, as if in agreement, placing his arm companionably along the back of her seat. His hand found its way to the far side of her neck. It looked like a caress. It was a grip of iron.

'Do you have any identification on you?' the soldier asked. Perdita groped in her bag and handed him her passport. She prayed he would notice how badly her fingers were shaking. *Just get me out*, she entreated silently.

The soldier scrutinised her photograph. 'Looks nothing like you. Can you tell me what you're doing out here at this time of night?' He peered at her, his eyes hostile. The automatic weapon he carried was on a level with her face.

Perdita hesitated. A second soldier moved into position behind the first, his firearm unambiguously trained at the driver's window. How to make a break from the car and not get shot—for the space outside suddenly seemed as dangerous as the space within. She was in turmoil. The British passport meant nothing, of course: she supposed every republican in the North had one of those. Might they not mistake her for IRA, too?

The RUC officer joined the two soldiers beside her. 'Can you tell me where did you hire this car?' he asked.

'In Dublin.'

'On holiday in Ireland, is it?'

'On business.'

'Show us the hire documents then,' commanded the first soldier.

Straining to pull free of her captor, she reached into the glove compartment. As she did so, she realised she could have pretended the documents were in the boot. Was it too late? Now she must do it: calmly, slowly, get out of the car. But her captor's gun was somewhere close to the left of her; theirs eight inches to her right. She felt incapable of movement.

The first soldier spoke again. 'Not much business in these parts. You're a long way off the road, aren't you?'

As she was about to pass them the papers, her fingers closed on her press card bundled up with them. Her brain unfroze. 'Here you are.' She handed the car hire papers and the press card through the window. 'I—I was at Keady,' she said. It was a massive gamble. She felt her captor beside her stiffen and grip her neck again, but she looked at the RUC man steadily.

He took the documents and examined them with care in the torchlight; then he turned and showed the press card to the soldiers and they conferred for a few moments. Eventually, he returned to the car. 'You was reportin' on Keady?'

'I was,' she said, wondering how this would play out with the man beside her. Then she heard herself say, 'Sorry, officer. I'm really tired. I'd like to get going, please.'

'That's a bad business, so it is.' He handed back the documents. 'Thank you, Ma'am, they're in order,' he said. 'Safe journey now.' And he waved them on.

They drove without speaking. With the soldiers behind them, Perdita could not believe what she had done. They had only to have ordered her out of the car, she screamed to herself silently. They had only to *ask* and she would have had no choice but to comply. But they had not taken their chance and she, from cowardice, had blown hers. She had joined the man beside her in complicity with a murder in cold blood. For all she knew, he and his comrades had done the Keady bombing, too. Perdita wondered if there was anything he could ask of her that out of fear she would not do. She bit her lip, willing herself to resist, or at least to conceal from him her state of mind.

'So what happened?' he asked at last. 'You could have turned me in back there.'

'I didn't,' she said angrily, 'because I didn't want to prove you right!'

He threw back his head and laughed. 'And that's the other thing about you Brits: your stubborn arrogance!'

A couple of miles further on, they reached a farm track winding up a hill. 'Turn here,' he instructed. Was she to be shot now? They bumped up the path that led eventually to a cluster of cottages. 'Stop.' She obeyed, took her hands off the steering wheel and held on to the seat in expectation. She was shuddering again and could not turn to look at him. He leaned over, removed the keys from the ignition. 'Wait there.'

He got out of the car and came round to the driver's door to lock it. Then he disappeared around the side of one of the cottages. Perdita knew this ought to be her second chance to get away, although there was no cover and she doubted anyone would harbour her if her captor were known here. Nonetheless, she felt she must at least make the effort to escape and leaned across to try the passenger door. As she had expected, the car had central locking. Besides, within a minute the man returned followed by a sleepy-looking boy tucking his shirt into his jeans. The boy went to a clutch of motors drawn up on the verge, reversed one of them noisily onto the track and threw the keys to Perdita's captor who in turn gave the keys of the hire car to him. 'In,' he ordered Perdita.

'Can I—can I get my things?' she asked. She was thinking chiefly of Daniel's precious memo.

'Get the bags,' the man ordered the boy. 'But leave the tapes.' He added something in an undertone that sounded like, 'friggin' shamrock'.

'Tank's full,' said the boy as they got in. He nodded at Perdita. For a moment, she felt lightheaded with relief: there was no sign of the gun—though she realised he had probably stowed it... wherever it was they stowed them.

This time the man drove. He drove deftly, easing the old saloon over the ruts in the farm track and out onto the road where their progress was now considerably faster. As the engine warmed and the heat came on, Perdita sank into the soft, cracked passenger seat and wondered if she were a hostage. She sensed a curious fatalism. The possibility of imminent death seemed to have receded.

'So, what was that ID you gave him back there?'

She was on her guard at once. 'It was my press card,' she said.

'And what exactly were you "reporting" on at Keady?'

'I wasn't at Keady.' She suddenly felt too tired to explain.

He turned to look at her in the darkness. 'So why did you say you were?'

She sighed. 'I just wanted to give them a reason for being out here, so they would, you know, send me on my way.'

'Why?'

'Because I don't like having guns pointed at me!' she burst out.

He said softly, 'But I have a gun too, don't I?'

She didn't answer. They drove for several minutes in silence.

Perdita could tell neither in which direction they were heading nor even which side of the border they were, though after a while the sight of a red post box told her they were still in the North and this made her wonder about the identity of her captor. Why he had murdered Brian Doherty, she could not begin to guess. She examined him covertly. There were no clues. He was in his mid-forties, tall, lean, with a straight nose and wavy dark hair. He wore jeans, the dark jersey and the battered black leather jacket she had glimpsed through the serving hatch in the dining room. His allegiances might be a mystery but there was no mistaking his role. He was the killer. She had watched him take aim. He sensed her gaze and she quickly looked away.

'Okay,' he said at last. 'Question time. Who are you?' His voice was businesslike now, not oppressive.

'Does it make any difference?'

'You bet it does. Are you Special Branch, or what?'

'I told you: I'm a journalist,' she said.

'I don't believe you! That must've been some kind of British police card that got them off our backs!'

She rummaged in her bag and took out the press card, reaching up for the overhead light to hold it in front of his face. 'I make films, documentaries, for British television.'

He took his eyes off the road for a moment to scrutinise the card, its black lettering PRESS unmistakable.

'And what *documentary*,' he gave it a sarcastic twist, 'are you making tonight?'

'It's about linen and tweed.'

'Go on.'

'I've driven from Dublin. I'm on my way to Belfast. A man I don't know suggested I go and see Brian Doherty. I did so, since it was more or less on my way. And I met you.'

'Is that all?'

'Broadly, yes.'

He frowned. 'Did Dublin send you?'

'Dublin?'

'No, of course not. What did you say your name was?'

'I didn't. It's Perdita Burn.'

'Byrne? So it's a good Irish name you have!'

'No. Burn. A village in North Yorkshire.'

He cast her a sidelong glance. 'You look Irish, at any rate,' he observed. 'For a frightened woman, you don't do yourself any favours, do you, Mrs Burn?'

She couldn't look at him. 'There's no point claiming to be what I'm not.'

'It would be more understandable if you had tried to,' he said quietly.

'But when you discovered I was lying, you'd wonder what else I'd been lying about.'

'A true Brit,' he growled. He said nothing further for a few moments. Then he asked, 'You come from a literary family?'

'I do not,' she said. 'My father was in the Navy.'

'A merchant seaman, was he?'

'No.' She hesitated. 'The Royal Navy. He wanted a son.'

He threw her another glance. 'And he got a fighting daughter!'

'I'm not a fighter,' she said.

'No, of course not. You make films about Ulster linen.' She was silent. 'It's a strange name for a wee girl,' he said thoughtfully. 'Where was your father stationed?'

'Malaya. We travelled around quite a bit when I was little. After that it was Plymouth mostly.' Why was she telling him all this?

'Was he never in action?'

'Oh yes,' she said. Then she added, 'He was killed in the Falklands.'

'Well, well.' The man spoke softly, to himself almost.

'And I wonder what he thought of that particular little war?'

'It was his last tour,' she said. 'He was due to retire. Overdue.'

'And what did *you* think of it?'

'It isn't a little war when your father gets killed in it.'

'Not a stupid little war? A pointless bloody war?'

'I don't want to discuss it,' she said shortly.

He shrugged. They drove in silence for a few minutes. 'So, Perdita Burn, tell me,' he resumed. 'You must know that you're going to have to tell me why you were on your way to meet Brian Doherty?'

'I don't know,' she said. 'I mean that. I met a man at a conference on Irish tweed in Dublin who said it would be useful for me to go and see him.'

'Why?'

'I don't know,' she repeated. 'I telephoned him and was instructed to go to the house at ten tonight.'

'And what did you do when you arrived?'

Without the slightest hesitation, she answered, 'Before I even got to the front door, the house went up in flames.'

He said, 'Did it now?'

'Yes,' she asserted.

'And naval officers' daughters don't tell lies, do they, to save their skin?'

'If I'd wanted to lie,' she pointed out, 'I would not have told you my father was in the services.'

'Maybe,' he agreed. 'And maybe not. You already know far too much. So tell me, who was the man who sent you?'

'A man from the North. He runs a linen business.'

'What's his name?'

'Ian Frazer.'

'*Frazer* sent you?' This piece of information seemed to startle him.

'You know him?'

The man didn't answer. His eyes narrowed. She could see the contours of his face set in a frown. There was a long pause. When he spoke again his voice had an edge to it that made her go cold. 'You knew him before.'

'I told you. I met him by chance today. Yesterday. I didn't know him at all.'

The man said, his voice like a razor, 'If Frazer sent you to see Doherty it was not about Irish tweed.'

'I don't know.'

'You do—fuckin'—know.'

Without warning, he swung the car off the road, down a track through a field gate and lurched to a halt. Perdita stared fixedly in front of her. Inside she was screaming again with fear. The man had Doherty's blood on his hands. He had burnt down Doherty's house. What did it matter to him if there were more? He turned to face her. One of his arms shot out. She ducked away, but his hand merely reached past her to lock the door. He spoke with urgency. 'Listen to me, Perdita Burn, you're not in your English drawing room now, with your codes of decent conduct and your certainties and your hypocritical fuckin' lies. You're here in a field in South Armagh and it's time for some straight talking, because the way things stand your life is not safe. D'you hear me now?'

'Yes.'

'Good. First question. In what context did Ian Frazer send you to see Doherty?' His hands grasped her wrists. His face was inches from her own. She raised her head and tried to look him steadily in the eye.

'There was a misunderstanding.' She could hear her voice tremble. 'While I was talking to him, to Frazer, about the industry—textiles—a message came through from someone I had been trying to get hold of earlier in the day. Frazer overheard the name. It was not someone you would normally contact if you were—'

'Who was it?'

Perdita hesitated. Was the introduction of Sinn Féin into this interrogation going to make things better or worse?

'Who the fuck was it?'

'Fionnuala James,' she said.

She watched for his reaction but his face was impassive. 'Go on.'

'When he heard it, Mr Frazer said something like—I can't exactly remember—that if I was going to contact republicans, these were the men I ought to speak to.'

'Did he now?' muttered her captor, half to himself.

'Well, something like that. So then he gave me Brian Doherty's number.'

'Who else did he name?'

'No one else.'

'You just said "men".'

'Doherty's was the only name. I'd had a lot of difficulty getting hold of Fionnuala James. I'd been trying for several days. I had to leave Dublin. I have to be in Belfast tomorrow—today—so I thought I would contact Mr Doherty on my way. I wish to God I hadn't,' she added passionately.

'And why were you, the maker of a film on Irish tweed

and Ulster linen, so keen to speak to Fionnuala James?'

'It was nothing to do with the film. It was an—an errand. For someone in London. It was unconnected. Ian Frazer misunderstood. Now I'm wondering if he was setting me up for this.'

'He was setting you up for something, all right,' the man said harshly. 'But not for this. Stop snivelling.' She had started to cry. 'Did you speak to Fionnuala James before you left?'

'When I was able to call back, no one was there. I left her a note.'

'You told her you were going to see Doherty?'

'No. I didn't know I was at the time. I told her I would try and reach her tomorrow.'

'Okay.'

'You're hurting my wrists,' she said. His grip relaxed. He turned back to stare through the windscreen. He rubbed his face with his hands. He looked very tired. At length, he said, 'I don't know what the hell to do with you.'

He started the car once more and reversed out of the field. Perdita wiped her eyes. They resumed their journey. She wondered what the time was.

'Why did you tell me that about your father?' he asked after a while. 'About being in the forces?'

She didn't know. She was still wondering herself.

They drove in silence. Suddenly he said, 'Are you a Christian?'

'What do you mean?'

'I have a friend,' he said, 'who was once on the run. Well, he was many times on the run but on this particular occasion he and his comrades took over a house for a while which belonged to a Christian family. They were Protestants. When my friends left, they prepared to take one of the sons of the family as hostage with them, to ensure the silence of the others, but the mother pleaded with them not to do so. My friend, who had trained as a priest in his youth, got them to swear on the family Bible that if he agreed to leave their son behind, they would not contact the RUC for seventy-two hours. They kept their promise.'

She had heard this story. It confirmed her assumption that he was IRA. She said, 'I'm not a Christian, but I won't go to the police.'

'On what, or by whom, then, will you swear?'

'I will not swear,' she said. 'It has no meaning for me. But I will not go to the RUC.'

He spoke low and urgently. 'You must not underestimate the danger to your life, Mrs Burn. Why will you not do as I say?'

She gave him a withering look. 'Because I'm being straight with you,' she said. 'Heaven's sakes! If I'd wanted to, I could have turned you over to the army back there!'

He grunted. 'But you were scared of them.'

'I was more scared of you! Of course I'm bloody scared! But what's the use of doing something I don't believe in? I've told you I won't report this, and I won't!' She decided to take a risk. 'Could you not telephone Fionnuala James, at least?'

'Would she vouch for you?'

'How could she? We've never met. But if she chose to, she could tell you why I had gone to see her.'

'Why won't *you* tell me?'

'Because I don't know who you are.'

'But you would do anything to get away from me?'

'Only if I thought it would work!'

He said nothing. They had come to a small town. She saw a green telephone box. They must have crossed the border again. Where on earth were they? The streetlights lit up her watch. It was almost two am.

'Why should I trust you?' he asked at last.

'I give you my word,' she said. It sounded hopelessly pompous.

'What kind of word is that? The word of a middle-class Englishwoman with a name out of Shakespeare and a father in Her Majesty's Royal Navy. Who says she's not a Christian. Who comes from a nation of liars and cheats. Who condemns the cause of Irish republicanism because, from where she stands, "violence is wrong". Am I right?'

'If that's the way you want to see it,' Perdita said.

'Oh? That's the way it is! You can afford to condemn "violence". You've never had to struggle for anything. You haven't had to contend with being starved, being harassed, being oppressed by your neighbours, being forced to take the shit jobs—or no jobs—just because of your name and your religion. Easy for you to preach democracy, when you've invented the rules for it. All democracy has ever done for us in the North of Ireland is screw us to the ground. We are violent, Perdita, because we have been driven to it. And we've been driven to it by you.'

To be subjected to a political homily at this point of the evening made her want to scream. With a great effort of will, she attempted to keep her voice neutral as she said, 'But now you're moving away from all that. Aren't you?'

'We are,' he agreed. 'You all make it sound so simple. But it's not done overnight. As you see.'

Perdita was not about to question him on the Keady bomb. She said nothing. No point in trying to reason with him.

They had been driving through the outskirts of the town and had reached a railway station. He now pulled up at the mouth of the station car park. There was just one car parked neatly in the nearest bay. Perdita started. It was her hire car.

'You are not to touch it or go near it,' he told her. 'If you do, you will be a major suspect for the business last night.'

'What about the roadblock? Won't they come for me in any case?'

He shook his head. 'They wrote nothing down. There will be no record you were stopped. But should they find the driver who gave you directions, that hire car will be red hot. D'you understand what I'm saying?'

'Of course,' she said. 'But why are you protecting me?'

'Oh, it's not you I'm protecting,' he told her. 'Were you taken to Castlereagh, I'd not give a flying fuck for my chances. They'd have you talking inside five minutes.'

'Well, thanks,' she said.

He turned to her, his eyes alight with urgency. 'Make no mistake, Perdita. It is not a picnic. Your English voice would get you nowhere in there: they'd see you as a defector. To them, defectors are scum. Defectors are worse than us.'

She nodded. She could believe it.

He resumed his instructions. 'In the morning, you take the train to Belfast. You call the hire company. You tell them you left the car here at nine o'clock last night. You tell them you left the keys under the sun visor. The papers are in order. Anything that happened to the car after that—you know nothing.'

He reversed, turned and drove on into town. Suddenly, Perdita smelt the sea. He took her, moving slowly as he sought the street names, to a house near the seafront. Outside, a small, lit sign: 'Cooley Point. Irish Farmhouse Breakfasts. Vacancies'. 'You can wake them,' he said. 'No problem. Tell them you were stranded. Your car broke down. They like wee English girls. Go. Oh, and listen, ah… I'm sorry about all the language. You know?' He gave her a single wry smile. Then he reached into the back seat for her bags.

It was all so sudden. Dazed, she unlocked the door and opened it. She felt she should say something. 'I promise—' she began.

'Okay.' He cut her off. 'Now get out, would you? I haven't got all night.'

She clambered stiffly out onto the pavement, picked up her bags and shut the car door. Without so much as a glance at her, he drove away.

Chapter 5

When Vernon Potts joined the press office, Daniel had found him quite matey. He had seemed to take an interest in Daniel's life outside the office and they'd eaten their sandwiches together from time to time in St James's Park. Daniel had even shyly revealed his passion for second-hand books, and Vernon had said he was rather keen on them too, though when Daniel asked what he collected it quickly became clear Vernon was merely being polite.

Recently, however, his colleague had been pretty standoffish. Daniel put it down to the publication of the latest long-range rocket artillery review, which seemed to be having a corrosive effect on Vernon's nerves. Long-range rockets were Vernon's speciality, apparently. With the retreat from Germany, gunners were flocking home with multiple rocket launchers and 45-tonne tracked AS-90 self-propelled guns.

They needed somewhere to fire them. Vernon had no patience with anyone who raised objections to their loosing them off in Britain's national parks. The storm of protest from ramblers, archaeologists, entomologists, poets and the National Trust goaded him to fury.

'Poets?' Daniel asked with interest.

'God, yes. You wouldn't believe the fuss. The Wordsworth Society's in a lather because William and Dorothy spent ten minutes in Jedburgh. Swinburne, whoever he is, stayed somewhere near the A1—I mean, we're talking the 1850s here, not last August bank holiday.'

To Vernon had fallen the task of coordinating these submissions and preparing for publication the Ministry's reply. Today was to be the news conference at which the minister would make a statement and only this morning, Vernon complained to Daniel, he had found in the file a submission from the RSPB about the Great Grey Shrike, a bird he had never heard of. Some halfwit was bound to raise it this afternoon. Daniel tried to be sympathetic, while silently willing the Great Grey Shrike to beat off the AS90.

In part, Vernon's distraction suited Daniel because it relieved him of having to account for his own preoccupation, but for once he would have welcomed the chance for a chat. In the few short weeks of his tenure in the department, Vernon seemed to have made it his business to find out about everything and everybody; he might well know who, or what, occupied Room 501—the destination of Daniel's mysterious memo—without being interested enough to bother asking why he wanted to know. Now, as the hour of the news conference approached, Vernon sharpened his pencils, took his T.A. tie out of the filing cabinet and bustled out with a self-important sigh.

Once he had gone, Daniel sat for a minute or two savouring the calm that had descended on the press office. But all too rapidly his own preoccupations came flooding back. Since the bomb at Keady, everything had attained a currency that Daniel found terrifying. He fervently wished that Vernon could have been someone else—anyone in whom he could confide. In his anxiety, he had even attempted to reach Perdita by leaving a message at her home, a move he knew to be foolish. But there was nothing to be done. He dragged his attention back to the half-opened pile of mail in front of him and mechanically reached for the next envelope.

*

Perdita woke to the sounds of a morning fairly advanced. She swung her feet from the squashy bed and went to the window, drawing back the sprigged curtains. Women with pushchairs and wheelie-shopping bags were coming and going from a small baker's in the street beneath. A black and white dog threaded its way purposefully between them, and at the crossroad the view opened out to the glittering sea. Perdita gazed at it in disbelief. In the hall below, a telephone rang. Footsteps hurried up the stairs.

'Mrs Burn!' A knock at the door. 'Telephone for you.'

'What?' She had no idea herself where she was, nor even if this was the east coast or the west. She threw her kimono around her. 'It's not possible!' she told the man on the stairs, though the remark was addressed entirely to herself.

But there was no mistake. 'Perdita Burn?' A brisk, female, Irish voice.

'Who's this?' asked Perdita.

'Fionnuala James,' said the voice. 'I received your note.'

'How on earth—?'

'You're to contact the advice centre as soon as you reach Belfast. This needs to be discussed as a matter of urgency. Our publicity officer is aware of the situation. Speak to Ray.'

'Where am I?' Perdita couldn't stop herself from asking.

The briskness in Fionnuala James's voice became positively withering. 'In Dundalk, of course. You will find there is a train in one hour. I must tell you we are less than happy at your... visit last night.'

'*You* are? How the hell do you think I feel?'

'You do not make arrangements behind our back.'

Perdita was furious. 'I was just trying to do my job! I wouldn't have gone there if you hadn't been so elusive yourself!'

'You will receive absolutely no cooperation from us unless you make approaches through the proper channels. I want that understood. Now hurry up or you'll miss your train. Ray will be waiting to hear from you.' And she was gone.

Perdita made her way to the station, discovering to her annoyance that there was more than one train to Belfast; that the journey would take not much more than an hour and she need not have hurried. What was it about these people: their bossiness and their rules? In a small act of defiance, she opened the door of her hire car and retrieved the tapes from the back seat. But as they pulled out of the station, she was struck by the alarming possibility that Mrs James had designated this train because there would be some kind of communication during the journey. Nerves still jangling from the horrific events of the night, it occurred to her that she might be approached, threatened—she couldn't imagine what might happen, or how—but she was, after all, the witness to a hideous crime. They had no reason to trust her. Someone must want her silenced. She glanced nervously around the carriage and shifted her seat closer to a knot of elderly women who appeared to be out on a jaunt.

Well, of course, now she must go to the police. It was absurd to keep her word to a killer. But as soon as she had made this decision, she began to feel more, not less, uneasy. First of all, what was she to tell the RUC about her reason for visiting Doherty's house the previous night? If Doherty had been some kind of dissident republican, as Frazer implied he was, it might be difficult to convince them of her own innocence. She would have to explain about Daniel and the document, and that was impossible. Her captor's words came back to her: *to the RUC, defectors are scum. Defectors are worse than us.* Oh God, what had possessed her to go blathering on to him about her family? She frowned, forcing herself to prod the fearful bruise of last night; to think back to how much she had told him. Was it perhaps some survival thing, some weird instinct that the more he knew about her, the harder it would be for him to shoot her dead? And, worse than that, she had made him an undertaking. Oh, she knew perfectly well what his game was, challenging her sense of honour with that story of the Protestant family who kept their promise. She wasn't going to fall for that! All the same, she *had* given him her word, and that was not nothing, even to a terrorist. Besides, if she felt herself to be at risk now from her captor and his people, how much more real would be the risk once she had betrayed them? Perdita stared bleakly through the window. The police were out of the question. She had embarked on this business and she would have to see it through on her own. She forced herself to calm down. Whoever he was, the man clearly had a direct line to Fionnuala James. As she had tartly reminded Ian Frazer, Sinn Féin was a legal organisation with, it appeared, a tight code of discipline. No harm could come to her if she played straight with them. Could it?

To distract herself from these unsettling thoughts, she searched the map for clues of their route the previous night. In her ignorance she had not realised how idiosyncratic was the border at this point; the southern county of Monaghan reaching up into Northern Ireland in a manner which seemed nothing to do with geography. Her captor must have wanted to avoid the South Armagh border in the wake of the Keady bomb and the fire, so they had probably driven in a wide circle to get back to Dundalk, a stone's throw from Cullabeg and the start of their bizarre journey.

The *Irish News* she had bought at the station was full of the Keady bombing but it had obviously gone to press before the fire at Cullabeg. The terrifying night, with its culmination in the clean, comfortable room at an ordinary seaside boarding house, began to play tricks on her mind. The phone call from Fionnuala James, she realised, was the only proof that her captor actually existed. As for Brian Doherty, the mystery of Ian Frazer's connection to him was unfathomable.

Perdita reached for her notebook and began to list the

duties of the day. Car. That was the first thing: she must make the call to the hire company. She decided to do it from a public telephone, although she knew the RUC would have no difficulty tracing her if they wanted to. Secondly, she must contact Ray at Sinn Féin. They would have to take her more seriously now. Third, her meetings, already scheduled. Oh God, the stupid film... fourth, Daniel. Perdita gazed out at the tawny countryside, pleasant, unexceptional, wholly unlike the mysterious terrain near the border. She needed an ally, a confidant. Nick? Not any longer. Nick had made it pretty clear that he was stepping back. Jeremy then? Certainly not. Hugh? No: well, maybe. Ian Frazer? Was he friend or foe? As the train wound through the outskirts of Belfast, its spires and slate roofs glinting beneath the great shadow of the mountain, Perdita thought she had never felt so alone in her life.

'I'd like to speak to Ray, please.'

'Wait 'til I see if he's there.'

Perdita waited. The Radio Downtown Belfast news summary was playing beside the telephone. And here it was, at last: '*A body has now been recovered from the wreckage of a burnt-out house at Cullabeg, South Armagh. The fire occurred just hours after yesterday's bombing at Keady and RUC sources believe it to be an arson attack. They are not ruling out a link between the two incidents...*'

'Hello there?'

'Ray?'

'He's not here right now.'

Perdita took a deep breath. 'I'm phoning on the instruction of Fionnuala James. She said it was urgent that I talk to him.

When will he be there?'

'It's hard to say. Later, maybe.'

'Will you give him a message, please? Will you tell him I need to speak to him today?' On the point of giving them the hotel number, she hesitated. 'I'll be phoning back.'

'Okay. It's Miss Burn, is it?'

'How d'you know?'

'Sure, we're not daft,' said the voice, with a laugh.

By the time she had rung off, the news bulletin was over.

When Perdita entered Ian Frazer's office, she found he was not alone.

'My dear Perdita!' He strode round his large desk to greet her. 'How very good to welcome you to the North.'

'Thank you,' said Perdita, a little surprised at this chummy reception after their acrimonious parting in Dublin.

'May I introduce Milton Lithgow?' Frazer continued, a light hand at her elbow steering her to the window from which Lithgow had turned to survey her.

'I'm delighted to meet you,' Lithgow said, shaking her hand and peering greedily into her face. It took a moment for Perdita to place him, remembering only that he was one of a clutch of Unionist MPs. 'I shan't intrude on your *tête-à-tête*,' he added. 'I was just fascinated to meet you and I wanted to say how thrilled I am at this time of turning swords to ploughshares, as it were, that a British television company wants to make a film about what's right in our lovely province instead of dwelling on what's wrong with it.'

'Well, I only arrived in Belfast this morning and I'm amazed at the changes,' she responded. 'It's almost as if there

87

had never been a war.' She watched their faces as she said it.

'Come, Miss Burn, you're speaking like a nationalist,' Frazer chided her. 'We prefer not to regard our little local difficulties as a war but as the work of a few fanatics.'

'Well, a few fanatics that kept you busy for thirty years,' Perdita said lightly. 'You must be hopeful that the worst is behind you.'

'We pray it is. We pray it is,' said Lithgow absently. 'At least, we hope the Troubles are behind us, even if the Peace still proves elusive. How much do you know about Ulster politics, Miss Burn?'

'Almost nothing,' Perdita confessed. 'I prefer to stick to textiles.' She looked at Frazer expectantly, hoping for an initiative that would get rid of this old buffoon. Frazer declined to take the cue.

'When we last met, however, I had the impression you were fairly new to the world of textiles also,' he said sweetly.

'I admit it,' agreed Perdita. 'That's us journalists all over.'

'You're upsetting her, Ian,' said Lithgow. 'He's no idea how to treat a lady, Miss Burn. He lacks the experience.' His tongue appeared briefly between rather yellow teeth. 'And now I must leave you two together. I can't abide one more minute without a cigarette. This man forbids me to smoke in his office.' The entire speech was delivered to Perdita in an intimate tone. He patted Frazer on the shoulder and touched Perdita's hand, the briefest of gestures that made her recoil. At the door, he turned. 'Are you positive now?' he said to Frazer, businesslike again.

Frazer nodded. 'Believe me, Milton. We can do better than that.'

Then Lithgow was gone.

Perdita moved to the window and took his place, gazing out. Ian Frazer certainly knew how to create a pleasant working environment. The main building was a refurbished early nineteenth-century mill, which he had restored with taste and care. Within the walls of his semi-circular office, no expense had been spared. The wide floorboards had been polished and exposed, setting off two fine antique rugs. Perdita found the place uncomfortably attractive, and Frazer's evident affection for it she found attractive, too.

'Circular offices—' he indicated the room around them. 'You've no doubt seen them in the Lancashire mill towns. They were constructed for the managers around the mill chimneys for warmth. It was the only place,' he added with a note of self-deprecation, 'the *only* place in the entire factory that received any heating. Can you imagine? It's the reason I installed such a splendid system on the shop floor, so I could take this beautiful room with a clear conscience.' He waved her toward the sofa and threw himself into an armchair upholstered in terracotta linen. 'So, welcome to the new Northern Ireland, Perdita Burn. Admit it. You're impressed. I can see you are!'

His secretary arrived with tea; silver teapot, white bone china cups and saucers.

In her head Perdita was trying to frame the questions about his terms of employment and recruitment policies in a manner that would not antagonise. This countryside she knew to be devoutly loyalist; red, white and blue painted signposts and kerbstones in the surrounding villages a permanent celebration of fealty to the British Crown.

As if reading her thoughts, Frazer watched the young

woman lay out the tea things and then said, 'Thank you, Sinéad,' with a little emphasis on the girl's name, adding to Perdita, 'Ask her where in Belfast she comes from.'

Sinéad was evidently used to this. 'I'm from Twinbrook,' she said.

Perdita was surprised. To employ Catholics from the heart of a nationalist enclave was impressive. 'How do you get here?' she enquired.

'Sure, there's a works bus leaves from the Dublin Road each morning,' Sinéad told her. 'It's free. It's grand.' She beamed at them both and left.

'West Belfast once had a proud tradition of flax spinning and linen production,' Frazer explained. 'I believe her father and grandfather worked in it. But all the same it can't be easy here for Sinéad: she has a sister in Maghaberry.'

Perdita was startled. 'What's her sister convicted of?' she asked.

'They call it shoplifting,' said Frazer. 'That's the republican idea of a joke, by the way: didn't she lift Marks & Spencer's a good ten inches off the ground just down the road there, at Lisburn!'

'A bombing?'

'The store was closed. No one was killed in it. She'll be out in a couple of years. Strain on the family, all the same.'

Perdita sipped her tea reflectively. 'So the bus from West Belfast is a deliberate policy?' she asked. Privately, she wanted to know *why*. Was this energetic entrepreneur, this new Victorian, a genuine philanthropist?

'Well now, Mrs Burn, am I knocking down a few of your preconceptions here?' he challenged. 'Am I not quite the mad loyalist ogre your friends had led you to believe?'

'I don't know what you're talking about,' Perdita said evenly. 'Who do you suppose I would have asked since yesterday?' For a moment her captor's face flashed into her mind.

'Well, you may not have done your homework on me, but I at least pay you the compliment of checking up on you. And let me tell you, Perdita Burn, if this is a film about tweed, linen and the peace dividend then the Pope's a Protestant.'

Perdita shrugged. 'To be honest with you, Mr Frazer, I wish it was about more. But it isn't.'

'So tell me why is Perdita Burn, scourge of governments, champion of lost causes, interviewing me about my textile business?'

Perdita sighed. The world had changed, she told him, amused at herself for channelling Jeremy. No TV company was going to pay for big investigations any longer. She was a working mother with a mortgage to pay… 'But since you're asking me straight questions,' she hurried on before he could interrupt her, 'I have one for *you*. What on earth were you doing sending me into a booby trap in South Armagh last night?'

Frazer frowned. He didn't follow.

'You give me Brian Doherty's number,' said Perdita. 'I call him. We make an appointment. I arrive at his house and find myself in the middle of a conflagration.'

As she spoke, Frazer's eyes widened. '*You* were there?'

'Had I arrived fifteen minutes earlier, one of the charred bodies they recovered from the ruins this morning would probably have been mine. Who was this man, and what were you doing sending me to visit him?'

'What happened to you?' Frazer sounded as if he were playing for time.

'Never mind what happened. I got away.'

'Were you questioned by the police?'

'What's that to you, Mr Frazer?'

Frazer jumped up from his chair and went to the window. After a moment he said, 'It was a bad night for peace in Ulster. That I can tell you.'

Perdita watched him, his fingers clenching and unclenching behind his back.

'He was a good man,' Frazer said. 'A republican, but a straight republican. Yes, there are a few. A man who had the good sense to see that prosperity and peace are inseparable.' He turned back to face her.

'So?' Perdita prompted.

'Many of us who have worked for peace in Ulster for a long time—oh, a *long* time, let me tell you—have reached across the divide and built-up contacts with each other. In that way I met Brian Doherty. Now I mourn him as a friend.' Perdita said nothing. 'South Armagh,' Frazer went on, 'is just about the hardest place for anyone to control. They've a breed of terrorist down there would make your hair stand on end. They're gangsters, murderers and of course over the years they've made a mint of money with the racketeering. As you may know, those men down on the border are always the last to agree to a ceasefire: they're making fortunes out it, Perdita. They'd do anything to break the peace.'

'The Keady bombing,' Perdita ventured. 'They're saying there's a link.'

'Indeed. Now the IRA have their own warped code of justice, as you know. They're like the Mafia. Doherty was policing the ceasefire in South Armagh to make sure it wasn't broken.' His voice thickened; he jumped to his feet and went over to his greatcoat hanging on a stand by the door, felt in the pocket and took out a white laundered handkerchief. 'I hadn't spoken to him for a number of weeks, but my guess is this: terrorists bombed Keady. Doherty knew who they were. So before he could discipline them they got to him.' He dabbed at the corner of his eyes and looked over at her with concern. 'Well, I'm very sorry you had to witness it, Perdita,' he said more softly. 'And as an apology for sending you into the lion's den—and to cheer you up after our gloomy conversation here—I absolutely insist on taking you to dinner.'

Perdita hesitated. She had a nagging sense that this man needed to be kept onside, but at arm's length. 'You're very kind, Mr Frazer, but I lost some time this morning after the excitements of last night. I've work to do and I'm very tired. Thank you, though. Perhaps another time.' The plea of exhaustion was genuine.

'A date in the diary, then.'

'Yes, I'd like that,' she said, telling herself she could sidestep it later.

'Excellent.' He came towards her, the intense blue eyes looking deep into hers. 'The pleasure will be all mine.'

CHAPTER 6

The door buzzed. Perdita pushed it open and found herself in the hallway of what seemed to be a derelict house. A man in a t-shirt was coming down the stairs. Perdita shivered. The place reeked of damp.

'To your left,' said the man. 'Just push the door now.'

Perdita did so and found herself in a small waiting room warmed by a Calor-gas heater and brightly lit. The padded seats around the walls, empty save for a young woman sitting in the corner deep in a puzzle book, looked as though they had come from a long-defunct departure lounge. To one side of the door an elderly man sat before the screen of the security video, homemade from an old black and white Hitachi TV. A knot of cable looped through a hole in the wall. 'You'll be for Ray,' he informed her. 'He'll be right back.'

Perdita sat down to wait. Understanding the psychology

didn't make it any easier to accept. Forcing herself to be patient, she studied the walls, festooned with posters and leaflets that fluttered in the draught whenever anyone opened the door. Irish classes. *De-commissioning: Tactics, Facts and Falsehoods—Come and take part in the debate.* Attendance Allowance: Can You Claim? And the ubiquitous '*Tiocfaidh ár lá*', 'Our Day Will Come'. A set of curling photos mounted on green card with an orange border told of a trip to Donegal for 'the partners and children of POWs'; faces habitually pinched and pale creased with delight around an elderly blue Transit. So young, Perdita thought, you could barely tell which were wives and which daughters. So many blighted lives.

'That there's me you're looking at,' said the girl in the corner suddenly. Perdita turned to her. She had put aside her puzzle book and was smiling wistfully. 'Sure, we had a grand time. Four whole days. First holiday me and my wee boy ever had.'

She didn't look old enough to have a child. 'Which is you?' asked Perdita.

The young woman crossed to the photos. 'My hair was shorter. See? And that's our Sean.' She pointed at a terrifying four-year-old, his head almost shaved, pinning the neck of a friend in a stranglehold. 'He looks ferocious,' she went on, as if seeing her son through Perdita's eyes. 'But he wouldn't hurt a fly. He's like his da, the big softy.'

'Is his dad in prison?' asked Perdita, curious.

'Oh sure. All the kiddies' daddies are. Mostly in the Kesh or Maghaberry. There's a few in England. Sean's Daddy's in England.' She spoke without apparent rancour.

Perdita looked at her. 'Hopefully, with the peace, they'll

release him soon?' she said lamely.

'Not him. He'll be one of the last.' The young woman gave a disconsolate laugh.

Perdita hesitated. Then she ventured, 'What's he in for?'

'Bombin'.'

'What's his sentence?'

'Life.' She spoke with a matter-of-fact pride.

Wouldn't hurt a fly? thought Perdita: men who went on active service to England were the elite. Before the peace, he would have been expected to serve at least twenty years; almost as long as this young woman's life so far. It was probably deserved, she told herself, but it was a hard sentence on his wife and son. 'Are you able to visit?' she asked.

'Hardly ever. His mother went over last Easter. Sometimes we get the Green Cross. I've been twice in three years.'

'It must be terrible not seeing him.'

'I hate going,' she confessed. 'The journey so complicated. Sometimes you get there and they've moved him. You have to go chasing around the country. It's that expensive. The screws treat you like muck: it's like you're some tart, not his wife at all. And they get unsettled, too, the men. Sometimes they say it's easier not to be reminded.'

Perdita felt the leering English prison officers to be her personal responsibility. When would the war end for this family? She wanted to ask more questions but the door opened and a thin man with spectacles came in.

'I'm Ray,' he announced to Perdita without ceremony. They shook hands. 'Fionnuala said you have something to show me.' He sat down. Perdita was taken aback. Surely the matter was confidential? Did he expect her to discuss Daniel's memo right here? She reached for her briefcase but her fingers hesitated on the buckles.

'Never mind Niamh,' said Ray, nodding towards the young woman who had picked up her puzzle book once more. Niamh looked up and grinned. 'Sure, it's all nonsense to me,' she said. Perdita sighed. The story of Niamh was still at the front of her mind. She took out the photocopy of the memo she had made in Dublin and handed it without comment to Ray. She had blocked out some parts of it, keeping Daniel's original copy intact. Ray's expression remained impassive. When he had digested the names and dates he inspected the headed paper. 'You received this, when?' he asked at length.

Perdita briefly explained, omitting any mention of Daniel.

Ray pursed his lips. 'I would say it's a fake,' he said dismissively. 'It's easy to forge a photocopy, so it is.'

Perdita was becoming irritated. 'This document contains privileged information,' she pointed out. 'It *predates* the Keady bomb.'

'I'm aware of that.'

'So whether it's fake or not is irrelevant,' she continued. 'Whoever wrote it knew what they were talking about.'

'What are you saying?'

She looked at him, exasperated. 'Fionnuala James took it seriously.'

'It's her job to take things seriously.'

'So what's your explanation of it?'

'Collusion is one thing. It's always gone on. But this is too blatant.'

'Then how do you explain the fact that the MOD apparently had prior knowledge of an IRA bomb?'

'Who said it was an IRA bomb? You know nothing about it.'

'Well, whose bomb was it then?'

'The IRA absolutely deny responsibility. And if you know anything about them at all, you will know they always claim liability where it's due.'

'So whose bomb does the IRA think it is?'

'I don't speak for the IRA. I'm nothing to do with the IRA.'

Perdita willed herself to be calm. 'I know that. But you must be aware, in all the fallout from this damaging incident— damaging to *you*, after all, and to the peace process—where the IRA is attributing this bomb?'

'You'd have to ask them yourself.'

'All right,' she agreed. 'So how do I do that?'

'I can't rightly say.'

'Can you make enquiries?'

'I'd have to refer it up.'

'I'm here for another five days.'

'It's tight. I'll see what I can do. Can I keep this?' He held up the memo.

Perdita hesitated. 'Is that necessary?'

Ray looked at his watch. 'I can't hang around,' he said. 'If you're not prepared to trust us, how d'you expect us to trust you?'

Perdita was annoyed she hadn't foreseen this. Then she nodded. 'Okay, if you must,' she said uncertainly.

Ray examined the document again. 'In fact, I would need the unredacted copy, the complete document.'

'I'm afraid you can't have that.' She wasn't going to give

them anything that might lead back to Daniel. 'My source was genuine: you'll have to take my word for it. This one has all the information you need.'

'Have it your way,' he shrugged. 'But that there makes my job more difficult.'

'Well I won't *have* a job,' she smiled sweetly at him, 'if I go passing classified documents to an illegal organisation. I'm sure they will be interested enough to discuss it with me.'

'Don't count on it,' he said tartly. 'They're extremely busy just now.'

She wanted to ask why a bunch of paramilitaries should be so particularly pressed in the middle of a ceasefire, but said nothing. They both stood up.

'I'll contact you at the hotel,' he told her. 'But don't hold your breath.' He moved to open the door for her.

'Goodbye, Niamh,' she called to the girl in the corner.

Niamh glanced up from her book. 'Ray, you old misery, can you not show her a good time while she's here? Get her along to the quiz tomorrow night. It's great *craic*,' she told Perdita.

Ray hesitated, his hand on the door. He looked irritated and shy. 'Would you be free tomorrow evening?' he asked.

Perdita made a hurried calculation in her head. She was due in Dungannon tomorrow and would not be back till evening, but this was no date. It was a chance to pin him down. 'I'll be free after eight,' she said.

'If you're interested, the quiz is at the Felons. I'll be able to give you an answer by then, shouldn't wonder. You might find it instructive,' he added with the first smile of the afternoon.

'Thanks,' she said. 'That'd be great.'

'Whenever you get to the door tell them you're with Ray from the Advice Centre. Come at eight-thirty.'

The Felons Club was a purpose-built fortress on the Falls Road. Despite the ceasefire it retained a security system which outshone that of the Sinn Féin Advice Centre, though architecturally the place looked more like a nightclub in Siberia. The Belfast City cab driver who dropped her there was concerned. 'Watch yourself, now,' he said. 'It's no place for wee girls.' She guessed he meant, but did not say, wee English girls.

'It's fine,' she reassured him with a confidence she did not feel. 'I'm meeting friends.'

The foyer was full of the inevitable young men with biceps and short-sleeved t-shirts despite the icy draught knifing through the double doors. One of them raised a questioning eyebrow at Perdita.

'Ray from the Advice Centre?' she asked.

'Not here yet,' said the young man. 'Liam!' he called to a colleague stationed closer to the bar entrance. 'Did you see Ray yet? From the Advice Centre?'

Liam shook his head.

A third man turned on hearing Ray's name. 'Is that the journalist from England?' he shouted across the hubbub. Several people turned to stare at Perdita, who blushed. This man was older. He wore a grey suit jacket over his t-shirt.

'I have some ID,' Perdita told him, reaching into her bag as he came over to her. The man shook his head, smiling. 'That'll not be necessary. Ray told me to expect you. He'll be along later. Go right on in.'

Although she had half expected it, this was alarming. The Felons was not a club you dropped in at alone. Its members and their families all knew each other by virtue of the fact that membership was confined to convicted republicans. She edged through the crowd at the door and found a space standing against the wall from which she could take in the scene before her. The quiz was already under way. Its participants sat in large circles around small tables bristling with glasses. The glasses were continually replenished by a stream of waiters who memorised huge orders, counted change and sashayed through the throng flourishing trays of drinks without spilling a drop.

'For six points,' boomed a voice from the loudspeakers. 'This is one for Table 9: Danny's Boys. Are you listening to me now, Danny? It's a historical one. In what year did the Fenians re-organise as the IRB?'

'1858.' A chorused answer.

'No. It was 1873!' someone protested, and was immediately overruled. Of course, they studied Irish history in prison. My God, Perdita thought, they're all terrorists. And am I their enemy?

'Okay, here's a historical one for you then, Felim!' came the even-tempered voice—Perdita couldn't see where the questions were coming from. 'For Table 8. Six points. Who sang *Love on the Rocks?*'

No one knew.

'Shame on you. Open it to the floor!' instructed the quizmaster. Hands shot up all over the room. 'Okay, Mary Moore?'

'Neil Diamond.'

'Cheat! Cheat! She's your auntie!'

'There's no law,' rejoined the quizmaster, nettled. 'She had her hand up first. Neil Diamond it is. Next question: Table 7.'

Across the room, Perdita saw someone waving in her direction, but such was the commotion in the bar it was a few moments before she realised it was Niamh. Niamh now stood up and beckoned. Perdita began to make her way tortuously around the tables to the group in the centre where Niamh was sitting.

'Gerry. Gerard! Would you ever get the lady a stool!' Niamh commanded a yellow-faced youth to her right. 'That's me little brother,' she explained to Perdita.

He looked at her balefully. 'And where will I do that? Will I conjure one out of the air? Hello there, missus,' he said, standing to greet Perdita as she reached the table. 'Would you sit here, please? No!'—silencing her protest. 'I'm away to the other bar. I've had enough. You can answer for me!' And with a quick grin, he was gone.

Niamh attempted to make some introductions, but the contestants were barracking the quizmaster and no one could hear above the din.

'Order!' came the quizmaster's voice. Next question: Table 5, the No Hopers.'

'Jesus, that's us!' Niamh hissed.

'Two parts to this question: three points each. First part: at whose house in London did the British government meet representatives of IRA and Sinn Féin during the 1972 ceasefire?'

'Willie Whitelaw's, was it?' asked a man *sotto voce* sitting next to Perdita.

'Paul Channon's, I think,' Perdita told him, grateful for her speedreading of some Troubles history before starting the film.

'Are you sure, now?'

'No! But that's the name that came into my head,' Perdita whispered.

'Never heard of him,' said an older woman doubtfully.

'D'you give up, Table 5?'

'Was it Paul Channon?' called out the man.

'Well done, No Hopers. Some debate on that, I fancy. Second part: and what do the letters IRA stand for?'

As the bar erupted, Niamh said to Perdita, 'He's brilliant, this fella doing the questions. He was years in prison. He was a great support to my Connor when Con was first convicted and going through a bad time; they were together in Albany. Con says he's deep, you know? A thinker. Used to talk to them, like, about philosophy and history and all sorts. But he'd have them in stitches, too.'

'Who is he?' Perdita asked. She still hadn't seen him, but there was something eerily familiar about the voice.

'Joseph McGrail. He's very senior.'

'I can't even see where he's sitting.'

'There. Through there. Up at the front... Jesus, he's that sexy, too. If he'd been my husband, I'd not have left him for a single night after he came home! That was a dreadful business when Caitlín got arrested. There's been nobody since, you know. Sure, he really loved her to bits!'

Perdita looked, but could see nothing except the backs of the other competitors. Then she caught sight of Ray. He was leaning at the bar talking earnestly to a slight, elderly man with a shaved head. 'There's Ray,' she said.

'Oh aye. That there's Curly Hughes he's talking to. They call him Curly because he's no hair. That's prison for you. People say Curly's a sticky,[4] but he's a good man.'

'Niamh's got a soft spot for Curly,' teased the man sitting next to Perdita.

'Sure I have!' Niamh agreed. 'Didn't he get me a house! Down at the Executive, pestering them every day till they gave in?'

'Typical Official IRA tactics!'

'*Get away!* If he really was a sticky, he wouldn't dare show his face in here. Come on now. We're supposed to be concentratin' on the quiz.'

'...a political one for Table 3,' called the quizmaster. 'What is the name of Postman Pat's dog?'

'Cat! It was a cat!' they all chorused.

'You been inside too long, Joe!' shouted a contestant. 'Poor wee Fionn got read the essays of Pádraig Pearse, so he did!'

'Sure, I didn't write the questions!' parried the quizmaster equably.

For all the heckling, everyone was taking it seriously. Perdita thought about pub quizzes at home. Here was something else in Ireland, familiar and yet infinitely odd. As she listened, tiredness began to wash over her. It had been a long day. She wanted to know if Ray had an answer for her and then she wanted to go home to bed. She tried unsuccessfully to catch Ray's eye.

---

4 Sticky: a member of the Official IRA.

The quiz began to draw to a close. Representatives of the three leading tables were called up to the front and were now having a final shootout. The questions had become more difficult. Many sitting at the back had stopped attempting to listen and conversations had broken out all over the bar. Suddenly Ray looked over and signalled to Perdita. He had clearly known where she was sitting all along. Curly Hughes was now nowhere to be seen but Ray had been joined by two women. He introduced his wife, Sheila, when Perdita came up to them. Sheila and her friend were teachers. They were discussing Stephen Rea's performance in *Uncle Vanya*, which had also gone on tour to London. Perdita, who had loved it, joined in, but her head was aching. Eventually she said to Ray, 'So, is there news?'

'There is.' Ray was almost scowling. 'You're in luck.'

'They'll see me?'

He nodded. 'They will. Frankly, I'm surprised. You seem to have something of a reputation.'

'I do?'

'They don't see everybody.'

Sheila had tactfully buried herself in a fresh conversation with her friend.

Perdita's headache receded. 'When?'

'Tomorrow. Five pm.'

'Okay.' Her afternoon meeting should be over by three-thirty.

'The Glen Road shopping centre at the end of the Falls, just this side of the Ringway. McCaffrey's Bakery. There's a couple of tables. Take a cup of coffee and wait there.'

She smiled. Trust Sinn Féin. 'Shall I have two spoons of

sugar in it?' she asked.

'I'm sorry?'

'It doesn't matter,' she said hurriedly. 'Am I to read the *Irish News*, or something?'

'That won't be necessary. You've been seen.'

She glanced around self-consciously. Of course they were here, watching perhaps at this very moment. 'Excellent, Ray. Thank you,' she said.

'No bother,' he said, in a voice that conveyed it clearly had been. Perdita wondered how Sheila put up with him. He started to say something further but it was drowned in an explosion of catcalls and applause. The quiz was over. She turned towards the corner where the victors were now being presented with vodkas and pints of Guinness on the house. The quizmaster, the legendary Joseph McGrail, was surrounded by a laughing knot of friends and acquaintances. She still couldn't see him but she caught the expressions of those at the outside of the group, their faces alight with respect. The press of people, women as well as men, began to shift in Perdita's direction, towards the door. Then she saw him. She had grown in certainty that it *was* him as the evening progressed; the distortion of the loudspeakers was insufficient to disguise the voice she remembered so vividly from the dark car. He was laughing, intimately she thought, with a woman as he passed her, but as if drawn by Perdita's gaze he raised his eyes. The laughter died momentarily. For a full three seconds they stared at one another. Then the crowd swept him on. Perdita stole a glance at Ray, but he was buying drinks and had noticed nothing. She drank hers as quickly as she could and wished them goodnight. At the door, the man with the jacket winked at her. 'Was it better *craic* than in London?'

'It was,' she told him. 'It was brilliant.'

Perdita's meeting finished early the next day, and glancing at her watch she calculated she would have time for a little research before her date at the bakery. Making for the Sinn Féin bookshop on the Lower Falls, she found, as she might have expected, a considerable display of histories of the Troubles, amongst them a rich seam of American publications unavailable on the British mainland. Cursing the books without indexes, she began to hunt for references to dissident republican groups, cross-sectarian initiatives and for—the name started out at her from a new edition of Dominic Magee's authoritative history of the Provisionals: McGrail, J. Perdita looked through each reference.

Joseph McGrail had a youth mirrored by hundreds of other Irish nationalists of his generation. Born and brought up in Derry. History studies at Liverpool University interrupted by the Bloody Sunday massacre of 1972. Joined the Provisional IRA and because of his ability and knowledge of England, sent on active service to London just two years later. Convicted of planting bombs in central London between 1977-81, the first major incidents since the conviction of the IRA active service unit captured after the Balcombe Street siege. One of the masterminds behind a spectacular escape from prison in 1985—yes, she vaguely remembered that. Settled in Dublin, where his wife, Caitlín O'Connor, *q.v.*, was able to rejoin him (one son, Fionn, b.1986), but returned frequently undercover to Belfast—what a nerve, she thought—where he was part of a senior strategy team within the Provisionals. Re-arrested in the North in 1992 and returned to England to finish serving his original sentence. Released 1995. (That must have been under the early release scheme extended by the British Government after the '94 ceasefire, she supposed.) Well, it was some cv. She closed the book and returned it to the shelf. She felt sick.

She was about to leave the shop when she remembered she had not looked up McGrail's wife. O'Connor. O'Connor... Caitlín O'Connor had also been on active service in England. She was wanted for a string of offences in the seventies and eighties but had never been caught. The British tabloids had christened her the 'miniskirt bomber' because of a short green skirt allegedly found abandoned behind the hot pipes of a safe house in Cricklewood, North London, from which she had had to make a speedy getaway. The epithet had added to her reputation as 'the IRA's sexiest weapon'. Magee had a picture reference. Perdita turned to it: a young woman with a cloud of dark hair and blue eyes smiled fuzzily from the page. Yes, thought Perdita, she was certainly beautiful. Then she caught the heading at the top of the page of portraits: *Dying for Ireland.* So this must be the 'dreadful business' alluded to by Niamh: she turned back to the text. Caitlín O'Connor had returned to the struggle in 1995. She was shot dead in 1996 by a security guard during an attempted escape from prison in Frankfurt, where she was awaiting extradition to the UK after being arrested near a British Army base in Germany.

Perdita paid for her purchases and left the shop, sunk in thought. She reached into her bag for the Belfast street map. Although she had not given much thought to it in advance, she realised she was feeling apprehensive as she set off for her rendezvous.

The Glen Road shopping centre was constructed of weeping concrete and to Perdita looked thoroughly British; built in the 1970s, it seemed to come from the same stable as the earlier, unlamented Divis Flats.

McCaffrey's was the less appealing of two bakeries on the ground floor. It sold not wheaten farls and potato cakes but iced slices and cream horns. A badly engineered track of Daniel O'Donnell singing *Leaving is Easy (When Loving is Hard)* played in the background. Wincing at the prospect of spending half an hour here, having arrived earlier than she meant to, Perdita obediently ordered coffee and sat down to wait. Why had Caitlín O'Connor, the mother of a nine-year-old son, gone back to active service at the very time McGrail was released from prison? *That poor little boy...* how could any mother do such a thing? And why? Had she and Joe fallen out? The girl at the Felons, Niamh, had hinted Caitlín was the one to leave; that he had been devoted to her. *Come on*, she admonished herself: just because *you* wouldn't have done it—which is why you're not a revolutionary! And besides, it's none of your business.

She had half-expected her contact would be Curly Hughes, since he was the man she had seen talking to Ray the night before, but when the call came it was from a stranger. She looked up from her newspaper to see him pause at the table. He nodded at her, a slight narrowing of the eyes, and passed on to the counter to buy a couple of sausage rolls. Was that it? Perdita folded her paper and stood up uncertainly. Without a glance in her direction the man took the paper bag with grease already seeping through it and left the shop. Perdita followed. Her heart was thudding now. At the entrance to the shopping centre a black taxi appeared in the dusk and drew level with the man. He climbed in. Perdita caught up with him and peered uncertainly through the window, whereupon he leaned across and opened the rear door for her. She had heard of people being blindfolded on such journeys, but her guide neither moved nor spoke. Was he the right man? It was both nerve racking and faintly absurd.

In the event there was no need for a blindfold. The cab ground its way up the Shaws Road and plunged off to the left through a twilit maze of small streets of identical semi-detached houses, round and round, so that she knew she would never have been able to find the place again.

They stopped at last beside a line of boulders that ran round the perimeter of a block of low-rise flats, one of several they had seen along the way. The man, still without a word, got out and Perdita followed. The street was deserted. He led her up two flights of acrid stairs built around a well with no light, save for some concrete lattice-work blocks that let in a moaning wind and a dappled yellow glow from outside; then along a walkway, past windows and doors, several of which were boarded-up. From the courtyard beneath came a reassuring squeal of children playing in the dark. Beyond them, far below, she could see the lights of central Belfast. At the last door on the passageway her guide stopped and rat-tatted once sharply with the flap of the letterbox. The man who answered, stood back in the unlit hall to allow them to pass. The flat was achingly cold and, though she could see nothing, struck her as empty, unfurnished. She followed her guide down a short corridor to a closed door. He knocked and walked in.

The room, a bedroom, was lit by a lone bulb. In one corner was a chair with a padded seat and wooden arms. It faced a single bed, pressed up against the opposite wall and covered with a stained blue eiderdown. The only other object in the room—she was glad to see it—was an old-fashioned dalek-shaped orange paraffin heater. Condensation dribbled down the window pane. A man sat on the bed, his face in shadow.

'Please sit down,' he said.

Perdita took the armchair. On the instant, she recognised his voice again and she felt a lurch of fear. Once more it was her captor, the quizmaster, the man she had just been reading about, Joseph McGrail. Her guide perched on the end of the bed.

There was no preamble. 'This document,' McGrail said. It was lying on the bed beside him. 'Why have you brought it to us?'

'Because I want to find out what it means.'

'But why should we know? This document comes from the British government.' His voice was quiet, impersonal. They might have been strangers, yet she shrank from his presence in the shadowed corner as if they were back in the car.

'Weren't the IRA behind the bomb at Keady?' she asked.

'Have they said they were?'

'How could the British government know in advance about the Keady bomb?'

'Perhaps they planted it.'

'Is that what you think, then?'

'I'm not going to discuss what we think. That's not your business,' he said. 'But it seems to me the question you should be asking is why *you?* Someone is trying to set you up. Your government contact. He's going to get you into a lot of trouble.'

'No one's setting me up,' she said. 'I think he's the target.'

McGrail shrugged. 'You or him. Have you asked him why? If you approach the problem from that end maybe you'll find an answer to some of your questions. You won't find answers here.'

She was seething with frustration. There must be more to learn than this. 'Doesn't it suggest some kind of collusion?' she asked. 'The memo?'

McGrail ignored her. 'The taxi will take you back, Mrs Burn, though regrettably not to your hotel. These fellas can't go there. He'll drop you in the centre.' He stood up and with a gesture to her silent guide indicated he had nothing more to say.

'Why did you go to the trouble of seeing me?' she asked, her eyes searching his face angrily. The meeting had been a waste of time.

He laughed; said nothing. The guide went out into the corridor. Perdita started to follow, but McGrail said, very quietly, 'Wait.'

She turned back to him. He was right behind her, leaned past her to push the door half-closed. In the cramped room they were forced to stand close together.

She was aware of the guide, waiting in the corridor, chatting to the man on the door. McGrail spoke softly: 'I wanted to warn you.'

'*Warn* me?'

'Frazer. Don't touch him. Don't trust him.' Gone was the tone of indifference.

'He'll be in my film,' she said, confused. 'The linen mill.

112

His new employment practices.'

'Yes, yes. Do what you have to do for your stupid film. That mill of his is all shite. If you were to do something half-useful you might enquire where he gets the money. But you won't do that. Do what you have to for those TV people in London and then get out. Don't let Frazer use you. Well, of course, he is using you. He's getting valuable PR out of it.' He spoke low, rapidly, his demeanour altogether changed. His dark eyes glittered with the urgency of what he had to say. She wondered what the two men in the corridor would have made of it, had they seen. 'But don't let him have any kind of power over you,' McGrail continued. 'The man is ruthless. You know of his connection with Brian Doherty. Believe me, whatever he tells you is false. Do your film and leave Belfast. Forget the rest. Forget this document.'

'What do you know about the document?' she asked urgently, sensing one last chance. 'There's something you're not telling me!'

He hesitated. 'There's dirty business in there,' he muttered. 'Stuff you cannot know and must not ask. Don't touch it. And, believe me, Frazer is in it somewhere. Not directly, but a part of it.'

'It's not possible!'

'There's others, too. They're using your man for some reason. I think they must be using you.'

She hesitated, desperate to discover more. 'Is Milton Lithgow, the MP, involved?' she asked. She had had a powerful feeling that it was no accident their paths had crossed at the mill two days ago.

'Hear what I'm saying, Perdita: keep clear of the whole lot

of them. You are on ground more dangerous than you know.'
He laid his fingers on her arm for a moment to emphasise his
words. 'Now, get along with you.'

Shaken, she turned and left the room.

*

Just as he was starting to feel a little calmer, a second document
arrived in Daniel's mail. He held the single sheet of paper in his
shaking fingers. What was this? Were they trying to unhinge
him? What was he supposed to *do*, for God's sake? Vernon
was drafting a press release, his two typing fingers tumbling
haphazardly onto the keyboard. Occasionally he would stop,
read to himself what he had written and exhale with a hissing
sound through clenched teeth. Daniel stuck a Post-it note
over the code in the corner of the document, rose from his
desk, walked calmly to the photocopier and copied it, keeping
one eye on Vernon. Then he re-sealed the envelope with the
original memo inside and slipped the copy into page seven of
a paper on procurement.

'How d'you spell "renege"?' asked Vernon.

Daniel spelt it.

'That's wrong,' Vernon told him. 'There's definitely a *u* in
it somewhere.'

'If you insist.'

Vernon looked up impatiently. 'What's that supposed to
mean?'

'The *u* is archaic.'

'Don't be ridiculous.'

'Whatever,' Daniel said.

'Bugger.' Vernon reached for the dictionary.

'Big word for the hacks,' Daniel observed.

'It's the right word,' replied Vernon crossly. 'Okay, that's it.' He peeled two sheets from the printer. 'I've got to drop this off before eleven.' And he strode from the office.

As soon as his footsteps had died away, Daniel put the paper on procurement, the copied document inside it, into his briefcase. Then he buried his head in his hands. What ought he to do? Something horrible was going on. The new memo was laid out in the same way with the same heading as its predecessor, but contained just a single name and date. *Why* was he being sent these things? Perdita seemed to think he was being framed, but his own view was that someone was passing him the information in the hope that, as a press officer, he would be in a better position to leak it. Daniel felt torn in two. On the one hand, he didn't want anything to do with it and the idea of breaking a cardinal rule of his service sickened him. On the other, he recoiled from the notion of his department staging a cover-up on this scale. If someone who shared his abhorrence were risking their neck to get the evidence out, he felt a strong duty to pass it on. He examined his motives again. Baldly, the easy option—to do nothing—came down to cowardice. He must be brave.

And in any case, there was one action he could take that might help him decide. He picked up the envelope in front of him and held it delicately by two diagonal corners, thinking. Then he re-addressed it to Room 501 and left the office. His search for the mysterious room, prowling the corridors in his lunch breaks, had proved fruitless, yet it had to be *somewhere*, by virtue of the fact that it was listed in the directory. Daniel had had enough of creeping around the fifth floor. There was a much simpler way to find out.

'It's a sort of mystery,' he said to Christine in the post room. 'I get these letters addressed to me, you see, but they're really for someone else in a different office. Do you know anything about it?'

'Nothing to do with me,' she said. She was rapidly sorting mail as she spoke. 'If they can't address'em right, it's not our fault if we deliver'em wrong.'

'I just wondered where you usually send things addressed to Room 501?'

'We send it to the right room, dear. The room on the envelope.'

'But what if the room doesn't exist?'

'What d'you mean, doesn't exist? You're confusing me now. I've got all this to get through and I'm on early lunch today.'

'I'm sorry, Christine. Perhaps you could just tell me, if you received this envelope—' he held it out to her. 'Well, perhaps you could just show me where you would put it?'

Christine wiped her hands on her khaki nylon overall and took the envelope. '501? Oh well, you should have told me it was a 501. All mail for 501 goes in the tray, doesn't it?' She tossed Daniel's envelope into an old-fashioned wooden filing tray on a shelf behind the counter where she was sitting.

'And where's that for, then?' Daniel asked.

'Ooh, you are a nosey sod. How long have you been working here?' She squinted at the ID hanging around his neck.

'Come on, Christine. You know me,' said Daniel.

'We don't deliver what's in there,' she told him darkly.

'So what happens to it then?'

'Well obviously. They come and get it, don't they?'

'Who do?'

'We never see them. Listen, you never heard this from me. It just goes. Fairies in the night!' She looked at Daniel and burst out laughing at her own joke. 'Well, that's what they say about them lot, ain't it!'

*

On Friday evening, Perdita's research trip was over. From Aldergrove Airport, she phoned home.

'That man called again,' Daisy said. 'You know. The Daniel person?'

'Was there a message?' Perdita asked.

'He just said to tell you—hang on, I wrote it down— "there's been another one".'

'All right, love. Thanks.'

'Does that mean anything to you?'

'I think it does.'

'He sounds flaky to me, Mum.'

'Listen,' said Perdita. 'They're calling my flight. I'll be home in two or three hours.'

'Can we have a takeaway?'

'I can think of nothing nicer.'

Chapter 7

Hugh Williams and Milton Lithgow sat in a corner of the library looking over the club garden at the back of Pall Mall. No danger of the Macallan not being old enough here. Hugh was drinking coffee since it was three o'clock in the afternoon. The coffee was foul; it must have been stewing since lunch. Between them on the table lay a sealed A4 envelope of Lithgow's. Hugh hoped it contained something good for him. He could ill afford the time.

'Your man, now,' Lithgow said, after a lengthy discourse on some fishing dispute, which had been exercising his constituency.

'Blakemore.'

'That's right. Remember I mentioned he has a queer past. Well now, Blakemore's lover is a civil servant—MOD, no less.'

'Ex-lover,' corrected Hugh.

Lithgow waved away this detail and leaned forward. 'He's been leaking information to the television. He was arrested this morning.'

Hugh found Lithgow's conspiratorial air annoying; besides, he hated the bloody television. 'I don't know people in that world. Any idea which company?'

'Hugh, my boy. It's on your doorstep!'

'A Murdoch company?'

Lithgow was agog with anticipation. He fairly snuffled. 'You know, Hugh, had I a wife like yours, I would have hung on to her.'

'What's Perdita got to do with it?' Talk of Perdita always irritated him.

Lithgow's nose quivered. His little eyes danced.

'You're not saying *Perdita's* got hold of this—this leak?' Hugh was incredulous.

'Heavens, the boy is slow today! I am. She has.'

'It's impossible,' Hugh broke in. 'She knows nothing of that world.'

'She's learning.'

'Her interests are all, you know, environment, nuclear stuff. Lunatic fringe.' Hugh had always felt comfortable in the belief that Perdita had never addressed a serious issue in her professional life.

'She has received a document,' said Lithgow.

'What was it about?'

'I can't say. I have no knowledge of it.'

'She's in deep water.' Hugh attempted to hide his satisfaction. 'Does she know this, er, whistleblower?'

'My understanding is that they have met, but they don't know each other well.'

'So why did he choose her, I wonder?'

Lithgow shrugged. 'He's a press officer. And I believe she's not unknown in certain circles.'

'Really?' Hugh found this notion depressing. 'She won't know what to make of the story; it'll be lost on her.'

'What a pity,' commented Lithgow. He leaned back in his chair and narrowed his eyes. 'Such a waste of good information. Maybe she needs a little help from the family.'

Hugh grunted. He didn't have to stop and think for one moment about that. 'I'd better start with the press officer. Arrested this morning, you say? How long can the police hold him for?'

Lithgow shook his head. 'They've got him under the OSA so, unless they charge him, I believe it's just the seven days.'

A whole bloody week? Hugh pulled a face. It might well break the deadline for his piece: that was the trouble with working on a Sunday newspaper. Still, he reminded himself, he would have an exclusive when it did go out. 'What's our chap's name?' he asked.

'His name?' Lithgow touched the envelope lying on the table and slid it towards Hugh. 'I can do better than that.'

Hugh opened it. It contained several sheets of paper with Daniel's name, address, description, full cv, place of work, a list of friends, haunts and interests and his duty roster for the coming month. It also contained the photograph from his ID card. 'Can we use this?' Hugh asked, turning it over in search of the copyright.

'I think you'll find they took the precaution of obtaining

a clearable picture.'

'Good man,' said Hugh softly. He gave Lithgow the appraising, straight-talking look he reserved for hard questions. 'Can you get me a copy of whatever it was he leaked?' The request hung in the air.

'My dear fellow!' Lithgow spread out his empty hands. 'I have to leave you some work to do. Besides, I'm sure your ex-wife will be happy to oblige.'

Hugh said nothing. He would start with Daniel Booth. And no putting a junior reporter on to it. Lithgow's disclosure had rekindled a fire in his guts that he had not experienced of late. This one was for him.

*

'They held you *how* long?' Perdita could not believe what she was hearing.

They were drinking tea in Daniel's kitchen. Daniel had called her from a telephone box. He didn't mention his arrest on the phone, but sounded so shaken that Perdita had immediately agreed to pick him up, surprised at the location: Queen Mary's Rose Garden in Regent's Park. Although the possibility they might be seen together was discomfiting, she wanted to find out what had happened.

Squirrels scattered over the lumpy grass as she stepped through the worm casts, past the beds where a gardener was uprooting one of the summer displays. A mound of dying bushes, some still carrying a gnawed bud, lay on the path nearby. Perdita did not see Daniel at first. Then a movement from one of the benches around the periphery caught her attention and she approached with mounting alarm. This time, the English angel looked as if he'd just been told there's no God.

He made no move to greet her, saying only, 'Please will you take me home, Perdita?'

Her misgivings were instantly quashed. 'Of course,' she said, deeply puzzled.

He offered no further explanation and, beyond giving brief directions, seemed to need to travel in silence. She asked him nothing until, rounding a bend on the third-floor landing of the Chalk Farm mansion block in which he lived, they both stopped short at the sight of his lopsided front door, which had been roughly mended.

'My God!' she cried. 'What happened, Daniel?'

They approached the door with caution. Daniel said softly, 'They came for me, you see.' Then he turned to Perdita with a giggle. 'D'you think it's an insurable risk? What do I put on the claim form?'

Perdita didn't reply, but shot him a look of disquiet. Inside, a superficial examination of the flat revealed everything to be in place, but as soon as they opened drawers and cupboards it became clear, unsurprisingly, that the search had been thorough.

Daniel grew increasingly agitated. 'One moment,' he said.

She followed him into the second bedroom, where floor-to-ceiling bookshelves occupied two walls. 'Bit of a hobby, this.' He threw her a self-conscious smile and reached up to run his hand along some narrow volumes on the second shelf down. Over his shoulder Perdita could see they were a set of county guides to England with illustrated covers; some of them looked pretty old. Daniel's fingers twitched as he searched for one particular volume, found it and removed it, wiping his sweating palms on his jumper before opening it with care. 'Wiltshire,' he said. 'One of the fatter volumes, you see.' He glanced up, as if expecting her to understand why this was important. 'I have the earlier edition, 1925, but in 1968 they completely re-wrote it—much more detailed; photographs by John Piper.' He was gabbling as he riffled through the pages.

Perdita watched him, frowning.

After a moment or two, Daniel's trembling fingers found what he was looking for. He sank into a chair with a small cry. 'They didn't get it!' He was weeping with relief. 'Didn't find it! The philistines didn't think to look!' He held it out to her. She saw the heading, the layout and typeface unmistakable to her from the first leaked memo: this must be the second. 'Take it!' he said.

But Perdita backed away. 'Not now, Daniel. Let's finish what we're doing first. Then let's talk about it.' She didn't want the beastly thing. She had made up her mind on the flight home: after her experiences in Ireland she wanted nothing more to do with any of it, neither the documents nor with Daniel himself. She admired his courage and was sorry for the trouble it had got him into. But she'd done her best to investigate his secret memo and didn't feel she owed him anything further. It was time to walk away.

He obediently put the photocopy back where he had found it and they continued from room to room, Perdita watching from each doorway as he made his inspection. The paper lining drawers and shelves had been clumsily wrenched aside. Socks bulged out at him, re-wrapped in untidy fists.

A concertina file in which he kept personal papers had been removed altogether. Daniel even found this amusing as he envisaged them scrutinising his gas bills. He was so thankful they had not found the one incriminating document, that he seemed to be taking the rest in his stride.

They had completed their tour and were about to return to the sitting room when there was a sudden noise from the bathroom along the passageway. They both heard it, a muffled thud. Daniel moved towards the closed door. Their eyes met for a moment, his hand on the latch. The sound came again: something, or someone, was in there. Perdita froze. But Daniel whispered, 'Ah, maybe—' and opened the door gently. Perdita held her breath, watching as he sank to his knees and hauled a reluctant bundle out from within. He squatted back on his heels, cradling it in his arms; Perdita caught sight of a round, golden eye. 'Lalibela,' he explained. 'Poor love.' The cat hunched in his arms for a moment, then caught sight of Perdita, scrabbled free and shot back into the bathroom. 'Bastards,' he said. Then he looked over at Perdita sheepishly. 'I was so caught up in my own miseries, I'd forgotten all about her. How could I have done that?'

When they had assured themselves that physically, at any rate, the flat was intact, Daniel went to the kitchen to make tea. While the kettle boiled, he opened a tin of cat food and carried a fresh bowl back to the bathroom, setting it just inside the door. Perdita watched as he moved around, gradually reclaiming his own space. Only when they had settled with their tea at the kitchen table, did he begin to explain—disjointedly at first, having lost the practice of speech—how he had been held in a police cell at Paddington Green.

'I'm sorry,' he said. 'I shouldn't have rung you, should I? Contacted you. If they're watching me?' He hesitated. 'I—I don't want you to think there's no one else… that I don't have anyone… you know, it was just that I—I would have had to explain to them *why*—and I couldn't. Not at the moment. So…'

Yes, she told herself: it must be lonely being a whistle-blower. Perhaps one even felt shame, though goodness knows it was honourable enough. She leaned across and touched his arm. 'It's fine,' she reassured him. 'I understand.' On one subject she was able to put his mind at rest: there had been nothing in the news at all. The investigation was evidently at an early stage.

They talked, guardedly on her part, about her research trip to Ireland. Perdita was certainly not going to tell him what had happened on her night at the border, although she did say she had met republicans in Belfast. Daniel was holding something back and until he told her what it was she couldn't confide in him. Indeed, every instinct was confirming her decision to walk away.

'I suppose you want to know about the new document?' he was saying.

Perdita sighed. 'Maybe that's not a good idea—after this.'

'There isn't much, anyway,' Daniel said. 'One date. One name alongside. I think it's a place in Scotland.'

'In *Scotland?* Why on earth would they want to blow up Scotland?'

'Well, maybe it's not. Maybe there's somewhere with that name in Northern Ireland.'

'The North of Ireland,' she said, absently.

'Sorry?'

She dragged herself back to the present. 'You're being very brave, Daniel,' she told him. 'I'd have been in a terrible state if they'd come for me.' She poured him more tea but, when he drank it, she noticed his hand was still unsteady.

There was a slight movement at the door. The cat made an appearance and sat washing her wrists for a few moments, then she rolled on her back, stretching her elegant toes, before jumping onto Daniel's lap. She threw Perdita a disgusted look, turned around twice and settled down with a loud sigh, purring furiously. He bent to kiss the sandy-coloured fur. 'Abyssinian, you see,' he said. 'Hence the name. She can come and go along the parapet, thank goodness, so she won't have been shut in there, but all the same she must have been ravenous.'

'And traumatised,' said Perdita sympathetically. She had grown up with cats. 'What a fright: poor old Lalibela.' She was pleased to see Daniel calming down. But Perdita herself was growing fretful: this was Daisy's last day in London before returning to Leeds; she wanted to go home. One question burned inside her: she could not leave without asking it. 'Daniel?' she began at last.

'Yes?'

'What's going on?' She said it as gently as she could.

'What's what?'

She could sense him brace himself. 'Why you? What have they got against you? Why involve the police when no one's heard of any crime?'

There was a long silence. She waited.

'You were right,' he said at last. 'You know, when we first met, you said you thought I was being set up? I honestly didn't know I was. It didn't even cross my mind. Then I did consider the possibility, but it seemed so ludicrous...'

'And now?'

'Something the police said today. It still doesn't make sense. People are so small-minded!'

At last, she thought. She tried to eliminate the edge from her voice. 'What did they say, Daniel?'

'It was right at the end. The only thing they asked me that they couldn't have got from my personnel file. One of them mentioned a group. A gay lawyers' group, back in the late seventies. I came across them when I was a student: about 1980. They used to produce rights leaflets and that sort of thing. It was all sound stuff. I knew a few of them.' He paused.

'And?' she prompted.

He dropped his gaze, massaging the cat's front paws. 'Well, clearly the police are on to it.'

'I'm sorry?' Perdita was disappointed. 'You've lost me. What's so incriminating about that?'

'Exactly. You may well ask!'

'Come on, Daniel,' she murmured. For a moment neither spoke.

Then he said, 'You see, I was having a relationship with one of the lawyers. He became an MP. He's a minister now.'

'Is that so sensitive?' Perdita asked.

'It wouldn't have been.' Daniel's voice had dropped to a whisper. 'But he's married since. Apparently he never came out. I don't know what he told his wife, but no one else seems to know.'

'It really shouldn't be an issue, should it? Heaven's sake! It's been legal for thirty years!'

'Not in Northern Ireland.[5] And you lead a charmed life in the media, you know. The rest of us are still catching up.'

Something nudged Perdita's memory. Her unwelcome encounter at the Travellers' Club. The minister her husband wanted to see. The man who married late. 'It's Clive Blakemore,' she said. 'Isn't it?'

Daniel nodded shyly.

'None of which adds up to anything,' she said slowly. 'Well, a minor story in the *News of the World.*'

'Except—' Daniel added.

'Except,' she echoed, 'that he's a Northern Ireland minister now, and the ex-lover has been turned into a security risk.' They looked at each other bleakly.

'It happened,' he went on. 'But so long ago. It's so tenuous, I still can't really believe that's what they're after. We never lived together or anything, and then I met Alex,' he hesitated, 'my partner. I haven't even seen Clive now for, I dunno, must be fourteen years? *I have no contact with the man,* for God's sake! How can they say I'm a liability to him?' Then, seeing the expression on her face, he added, 'Oh dear. I suppose that sounds awfully naive.'

Perdita leaned across the table and gave his arm a reassuring squeeze, reflecting that none of us can choose our lovers with foresight. 'Don't worry,' she said. 'I can't use any of this. If I don't publish your document, they've no proof you passed it on to anyone, have they?' He smiled gratefully. But they both knew that the damage had probably been done.

---

5 Homosexuality wasn't legalised in Northern Ireland until 1982, and the age of consent, initially, was 21. So in Northern Ireland their relationship would have been illegal, as Daniel would have been 18/19 at the time.

With his admission about Blakemore her irritation had dispersed, but her resolve became clearer. 'Listen to me, Daniel,' she said firmly. 'What we are doing—these documents—it has to stop.'

From his abject demeanour when she met him in the rose garden, she had imagined he would jump at the chance to extricate himself. But his head jerked up and his eyes blazed. 'No,' he cried. 'No!'

For a moment she was caught off guard. 'Are you crazy? If the leaks continue, they'll have you and—forgive me, more famously—they'll have Clive Blakemore where they want him, presumably: out of office.'

'But who are *they?*' Daniel exploded. He jumped to his feet and walked out of the kitchen, scattering the cat as he went. Perdita followed him into the sitting room. He threw himself on the sofa. 'Don't you see, Perdita, if we run away now, whoever "they" are will be able to do this all the more? We live in a decent society and we're doing nothing wrong. We're exercising our legitimate right to say *No, we're not standing for this*.'

'Daniel.' She knelt on the floor at his feet. 'Daniel, the memos must be fake. We're being used. We mustn't play into their hands!'

'But we can't just go back into our box: we have to expose them!' he argued. He thought for a moment and then continued, more calmly, 'You can do what you like, Perdita. But I've got to see this through. They arrested me, but they didn't charge me: they had to let me go. They've nothing on me. The law stopped them dead. This intimidation—it doesn't happen in England. There are—' he waved his hand, groping for the phrase, 'checks and balances. The police are just cowboys and they're not going to get away with it!'

But who's briefing the police? she asked herself. Aloud, she said doubtfully, 'You've got more faith in the system than I have, then.'

'Maybe I have,' he acknowledged. 'But the system isn't something invented by other people. We get the system we deserve.' He was calm now. 'We have to take responsibility for it,' he finished quietly, 'and expose it where it's going wrong.'

He was right, of course—but, for her, the primary responsibility was to Daniel himself: he had passed her a memo and had been arrested for it. She had a duty to protect him, her source, and she had already decided that the best way to do that was to drop the whole thing; get out of his life. He had mentioned a partner, so hopefully his world wasn't entirely solitary: that was reassuring. She considered him thoughtfully, trying to imagine how he would appear to the general public. Would they see him as a champion of ethical government—or a traitor? She just didn't know.

Then Daniel said softly, 'And besides...' he paused, thinking. '...even if it was a fake, how did the writer of the memo know there was going to be a bomb at Keady?'

It was the very point she herself had made to Sinn Féin. For a smear campaign it had been chillingly thorough. Reluctantly, she was forced to acknowledge that it would be wrong simply to walk away: she couldn't let him face the consequences alone—this much she owed him, at least.

'Listen,' she said firmly. 'You need a solicitor.'

Daniel flinched. 'Do I? When I haven't been charged with anything? It'll mean putting the whole thing on the record.'

'Yes,' she agreed. 'But as you said yourself, you have rights too. You need to know what's what... in case they come back,' she added gently. 'Ask the people at Liberty—you know, the pressure group. Even if their lawyers can't take you on themselves, they'll send you to someone you can trust.'

She got up and went to the sitting-room window, staring down into the street again, where the wind blew a drift of leaves through the dusk. She needed to get away now, go home to Daisy.

On the opposite side of the road, a man was locking a parked car. He turned and looked up at the building, staring straight at the window where Perdita stood. For a moment it seemed as if their eyes met. Flesh prickled at the back of her neck. She drew away. 'Daniel—' she warned.

The note in her voice brought him to his feet. But he reached the window only in time to see the top of the man's head as he crossed the street and disappeared beneath the jutting parapet of the entrance porch below. She took Daniel's cold hand in hers.

'I'd better not be seen here,' she said. 'Whoever it is.'

'He'll ring the bell downstairs,' Daniel assured her. 'If it's me he wants.'

'The police didn't bother.'

As they both considered this, the doorbell rang.

'I'll leave,' she said. 'He won't know I've come from this flat.'

'No, wait. You can hide out there.' He indicated the flat door.

'He might do another search!' She grabbed her coat and bag from the kitchen. The doorbell rang again. 'Answer it, Daniel!'

Daniel picked up the Entryphone receiver. His hand was shaking but his voice was steady. After a moment he said, 'Oh hello, Vernon. Just a second.' His eyes met Perdita's in alarm. Then he spoke into the mouthpiece again. 'I'm afraid the buzzer's a bit dodgy. It may not work. Hang on a minute.' He replaced the receiver. 'It's okay. It's a chap from work. God knows what he wants. He mustn't see you, though.'

Perdita shook her head. 'Does this building have a fire escape?'

Daniel nodded. 'There's a little staircase up to the water tanks and the roof. He opened the front door and pointed at a door to the left of his. It had a circle of plain glass cut into it at head-height. 'Up there. Wait till I've got him inside, then you can dodge back down.'

'Hide the second mug!' she hissed at him.

'Wait a minute. Hang on. I want to give you something.'

'Send it,' she told him. 'You haven't time.'

'I daren't. It's the name from the latest document.' He felt in his pocket, pulled out a bus ticket and wrote on it. As he did so, the doorbell rang again.

'Let him in,' she said, taking the scrap of paper from him. 'You can't leave him down there.'

Daniel pressed the remote locking mechanism. Three floors down, in the hall, they heard the street door slam. 'Write your number in Ireland,' Daniel implored. 'It's terrible not being able to get hold of you.'

She whipped out her Filofax and leafed through it with shaking fingers. They could hear heavy footsteps starting to climb the stairs. Perdita tore the bus ticket in half and wrote

132

the number of a small hotel near the university. 'It's safe to call there,' she promised as she handed it to him. 'It's not one of the big places.' Then, stuffing her half of the ticket into her pocket she stepped out onto the landing. Below them, the footsteps had reached the second floor. 'Take care of yourself, Daniel,' she said, giving him a quick hug. 'Don't do anything wild.' Then she pushed against the swing door to the service stairs.

It was locked. Daniel came behind her, put his shoulder to it. The door was rigid. 'Can't be!' He was almost crying. 'It's always open!'

'Not today,' said Perdita briskly. There was no time to dodge back inside the flat. She turned instead to smile at Daniel's visitor who now came into view around the bend in the stairs. She took in the brief impression of a thickset man in his forties with grey flannel trousers slightly too short. Then she turned brightly back to Daniel. 'All right then, Mr Booth, I think that's all we can do for today. Goodbye. Goodbye!' she repeated to the man on the stairs, feeling his curious eyes upon her as she swept past him with a wave of the hand.

In Daniel's last words, as she clattered out of sight, she was relieved to detect a degree of composure. 'Sorry about that. Something seems to have happened to the buzzer.'

Perdita left the building feeling unnerved. As she forced herself to walk calmly to her car, parked directly beneath Daniel's windows, her flesh crept with the overwhelming sense of being observed. This feeling persisted so strongly that, anxious as she was to get home, she went the long way round. As she drove, she reflected on what she had learnt that afternoon: Daniel's arrest; his connection to the minister; the partner he had not called today to come and fetch him; his wretched new document. Her dismal failure to detach herself from the story.

It was only later as she drained linguine to mix with Daisy's favourite roast aubergines and peppers, she remembered Daniel's bus ticket in her jacket pocket.

'Mu-um…?'

'We'll want more parmesan than that, love.'

'Where are you going?' Daisy complained. 'It's ready.'

'By the time you've done the cheese, I'll be back.'

In the hall, her fingers slightly oily from the aubergines, she fished the ticket from her pocket. The writing was in pencil, and faint. Perdita carried it back into the kitchen and examined it under the light. It was not a place in Scotland. What she read there, made her let out a small cry.

Daisy spun round, flakes of parmesan snowing down from the grater onto the floor. 'What's up, Mum?'

'Oh, sorry darling. It's nothing.'

'It's not nothing. Are you okay?'

'I'm fine. I just got a bit of a shock. Are you ready?'

'What shock?'

Perdita returned to the colander where the linguine were threatening to congeal. 'I'll serve it straight onto the plates, shall I? Please could you bring them over here?'

'*Mum*—' There was an ominous note in Daisy's voice, but she brought the plates obediently.

'Hang on. This one needs a bit more.'

'You can't wriggle out of it that easily.'

'It's really not important, Daisy.'

'It's that bloody film, isn't it?'

'The film is about linen and tweed, my love.'

'So you keep saying. Sounds more like *The X-Files* to me.'

Along the hall, the telephone rang. 'Bother!' cried Perdita. 'Why does this always happen with pasta? Every time!—Hey, where are you off to? Leave it, darling.'

But Daisy was halfway down the hall. 'I'll get it,' she called. 'I opened the bottle. It's on the table.'

Perdita was pouring wine when she heard Daisy wail, 'Oh no, it's that *thing* again!'

'What thing? Come on, it'll get cold.'

'Mum, come and listen!'

Perdita walked down the corridor with a wine glass in her hand. She took the receiver from Daisy with a quizzical frown.

'It's our answer-machine!' Daisy said. 'It happened twice while you were away.'

Perdita listened. At the other end of the line she heard her own voice on the answer machine, playing back to her. 'What on earth....?' She rang off. 'Well, I don't know what that's about, but come *on*, sweetie. The pasta will be ruined.'

'Anyway,' said Daisy as they sat down at the table, 'whatever it is, it's weird. And I tell you, after a while the telephone will sort of jangle again, as if someone's ringing off. You'll see!'

'It's just a fault, love. If it goes on, I'll call BT.'

'It's creepy,' Daisy said. 'Started as soon as you got to Belfast, as a matter of fact. It's like we're being listened-to, or something.'

'Don't be silly, Daisy. It's nothing like that.' Perdita picked up her glass again.

Daisy watched her. 'So why is your hand shaking?' she asked.

When they had finished eating, Daisy returned to the subject again. 'That film isn't just about linen and tweed, is it, Mum?'

'When you graduate, Daisy,' said Perdita, 'what will you do?'

'I think this is the most scary thing you've done, you know,' Daisy told her seriously.

'It's a film about *linen!*'

'It can be about fried eggs, or—or ashtrays for all I care,' Daisy burst out. 'It *frightens* me!'

'I promise you, Daisy. I'll be all right.'

Perdita cleared the plates and they talked about other things. Suddenly, Daisy said, 'So what *was* that note you were reading before supper?'

'I believe there are good openings in interrogation,' Perdita remarked. 'They're looking for your sort of skills.'

'Shut up. No deviation or prevarication. Is that right, by the way?'

'Is what right?'

'Is that what prevarication means?'

'To prevaricate is to equivocate. To answer evasively.'

'Good. So what *was* on that piece of paper?'

'Nothing. A name.'

'A name that made you scream!'

'I did not scream,' said Perdita patiently. 'I just made a surprised noise.'

'I'm going to read it,' cried Daisy. She jumped up from the table and threw down her napkin. Perdita let her go. In a moment she was back.

'What does it mean?' she asked, peering at the name on Daniel's bus ticket.

'It's just a name, and a date.'

'Is it a place?'

'It might be. Or a person.'

'Who is he? Have you met him?'

'Lithgow? He's just a fellow,' Perdita said.

Along the hall, the telephone jangled and was silent.

Chapter 8

Vernon's unwonted mission to Daniel's home seemed to be to tell him, among other things, that he would be expected back at work as usual the following week. He didn't refer to the reason for Daniel's absence, and Daniel was none the wiser after his colleague had left as to how much, if anything, he knew. They discussed office matters, with Vernon as incurious as ever about Daniel's affairs. Accordingly, he returned to work on Monday and gingerly picked up the threads of his former existence, in which he felt he was now playing a temporary role, like an understudy at the theatre. He expected a summons from the personnel department, or at least to be briefed by his manager, Major Tiffin, on what might happen next, but the entire incident was never mentioned. He found it disconcerting.

At the end of his third day back, the Wednesday, Daniel

left the office and turned right along Whitehall into a slicing wind. His habit was to cross Trafalgar Square where tonight knots of Manchester United supporters were stamping their feet and breathing into their cans of Boddingtons. The 24 bus edged its way around the square and stopped. A crowd of people pushed on to it. Daniel went upstairs and found a seat by a window. Almost immediately someone sat down beside him. Daniel was slightly surprised—there were plenty of empty window seats.

'It's Daniel Booth, isn't it?' The man sitting beside him had turned towards him and was leaning forward. Daniel was trapped. 'Let me introduce myself. Hugh Williams. I work for *The Sunday Times*.'

For a crazy moment it occurred to Daniel that this might be nothing more than a casual proposition, wondering briefly whether things like that even happened any more. Not to him, at any rate: the man knew his name. Daniel tried to get a look at his face. He was thickset, handsome, fiftyish, with a good deal of smooth hair at odds with his puffy features. But the three-quarter-length Mulberry coat with its expensive suede collar told its own story. This was no ordinary reporter.

'I hope you don't mind me barging in on you like this,' said Hugh. 'I thought I would take the opportunity.'

'For what?' Daniel asked.

'A little chat.'

'Why?'

They were sitting unnaturally close, side-by-side on the narrow seat. The bus was edging up Charing Cross Road. 'Tell you what,' Hugh said, affably, 'How about a drink?' He made to stand up.

'I don't want a drink. I'm going home.'

'Put it like this,' said Hugh. 'You're going to have to talk to me one way or another. I think it would be more pleasant in a pub.'

'It wouldn't be pleasant at all. What d'you want with me?' Daniel was stalling, clinging to the possibility it might be something harmless.

'I believe you know my wife,' Hugh said, watching Daniel's face carefully. 'Well, ex-wife: Perdita Burn.'

Daniel was startled. He knew nothing of Perdita's private life, but certainly would not have imagined her married to a man like this. If this were Perdita's former husband, was it good news or bad? Friend or foe? Perhaps something had happened to Perdita. 'All right, then,' he said warily.

Hugh led Daniel down Manette Street and into Soho. They found a table in a barn-like pub in Greek Street and Hugh bought drinks. Daniel, his head full of questions, asked none of them. Hugh slung his coat over a chair. Daniel kept his on, buttoned up. Hugh started talking about the football match, a subject on which Daniel could not have enlightened him even had he wanted to. He looked at his watch. Hugh noticed and changed tack.

'One of the things I do,' he began, leaning back in his red-plush bench seat, 'is political profiles.'

Daniel said nothing.

'Fresh administration. Most of them new boys. People the public still haven't heard of. Where have they been in the wilderness years? Lots of furrows to plough. Uncharted waters for me, most of it.' Even in his anxiety Daniel noted the mixed metaphors. It was a long time since he had read *The*

Sunday Times from choice: its former esteemed editor would not have approved, he thought mournfully. Hugh was still talking. 'One has to speak to as many people as one can find who were acquainted with the subject in his or her younger days. Wilder days, sometimes.' He leered at Daniel. 'I bet you never thought your old friend Clive, Clive Blakemore, would end up a minister?'

So that was it.

'I didn't think of it one way or another,' said Daniel.

'You did know him?'

'I knew people who knew him.'

'Are you saying you didn't know him directly?'

Daniel's mind was racing. What to say. Whether to lie. And what the hell was the wretched man driving at anyway? 'We moved in a similar group for a while, but it was years ago. I knew him slightly.'

Hugh swilled the ice around his glass, apparently considering his next question. Then he raised his eyes and said, 'Does that mean that when you went to bed with him you were strangers? It was a fling?'

'Who says I went to bed with him?' asked Daniel quietly. There was a boiling sensation in his chest.

Hugh returned the shot. 'Are you saying you didn't?'

'I don't have to sit here,' Daniel protested, 'and answer prurient questions about my distant past.'

'So you're not denying it, then?' Hugh kept his tone chatty.

Parry question with question; a good ministerial stalling tactic. Daniel had observed it often. 'Who told you this stuff?' he demanded. 'I'm sure you didn't get it from Perdita.'

'Oh, you've told *her*, then?' Hugh sniggered to himself.

This was proving easier than he had imagined.

'What?'

'She couldn't tell me unless you'd told her. And if you told her, it must be true, mustn't it?'

'I didn't say that!' Daniel realised he was raising his voice.

'Well, if it wasn't true you wouldn't be so bothered about it, would you?'

Through the engulfing fogs, Daniel clutched at ministerial tactic number two: when cornered, claim moral high-ground. 'This is a total invasion of my privacy. I thought *The Sunday Times* was supposed to be a serious newspaper. Of what possible concern is it to your readers what I did in my youth?'

Hugh laughed softly. 'Oh, I think it's of very great concern, don't you? I would say it's directly in the public interest.'

Daniel jumped up. 'This is ludicrous,' he said. 'It's not in the public interest at all. I bet you haven't been stalking Clive Blakemore and asking him questions like this!'

'You're not denying, then, that you had a relationship with him?'

'What does that mean?' Daniel groaned. 'Go and ask Blakemore if you're so keen to know. I have nothing to say on the matter.'

Other drinkers were starting to turn in their direction.

'Sit down, Daniel,' said Hugh evenly. 'You're drawing attention to yourself. I want to ask you something else.'

'I'm not answering your bloody questions!'

Daniel turned to leave, but Hugh's voice took on a warning edge. 'I know about the document, Daniel. It's for your own good you need to stay and hear what I've got to say.'

Daniel hesitated. The barman was drying his hands,

looking over at them. He started to move in their direction.

'Sit down!' Hugh commanded again. 'I want to help you.'

'Is there a problem here?' asked the barman as he approached their table.

'It's fine, thanks,' said Daniel morosely. He sat down, glaring at Hugh. The barman retreated. Neither spoke for a few moments.

'So?' Hugh prompted at last.

'What document?' said Daniel.

'Oh come on. You're not in the press office now.'

'It's none of your business,' Daniel told him. 'I'm not prepared to discuss it with a journalist.'

Hugh chuckled. 'You discussed it with my wife.'

'Who are you, really?' Daniel asked. 'And how did you hear about me?'

Hugh regarded him. 'I'm sure you wouldn't expect me to reveal my sources?' He allowed the irony to hang in the air.

'Did Perdita tell you? I can't believe Perdita would have said...'

Hugh's smile broadened. 'So you don't deny it, then? You have received a confidential document and you have passed it to my wife?'

'I didn't say that!' It didn't sound convincing and Daniel knew it.

'Poor Daniel. You're not married, are you? You can't understand. It's a special bond. Deep. It doesn't end just because the marriage is over. She wouldn't see it as a breach of confidence.'

Daniel was struggling to take in the extent of Perdita's betrayal, if that's what it was. Hugh's taunt washed over him unnoticed. He simply couldn't believe Perdita would do this. He said nothing.

'So let's be straight with one another,' finished Hugh.

Daniel snorted.

'I'm wondering,' Hugh pressed on, 'have you asked yourself why this document was sent to you?'

Everyone wanted to know that. Daniel was silent.

'Has it occurred to you that it's not you they're after?'

'Of course it has,' Daniel replied. His disordered mind was starting to compose itself. He paused, wondering furiously how much damage he had already done; trying to reason with himself how much was safe to say truthfully and how much falsely. Hugh was content to wait. 'I went to my senior officer about it,' Daniel began. 'He told me what to do and I did it. The whole thing was a mistake. I forwarded the documents to their correct destination.'

'More than one?'

Daniel stammered, 'No, no. One document. I took it to my boss. It was just an error. There was nothing improper about it.'

'Until you copied it and passed it to my wife.'

'Where did you get that from?' Daniel bit back his words. There was only one person who could have told. He would never have believed it of her. He had trusted her. Well then, she could stew. 'Because whoever said that is lying,' he added.

Hugh raised his eyebrows. 'You're saying it's not true?'

Ministerial lesson number three: lie when it's unprovable. 'It's not true.'

'Look,' said Hugh. 'I could really do with your help. I'm not interested in you or what you have or haven't done. I'm interested in Blakemore. Why do you think someone is trying to discredit him and using you to do it?'

'You'll have to ask him,' said Daniel. 'I haven't seen or heard from Clive Blakemore for fourteen years.'

Hugh smiled. It was a very precise period of time. Daniel had clearly been asking himself the same question.

For a while they discussed Lawyers for Gay Rights. Or rather, Hugh discussed it. Daniel sat in stony silence until he could bear it no longer. 'It's a human rights matter, for God's sake!' he broke in at last. 'Not that I'd expect you to understand what that is. And besides, who cares, frankly, if someone turns out to have been gay in the late seventies? It's a non-issue.'

'Early eighties,' Hugh corrected him. 'You must excuse my ignorance, but is it usual for people suddenly to become heterosexual in middle-age? I mean, boys at public school are one thing. Not that I'd know,' he added hastily. 'I'm a grammar-school boy, me. You hear what these chaps get up to.' He laughed heartily. 'But Blakemore must have been in his late twenties by the time he met you... I say, are you off?' Daniel had stood up again. 'Listen,' said Hugh hastily. 'I didn't mean to be—Daniel, please understand. I'm on your side. I want to try and help you if I can.'

'No you don't,' said Daniel. 'But get this straight. I did not have a sexual relationship with Clive Blakemore. And if you suggest in your tacky newspaper that I did, I shall sue.' He turned and left the bar. It was not immoral to lie to a man like this. As he walked back to the bus stop and began to wait a second time for the number 24, he almost believed it to be true. It was thoughts of Perdita that made him sick at heart.

*

The day after his meeting with Daniel, Hugh stalked into Perdita's office as she was preparing to go for lunch.

'You've seen Daniel?' Perdita stared at him in horror and disbelief.

Hugh didn't bother to reply.

'It's nothing to do with you!' cried Perdita. 'It's not your story and it's not your business.'

'It is now,' Hugh smirked.

'Who put you on to it?'

'Well, of course, Daniel thinks you did.'

'*What?*'

'Naturally. Once I'd told him who I was.'

'You used that? You got his confidence by letting him think—'

'Darling, you can't make a film out of any of this,' Hugh said.

'You know nothing about it!' Perdita was appalled.

'I know enough to do the story,' he said evenly.

'What story? The story's very complicated. You can't publish it half-cock.'

'The story is simple, Perdita. It is in the public interest. The public has a right to know.'

'*Whose* public interest, Hugh?' They glared at each other. His eyes were bulging slightly. She was sure they never used to; what did it mean? Thyroid? 'You don't look well,' she told him. 'You ought to eat more vegetables.'

'Perdita. He's leaking top-secret memos to the press. He's got a connection to a minister in one of the most sensitive departments. It's serious!'

'No. No, Hugh. Listen to me.' Why, she was wondering,

do I still lapse into mothering him, this great fat white boiled egg of a man? 'You're being sold a line. Hasn't it occurred to you? Blakemore's the target and Daniel's the weapon. And now *you're* being used.'

Hugh gave Perdita a pitying look. 'You don't believe that?'

Perdita thought she could detect a crack in his composure. 'Think about it,' she pushed on. 'Someone wants to get rid of Blakemore. They dig around in the dustbins and the best they can come up with is a squeaky-clean civil servant with whom he apparently had an affair fifteen years ago.'

'Did he?' said Hugh quickly. 'That's interesting.'

Perdita faltered. She assumed he had been told that. 'Well, if he didn't, what's the connection supposed to be? If they can claim a connection, they can use it against the minister. Trouble is, there's not much wrong with a straightforward affair. Nothing that'll lose Blakemore his job. So they have to corrupt the civil servant. Right?'

'This is typical of you, isn't it, Perdita? Woolly left-wing conspiracy theory. It's irrelevant. The civil servant is corrupted.'

'He's not,' Perdita insisted. 'You're the one who's about to damage him if you publish that document.' She was gambling on the likelihood he hadn't been told about the second one.

'I never said anything about publishing any document. I haven't seen it. All I know is that he intercepted classified material that was not for him.'

'Wrong. Someone sent it to him deliberately.'

'He copied it and passed it to you,' said Hugh. It was a statement, not a question.

147

'Who says?' she asked. Daniel would never have admitted that.

'I've been told. You're not going to deny you've seen it, are you?'

Perdita thought for a moment, weighing the options. The one thing that might stop Hugh publishing his stupid piece was if he knew what the first document contained. The MOD's prior knowledge of the Keady bomb: now there was a story worthy of investigation. His contacts were better than hers for that. The name in the last document: could she trust Hugh with it? It would buy her time… but then she would have given him the corroboration he needed that Daniel had shown the documents to her. Catch 22. 'You're misinformed,' she told him. 'Who told you Daniel had passed me a document?'

Hugh hesitated. 'He told me.' It was an old trick but it generally worked.

Perdita caught the hesitation. 'I don't believe you,' she said, watching his face intently. She felt breathless. To think they could have been married, shared pillows and washing machines, had a child together, and it should be reduced to this.

'That's your problem.' He shrugged. He was angry.

She was on the offensive now. 'Who put you on to Daniel?'

'You don't expect me to tell you, do you?'

'Whoever told you, he or she is your real target,' Perdita said. 'There are traitors, Hugh. Blakemore is an elected representative. They're trying to bring him down.'

'Who is this *they?*' he broke in impatiently.

She ignored him. 'Haven't you thought to ask why?' she finished.

'That's not at issue here.'

'Well, it damn well should be!'

'This is how political journalism works, Perdita. People tell you things they think it is important the public should know. I seem to remember it's a system you've been happy to employ in the past.'

'Hold on to your story,' she begged him. 'There are bigger issues.'

'Are you going to tell me what they are?'

'How can I? I can't trust you!' She looked at him in dismay, but there was nothing in his face that acknowledged the insult. On an impulse, she said, 'Take me with you to meet your source!'

'I can't do that. You know I can't.'

'Ask him, then.'

'Will you tell him things you won't tell me?' he challenged.

She considered for a moment. 'I'll hear what he's got to say.'

He slapped the desk suddenly, exasperated. 'For Christ's sake, Perdita, don't be such a dog in the manger! You can't use any of this stuff in your film.'

'It isn't always a question of *using*,' she corrected him. 'It's a question of understanding. In fact, it might turn out to have a bearing on what I'm doing.'

'So you're "checking it out in Ireland", are you?' His tone was heavy with sarcasm.

'It's none of your business. And get out, Hugh. I've a meeting at two and I've had nothing to eat.'

He stood up to go. 'You'll regret this, Perdita, not being straight with me,' he said. And he left the room.

Perdita picked up the phone. She desperately needed to talk to Daniel. No good, of course. She would have to wait until the evening.

Hugh strode out into St Martin's Lane in search of a taxi. Then he dialled a number on his mobile phone, an idea forming in his mind. Lithgow had told him the name of the department within ITV that had commissioned Perdita's film. In a couple of minutes, Hugh had elicited the information that the commissioning editor was Jeremy Jordan. Hugh smiled to himself. 'I've changed my mind,' he told the taxi driver. 'Can you take me to Gray's Inn Road?'

'Daniel, I've got to see you.'

'What for?' asked Daniel bitterly.

'That bastard, my husband—'

'You told him.'

'I did *not* tell him!'

'No one else can have told him,' Daniel pointed out.

'They must have.' Perdita was torn between discretion on the open telephone line and the need to convince Daniel of her loyalty. 'They must be using Hugh to get at you,' she said. 'It makes sense.'

Daniel had spent a sleepless night. The raw sensation of betrayal still gnawed at him. 'The only thing that makes sense to me,' he said, 'is that I tell you something in confidence and a couple of days later your ex-husband turns up out of nowhere and repeats it.'

'It wasn't me, Daniel. Please listen. It has to be the same source as whoever sent you the memo in the first place. I need to know what you told Hugh. I've got to see you. We must talk. It's vital—for you.'

'No, Perdita. I made a big mistake with all this. I'm not talking to anyone.'

'It's too late, Daniel.' She knew he meant it. 'I'm trying to help you.'

'That's what your husband said, too.' Daniel gave a short laugh. 'Sorry, Perdita.' He cut her off. When she re-dialled, the number was busy.

Perdita arrived at work the next morning to find herself summoned to the Network Centre. She walked into Jeremy's office with a deep sense of foreboding, which turned to incredulity when he told her he had had a visit from Hugh.

'I don't know what the hell it's all about,' said Jeremy as soon as she had taken this in. 'So I thought you'd better come and explain.'

Perdita was seething with rage. 'He has absolutely no business coming to see you!'

'That may be right,' Jeremy conceded. 'But I want an explanation all the same.'

'He told you I've received some leaked information—?'

'Which you may be planning to use in your film. Are you?'

'No,' she said. She was frowning. 'It's nothing to do with the film.'

'But you've been researching it on our budget?' She was silent. 'Well, have you, or haven't you?'

She jumped up and paced around his large office. Then she turned back to face him. 'There is a textile manufacturer,' she told him. 'He's a very influential man in the North and he will have to be a major interviewee in the film. If he's up to his neck in political shenanigans you'll thank me for checking it out.' In truth, she had not until this moment taken McGrail's warning seriously.

Jeremy sighed. 'The thing is, Perdita, as I've told you before, our viewers and advertisers aren't interested in political investigations. I gave you this film because Nick has a high opinion of you and I assumed you could do a quick and efficient job. Perhaps I was misguided. Perhaps you can't look at a subject straight-on because you come from a generation of filmmakers that sees conspiracies in everything...'

How dare he? She felt a white-hot anger explode in her head. For a moment she considered walking out on the commission then and there, but instead she took a deep breath. 'Quite apart from the story itself, there's an important compliance issue: I'd have thought you'd be grateful. My object is not to make a fool of myself or of ITV...' She paused. 'Or of you.'

They were silent, watching each other. If it were Nick, she thought, I wouldn't be having this argument. Oh, she would have had to justify herself, of course—quite properly. The difference was that their discussion would have been founded on mutual respect.

'This document,' he resumed. 'The one you've been leaked. Hugh Williams says the story is about to break. Are you going to be involved in that?'

'I've told you,' she assured him. 'I'm not using any document. I don't know where Hugh's got that from.'

He hesitated, frowning. 'Okay,' he said at last. His tone softened. 'As long as you're not part of it. We don't want the network or WGBH involved in a contempt charge. Boston would hit the roof. I wish you'd told me this earlier, Perdita. I felt foolish having to hear it from him.'

'Had it been an issue, you would have heard,' she said crisply. She picked up her coat.

Jeremy looked stern. 'Promise me now, no more conspiracy theories!'

'Five years ago,' said Perdita, 'this wouldn't have happened. We've got a huge bloody scandal staring us in the face. We've got the big story you and Nick were looking for, Jeremy. And we just have to turn our backs on it.'

'Do the linen film,' Jeremy instructed. 'I'm not stopping you from staying on afterwards if you want to wade about in some Irish bog. It's just that you won't get a commission for it.'

CHAPTER 9

On Saturday night Daniel had supper with his friends Michael and Ben at their flat off Clapham Common; fillet of brill in red wine, followed by clementines and dates.

'Christmas food...' said Daniel wistfully when they had finished.

Michael had been watching him with concern. 'Something's up, isn't it?'

'Yes,' said Daniel.

'Do you want to talk about it?'

'I'm sorry. For being rotten company, I mean. No, I'm afraid I can't.'

'Is it to do with work?' Michael asked.

'What d'you mean, you can't talk about it?' Ben broke in.

'If it's to do with work, Ben, maybe he can't,' Michael reminded him.

'Is that it?' Ben asked Daniel. 'Official secrets, that sort of thing?'

'I suppose it is,' Daniel replied.

'I say, how thrilling!' said Ben, mock Biggles accent. Michael gave him a stony look and Ben added in his ordinary voice, 'Well, it's all bollocks. Can't you get a transfer to the Department of something more cuddly—Ancient Buildings, or whatever it's called?'

'Culture, Media and Sport,' Daniel said. 'I wish!'

'Whatever. You need a new job.'

'Yes, I do,' agreed Daniel. 'Um, one thing.' He paused, embarrassed about what he needed to say.

His friends waited. Michael was frowning.

Daniel fished in his pocket and brought out a key. 'I, er, want you to have this,' he said. 'Spare key to my flat.'

'What on earth for?' Ben asked.

'It's just in case... Would you mind? You know Lalibela?'

Michael and Ben looked at him, puzzled.

'The kitten we got when Alex had to stop work? He adored her... Got awfully fond of her myself. I mean, it probably won't be necessary, but just if anything should happen?' He couldn't look them in the eye as he said it.

'What sort of thing?' Michael asked.

'Oh... I don't know. Just in case I have to—to go away at short notice. You wouldn't mind taking her in for a while, would you? You're not allergic or anything?'

'Stay over tonight,' Michael urged him. 'You don't want to face the tube. No need to tell us. Just be here.'

'Thanks, but I ought to go home. I'd rather go.' Daniel put the door key down on the table and picked up his coat and scarf.

'We'll look after her,' Michael promised. 'Don't worry. She'll be safe with us. But I'm sure it won't come to that.'

*

For a Sunday, the terminal around the shuttle was surprisingly crowded. Perdita bought three newspapers and heaved bags and papers on to the X-ray belt. Sitting in the departure lounge reading *The Observer,* her eye caught a piece in brief half way down page three:

The future of Northern Ireland Minister Clive Blakemore is in question this weekend following the suggestion of a link with a civil servant at the MOD. The civil servant is allegedly in breach of the Official Secrets Act.

Perdita froze. This was far sooner than she had imagined. Was Daniel back in custody, then? She reached for *The Sunday Times*. Hugh had his scoop all right: it was front-page news. Where had he got his corroboration? Surely Daniel had not confessed to leaking the documents? She ran her eye down the columns. Her name, or that of the TV company, did not appear:

...alleged to have passed at least one top secret memo to a television company. An ITV spokesman confirmed the existence of such a document but said it would not be published.

Who was that? Perdita frowned. What spokesman? Had that sneak, Jeremy, confirmed it to them, then? He knew nothing first-hand: they couldn't have published on the strength of that, could they? *The Sunday Times* had gone to town on Blakemore. Inside pages carried Hugh's profile alongside several of the moody portraits of the minister shot for the piece by one of the newspaper's award-winning photographers. Would he have posed for those, Perdita wondered, had he known the context in which they were to be used? An inset cv read, she thought, like an obituary. Some junior reporter had done a cuttings job on Lawyers for Gay Rights and written it up as though it had been a major subversive force:

...fomenting strife in work places up and down the country where homosexuals claimed they were subject to discrimination.

There was nothing of the mildly practical rights guides; of the judicial reviews and test cases, hard-fought and soundly won. A fuzzy snapshot purported to show Clive Blakemore at a rally in 1979 and there were several stylish wedding photographs from 1993. Curiously, Daniel's name was not mentioned. That must be a relief to him, at least: perhaps there was a problem with the lawyers. She longed to be able to speak to him and wondered, as she had before, about his partner, Alex. Clearly, they didn't live together but she fervently hoped he was still around. As for the minister, if this were a smear campaign, to what end was it? Blakemore was doing a good job, as far as she could tell. The Murdoch press had seemed to support New Labour in the election, but it looked as if it hadn't taken long to revert to type. From their point of view the story had everything: Labour sleaze, gay sex, betrayal of country, betrayal of family values. It presented a first-rate opportunity to undermine the new government, which had won power on a decency ticket.

But then, in whose interest was it to destabilise peace in Ireland? Perdita's thoughts kept returning to a theory she had toyed with ever since Daniel's account of the mysterious Room 501. She understood there had been a turf war between the British Security Service, MI5, and the overseas intelligence service, MI6, over who should be operating in Ireland—a power struggle that was said to be settled now. Yet, throughout the thirty years of the Irish Troubles, there had apparently been a history of such disputes between the many confusing subgroups within the British security services and military intelligence. Might some version of this antagonism still be going on? Well—she shook herself awake—whoever they were, they could be looking for her as well. As the plane banked and dipped in preparation for landing, Perdita tried to steady herself for detention at the airport; but there was no hand on her shoulder, no posse barring her way at the car hire desk. As she left the building and made for the car park, she fought an impulse to turn back and harangue them for ineptitude.

Perdita switched on the television news as she unpacked. Clive Blakemore lived in a stylish Georgian house in his Midlands constituency. He was pictured outside it now with his wife Sarah and their two children, Charlotte, four, and Emily, eighteen months. The little girls brought tears to Perdita's eyes, thinking of Daisy. *You bastard, Hugh,* she murmured. Sarah Blakemore, close by her husband's shoulder, looked steadily into the camera. She still practised part-time as a solicitor in West London so the family must do a great deal of commuting. If there were nannies, which there must be, Perdita thought, they were well concealed.

'I simply can't see its relevance,' Sarah Blakemore told the interviewer. '*If* my husband had any such relationship before

I met him, it was in the distant past.' She gazed across at her husband with a warmth that Perdita found briefly distracting. Lucky people, she thought.

The next question recalled her attention to the screen. 'So that means you have no problem with your husband's male ex-lover being a security risk?' the female reporter was asking. God, they didn't mess around, these young women.

Sarah Blakemore didn't even flinch: she let the question hang in the air, for its full effrontery to reach the viewers. Then she replied quietly, 'I didn't say that. I meant that I set more store by my husband's word than that of *The Sunday Times.*'

The problem arises, said Perdita to the television, when your husband *is The Sunday Times.*

Blakemore's denials were equally robust: the civil servant was no more than a name to him from a pressure group he had supported long ago. If they cared to check, they would find he had a distinguished record of campaigning on a wide range of civil liberties issues. 'I think the question you should be asking is who is behind this crass smear campaign? They will have to do better than this. We are on course for a lasting peace in Ireland. I am confident about the future.'

Perdita wondered if there would be a report on Daniel, but there was still nothing. Poor Daniel: he wouldn't know what had hit him. She felt wretched at the very thought of him, and of the rupture engineered by Hugh. She longed to make it better between them, yet there was nothing she could do from here.

As she headed out of Belfast a couple of hours later, she reviewed once again the necessity to go and see Lithgow, racking her brains for any course of action that would not so clearly expose Daniel and the existence of a second document. Given the care she had taken, up to now, to deny that any classified information had been passed to her, Perdita knew this would open herself and Daniel to serious trouble. But of course she must warn Lithgow—and his security people would have to inform the police. As a journalist, she would be caught either way: guilty of breaking the law herself if she failed to report an impending crime. The alternative—to keep quiet and rely on the likelihood that the second document was a hoax and that there would be no assassination—was out of the question after the Keady bomb. She couldn't have it on her conscience. Besides, she had picked up one or two strategic tips from Hugh over recent days.

Milton Lithgow lived in a chilly mansion at the heart of his constituency, midway between the coast and the lough. It should have been a romantic spot, but was in fact a street of similar detached houses framed by laurels and rhododendron bushes, unutterably dreary at this time of year. The curtains in the dark front windows were pea-green and gold. She suspected there would be a housekeeper.

Lithgow received her expectantly in a room overfilled with mahogany furniture. The electric fire had only recently been switched on and Perdita suppressed a shiver.

'My dear Miss Burn. I can't say how honoured and delighted I am to renew our acquaintance. Mrs Lawson, tea in here, if you will. Or can I tempt you to something stronger?' he asked Perdita.

'Tea would be lovely, thank you,' Perdita said. 'It's so

kind of you to see me at a weekend. I won't take much of your time.' For the first twenty minutes she made play of interviewing him on the subject of linen, employment and initiatives with the Republic. Then she put her notebook aside and asked him what he thought of the trouble that had burst that day upon the Northern Ireland Minister.

Lithgow's knowing smile told Perdita he had guessed this was why she had really come. 'Indeed, it is a terrible thing, a terrible thing,' he said, his chins wobbling, 'when a good man, an honourable man, finds himself the subject of scandal. Which of us can cross our hearts and say we have no skeletons in our cupboard, Miss Burn? Yet do they render us unfit for office?'

'That sounds as if you believe it to be true,' said Perdita. She was receiving the powerful impression from his answer that the news was not fresh to him that day and asked if there had been rumours at Westminster before the story broke. Rumours... well, Lithgow was suddenly concerned with the lighting of a cigarette; Westminster was a cauldron, as she must know, of rumour and speculation, half of it never substantiated. Yes, there had been certain innuendoes about a lover, a leak...

The moment had come. Looking at him steadily, she said, 'I don't know if you are aware, Mr Lithgow, that my husband—former husband—is the journalist who broke the story?'

'Why, no!' Lithgow gazed at her in disbelief. 'My dear Miss Burn, I had no idea. Good gracious!'

'I merely mention it,' she continued, 'because, of course, there is another story behind the scenes. You know there are always things they can't publish.'

Lithgow was nodding vigorously.

'My ex-husband told me he is aware of the information the civil servant is supposed to have leaked. Of course, it's classified—'

'Naturally.'

'Perhaps you know already?' she asked hopefully.

He shook his head. 'That part is very hush-hush.'

'It seems the document, or documents, are about IRA atrocities,' Perdita pushed on. 'My husband told me they list incidents, he didn't exactly say what, but one is still in the future.'

'Very shocking. These people are animals, of course.'

'It sort of arose in conversation when I said I was coming to see you. He said perhaps I should warn you that the latest document—the future atrocity—appears to concern yourself.' It came out with something of a rush.

Lithgow, who had been nodding absent-mindedly, froze for a moment. Then he collected himself and laughed. 'My dear Miss Burn, how charming you are.'

'No, I mean, it's serious,' Perdita said. 'It's very soon. In three weeks' time, in fact.'

'And what form, pray, does this threat take?'

'As I understand it,' Perdita replied, 'it comes with no more detail than your name and a date: November the twenty-seventh.'

Lithgow was silent for a moment. He drew deeply on his cigarette. 'I have nothing to fear from such madmen,' he said at last. 'There have been threats before. There will be threats again.'

'I thought—*he* thought—you should be told,' she persisted. 'Because in other instances, information from the same source has proved correct. Apparently.'

'My dear girl. I am most grateful for your concern.' He peered at her beadily. 'I will, of course, telephone your husband and thank him also.'

This was what Perdita had been dreading. If Hugh discovered she knew the contents of the documents, he would have further corroboration that Daniel had leaked them to her. To an extent the damage was done: there had already been some kind of verification that had enabled the media to run the story. She regarded Lithgow coolly. 'Hugh was anxious not to speak about it. He now finds himself in a delicate situation: he has undertaken to the newspaper's lawyers not to divulge the contents, which is why he asked me to pass on the message in person. You can call him if you like, but for both our sakes we'd rather you let it pass.'

'In that case,' Lithgow said, 'I would like to issue you with an invitation, an expression of my gratitude. What was the date you mentioned?'

She repeated it.

'Let me see. Let me see.' He shifted his bulk sideways in the chair and reached into his jacket pocket for a small diary. 'On the twenty-seventh I am in Belfast. I'll be addressing—' He fell silent. It crossed her mind that he did not trust her with the information. 'I will be free by eight-thirty pm. I invite you to a late supper, my dear. To celebrate my survival. Are you staying at the Europa?'

'Not this time,' she said.

'Really? How very advanced you are. Well, I invite you to have supper with me at the Europa Hotel at nine o'clock. That's a date. Write it down.' He waited imperiously. She was forced to take out her diary and record it. Well, she could think of an excuse later. 'And I will get you drunk,' he finished. 'It will do you good. We can laugh about the terrorists.'

When she had gone, Lithgow, his brow deeply furrowed, bustled into his study and picked up the telephone. Hunting through a tumble of papers, he found Hugh's business card. He dialled the number, but it went straight to voicemail. Lithgow hesitated. Then he called a second number, which he did not need to look up.

'Curious thing,' he said, when the receiver was lifted at the other end.

'Ah, Milton. Good evening.'

'Leaked list of IRA atrocities.'

'Uha?' said the voice languidly.

'My name on it anywhere?' Lithgow asked.

'I'm sorry?' Disbelief at the other end of the telephone.

'You heard.'

'My dear fellow!'

'I'm hearing there's more than one document.'

'Of course there isn't.'

'Sure about that?' Lithgow pressed.

'Why would there be a second?'

'Thought not.'

'Are you all right?' The voice was concerned.

'I am now. Tell you later.'

'You're not getting cold feet?'

'Of course not.'

'It's going well, Milton. No need for a second.'

*

It was no surprise to Perdita when the subject of Lithgow surfaced two days later at the end of dinner with Ian Frazer. She had managed to turn the tables on him, converting his ambiguous invitation into a work meeting at the production's expense, and had chosen a newly opened *fin-de-siècle*-themed restaurant in the city centre. The place was typical of post-ceasefire Belfast. It catered for tourists, of course, but also to a breed of Irish men and women that Perdita had never encountered.

'Who are they?' she asked Frazer, gazing around at the well-dressed, self-confident and for the most part young clientele.

'My dear Perdita, not everyone in this city is as poor as your friends on the Falls Road, you know.'

Perdita attempted to hide her irritation by teasing him. 'Why should you imagine *they're* my friends any more than you are?'

'Believe me,' he told her, 'you've made it pretty clear you would not be sitting here tonight purely for pleasure.'

They both laughed. Then he said, 'Talking of unionists, which we were not, I heard you've been taking a keen interest in the welfare of my friend Milton.'

Perdita was instantly on her guard. As Frazer elaborated, she realised Lithgow had given him a detailed account of her visit. 'I wondered,' she said, 'what anyone would have against him—I mean, to risk the entire peace. Why?'

'You've answered your own question,' replied Frazer. 'They won't risk it. Milton Lithgow may have the style of a thundering old bigot—and, believe me, I would say that to his face. But Milton is a man of the world. He knows Ulster has to change and he will be right there at the forefront. He is not a target on anyone's hit-list, believe me. You are misinformed.' He sounded very certain.

'Well, I'm delighted to hear it,' Perdita said.

She was about to change the subject when Frazer continued, 'Perdita, I want to make a suggestion which I hope you do not take amiss. I think you should stop meddling in things that are nothing to do with the subject of your film and of which you have no comprehension.'

Perdita tried to swallow her annoyance. 'You're wrong,' she said seriously. 'This is everything to do with my film because I need to understand what's going on here.' Then, to deflect an awkward follow-up question, she added, 'What is it that gets you all going like this?'

'So I'm not the first?' He smiled knowingly. 'Forgive my lack of originality, but may I suggest that if others are warning you off, there may be some wisdom in it?'

'No,' she flashed back. 'I may be in the dark, but I'm pretty sure I'm asking the right questions.' Hugh, Lithgow, Joseph McGrail, all somehow linked by Daniel's documents. Could McGrail be right? Was Frazer implicated too? Her problem was she had not the slightest idea how.

'Or,' he suggested softly, 'that we see you in danger of doing yourself harm. Professionally... physically...' The possibilities hung in the air. *Was this a threat?* She looked at him, startled, but he continued after a moment, 'And we care too much about you to allow that.' He smiled, a smile with a purpose. The unease she had felt during their interview at the mill, returned sharply.

'Oh, I dare say I can take care of myself.' She was trying

to shrug it off.

'But this is Belfast. The rules are different here.'

'Well, the people are not from Mars.' She grinned at him. 'I guess I can muddle through.'

His gaze was steady. 'I get the impression that, like me, you are on your own,' he said.

Perdita cursed silently. 'Not exactly.' Her face was hot. 'I have an ex-husband who's quite a handful and a daughter at university.'

'You know what I mean.'

She fleetingly wondered whether to invent a boyfriend in London, but was not going to invite intimacy with Frazer by doing that.

'You English women go to such lengths to hide your vulnerability. And you aren't succeeding. Quite the reverse, in fact.'

A few minutes ago he had been patronising, perhaps threatening her. Now, she could no longer ignore it, the man was chatting her up.

'Come on, Perdita. Don't make it hard for me. From the first moment we met in Dublin, I found you extremely attractive.' His fingers brushed hers and lingered.

As she removed her hand, Perdita interrogated herself critically: had her behaviour with Frazer differed in any respect from the way she would have treated another interviewee? Had she sent out the wrong signals? He was gazing at her with an intensity that made her recoil. Beyond the desire—well, lust, most probably—there was something else in his pale eyes. It was menace.

'Rule number one,' she said lightly. 'Don't sleep with

the contributors.'

'Nonsense,' he murmured. 'Why not?'

The attempt at humour had been unwise. 'It's a professional relationship,' she told him briskly.

'Rules are there to be broken,' he persisted. 'It would be our secret.' This time his hand closed over hers.

She pulled her hand away a second time, more sharply. 'Ian, the answer is no.' The man was an utter creep.

'Don't play with me. You've been making your feelings pretty clear.'

At that, her thoughts came back into focus. No, she had not led him on. Absolutely not. 'That's nonsense,' she said evenly. 'I've been having a nice evening. And so have you. Nothing more.' She caught the waiter's eye. 'The bill, please,' she said.

'I shan't forgive you.' The threat was unmistakable now.

'Yes, you will,' she answered confidently. 'When you see my film.' She gave him a bright smile and handed the waiter her card. A second waiter brought their coats.

'Is that it?' he asked. 'Are you sending me on my way?'

'It's late,' she said as they reached the street.

'A wee nightcap? I know somewhere quiet.'

'Thank you. But no.'

'A wee kiss, then.'

Before she knew what was happening, he had pinned her arms to her sides. As his mouth came towards hers, she twisted away from him with all the strength in her body and broke free, before turning back to stare at him, speechless.

'You'll regret it,' he warned her. He did not appear to be drunk and this was disturbing.

'*I* may regret it,' she managed to say. 'But *you* won't. Goodnight, Mr Frazer.' And without a backward glance she crossed the road to the taxi-office she had noted earlier. Escape by pre-arranged taxi had been one of the principal factors in her choice of restaurant.

CHAPTER 10

The taxi sped past the University and on up the Malone Road. The driver was intent on some instructions crackling at him over the radio, while Perdita, still reeling from what had just happened, re-examined her opinion of Frazer. Repellent, yes, but she was puzzled at the crassness of his assault.

Returning to the present with a jolt, she realised they had overshot the turning to her hotel and were still heading South. 'I think we've gone too far,' she told the taxi-driver, yawning.

'I'm sorry, Missus,' he said, glancing regretfully in the mirror. 'I'm sure you're ready for your bed an'all, but them's got other ideas.'

'What?'

'I would have cut through, but I'm not too happy on some of them wee streets this time of night, so I'm takin' you round the longer way. It's just as quick in the end.'

'I don't get it,' she said. 'I want to go to the Wellington Lodge, please. It's back there.'

'You see, ma'am, we're not going to your hotel just now?' He inflected it as a question.

Perdita was suddenly wide-awake. 'Who says?'

'It came over my radio, so it did.'

'I don't care! Please turn round.'

'It's an order, like.'

Perdita was suddenly very scared. Was this this to do with Frazer? 'Who from?' she asked the driver. 'What are you talking about?' The prosperous suburban houses past which they were driving stood dark and shadowed behind neat, thick hedges. It must be almost midnight. She prayed for a red traffic light so as to jump out of the taxi, but they were speeding now; the wide road was deserted. In this city, on the wrong street, at the wrong hour of night, the war lived on.

'Sure, it's no problem. It's okay,' the driver muttered. But he avoided her eyes in the mirror. Soon they were on a major road skirting the city. After a mile or so, the taxi turned abruptly at traffic lights, then again off the main road into a labyrinth of streets and closes, partly Victorian, partly 1960s redevelopment. Perdita, her eyes strained at the window for clues as to where they were, could distinguish nothing. Her overwhelming thought was that Frazer had decided to wreak revenge for her rejection of him; it was exactly the kind of power game she imagined he would find amusing. Far from being comforted by the possibility, it terrified her. *You'll regret this*, he had said. No, it was nonsense. She now knew Frazer capable of violence, but not like this. Frazer would take her to his mill and ravage her on an antique sofa, not in a back street with dustbins.

For this was where the taxi now stopped. The driver switched off the engine. She could hear nothing except water dripping from an overflow. They had parked towards the end of an alley that ran between high walls and fences. Where were they? Even in the neutral city centre taxi firms still divided along sectarian lines. Dangling from the mirror of this one was a St Christopher medallion. Protestants wouldn't have those— would they? If this were a nationalist taxi, it had nothing to do with Frazer. She gazed out of the window, hunting for graffiti, but there was nothing to enlighten her. Indeed, she wondered, what did it matter where they were: was one community any less dangerous to her than the other? The window was starting to steam up. She wiped away the cold moisture and suddenly saw, out of focus, a piece of tattered bunting hanging from a lamppost. She rubbed at the smeared glass in frustration and peered again, straining to determine the colours. As she did so, a light wind obligingly blew an aluminium can across the alley. Faded and torn from some long-ago summer, the bunting now fluttered. Perdita saw it was her own flag, her own colours. So, if she was right, a nationalist driver had brought her to a back street in loyalist East Belfast at the dead of night. *Why?* Perdita, terrified now, was forced to acknowledge she understood not a single thing about this country. In the mirror, she saw the driver frown. He glanced down briefly at his watch then up at the mirror again, gazing fixedly past her at the darkness behind. Seconds ticked into minutes. She covertly tried the door-handle. It wouldn't open.

'For goodness' sake,' she burst out at last. 'What are we doing here? What are we waiting for?'

'If I knew, I swear I'd tell you,' the driver said. 'Don't be thinkin' I like it here any more than you do!'

'So let's go!' she cried.

The driver threw her a look, but said nothing.

The temperature was dropping inside the cab. Her armpits felt sticky with cold sweat. Please don't let there be guns, she prayed.

Perdita had opened her mouth to ask the driver to turn on the ignition and run the heater, when she saw his expression in the mirror change. A look of relief. He released the central lock. Behind her she heard a light sound, indefinable. The hairs seemed to sharpen and rise at the back of her neck. She fought the impulse to turn her head. A man slid into the seat beside her, closing the door with a soft click. She shrank away. No one spoke. She was conscious of him catching his breath; he must have been running. Now it seemed the three of them were waiting for something more. In a few seconds, a hooded figure slipped across the mouth of the alley in which they were parked. It was followed by a second. She caught sight of an automatic weapon silhouetted against the more luminous dark of the cobbles beyond and a small sound escaped her. A sharp intake of breath from her fellow passenger enjoined her to silence. More figures were crossing, all hooded, unspeaking and apparently armed. With the disappearance of the last, her companion whispered, 'Now watch.' Twenty seconds passed. Then an entirely different kind of figure appeared, crossing in the wake of the others; a portly figure, not hooded, with a rolling gait, stopping at the far pavement edge to light a cigarette. Even had he not done so, she would have recognised him anywhere. Lithgow.

They waited a further full minute before the passenger commanded in a low voice, 'Reverse, Francie.' The driver started the car and reversed slowly the length of the alley. 'Now get the hell out with you,' the passenger said. They drove at a moderate pace, slowing at cross-roads, until they reached a major thoroughfare with lights. Perdita turned to look at the man beside her for the first time. He pulled off the dark knitted cap he was wearing and ran his hands through his hair, grinning broadly. It was McGrail.

'How're you doin', Francie?' He leaned forward, ignoring Perdita, his hand closing affectionately on the driver's shoulder.

'Sure, I'm doin' grand, Joe. I just got out. It's good to see you, so it is. Been a while. Long Lartin, was it?'

'Was it that far back? I was in Albany another two years after that.'

'Heard you was out.'

'Aye. A while now. Good to be home.'

'If you required a taxi,' Perdita said, 'could you not have found one without me in it?' Her voice was shaking, although whether with relief or anger, even she was unsure.

He turned to her then. 'Forgive me. When I heard young Francis here was driving, I couldn't resist the opportunity of giving you a sightseeing tour.'

Perdita was attempting to recover her equilibrium. 'You might have warned me.'

'I'm afraid these things are not set up by appointment. I wanted you to see him in his natural state.'

'You mean Lithgow?'

'Well, you said when we last met that you had an interest in him.'

'That doesn't mean I was asking to be taken at the dead of night to a loyalist area for a rendezvous with Lithgow and fifteen armed men!'

'You were in no danger tonight.'

'…in a nationalist taxi, I presume!'

'Believe me, Perdita, they were all so busy getting off on the drill and the weapons they wouldn't have noticed a nationalist taxi if it hit them between the ears.'

She was not convinced. But curiosity was getting the better of her. 'So, what was going on back there?' she asked.

'Ach, he's their daddy. He likes to keep an eye on them. It's said when he's not hanging around the poor wee kids in the boys' home, he's quite partial to the raw recruits. They meet fairly regularly, for drilling. Keep their eye in. He likes to watch them on exercises. It makes him feel young again, I shouldn't wonder.'

Was he joking? 'It seems kind of foolhardy for a mainstream politician,' she said.

'Lithgow's no Einstein,' McGrail explained. 'And he knows he's on home territory.'

'What about patrols?'

McGrail shook his head. 'No army patrols in loyalist areas these days. If the RUC saw anything they'd look in the other direction… By the way, did you introduce yourself to Francis, here? Francie's an old friend of mine. We go back, don't we Francie?'

Francie nodded at her in the mirror. 'How're you doin'?' he said, as if they had only just met.

'Francie,' McGrail went on. 'This is Perdita Burn. She's a film director. She makes documentaries for the TV.'

'Is that so?' Francie looked at Perdita again. 'That's an interesting job, so it is.'

Perdita turned from one to the other. She found it weird. What was McGrail's game?

'Francie's a modest fellow. He'd not tell you himself, so I'll have to say it for him. If you want to do any undercover filming, now, Francie's your man. Electronics, no problem. Digital systems. Hidden mics. Cameras with pinpoint lenses—you name it.'

McGrail's exuberance, so different from his demeanour at their last meeting in the West Belfast flat, infected her in spite of herself and she laughed. 'Well, thanks,' she said. 'I wasn't planning on doing any secret filming but, if I do, I'll bear it in mind.' She preferred not to speculate how his skill might be employed by the republicans.

While he had been talking, they had left the city centre and were driving through the suburbs. Perdita stared nervously out into the darkness. She had spent too long travelling at night with this man. 'Where are you going now?' she asked. 'Will you please take me back to my hotel?'

'We will,' McGrail promised. 'We will. I just wanted to show you our fat friend in his true colours. To prove to you that you should stay clear of him.'

'In the same way as you warned me off Frazer, you mean?' she shot back. In truth, she was fascinated by this revelation about Lithgow, an elected member of parliament, but she resented McGrail's tone. What right had he to dictate her opinions?

'That is no joke, Perdita. You must keep clear of Frazer. D'you hear me now?' He had picked up her anger and matched it with his own.

'Why?' she demanded.

'Because there are more things than you know. That's why.'

'You have no right—'

'I have a right to save your friggin' life if I want to!'

It was not the raised voice, but its urgency that silenced her.

With barely a pause, he continued, 'Was it a good dinner, by the way?'

She turned to stare at him sharply.

He was delighted with himself. 'Perdita, there's not a wee English girl takes a piss in Belfast but we don't know about it.'

'It was fine,' she said flatly. 'It was work.' She was furious.

'Did he make a pass at you?'

'I don't need to tell you since you already know everything that happens to me.'

'Fair enough. He did and you said no. Am I right?'

'The hotel, please, Francie,' she implored the driver.

'Oh. He did and you said yes, was it?'

'I did not!'

McGrail chuckled. 'I knew you wouldn't,' he said.

They drove in silence for a minute or two, until McGrail asked, 'So after your experience with him tonight, did you change your mind on him at all—on Frazer?'

'We'll have to agree to differ on Mr Frazer,' she said stiffly. 'I've done a lot of research on him. Whatever his abysmal treatment of women, he's done a great deal for the nationalist community.'

'He would end the peace tomorrow, were it up to him.'

'Prove it,' she challenged.

He was getting cross again. 'Okay, Ms Brit Feminist Know-all. I'll tell you about Frazer. But first I have to explain who Brian Doherty was and who Milton Lithgow *is*—men on opposite sides who both want the same thing: that peace should fail.'

'Frazer told me already,' she said. But she was listening closely.

'*What* did Frazer tell you?'

'Dissident factions in the IRA. He said Doherty was killed by one of the groups trying to start the war again.' She turned to him. 'Are you?' she asked.

'Is that what he told you?' McGrail's voice was quiet and dangerous. He didn't answer her question.

With a sudden resurgence of fear, Perdita wondered if she had gone too far—effectively telling him she knew he had shot Doherty. 'Th-that's how he claimed an acquaintance with him,' she stammered. 'He said they were both working for peace.'

McGrail let out a mirthless laugh and shook his head. 'I'll bet he did.'

Then he began speaking and she realised this was the real reason he had brought her out here tonight. He told of Doherty's role as an agent—for the security services, police special branch, who knew?—not only informing on republican activities, but instigating operations of his own and working as an *agent provocateur* within the fiery South Armagh republicans, to stir up discontent against the peace process and organise the dissidents against the leadership. He explained that men like these were sustained financially and ideologically by powerful interests across the North, and beyond.

'And for this,' she ventured, 'Doherty was killed.' *By you. In cold blood*, she added to herself.

'Indeed,' he said. He turned to look at her. He made no further attempt to justify it.

'How can there be powerful interests that don't want peace?' she asked. 'It doesn't make sense.'

'Not for the country as a whole,' he agreed. 'But men like Frazer and Lithgow aren't motivated by that.'

'By what, then?'

'For all his lip service to the peace talks, Lithgow will fight tooth and claw against change. Did you read of a movement called Tara in your researches?'

Perdita frowned. 'The Hill of Tara? Where the Irish kings were crowned?' How could this be connected to an Ulsterman like Lithgow?

McGrail grinned at her confusion. 'Oh, don't be thinking we nationalists have a monopoly on Irish mysticism! Tara was the name of a quasi-religious Ulster organisation, which was also paramilitary. What was their motto now?' He closed his eyes. '*We hold Ulster that Ireland might be saved and Britain reborn!* Snappy, don't you think? Tara was dreamed up in the 1960s by a man called William McGrath who used it as a lure for young men and a front for his paedophile activities. You'll have heard of the Kincora boys' home, no doubt?'

This time Perdita was able to say she had; a notorious care home for young boys in Protestant East Belfast that had been the focus of a paedophile ring in previous decades.

'Well, Lithgow was one of McGrath's young Turks. He wriggled out of the scandal then, but he's still up to his neck in all the Orange Order bullshit, and worse. He's out there now smooth-talking small victories through the House of Commons—believe me, he's good at it—victories that block the path to peace.'

It sounded like pure propaganda. Perdita wasn't going to fall for that, but McGrail caught her sceptical glance and pushed on with his explanation. 'No. Think about it, Perdita. Peace—not tomorrow, maybe not in my lifetime, but in the end—will mean some kind of a united Ireland: anathema to certain Brits and Ulstermen alike. These fellas want to preserve the Ulster way of life. Don't they see it as their mystic duty to stay British and prolong the war? Most Brits don't understand our politics, anyway. To them, Ireland is boring. So Lithgow can operate under their noses, giving credence to the whole thing—and do it with the blessing of certain parts of the Security Service.'

'Oh, for goodness' sake,' she burst out. 'That's all in the past, isn't it?'

He sighed and turned away from her. 'Come on, Perdita. You have the evidence in your man's document you showed me, don't you? If you won't hear it from me, then go and find out for yourself. Not in London,' he added fiercely. 'You won't find it there, but go and do your homework. This is stuff you need to know.'

Perdita bit her tongue, annoyed with herself. She ought at least to let him give her his version of events. She resolved to be less dismissive if he told her anything more.

They travelled on in uncomfortable silence, but she was relieved to notice they had left the dark suburbs and were driving through an industrial area. No instruction appeared to have been given to Francie by McGrail; until it was, she assumed her own request would be ignored. She was past tiredness.

'How *is* your man in Whitehall?' asked McGrail after a while.

She was instantly on her guard. 'How d'you mean?'

'When we last spoke you were concerned for his safety, I believe. I couldn't help thinking when the minister, Blakemore, was linked to a security leak, was your man the civil servant cited in the case?'

She turned to him, her eyes wide. 'Listen. Not a word about that. Forget it. Please!'—and immediately regretted confirming McGrail's supposition. The idea that the republicans might hold Daniel's future safety in their hands had plagued her since the story became public.

'It goes without saying,' he replied shortly. 'Was he arrested, then? The press didn't report it.'

'I don't know what's happened to him,' she confessed. 'He certainly isn't returning my calls. I'm worried sick about him.'

He shot her an admonitory look. 'You should watch yourself. It's surprising they haven't come for you.'

She disliked sharing confidences with McGrail, but he had guessed it all in any case. 'My editor said we were not publishing,' she explained. 'Maybe that's why.' Or rather, she thought to herself, they know perfectly well that I'm here and will pick me up as soon as I get back to London.

'How many documents was he supposed to have leaked?' McGrail asked casually. 'I think it was two, was it?'

'They didn't say.' Perdita had read every newspaper she

could find.

'Did he not show you a second?'

She was suddenly wary again. 'No. What makes you think that?'

He shrugged. 'I just thought there might have been another one. I wondered what it said.'

She came to her senses. He was fishing for information and she was certainly not going to give him any more. 'I know nothing about that,' she answered. She looked straight ahead of her, cursing herself for treating this man as if he were an ally.

He burst out laughing. 'Perdita, of course you do. You just don't trust me.'

She said nothing.

'You trusted me with the first one!' he reasoned. 'You got me interested! You can't go coy on me now.'

'I'm sorry,' she told him. 'Everything's changed. I had no idea it was all going to move so rapidly.'

He said nothing. She knew he was displeased, but he had the grace not to push it. 'You see,' he continued after a moment, 'they are all linked, these things I've been telling you. All linked to your man's document.'

She turned to him in disbelief. 'What things?' she asked. 'How?'

McGrail looked at her, weighing up his answer. Then he shook his head. 'I'm not going to tell you, Perdita. This stuff is too important. If you hear it from me, you'll not accept it. You need to make the connections yourself.'

'Tell me anyway,' she argued, 'and I'll decide if I believe it or not.' In truth, she badly needed to know. She was also alarmed to realise that despite his cranky ideas about collusion between the British state and Ulster paramilitaries, this volatile man for some reason compelled her respect, the way she had seen it on the faces of his followers after the quiz at the Felons. She was deep in the mire and she suspected he was the one person who could help her make sense of it.

But he shook his head. 'No.' She had offended him, and Perdita wondered again if she ought to be fearful. Yet surely he was not going to kill her now: she had the unnerving suspicion that the deadlier threat from these men of violence—to her, at any rate—came not from their guns but from their sense of irony. She must beware of that.

Frowning, she asked, 'So... are you at least going to tell me how Ian Frazer fits in to all this?'

McGrail thought for a moment. 'Frazer is both simpler and more complicated than Lithgow,' he said. 'Yes, he's tied up in what I've just told you: he's making too much money out of it to want to end the war. But he's no time for the mystic Ulster bollocks: he is motivated by power and by pure greed.' He paused. 'This much I will say: linen is not Frazer's business.' She could sense him looking at her; this was important to him. 'Linen is his toy, his respectable face.' He recollected himself and his voice was cold again. 'But then there's no point telling you where his real wealth is generated, because you won't believe me.'

'No, I probably won't,' she responded drily. 'I suppose you're going to say it's drugs.'

'I'm not going to discuss it, Perdita. But hear this: if you put him in your film as a champion of good old Irish traditional industry and equal opportunities, you'll have a flock of

Ulstermen hooting with derision. You're wrong. You're walking into it. And I can just see you about to make a real big fool of yourself. I tell you, you have a reputation to maintain and this is not worthy of you.'

The challenge, delivered quietly and with authority, knocked her completely off balance. Much as she wanted to dismiss it, Perdita was stung. Partisan he might be, but McGrail knew this territory. She said nothing for a while, turning over what he had told her about Frazer and Lithgow.

They were back in the centre again and, though there had been no discernible instruction from McGrail, were at last approaching Perdita's hotel. 'If greed is the simple bit,' she asked, 'what's the part about Frazer that's more complicated than Lithgow?'

'The complicated part,' he said, 'is that the man is clever, rich, plausible, sexy and very well connected. The complicated part is that smart British journalists come along and make films about how much he's doing to combat sectarianism. And even if they might want to tell another story, the great British TV establishment wouldn't be interested in broadcasting it. The complicated part is that Ian Frazer can proposition the journalist over dinner, and when he comes on to her with unwanted embraces, she won't kick him in the balls because she needs to keep him onside. And the most complicated part of all is that there's no one to tell it to you but me, a convicted terrorist. Go now, quick. I can't stay here.' Francie had stopped twenty yards from the hotel in an unlit stretch of the deserted street. Perdita opened the door and got out. She looked back at him. She had nothing to say. 'But one day,' he leaned towards her and his eyes gleamed. 'One day I'll show you. I will prove it to you beyond all shadow of doubt. And then *you* will have to prove it to the world.'

Her dinner with Frazer had been Perdita's last scheduled appointment in Belfast. The morning after her encounter with McGrail she drove to Dublin. The news on the car radio was about the suspension from office of Clive Blakemore, pending an inquiry. She could imagine all too clearly Hugh's satisfaction at hearing that 'his' story was now top of the political agenda, and wondered once again where this left Daniel.

There were still a couple of people to see before the crew arrived. The southern sequences would be shot first and they would all then travel north. The recces went well and Perdita congratulated herself on being ready ahead of time. One thing could be said for the subject of textiles: no one was going to get hurt. There was nothing contentious at all. It might be boring to make but it was less complicated. She might even get a taste for it.

On the last day, she made for the National Library of Ireland and spent some time flipping through the catalogue on contemporary Irish history, north and south. Several recent accessions on the Troubles were startlingly up to date: a newly completed Boston College thesis about the Anglo-Irish agreement and the peace process contained a final chapter on the likely endgame of the conflict. She filled in an order slip and was told by the helpful librarian that, yes, it was still on site and could be at her desk shortly.

While waiting, she turned her attention to the Kincora boys' home scandal and found articles in Irish periodicals that filled in some of the detail. One referenced a book published in Ireland the previous year that told the entire story—both what was known and what still only suspected. The paedophile William McGrath had been sent to prison for a short time eventually, but the article she was reading claimed that the scandal was never properly investigated on account of the huge vested interests high up in the Protestant establishment in the North, and perhaps also in Britain. It seemed that anyone who tried to expose it—even British Army intelligence—was ordered off. And there, in the article's final paragraphs, she found what she had partly been looking for: the British Security Service, MI5, the writer concluded, used the Tara organisation—may even have authorised William McGrath to set it up—in order to keep tabs on right-wing loyalists. McGrath himself was strongly suspected of being an agent for MI5. Perdita gazed out into the reading room. It was wise indeed of McGrail not to tell her all this, for she would have dismissed it out of hand. Yet here it was, in a respectable journal.

An attendant trundled towards her with an old-fashioned wooden trolley, delivering books. He placed the Boston College thesis on her desk as he passed, breaking into her reverie. Perdita thanked him and started to leaf through it, searching for the final chapter. Dense and overly full of jargon (didn't anyone teach these students to write?) its advantage over the Kincora article was that it was laden with references, and she noted some of them down. But as she wound her way through its subordinate clauses, she began to understand that, crazy as it might sound, she must think in terms of a whole re-drawing of the fault lines in the Irish conflict. On one side, the present Labour government and the previous Conservative administration were lining up to end the war (although the student was careful not to call it that), along with the Irish government, Sinn Féin, Irish nationalists, many Unionists and the leadership of the Provisional IRA. Opposing them, dissident republicans were incongruously aligned with right-wing Ulster loyalists (that's Lithgow, she thought) and elements among the right wing of the Tory party at Westminster; each side backed from the shadows by the various branches of the intelligence services, some of whom were still in conflict with each other. So perhaps McGrail had not been giving her his own party line after all.

And where are you in all this, Joe McGrail? Perdita wondered, as she packed up her notebook and returned the thesis to the librarian's desk. What drives you? Is it a peaceful future for your country, or hanging on to power as a paramilitary leader? Instead of turning the people you call wrongdoers over to the police, you murder them in the name of peace and justice. Does that make it all right, then?

She needed time to absorb all this, and wandered along the banks of the Liffey in the mild air, lost in thought, joining the knots of lunchtime tourists and wanderers crossing and re-crossing the Ha'penny Bridge. It sounded implausible, but she was fast learning that in Northern Ireland the more improbable something seemed, the more likely it was to be true. Applying this thesis to her own story, it seemed the present Secretary of State was untouchable and would stand firm: no one would be foolish enough to get at her. But Blakemore, the relatively fresh-faced and least experienced of the ministers beneath her, might be fair game. If those who opposed the peace—she thought of them as the forces of darkness—could discredit him by means of a scandal, they would do considerable damage. Right now, it seemed they were well on the way to success.

CHAPTER 11

In the weeks following Hugh's article in *The Sunday Times*, Daniel had come to understand that nothing would ever be the same again.

On the day the piece appeared, his friend Michael offered him the use of his mother's small cottage on the East Coast. Daniel accepted gratefully and wrote a note to his bosses telling them he would be taking all the annual leave owing to him. On the Monday morning, he hired a car, packed Lalibela and a pile of books and drove east. After days of long walks, or exploring the English topography sections of the second-hand bookshops and watching the cat delightedly stalk spiders in the garden, he had grown ridiculously fond of the place and realised London was no good for either of them. He started to think about leaving the whole rat-race and coming to settle in Suffolk. By the end of his stay, he had almost forgotten the grim circumstances of his absence from work and caught himself glancing in estate agents' windows. Why, he could get himself a job at the Yoxford bookshop...

Such was his sense of wellbeing, he imagined he might feel just as optimistic once he returned home; but after a few hours back in the flat he caught himself listening. For the feet on the stairs. For the thud at his patched-up door. Daniel spoke to himself sternly: this was sheer idiocy. They had nothing to charge him with; he had done nothing wrong. Almost nothing. He lay on the sofa with his latest acquisition: *Suffolk* (written by Norman Scarfe, second edition 1962, with photographs by John Piper, Edwin Smith and others) and started to try and plan his new future, but try as he might he couldn't stop his thoughts from reverting to the question of what would happen next.

He found out the following morning. The letter came not from his manager but from the overall Director of Public Affairs and was very short, informing him simply that pending an internal inquiry his employment with the department had been suspended. It added unnecessarily that he was not to speak to the media on this or any other matter. No further explanation. Daniel felt patronised, locked-out and very alone.

His thoughts turned to the remnants of his family. Contact with his sister Mary was sporadic these days; they were fond of each other but she had moved to Queensland seven years ago with a man whom Daniel and Alex had solemnly christened The Homophobe (Daniel found himself smiling at that), and he knew Mary was embarrassed about keeping in touch. As for his father, Daniel had never come out to him. The old man lived an increasingly withdrawn existence in

Weymouth where he had worked all his life as an insurance agent. It was Daniel's mother, a teacher, who had provided the light and energy at home. Thank God, Daniel thought, she had not lived to see this.

What was he supposed to do now? His first instinct was to telephone Major Tiffin and ask. The telephone was answered by Elizabeth Hare, secretary in name to all of them, though in practice she worked to Tiffin alone.

'Hello, Daniel,' she said in the dispassionate voice he had heard her reserve for strangers.

He had been on the point of holding as friendly a conversation with her as the circumstances would allow and her tone caught him off-guard. 'How are you?' he asked instead. It sounded forced.

'I'm all right, thank you,' she answered, omitting to return the question. 'I'm afraid Major Tiffin isn't here at the moment.'

'Is anyone else around?' he asked, hungry not so much for news as for a friendly voice.

'Vernon's here.'

Vernon was the last person Daniel wanted to speak to, but it was better than nothing. 'Can I have a word, please?' he asked.

'I'll see if I can put you through.'

There followed a pause. She was not trying to dial Vernon's extension; there was no click on the line. Perhaps he was in the room with her. Daniel fancied he could hear the sound of her hand uncovering the mouthpiece before she spoke again. 'I'm afraid his phone's busy,' she said. 'I'll put you on hold.'

The line went dead without her saying goodbye. Vivaldi's *Four Seasons* drilled into his ear—and then stopped, to be replaced by a high electronic tone. They had cut him off. He started to re-dial, but his fingers were shaking and he threw down the receiver.

The day was passing. At dusk, Daniel forced himself to go to the supermarket, wondering how much food to buy. It seemed wasteful to fill the fridge if one were going to prison. On the other hand, there was the possibility of a long media siege. He considered the shelf of ready-washed salads, reaching the checkout eventually with almost nothing: cat food, a pint of milk, a couple of newspapers, ciabatta rolls (suitable for freezing), Chinese leaves and smoked haddock. He had never bought Chinese leaves before but they looked resilient. Once home again, he scanned the papers for information about himself and Blakemore but the story had gone quiet: a good bit of news management there by someone, he reflected, and was grateful. The only reference was a small story on page three of the *Telegraph*:

Detectives are moving in on the civil servant at the Ministry of Defence accused of leaking classified information to the media, following allegations of a link to suspended Northern Ireland Minister Clive Blakemore.

Well, that was ancient history, thought Daniel. Wasn't it?

The telephone rang.

'Daniel Booth?'

Daniel hesitated. 'Who is it?' he asked.

'Hi, Daniel. Brian here. Brian North? I'm a friend of Alex. We all met back in the Spring—on the Pride march. Remember?'

Daniel slammed down the phone. The Gay Pride march had moved to August that year and his dearest Alex was dead.

As he sat there for a moment, shaking, there was a ring at the door. Daniel ignored it. He ran down the corridor to his bedroom. Behind him in the sitting room the telephone rang a second time. By peering through the balustrade of the parapet outside his window it was possible to see out without being seen. Daniel craned his neck gingerly. He froze. There were hundreds of them.

*

Reluctantly leaving her film crew to enjoy a seafood supper, Perdita walked into the bar of the Europa Hotel to keep her appointment with Milton Lithgow. It was nine in the evening on the twenty-seventh of November. She had intended to tell him she would be out of town, but when his office had called hers to check the timing, the production secretary in London had confirmed that Perdita would be in Belfast that night.

'I'm *so* sorry!' she apologised to Perdita when she realised her mistake.

'Ach, it'll be fine,' said Perdita. 'I'll leave before the pudding.' But in truth she was dreading the evening.

Throughout the years of the Troubles, Belfast's foremost hotel had earned itself the doubtful accolade of being the most bombed hotel in the world. Perdita remembered in the 1980s how tight the security had been and experienced a slight frisson as she crossed the redesigned glass foyer that seemed to cock two fingers at terrorism. This was the date designated for Lithgow's murder, after all, and although mid-evening it was not yet over.

She had hoped to find him surrounded by cronies but to her

dismay she spotted him alone, perched impossibly on a high bar stool like Alice's caterpillar, no hookah but a large whisky beside him. On seeing her, his eyes creased malevolently and he prised himself off his perch with a practised twist of the gut.

'Still alive and kicking, as you see,' he greeted her, spreading his arms wide for inspection.

Perdita swallowed her revulsion and gave him a beaming smile, ignored what was probably an invitation to kiss his cheek and held out her hand. 'Congratulations, Mr Lithgow. I'm delighted to be wrong.'

He turned to the barman, ordered drinks and steered her across the room to a couple of empty armchairs. 'Sit there,' he instructed, indicating one, and eased himself into the second. He had chosen, curiously Perdita thought, the two chairs closest to the television, where the lead story on the BBC News—Kosovo, she knew from watching Channel 4 earlier—projected lights and shadows on to the side of Lithgow's face. It was distracting but, she thought, might at least bridge the gaps in a conversation that was bound to flag. She had no idea how she was going to fill an entire evening with this man. She decided to start with an apology for alarming him unnecessarily about the threat to his life, but he waved it away.

'Perdita (such a charming name. You don't mind if I call you Perdita?), one can never be too careful, my dear. My Special Branch man was most amused.'

'Is he here?' Perdita asked, glancing around hopefully.

'You'll meet him later. He's got some information for you, as a matter of fact, but I've given him the slip for now.' He leered at her.

'It must be tedious having your footsteps dogged every

hour of the day,' said Perdita evasively. She couldn't imagine Special Branch divulging anything really interesting to her; she was about to ask more, when a large explosion on the TV screen distracted their attention.

The waiter brought their drinks.

'Is it possible to turn it down a little, please?' Perdita asked him. The television had no visible controls.

'Certainly, Madam.'

'No. Leave it,' said Lithgow sharply. Perdita and the waiter stared at him. 'We shan't be staying long. You booked me that table, now, didn't you?'

'It's ready whenever you like, Mr Lithgow.' The waiter retreated.

With the end of the filmed report, the TV became less intrusive. Perdita glanced across at Lithgow uncertainly. Her plan was to use this unwelcome date to pump him about the Orange Order—maybe even mention Tara—but judging from his present edginess she would have to wait until he was considerably more drunk than he was at the moment. McGrail had not given her a satisfactory explanation of what Lithgow was doing with the masked men near the Shankill at midnight, but it was unlikely to have been constituency business. It would be instructive to hear his public view of such organisations.

The next item on the BBC was home news. The reporter was standing on St Stephen's Green with the lights of the Palace of Westminster behind him. Perdita turned to ask Lithgow a question but his attention was fastened on the screen. The scene changed to a block of Edwardian flats where, under the light of a street-lamp, a flock of reporters and photographers surged forward as the door opened and a figure was hustled out by police.

'Have you anything to say, Mr Booth?' called a voice from the throng. The figure averted its face, screened after a few moments by the open door of a car.

Perdita felt Lithgow's eyes upon her and understood everything. He had placed her where she had a prime view of the television and he had a prime view of her. This story had not made the seven o'clock news on Channel 4, yet Lithgow already knew of it. Tearing herself away, she threw him a smile. 'This must be the civil servant who leaked the documents,' she said. 'What a coincidence.'

He was examining her intently. 'Feel free to watch it, Perdita. I can see you're desperate for news of your friend.'

'My what?' How she loathed him.

'You heard, my dear.'

They watched the rest of the news report in silence. When the scandal had first hit the headlines, its focus had been exclusively on Blakemore. Now it was all about Daniel. According to the bulletin, Daniel was being arrested under the Official Secrets Act for passing classified material to the media. A document had been deliberately sent to him; a fabrication, the reporter explained. So her necessary warning to Lithgow had indeed provided corroboration that Daniel had leaked the memo. Although she had foreseen this might happen, the realisation hit her like a stone: they must have used the name of a person rather than a place on the second document in order to force her hand, knowing she would be duty-bound to disclose it. A simple trick and she had fallen for it—but then, what else could she have done, she wondered, supposing it *had* been genuine? And why had *she* not been arrested, too?

Perdita tried to take in the report as she struggled with these thoughts, the requirement to appear calm almost defeating her.

'Does that mean they'll have picked up Hugh, my ex-husband?' she asked, as blandly as she could, when the item ended.

'My dear, how should I know?' Lithgow was basking in her distress. 'Does it bother you so very much?'

Perdita was thinking of Daisy at her student flat in Leeds. Would she have to learn of Perdita's arrest from the television? Would the reporters track her down? She longed to call her, but Daisy had no phone. The image came back to her of Daniel, propelled toward the police van. His features had been in shadow but the angle of his neck told of agony within. She wondered at his former absence from the flat, the repeated calls she had made to his answer-machine from Dublin. In her mind she had thought of him in custody then. Had he been at home all along, ignoring Irish calls because he still blamed her for betraying him to Hugh? She was well aware she'd had no opportunity to give him any proof to the contrary. For security reasons she had never called from her home phone, left her name, number, or a message, yet the authorities must know of her connection from Lithgow himself. And, according to McGrail, Lithgow had links to MI5... The need to say something un-incriminating to him dragged Perdita's tangled thoughts back to the present.

'So, the document with your name on it, the one I warned you about, was fabricated to catch—to catch this chap?' she asked him.

'There was no second document, Perdita.'

'But your *name* was on it!' She could no longer keep the

irritation from her voice.

'I never took it seriously, as you know,' he said airily. 'But, yes, I checked it out. It's not as easy as you might think, in fact. There's all the boys in there: military intelligence, Special Branch, you name it. The word came back there had been no document whatsoever with my name on it. You—forgive me, my dear, your *ex-husband*—must have been misinformed.'

Perdita was confused. 'He—that is, Hugh—was very sure about it,' she said. Of course, she had not actually seen Lithgow's name on the document itself; but she had seen and recognised the new memo in Daniel's flat. The second document existed. And why would Daniel make up that name? It was impossible.

'Well,' Lithgow assured her. 'There was *one* document—that much is certain. It was a *sting*, I believe to be the expression—as they just said on the news. But I was in the clear,' he simpered. 'Come now. We must go and eat. I'm sure the excitement will have given you quite an appetite.' He levered himself from the chair and waved her in the direction of the restaurant. At one point, she turned to make a remark to him and caught a glint of triumph in his small eyes that killed the pleasantry dead.

The meal seemed interminable. Perdita's appetite for investigation, as for the food, had deserted her and she had no energy to quiz him on the dangerous subject of loyalism. The day, she felt, was Lithgow's and her only tactic was to retain a semblance of calm. Lithgow for his part appeared spent. He drank as heartily as he ate and as dinner progressed, torpor enfolded him. His eyes slipped back into his head and when Perdita experimentally relaxed her grip on the conversation, he appeared to drift off altogether. She stole a glance at her watch under cover of the table-edge: ten-forty. If only the service were not so slow. When the waiter trundled the dessert trolley towards their table, she gave him a glazed smile and shook her head, hoping to answer for both of them. But Lithgow woke abruptly from his slumbers and ordered bread and butter pudding with cream. The waiter retreated to the kitchen to revive it in the microwave and Perdita, screaming inwardly, settled down for another long wait, racking her brain for a safe, untried topic of conversation.

To add to her miseries, Lithgow seemed to be stirring again in his awareness of her. From the slits in his face, his eyes gleamed. 'You're a clever girl,' he said. 'But there's a lot you don't know.'

Perdita was about to reply when her attention was distracted by a slight commotion at the door. Two RUC officers had entered, followed by the Maître d', who nodded towards their table. Perdita, suddenly wide awake, froze. This was it, then. They were coming for her. Lithgow, sensing her change of focus, turned to watch them advance. It was to him that the RUC sergeant spoke.

'Forgive me for intruding, Mr Lithgow,' he began. He glanced at Perdita. 'I wonder if I could have a private word with you, Sir?'

Lithgow regarded the sergeant for a moment, grunted and lumbered to his feet. The RUC man drew him away from the table and began to speak in a low voice. Perdita watched their two backs, the hummock of Lithgow's shoulders. She found herself rolling the edge of the tablecloth where it lay on her knee into a tight coil. Her stomach had turned to water. This was about to be humiliating. They would fly her to England for questioning, presumably. The shoot would have to be abandoned. How was she going to explain it to the contributors, the production company, Jeremy Jordan? She turned to look behind her for signs of a fire exit, although escape, she knew, was pointless.

After a minute's conversation in which Lithgow appeared to be plying the police officer with short questions and listening to longer answers, he turned back to the table and said, 'My dear, a foolish business seems to have come up. I'm truly sorry to spoil your evening.'

CHAPTER 12

Perdita braced herself. Her face was hot.

'I have to go to my constituency with these officers,' Lithgow continued. 'Sometimes, the responsibilities of public life are most unwelcome.'

Perdita raised her eyes to his face. She didn't understand him. It was another few moments before she realised this was not about her, after all.

'I'm afraid I have no choice but to terminate our meal,' he was saying. 'However—'

'Please!' Perdita broke in. 'Think nothing of it. It's late and high time I left you in peace.' She smiled gratefully. 'I've so enjoyed—'

'You misunderstand,' he said. 'I wouldn't dream of turning you away. Are you forgetting that I promised you information? By accompanying me on this tiresome business, which I'm confident will take no more than a half-hour, you will meet my security man who has something of importance for you. He will join us at my office.'

The RUC sergeant stepped forward. 'If you'll forgive me, Sir, I think the lady would be better advised to remain in Belfast.'

'Nonsense!' Lithgow was warming to his theme. 'Come on, man. I have made this lady a promise. She is an English journalist for whom I have information. Am I to let her down?'

'I'm serious, Sir. Don't bring her,' said the officer fiercely. To Perdita it sounded like a warning.

'I shall stay behind,' she repeated firmly.

'You will *not* stay behind,' asserted Lithgow. 'Unless, of course, you are afraid to meet my man and hear what he has for you? I can tell you this much: it concerns your Mr Booth.'

Perdita hesitated, her thoughts in turmoil. Now Daniel had been arrested, she might just possibly be given an official explanation of his documents, an opportunity not to be missed. 'But these officers are saying—'

'I'm not interested in what they are saying. You are to come!' Lithgow gestured to the waiter, who hurried forward with the bill. Bread and butter pudding was off the agenda. Perdita tried to catch the sergeant's eye. His face was pale and set. A second waiter produced their coats and Lithgow swept out of the restaurant, the fingers of his left hand pincered into Perdita's elbow. She felt as if he were taking her hostage. Well, the RUC would protect her. She looked at them. They were all armed.

'Better travel with us, Sir,' the sergeant urged. 'One of our men will follow with your car.'

'I can drive myself, can't I?' Lithgow sounded disgruntled.

'Security, Sir. Can't be too careful,' said the sergeant.

A glossy unmarked police car was waiting outside. Perdita saw that with the driver, who already sat at the wheel, there would be six of them. 'This settles it,' she told them firmly. 'There isn't room for me.'

'The lady will be cramped,' agreed the sergeant.

But Lithgow increased his hold on her upper arm as he groped for his keys and handed them to one of the officers. 'The vehicle is large enough if one of you follows with my car. You go in front, sergeant. We can squeeze in the back with your wee man. We will be quite cosy.' The constable, who had said nothing throughout, was indeed slightly-built, Perdita noticed. Lithgow almost pushed her into the middle of the back seat and clambered in after her, exhaling heavily as though this might reduce his bulk. The driver slid his seat forward a fraction and Lithgow eased his bulbous knees towards the handbrake, finding it necessary to place his left arm behind Perdita's shoulders.

They moved out into thinning traffic and headed west, Lithgow's thigh pressed tightly against Perdita, who in turn held fast to the edge of the front seat for independent support. She was furiously regretting her own ineptitude. Of course she should have stayed behind! Nobody spoke. Within a very short time they had left the city and were speeding into the darkness. From her previous visit to the constituency, Perdita knew the drive would take less than half an hour. She turned over in her mind Lithgow's reasons for bringing her along, none of them attractive. The sexual possibilities she dismissed as too crass, even for Lithgow. Either he was still punishing her, or he simply wanted to show off. She wondered what the security man had to tell her and hoped that, after all, it would be worthwhile.

At a junction the car slowed and turned off the main road. 'Is it necessary to take the back way at this time of night?' Lithgow asked. It was a genial enough question, but Perdita thought she detected a note of unease.

'He was born around these parts. He prefers the high ground,' joked the sergeant.

The driver did not attempt to answer. Lithgow leaned heavily against Perdita as he reached into his pocket for cigarettes. She had wondered how long he would hold out. The fan was switched to full capacity—she could hear it now they were driving more slowly—and the heat was ferocious.

'Will I open the window?' Lithgow asked, feeling for the winder on the car door.

'Central controls,' said the sergeant. 'The locks are on, Sir. Security.'

Lithgow grunted but lit up anyway.

Perdita thought she would choke. 'Could you turn the heat down please?' she asked the driver, seeking out his face in the rear-view mirror. Lithgow's car had caught up and was now hard behind them; its headlights illuminated the interior of the police vehicle. Her question distracted the driver's attention for a moment and he returned her gaze. Perdita caught her breath. It was a *déjà vu*, but so vivid as to be uncanny. For a moment she was convinced she had sat here in the back seat before and seen the driver's eyes in the mirror; the slight frown in them. The car rounded a bend and the interior was plunged into darkness again. 'Certainly, Ma'am,' the driver said.

They continued into the night. Perdita's head was aching. The more she considered the promise of information, the less optimistic she felt. The likeliest explanation was some weird revenge trip of Lithgow's. She sat cursing Lithgow and cursing herself for taking the bait. She would be exhausted tomorrow.

Then unexpectedly they hit a stretch of straight road and the car behind lit their vehicle once more. Stealing a sidelong glance at Lithgow she saw a film of sweat glistening against the dark. The face of the man to her left was dowsed in shadow but by moving slightly forward she could see the mirrored image of the driver and again the impression of having met him before was so powerful that blood beat at her temples. Under the anonymous peaked green cap, she *knew* those eyes. From where? In the dark. In the mirror. With fear in her guts. In the back of a car that was safe enough when she climbed into it, just as tonight's car had been, but which took her to a place, scared and alone, where she was not safe at all. As if reading her thoughts, the driver's eyes now drew back to the mirror, met hers. *The order came over my radio*. In her imagination she remembered his voice. She stared at the face in the mirror and saw the answering recognition. For seconds he drove, blind to the road ahead; his eyes locked with hers, transfixed in the mirror, the shock for him clearly as tumultuous as the shock for her. This driver was not RUC. Then not one of the men in this car or the car behind was RUC. *How're you doin', Francie?* McGrail's words came back to her. This was McGrail's man. Francie's eyes narrowed as he watched her now: a plea, a warning. *Say nothin'*. Perdita looked frantically away. The car sped on through the darkness carrying a frightened Englishwoman, a fat, elderly loyalist politician—and who else? This was the date: 27 November. There *had* been a second document, after all. Why hadn't Lithgow realised? His bloody country. *His* bloody RUC. Why had he not taken care? The beads of perspiration were swelling on Lithgow's upper lip. Had he, too, registered the truth? *What can we do?* she asked herself desperately. There was nothing to be done.

The moment came without warning. With scarcely a break in speed the car turned left along a forestry track, drove a couple of hundred yards and crunched to a halt on a bed of gravel, Lithgow's car behind. There was a moment's silence.

'What's this?' demanded Lithgow. The three men in the car said nothing. Behind them, the door of Lithgow's car slammed shut. Francie released the driver's window and as it slid open a face appeared.

'Get out the vehicle.' The command was primarily to Lithgow. This was business.

'What for?' Lithgow's voice was rasping.

'Out. The both of yous.'

'Wait—' It was the driver, Francie, who spoke. 'Not her.'

'Are you out, or am I to pull you out?' The man outside the window ignored Francie.

'What's going on here?' repeated Lithgow a third time. Perdita could hear his effort to take control of the situation. 'Did you not tell me we were going into town?'

The 'sergeant' in the front passenger seat turned to Lithgow for the first time. 'The journey stops here, Milton. You were warned, Milton. But you carried on.'

'This is nonsense. You're talking nonsense. There's a misunderstanding.'

'No misunderstanding. Let's get this absolutely straight: this is as far as you're going. Get out, like the man says.'

It seemed to Perdita that the doors all burst open at once. The man beside her leapt out and ran round to Lithgow's side of the car to help drag him from the back seat. For a split second she considered hurling herself into the undergrowth, but the 'sergeant' was ahead of her, blocking the open door.

'Out!' he ordered.

Perdita's legs were shaking so badly she could scarcely stand. He gripped her arm and supported her round the back of the car to where Lithgow was now spreadeagled, pinned by one of the men while another went through his pockets. In the fierce light and shadow thrown from one side by the lights of Lithgow's car, Perdita saw him withdraw a squat pistol from the MP's left armpit. 'All that there training with the boys, Milton. Didn't do you no good in the end.'

Lithgow stuttered, 'You're crazy. You're going to have to kill her, too.' As an attempt at bravado, it was not impressive.

'Yes. Thanks to you, we are,' said the 'sergeant'. 'Well done, sir, for that fine feat of gallantry, attempting to use a wee girl for cover.'

'We have to talk,' said Francie urgently to his comrades.

'Not now, man.' The driver of Lithgow's car, who was apparently in charge, jerked the MP upright, pulled both arms behind him and snapped on a pair of handcuffs. The 'constable' pulled back Lithgow's head and bound a length of fabric tight around his mouth. Perdita, still in the grip of the 'sergeant', watched in horror as grotesque shadows on the enclosing trees magnified the action before her.

'And the woman,' ordered the man in charge, nodding

towards the gag. Next moment, Perdita found herself thrown forward, hitting the ground with a jolt. Pain shot through her as the gravel bit into her chin and she smelt, beneath it, the bitter, soft reek of leaf mould. Hands twisted her neck, raising her face far enough from the earth for a piece of cloth to be tied tightly over her mouth and nose. Frantic for breath she jack-knifed her body into a foetal position and her captor must have understood, for his fingers jerked her head around and slipped the gag away from her nose, yanking it tightly into a knot again. Her hands were also bound and she was pulled back onto her feet. The material that cut between her parted lips stank of sweat and something worse. For a few moments her body was racked with uncontrollable retching. The over-rich meal, so recently consumed, rose up her throat, burning and foul, threatening to choke her. A shove in the small of the back sent her reeling and she would have pitched to the ground once more, but for Francie who darted forward, caught her and now took her firmly from her former unseen captor. In the course of propelling her along—for they were on the move—he was breathing into her ear. At first, she recoiled from the touch of his mouth against her hair, but then she realised he was trying to tell her something. The hissed words refused to untangle themselves and she turned to look at him, frantic for hope, but his face was in deep shadow. She could make out nothing.

They had left the clearing and were stumbling into dense pine forest, guided from the front by the man in charge with a powerful flashlight. The 'sergeant' carried a bag and both he and the 'constable' had what she supposed were weapons slung on their shoulders. With every step, Perdita felt hope recede. She had never been able to imagine it: the way a prisoner must feel on the walk from the cell to the scaffold. How could one compel one's own legs to make such a journey? Hers felt detached, as though operating by remote control. She was aware of bones grinding into sockets; of knees and feet operating by levers and counterweights without any volition on her part. No one spoke until, after a couple of hundred yards, the track issued into a wide highway of clear ground that ran between the tall banks of trees.

The man in charge swept his flashlight over them. 'OK, Milton,' he commanded. 'Time to get diggin'.'

With a fresh lurch of horror, Perdita realised that what two of the men carried on their shoulders were not rifles but spades. This was somehow worse. The 'constable' freed Lithgow's wrists. The 'sergeant' shoved a spade into his hands. Lithgow had apparently lost all sense in his fingers, for he dropped the spade, earning himself a clout in the mouth from the flashlight. 'Pick it up!' barked the man in charge. Lithgow propelled his weight uncertainly forward and did so. 'Move, for Christ's sake. We haven't got all night!'

'First honest work you ever done, Milton!' This was from the hitherto silent 'constable'. Lithgow, still gagged, threw him a look of pure loathing. With deliberation, he started to dig. Perdita found the logic of it revolting.

Then the man in charge swung round to Perdita, the flashlight reeling crazily off the trees. 'And you!' he shouted. 'Get diggin', will ya? Give her a spade. We've enough delay on our hands as it is.'

One of the men held out a spade, but Perdita's arms were still lashed behind her back and there was nothing she could do. The man in charge appeared to have forgotten she was bound for he now stepped forward, seized her shoulder and forced her down onto the forest floor. 'And we've enough of your fuckin' Brit insolence!' he shouted.

But this time, Francie interposed himself. 'Listen, all of yous, this is complicated. You're to leave her be.'

'Jesus Christ, man. How can we?'

'You have to, I'm tellin' you. She's connected to—to *us*.'

'She's *what?*'

'I know her. I drove her one night, on orders. Watching that slob there getting off on his wee killers from the Young Militants, in fact.'

'You drove her?'

Lithgow gazed up at them in amazement. His eyes were bulging.

Francie continued, 'It was when your man here was under investigation. She was being shown stuff. She's trusted.'

The man in charge bent down close to Perdita. 'Is this true? You've met this man before?' He jerked his head at Francie.

Perdita stared at him. She saw Lithgow beyond. For all his terror, Lithgow's little eyes were triumphant. His expression said, *You set me up, you bitch.* She flinched as though he had spoken it aloud.

Francie was behind her now. He untied the gag. As the vile thing fell mercifully away, Perdita took a lungful of forest air. 'I've met him,' she said hoarsely.

The man in charge was unimpressed. 'So tell us his name,' he ordered.

Perdita looked at Francie, who nodded. 'His name is Francis. Francie,' she said.

The 'sergeant' now spoke. 'Means nothing! She's met Lithgow here. She's as well a friend of Lithgow's.'

'No, no.' Francie's blazing eyes were fastened on Perdita. 'She's not telling you how it is. She's helping us.'

'How?' Deep sarcasm.

'She's a film producer. She's making a big TV programme about all the grief the Brits are putting on us over the peace. She's being entrusted with important information, so she is.'

'But look at her,' argued the 'sergeant'. 'She's spending time with this load of gobshite here. He's giving her information, too. She's a Brit, Francie, when all's said and done.'

'She's a journalist, Francie,' growled the man in charge. 'And you're seriously suggesting we set her free to tell the biggest fuckin' story of her life?—"I watched brave Milton Lithgow die"? Jesus, man, are you out of your fuckin' head?'

'Belfast will go ape-shit, I'm telling you,' Francie assured him.

'Belfast will go ballistic if we send her running off back to the BBC to tell her tale.'

'She'll not tell,' Francie insisted. 'She's been tested before. She's sound.'

'How d'you mean: tested?'

'I have it on good authority. She—'

'Whose authority?'

'Very senior authority. She was in a situation. She didn't tell then. She's trusted. Ask her!'

Perdita saw their flashlit faces, their noses cast into beaks by the ghoulish, one-sided light. They wore no masks, for there were to have been no witnesses. She was painfully aware of Lithgow, of the terrified eyes above the gag that cut into

his puffy cheeks. But what choice did she have? 'I won't tell.'
She forced herself to look straight at Lithgow as she said it,
knowing that his face at that moment would haunt her as long
as she lived.

The small man, the taciturn 'constable', said simply, 'I
don't believe you.'

'Nor do I,' echoed the man in charge.

Francie rounded on him. 'Well *ask* them, for Chrissakes.
We keep her alive until you refer it up!' He produced a brick-
sized mobile phone from his pocket.

There was a moment's silence. Then the man in charge
said, 'Take her to the car.'

Everything happened very quickly after that. Francie
grasped Perdita's arm and without another word hustled her
back along the path they had come, before any of them could
change their minds. Behind her she heard spades hitting the
earth again. There were two of them digging now.

By the time they reached the cars, Perdita was shuddering.
Francie stopped, untied her hands and bundled her into the
back seat. Then he turned on the engine, locked the doors
and switched the fan to its maximum setting. The rush of air
dulled sound outside. Searching out his eyes in the mirror, she
stammered, 'Why does he have to die?'

'There's good reason.'

'I can't see the logic,' she faltered. 'I thought McGrail
was for the peace. If you kill Lithgow, won't it jeopardise the
whole thing.'

Now Francie seemed to want to talk, maybe to try and
justify what was happening. He said, 'Yes, it will do damage
to the peace process, but not as much as Milton Lithgow was

doing to sabotage it. And you need to know: this is absolutely not McGrail's operation, regardless of how it looks.'

Perdita forced herself to concentrate. 'Then why are you on it?'

'Let's say I am his eyes and ears.'

'So these men are… who, exactly?'

Francie shook his head. 'It's not your position to ask!'

She was sickened. 'If they're dissident republicans, why will you and McGrail not stop them?' He had not hesitated to shoot Brian Doherty, after all.

Francie's gaze slid away from her. 'The situation is complicated,' he said. 'I cannot tell you more.'

'Are you saying you're content to let this murder go ahead because at some level it *suits* you?' Perdita was unable to suppress her disgust. 'And it will no doubt suit you to blame it on the Continuity IRA, or whatever it is they call themselves!'

'Listen,' Francie burst out. 'I don't expect you to come crawling on your hands and knees or nothin', but I just saved your life out there in case you didn't notice, and we aren't out of the woods yet. In any sense,' he added.

'I know that. I'm aware of that. Thank you, Francie.' She wanted to say, *I should have done something for Lithgow and I failed.*

'Anyways, you don't know the full facts of it, so there's no point in discussing it,' Francie said. 'You're not of a mind to understand.'

Silence fell. The notion that McGrail could sanction, at whatever level, the murder of a public figure had done nothing to reassure Perdita; fear for her own life came surging back. 'He was such a creep,' she said through her tears. 'He insisted

I meet him tonight. I'd have done anything to get out of it.'
This thought made her weep in earnest. Then she grew quiet
again and they both sat there, listening. How long did it take
to kill a man?

It was a single shot, muted by the heating fan inside the
car, which was now quite hot. When it was over, Francie
turned down the fan. 'Just a shallow grave,' he explained. 'To
protect the body. They'll not be long.'

'So strange,' she said, half to herself. 'To protect the body,
but not the man.'

'From foxes an' that, I mean.'

'I know what you mean.' She was so tired. She closed her
eyes. And now it was her turn. God knew whether she would
ever get back to Belfast...

She didn't know how much time had passed when
Francie's voice roused her. Had she actually slept? She
shook herself awake and realised he was speaking softly on
his phone. When he saw she was listening, he got out of the
car and continued the conversation. After a few minutes, the
call ended and he leaned in through the window. 'It will be
arranged,' he told her.

'You mean: *me?*' she asked fearfully.

'They won't want the blood of a British journalist on
their hands,' Francie explained. 'That's what I'm bankin' on.
There'll be a deal. A trade-off, most like.'

*Yet McGrail is content to spill the blood of a British
MP*, she thought to herself. She couldn't begin to understand
how a senior republican like Joe McGrail could influence
the decisions of dissidents who opposed him, but she had
long since given up trying to understand these wheels within

wheels. She prayed that what Francie said was true: it was the only hope to sustain her. She reflected how much safer it would have been for McGrail to have killed her last time, in the car after the fire; yet he had chosen not to. 'Why did you even mention McGrail?' she asked. 'If I tell the police, it's you who'll get done for it.'

He was looking at her shrewdly. 'Aye, but because it's McGrail you'll not go to them, will you?'

'I won't need to. They will come for me.'

'I don't want to talk about it,' he cut in. 'I must be crazy to be saving you. I might well change my mind.'

She could sense he was not playing with her and was suddenly wide awake, on guard, her terror returning. 'Who will they call? When will they do it?'

'I'll try and get them away from here. It's too easy here.'

'You mean it's too easy to fire a shot and dig a shallow grave out here, if they choose to disobey orders?'

He said nothing.

'You could just let me go, Francie.'

'I could not!'

There was silence. She strained her ears for the sound of the men returning, longing for the nightmare to be over, yet fearing to hear them.

When they came, they were subdued, breathing heavily. The spades were hurled into the boot with a clatter. The man in charge now sat in the front passenger seat. The 'sergeant' took Lithgow's place on one side of her, the 'constable' got in on the other.

'Did you call?' the man in charge asked Francie.

'No signal.'

'Gi's that there.' He reached for the mobile phone lying above the dashboard, but Francie grabbed it first and held it out of reach.

'There's no signal, I'm tellin' you.' Francie stuffed the phone firmly into his right-hand pocket, turned the car and headed out of the clearing; Lithgow's vehicle was left behind.

They drove in heavy silence back down the track and out onto the country road. Then the man in charge said, 'Pull over.'

Francie stopped on a wide grass verge. The time was one-fifty by the dashboard clock. Perdita, wide awake now, clutched the seat to avoid touching the men on either side of her. This was it, then.

'I'll do it,' Francie said.

'No.' The man in charge held out his hand again, peremptorily. 'I want to hear this myself. Frankly, I don't believe it.'

Francie dialled the number and handed him the phone without comment. Perdita's heart was pounding. *Be there*, she prayed. Someone answered. She wondered who it was.

'It's us,' said the man in charge brusquely. There was a pause. 'Wake him, would ya?'

A long wait. Perdita wondered how they would manage the information on an open line. Then whoever they needed to speak to must have come to the telephone, because the man in charge said a terse, 'Hello there.' There was a pause. 'Aye, it's done. Except we had an audience…' The man in charge got out of the car, kicking the door shut behind him. Everyone waited. Everyone was tense. Perdita leaned her forehead against the seat in front. Outside, she could see the shadow of the man in charge. She saw him end the conversation, which was quite short. As he climbed back into the passenger seat, they were all watching him. He glared across at Francie. 'You bastard,' he said. What did that mean, for God's sake? Perdita wondered. But on either side of her she felt the other two relax.

'Come on,' said Francie. 'Tell her what he said.'

The eyes of the man in charge stayed on Francie's face. 'He said, "The driver is right".'

Perdita started to weep silently.

'Why?' The man in charge leaned towards Francie and spoke with menace. 'Why is the driver right? Why are we to put our trust in a fuckin' Brit journalist? Who's she shaggin'?'

'It's late, man.' Francie started the car. 'We're all tired. We're going home.'

'Is that it?' the 'sergeant' asked. 'Is she shaggin' someone?'

'No!' Perdita protested, through her tears.

'Don't talk to her like that,' said Francie. 'She is not. She is helping us.'

'Well, I don't want her fuckin' help!' The man in charge threw himself back in his seat. Francie pulled out into the empty road. It had started to rain. The wipers slapped against the rim of the windscreen.

'If she was someone's woman, it'd make sense,' commented the 'constable' after a moment or two. 'It's a breach of discipline, though I could understand it. But *this* I don't understand.'

'It's a serious breach of discipline,' echoed the 'sergeant'.

'She—is—no one's—woman!' Francie repeated. 'There is no breach of discipline. Now shut the fuck up, all of yous. This is nothin' but L.T.'

'Never wanted you on this operation in the first place.'

The man in charge glowered at Francie.

'Steady on now,' Francie shot back. 'Who let her get in the car with us? I didn't exactly hear you protesting. You didn't need to bring her.'

The man in charge muttered, 'I thought we'd lose him if we stopped her.' But even to Perdita it sounded like a feeble excuse.

'You fucked up,' said Francie shortly. 'Just tell me how does the blood of a British journalist serve any kind of cause? I've saved you from one massive scandal tonight, and you should have the grace to admit that!'

'It's her I'm worried about,' said the 'sergeant'. 'She'll spew out everything.'

Perdita turned to him. 'Listen. *You* know, because you heard me tell Mr Lithgow: I didn't want to come tonight. I tried to stay behind. And now I want nothing more to do with it. Just like last time, as Francie told you. I could have gone to the RUC then, but I didn't.'

They travelled without speaking after that, each man apparently lost in his own thoughts. The car rejoined the highway and within another fifteen minutes they had reached the outskirts of Belfast again.

It was Francie who broke the silence. He spoke in a voice that made Perdita aware that, since the call to senior command—whoever they were—the balance of power within the car had shifted. 'Lithgow's branch man will have been alerted by Lithgow's failure to show. We have to abandon this vehicle in the next minute and a half. Perdita, see that there?' He pointed to an all-night taxi office. 'Got it? When I stop around the corner, you can run back there. Okay. Here goes.'

He turned sedately into a side street and parked the car in the forecourt of a large pub. The three other men melted away into the darkness. Perdita clambered out after them. Her legs felt as if they would give way beneath her.

'Watch yourself,' Francie said. She turned back to thank him, but he, too, was gone. As she approached the taxi office, she heard the first helicopter overhead.

CHAPTER 13

Daniel had been answering questions. On the evening of his arrest, two men sat behind desks while he was given a lone upright chair in the centre of the room. His interrogators introduced themselves by name—Farrington and Hughes—of whom Daniel rapidly decided Farrington was the senior. They wore office suits. He noticed their shoes were not particularly shiny and, on the notion that a good deal of shoe-cleaning went on in the military, decided they were more likely to be civil servants than service personnel. The police had read him his rights when he was arrested, but no one had told him what he was accused of; the questions nibbled around the edges. What had he to say about his attendance at a conference on the civil service and the media in 1995? What were his motives for associating with the pressure group Lawyers for Gay Rights in 1981? Was he a practising homosexual?

'I have been a practising homosexual, as you call it, throughout my adult life,' replied Daniel. He could not resist adding, 'I'm a civilian.' He had an acute sense of the absurdity of all this—had been conscious of it from the moment he realised it was Blakemore they were after. Now he felt the need to express it, to hang on to some kind of identity. If he failed, he feared he would go out of his head.

The point about his civilian status was a serious one. Homosexuality was still illegal in the armed forces,[6] but *he* had broken no law. As a civilian under interrogation in a police station he would have had rights, but in this quasi-military environment he appeared to have none. There was no evidence of the interview being recorded and an early appeal for a solicitor had been brushed aside. He attempted to ask if this was still about the documents or whether they had something new against him, but the question was ignored. It was as if Daniel simply had not spoken.

On the first night, he was held not in a police cell, as on his previous arrest, but in the building where he was being questioned. Daniel guessed it must be something to do with the secret services, somewhere across the river; in Southwark, perhaps. A trip to the lavatories revealed two uniformed military police officers outside the door, and the realisation that his makeshift ablutions had to be carried out under the scrutiny of a third, who loitered by the urinals, watching impassively. Daniel splashed water over his face and neck and dried himself gingerly with paper towels. 'Can you get me a toothbrush?' he asked over his shoulder, more to break the

6   This is November 1997. Homosexuality became legal in the armed services in November 2000.

silence than anything.

The man grunted. 'I'll see what I can do tomorrow,' he said.

When the interrogation resumed next morning, Daniel could distinguish very little shift from the previous day. He knew from a stint at the Home Office in the 1980s that the Police and Criminal Evidence Act laid down strict guidelines for suspects in custody, but he could not remember what they were. There was certainly something about rests and food.

As the hours passed, he dropped the combative tone and tried to conserve his energy. When the subject turned at last to the allegedly leaked information, he asked repeatedly for reference to be made to his senior, Major Tiffin, insisting he had breached no rules, had consulted his boss and had concealed nothing. The photocopying he denied, as before, clutching at the reality that he had not passed the second document to Perdita, but merely told her the mysterious name, and the date beside it. There could be no record of that.

'You were under suspicion,' intoned Hughes. 'And therefore the document was sent in order for its progress to be tracked. Naturally, it contained no restricted information.' Given that the document revealed prior knowledge of the bomb at Keady, this was an extraordinary claim and, for a moment, Daniel teetered on the edge of pointing it out to them: the memo surely proved some kind of collusion, for heaven's sake! He took a breath to speak, but then remembered he was not supposed to have read the document. This information must have been divulged in the hope of catching him out. He must focus and take more care.

For a while he remained alert to further traps, but the questions slid away from the document again and he speculated that the real pressure would come when his resistance was lower. Sure enough, by the afternoon, he began to notice a curious dislocation in his head from what were logically his own best interests. Part of him longed to confess. He wanted to move things on, at least tell them he'd read the document and challenge them on the privileged information it contained. Yet each time the subject came up, he resisted; and each time the moment passed, he watched its disappearance with regret.

As time went on, he noted that they were referring to a single document. There was no mention of the second. At the third reference to the 'document', he heard himself say, 'You keep talking about one document. But you must know there were two.'

Farrington frowned. 'One document, Mr Booth. It was only necessary to send one document because it became clear you had passed it to a third party. There was no second.'

'But I'm telling you,' Daniel insisted. 'I received two. The first I took to Major Tiffin; the second I returned to the post room. I realised it had come from the same source as the first, and that it was not for me.' Didn't they understand *he wanted to tell them?* If he told them, maybe he could get out of the room.

This time, Hughes and Farrington exchanged glances. Farrington said, 'I'm afraid you're mistaken about that.'

'No, I—' Daniel was on the point of telling them what the second document contained. But this would have been fatal, of course. He forced himself to get a grip. Some people confessed. Some did not. He mustn't fall for their technique, whatever it was.

*

By the time she registered the knocking at her door, Perdita realised it had continued for some time. Cursing, she clawed her way from sleep and felt for the light-switch: five-fifty am. She had slept for little more than two hours: if it was the RUC, they had wasted no time.

'Ms Burn!' A woman's voice now accompanied the knocking.

Go away! Perdita buried her head in the pillows. 'What?' she groaned.

'Ms Burn. Room service.'

'I haven't ordered any room service.'

'I have it here.'

'I don't want it!'

'I need to bring this to you now.' The urgency of the voice penetrated her fuddled mind. Perdita swung her feet to the floor and stood up. The heating was only just coming on. In the split second before she reached the door it occurred to her the officers might be armed, though she was too exhausted to care. But standing on the threshold was a stocky young woman in a nylon overall holding a breakfast tray.

'I didn't order this,' Perdita said, glancing nervously past her up the corridor.

The chambermaid appeared to be alone, however.

'Will I come and set it down for you, please, ma'am?' she demanded, adding a little sharply when Perdita hesitated, 'It's heavy, so it is.'

'I was fast asleep,' Perdita told her, though she stood aside anyway. The maid entered and dumped the tray somewhat unprofessionally on the bed. 'There's been a mistake,' Perdita repeated. 'I didn't order this and I certainly didn't want to be woken before seven-thirty.'

'There's no mistake.' Instead of making to leave the room, the chambermaid closed the door and leaned against it. 'I'm sorry to wake you after your late night an' all, but the hotel will be crawling with police at any moment, as you must know. I have to be brief. I have a message from Joe.'

'Joe?' Perdita's mind was blank.

'You don't have to play dumb with me now, Perdita Burn. Wake up and listen.'

'Oh, from *Joe*—'

'*Listen!*' the woman cut in before Perdita could say his surname. 'You'll tell them that although you left with your man last night, they dropped you off here, at your hotel. You did not travel out of town with them.'

Perdita was wide-awake now. She looked at the woman, collecting her thoughts. 'So I lie about it, do I?'

'Sure you do!' hissed the chambermaid urgently. 'Can you imagine what would happen if you say you went along with them—that you was present at the scene?'

Perdita hesitated. She did not like being pushed into a course of action without thinking it through.

Seeing her indecision, the woman pushed on, 'Think of it for a moment, would you? How are you going to explain what happened in the forest there?'

'I would have told the truth,' Perdita replied. 'I was a hostage. They left me in the car. I didn't see the shooting...'

'But you *knew!*' the woman expostulated. 'For chrissakes, you all left the scene without Lithgow. And how on earth do you suppose they would have risked letting you walk free after that? You wouldn't just have been let go!'

'Maybe they wouldn't have wanted the blood of a British journalist on their hands?' Perdita suggested, echoing Francie from the night before.

'They'd already the blood of a British MP!' argued the woman. 'Jesus, what difference? Besides which,' she continued, 'we're assuming you came back here, when by rights, after that, you should have went straight to the authorities! That's a serious crime.'

Perdita considered it, disconcerted by this 'we', which conjured a picture of some cabal of republicans sitting up all night discussing her fate. But yes, it was true, she could well be held complicit for not reporting the crime. She had thought of herself as a witness, a secondary victim, but to the RUC she could see she might well be a suspect. 'So, what are you saying?' she asked cautiously.

The chambermaid stared at her for a moment, infuriated that she should even have had to argue the point. 'Okay,' she said at last. 'Here's what you do. You wake up this morning and you hear about the death on the news. Lithgow's Branch man will have alerted the authorities hours ago: they'll find him soon, shouldn't wonder. They knew you were seeing him last night?'

'Yes. And there was no security last night,' Perdita confirmed. 'But the reason I even got in the car with them was that Lithgow insisted his Special Branch man had some inform-ation for me that I... well, I needed it urgently. God, I wish they'd never let me get in that bloody car!' she burst out angrily.

'Yeah, well they did. So. No use moaning about it. And you will have been seen—it'll be on the Europa cameras—so you can't say you didn't go. But you did *not* leave town with them. Okay?' She paused, making sure this had sunk in. 'They simply dropped you off here.'

Perdita was warming to the idea. She nodded.

'So, you go to bed. You know nothing till you hear it on the news. They will come for you in any case. It'd look better if you went to them first.'

'Yes,' Perdita agreed.

'Right. But next they will ask you for descriptions of the men. You did meet them after all. You travelled in the car. So you need to know what you're going to say about that. The detail is important. Get it straight. And get it into your head beforehand.'

'I saw their faces in the hotel.'

'They were wearing caps pulled low on their eyes, were they not?'

'All police officers look the same, you mean?' Perdita could not resist the jibe.

The woman failed to smile. 'Well, could you describe them? You'll be asked.'

'I couldn't. I only saw the uniforms. Except one man was noticeably short.'

'You can say that. You have to appear to be cooperative.'

There they went again, Perdita thought to herself, forever hectoring you about what to do. 'I know how I have to behave,' she answered, with an assurance she did not feel.

'Oh, do you?' sneered the woman. 'Well, if I'm not

mistaken, you was about to go and blab to them that you witnessed the whole operation!'

'Come on,' said Perdita. 'You've just woken me up. I'm in one hell of a mess here—and it's not of my making.'

'Perhaps that's why Joe wanted to help you.' The woman was staring at her critically. 'I hope to God you're to be trusted!' she added. She had clearly formed the opinion that Perdita was not up to the task. 'So, as soon as it comes on the news, you go to Crumlin Road. You can tell them you're in shock. That's why you're having trouble getting it straight!' She didn't bother to hide her contempt.

'Well, I *was* in shock,' said Perdita irritably. 'I still am...' It was starting to dawn on her that she was in no state to handle a police interrogation. Who was this woman, anyway, bossing her around? 'Do you work here?' she asked.

'Are you kiddin'?' The chambermaid laughed. 'The networks run deep in this city, deeper than you will ever fathom.' Pride shone in her eyes. 'Mind what I told you now: you couldn't describe their faces.' She turned to leave, adding as an afterthought, 'And there was no names, mind.'

Then she was gone.

Perdita stood for a while trying to clear her thoughts. It was pointless to go back to bed. The woman was right: she must deny that she had left town with them. Her head felt at the same time woolly and translucent, disjointed fragments from last night flashing through her brain. She sank onto the bed beside the breakfast tray, absently scooping up the glass of orange juice that tipped perilously towards the counterpane. She must work out her approach to the police: that was a priority. Would they suspect her of luring Lithgow to his death? In her exhaustion she had overlooked this, yet it was all too obvious now. Even if she told them she hadn't left Belfast, she realised it could be hard to explain that the men had simply dropped her off. It meant lying, and lying was complicated, though (the chambermaid was right) less incriminating than sticking to the truth.

She swallowed the orange juice and went to turn on the shower. The early morning visitor had been appraising her and, like the men last night, was deeply suspicious that she had been let go. Francie had indeed taken a gamble. 'Aye, but *because it's McGrail* you'll not tell,' he had said. What was that supposed to mean? If McGrail had sent the chambermaid, did that imply it was McGrail's operation, or had he been called in to sort out the mess? Well, someone had saved her life out there in the forest, but there was no point speculating further: there were far more urgent things to think about now.

The crew was due to load at eight-forty-five according to the call-sheet, but if the police hadn't shown up at the hotel, she would have to go to them before that. Either way, she would not be filming this morning. Standing under the hot shower, Perdita shivered. She must warn the others.

'Yes?' When she knocked on his door, Chris Pope, the cameraman, sounded as dead to the world as Perdita herself had been half an hour previously.

'It's me,' she whispered. 'Sorry. I didn't want to phone you.'

'Oh, thank God!' Chris was instantly awake. 'Hang on a second...' He came to let her in. 'We were so worried about you when you didn't get back,' he said, as soon as she was inside. 'Are you all right?'

'Not really.' Perdita sank into a chair and gave him a brief summary of the night's events, wondering if she should be telling the truth even to him.

Chris stared at her, aghast, as her story unfolded. 'Bastards. Murdering bastards! That poor man. Jesus, Perdita, are you sure you're okay?'

Perdita started to weep. With her return to normal life, and Chris's natural, well-founded horror, she felt that at last she was coming to her senses. They had worked together a good deal over the years, in situations ostensibly far more dangerous than this; not least, a tricky shoot in Malaysia in 1993 on the notorious Pergau Dam affair, as well as on Helstone B. For the first time in weeks, Perdita realised here was someone she could trust.

'It's supposed to be a film about tea-towels, for God's sake!' he burst out. 'The most boring film we've ever done— and here we are in the thick of a murder! Why the hell do we have to get mixed up in it?' All the same, he reached for the remote and turned on the news, keeping the sound low.

'I tell you, Chris,' said Perdita through her tears, 'I just want to finish the shoot and get out of this bloody country.' Frazer and McGrail had been right. It was far bigger and far dirtier than anything she could deal with.

They hastily replanned the morning's shoot, Perdita asking him to get the office to postpone the interview scheduled for the afternoon, if she hadn't re-appeared by lunchtime. She had been keeping an eye on the screen as they talked and now put a hand on his arm. 'Oh God, hang on, Chris. It looks as if they've found the body. I need to hear what they're saying.'

When the news report ended, she stood up to leave, telling him on no account to pass on to the others what had happened to her. 'Or to anyone, Chris. Not to the office, either. I'm going to have to... handle it with the police.'

'Be careful, Perdita. If you can't say what really happened, that's dangerous.'

'What choice have I got?' she muttered. At the door, she turned back to him. 'Listen, did you happen to notice if there was anyone in reception when you went to bed?'

'No one. I wanted to ask them if you'd come back, so I went down to the desk about midnight. Not a soul around.'

'Good,' she said. 'Unless... Oh goodness, there'll be a camera, won't there?'

'There's not,' he assured her. 'I made a point of looking, the day we got here. Rather remiss of them, I thought.'

This was a relief. Her story was coming together. 'You're very observant!' she smiled.

'I'm a DoP, aren't I?' He shrugged. 'Goes with the job.'

By the time she took a taxi to the RUC station, Perdita felt she was regaining the initiative. Waiting in an interview room for the relevant officers to be summoned from elsewhere, she almost managed to persuade herself that since she had come to them and they hadn't had to search her out, it followed that they would accept her story. But it was not like that at all. An hour passed before the interviewing officers arrived, and by the time they entered the room her optimism had waned. No sooner had they switched on the tape and taken her through the preliminaries, her two interrogators launched onto the offensive.

'So you're asking us to believe, Mrs Burn, that the IRA gave you a lift back to your hotel?'

Perdita swallowed. This was supposed to be the easy bit. 'I—I didn't know they were IRA,' she stammered. 'I mean, I thought they were RUC officers, of course. It never occurred to me to question it.'

'Would it not have been more natural to put you in a taxi?'

'I've no idea,' she said. 'It—it didn't strike me as particularly odd. Well, was it? What would the police usually do in that situation?'

'We're asking the questions here, not you.' The officers had Belfast accents and were presumably RUC Special Branch, not British security services, yet their tone was much more intimidating than she had imagined it would be. 'Did you not find it odd that they should go out of their way?' the first man persisted.

Perdita looked puzzled. 'Well, everyone here is very... helpful. I didn't know if it was out of their way or not—but, even had I known, I'd have assumed it was because they were looking out for my security and wanted to see me home safely.'

'And what did Mr Lithgow say?' asked the second officer, who had been silent up to this point. 'Did he want you to go along with them?'

'Well, yes,' Perdita said, thankful that on this point she could tell the truth. 'He was sorry they had interrupted the evening, as he put it. He was very solicitous. So maybe that's why they drove me back to the hotel.'

'I didn't ask that. Mr Lithgow wanted you to go with him to his constituency, did he not?'

'It was mentioned,' said Perdita, cautiously. 'But it was

very late.'

'What time was it exactly?'

'Er, I couldn't say. But the restaurant was empty.'

'Did you not check the time?'

'No, I don't think I did. But we didn't start eating till after the Nine o'clock News was over.'

'Though you would have seen the time when you passed the very large clock in reception at your hotel?'

'I'm afraid I didn't notice.'

'Is that because you didn't return to your hotel, Mrs Burn?'

'I'm sorry?'

'I put it to you that you did not return to your hotel, but left Belfast with Mr Lithgow?'

'No.' Perdita managed to look taken aback. 'Why would I do that?'

'Because Mr Lithgow wanted you there, perhaps? Because his Special Branch man had some information for you back at the constituency office?'

Of course, she told herself, they would have spoken to Lithgow's man already. 'There was nothing so urgent that I'd have gone to meet him in the middle of the night,' she assured them.

'We have spoken to Mr Lithgow's security team. One of the men said he was expecting you to accompany Mr Lithgow.'

Perdita shook her head. 'Mr Lithgow did suggest it, but it would have been ridiculous at that hour. So we agreed I would contact them in the morning.'

'You didn't want to go with them because you knew there was going to be foul play.' This was the second man again.

Perdita frowned at him. 'What do you mean?' she asked.

'You heard.'

Perdita looked from one to the other of them. 'No!' she cried, in genuine outrage. 'They were police officers, so of course it didn't cross my mind.'

'If you thought they were police officers, why would you not have gone with them? I suggest you knew they were not.'

Perdita blinked at him. 'It was nothing to do with whether I would have trusted them. I've just told you: it was *late.*'

'You had seen their faces in the bright lights of the hotel.'

'Well, no. Not really.'

'What's that supposed to mean?'

'They wore peaked caps—RUC uniform. Their eyes were in shadow.' It all came out in a rush. Perdita hoped it didn't sound rehearsed.

'Come now, Mrs Burn. You must have noticed something!'

'I couldn't distinguish them. Except one was short for a police officer.'

'Did any of them use names to each other?'

'No.' She pretended to think about it. 'No, they didn't speak in the car.'

'So you all get into the vehicle together. How many in the car? You were in the back, was it?'

'I was in the back seat,' said Perdita. 'There were five of us.' Of this she was sure. 'Oh, and another man was behind in Mr Lithgow's car.'

'So, you had a whole convoy escort you back to your hotel?'

This felt like treacherous ground. Perdita wished she hadn't mentioned the man in Lithgow's car. 'To be honest, I didn't notice,' she replied.

'For a journalist, you're not very observant, are you?' commented the second man. When Perdita said nothing, the first officer resumed his line of questioning: 'And sitting close up to them as you say you were, could you see nothing of their faces—even driving through the city centre with the lights?'

'I was not thinking about how they looked.'

Then the second man, who had been watching her, said, 'Did you not see the driver in the mirror?'

'No!' she answered, a little too swiftly. She couldn't meet the officer's eye. All she could see was Francie, the shock of recognition.

'I suggest you did!'

She shook her head. 'The mirror...? No,' she said. 'I couldn't see his face. It can't have been at the right angle.' Even to her it sounded forced. The second officer was staring at her: she knew it must be all too obvious that her own face was shiny with perspiration.

'So they drove you, in silence, to your hotel, where you got out. Is that it?'

Perdita nodded. 'We—we said goodnight. I thanked Mr Lithgow for dinner. I thanked them for bringing me home.'

'And what happened after that?'

'Well, they drove away and I went into the hotel. That's all I know.'

'Are you sure now, Mrs Burn?' The first man was staring hard at her.

'I'm perfectly sure.' She gazed back at him.

'And the night manager can confirm your return, no doubt?' asked the second officer suddenly.

Perdita shook her head. 'I'm afraid he probably can't,' she

admitted. 'There was no one around when I got in.'

'No one on reception?' said the first man. 'Isn't that rather unlikely?'

'Well, it would have been after midnight, I imagine.'

'But you didn't see the clock.' Heavy irony.

'If there was no one in reception, how did you get in?' the second man demanded.

'They give us keys, er, to the front door to use late at night.' Perdita opened her bag and rummaged with shaking fingers for her room keys.

The second officer examined them and handed them back. 'So, when you returned to the hotel in the small hours of the morning—three or four in the morning, was it?—you were able to slip into the hotel unnoticed. How convenient for you.'

Perdita was instantly on her guard. 'What are you saying?' she asked.

'You knew what was to happen all along, because you had tipped off the IRA that you would be meeting Mr Lithgow at the Europa last night. You did not return to your hotel. You went with them. You were part of the plot.'

This accusation suddenly seemed to be coming from far away. Perdita wondered if she was about to faint. 'H—how can you possibly say that?' she heard herself ask. 'It's nothing to do with me.'

'You've got to agree it looks bad for you, Mrs Burn.'

Perdita dug her nails furiously into the palms of her hands as she tried to drag her brain back into gear. 'In what possible way does it look bad?' she asked, hating the catch in her voice. 'I—I accept a lift home from people I take to be the police. They drop me off at my hotel. That's the end of it! Now you're saying I'm a *suspect?*'

'I've no idea if you had a hand in the murder,' the second officer said. 'But you were part of it.'

From somewhere, Perdita gathered her wits. 'Are you accusing me?'

'Put it this way,' said the second officer. 'Has it not crossed your mind why a group of terrorists would simply take you back to your hotel when you had seen them, could identify them, could lead us straight to them? You seriously expect us to believe they would let you go, just like that?' He snapped his fingers in the air. 'That is not how these criminals operate, Mrs Burn. Their *modus operandi* would be to keep you with them. And then to silence you. I give you one more chance to tell us why they did not.'

Perdita turned helplessly from one to the other. 'I have absolutely no idea,' she said. 'Except that I had seen nothing suspicious. And... well, Mr Lithgow obviously saw nothing, either, otherwise why would he ever have gone with them in the car? When I saw it on the news this morning...' Her eyes filled with tears that were genuine enough. 'Can't you see, I came here because I wanted to help you? That poor man... '

The first officer cut her off. 'Calm down, Mrs Burn. We're merely observing that your account is inconsistent.'

'I—what's inconsistent about it?' Had she tripped up? Contradicted herself? Then, mustering her strength, 'If you're accusing me, I want a solicitor present.' It was meant to be assertive, but it sounded querulous, even to her.

The second man shrugged. 'You meet a British MP by pre-arrangement. The IRA miraculously know where to find him. They lure him away to his death after thoughtfully dropping you back to your hotel. We're simply pointing out that from where we're standing, you're right in the middle of it.'

'Listen, I'm a journalist doing my job. Why on earth would I want to murder a British MP?' Perdita's tears were now as much from frustration as from fear. 'There's nothing more I can say. I'm shattered. Do whatever you have to do, but until you've got more information, can I please go?'

'You're going nowhere, Mrs Burn, until we tell you. You may have been party to a murder. You will stay here while we investigate further.'

*

The light was already fading from the grey square of wire-meshed window glass when Farrington, the senior of Daniel's two interrogators, announced the first break of the second day. Daniel examined their faces. Farrington looked drawn but his younger colleague showed no sign of exhaustion. He hoped his own features betrayed as little strain, but on entering the gents, trailed by his jailer, a covert glance in the mirror revealed that his skin had a papery quality and receded into hollows he had never seen before. He was returned briefly to his room to find a mug of tea awaiting him, but it had clearly been there for some time. He forced himself to drink it, grimacing at its consistency. His head was aching, probably from dehydration as much as stress, and Daniel was annoyed with himself for not drinking water from the washroom tap.

'Please would you rinse that out for me and bring me some water?' he asked the jailer.

'Orders are not to leave you alone,' said the man doggedly.

'Well, give it to one of the chaps out there, then.' Daniel

could hear a pleading in his voice that he fiercely resented.

The man called out into the corridor, 'Prisoner wants some water.' He handed the stained mug to one of the guards.

'Interview resuming,' the guard responded. 'He'll have to do without.' The door opened wider and Daniel was marched back to the interview room.

He could tell as soon as he entered that something had happened. The two investigators had been joined by a third, a man he had not seen before. Farrington and Hughes sat upright in their easy chairs, their features set. The new man was different: younger than the others, dressed in a leather jacket and jeans, he leaned back in his chair with the air of an observer. Instinct told Daniel that this was a departure from the scheduled programme; a new urgency flowed from the other two.

'This, er, second document you say you received,' Farrington began. 'To whom did you pass it?'

'I passed it to no one except to the room number for which I thought—for which Major Tiffin told me—the documents were designated.'

'What room was that?'

'Room 501.'

'I suggest you *stole* the document. You kept it, and then passed it to a journalist who was not authorised to see it.'

'I did not steal it. I attempted to find Room 501 in order to deliver it myself, but the room did not seem to exist. I then gave it to the woman in the post room.'

'Did she recognise the destination?'

Daniel hesitated. 'Yes. She didn't exactly say, but there was some remark that made me think it was the Security Service.'

'What remark?' asked the new man, who had not introduced himself.

'I honestly can't remember. Something about it being a secret. I gave up after that. Well, presumably you know more about that side of things than I do!'

The interrogators glowered back at him. 'What happened next?' asked Farrington at last.

'Nothing. That was the end of it.'

'Who else did you pass the second document to, Mr Booth?' Farrington repeated.

'Nobody. To no one.' His eyes slid away from the three men. Vernon would have reported Perdita's presence at his flat, of course. He massaged the knots in the right-hand side of his neck with fingers that were damp with sweat. Ought he to pre-empt their next question and tell them about Perdita? No, of course not. There was nothing to link Perdita with the documents. He struggled to clear his aching head.

There was a pause. 'Tell us,' said the new man, his voice neutral, 'what the name Lithgow means to you.'

Daniel was tense again. He wouldn't be caught on this one. 'Nothing.' He attempted to shrug, but it came out like a kind of twitch.

'Come along, Mr Booth. You're claiming to be straight with us. Don't spoil it.' Unlike his colleagues', the new man's accent was unmistakably public school. Daniel couldn't work out who he might be.

'In what context?' he asked guardedly.

'How about the context of one of Ulster's most senior members of Parliament?' Hughes suggested.

'Him. Well, of course I've heard of him.'

'You thought I was talking about the document, didn't you?' said the new man, still from the depths of his armchair.

'I didn't read the document.'

'If you didn't read it, why did you think I was referring to the document when I mentioned the name Lithgow?'

'I didn't.'

'Oh? But I suggest you *did*, Mr Booth.'

'I—I was thinking about the word Lithgow and it meant nothing.'

'You saw it in the document and it meant nothing,' Farrington corrected.

'No!'

'You thought it was a place because the names on the first document had been places. So you weren't thinking of the Unionist MP whose name it was.'

Daniel shook his head; his thoughts scrambled. What were they bouncing him into? 'Look,' he said. 'If you're accusing me of something, I want a lawyer.'

'Who did you pass the name on to, Mr Booth?' asked Hughes.

'I passed it to no one!'

'You gave it to a journalist who came to your flat, didn't you?'

'No.'

'Do you know what the date is today, Mr Booth?' the new man interrupted.

Daniel thought for a moment. What was it? Was he becoming disoriented? 'Is it the twenty-seventh of November?' he asked warily.

'It *is* in fact the twenty-seventh. And what was yesterday?'

Daniel stared at him. What kind of trap was this? 'Yesterday was the twenty-sixth,' the new man continued. 'The date on the document. Right?'

'No, that's wrong,' said Daniel. His brain was reeling. The date on the document had been the twenty-seventh.

There was a long silence. Daniel felt breathless. What had he let slip? What could he now say?

'Really?' Farrington's eyebrows shot up. 'Perhaps you can put us straight, Mr Booth? What *was* the date on the second document?'

'What... what I mean is—' Daniel felt as if he were drowning. 'It can't be the twenty-seventh today. It—it must be the twenty-eighth by now.' Would it do? Did they believe him? He stole a glance at Farrington, whose expression was impassive.

'What was the date on the second document, Daniel?' asked the new man, quietly.

'I didn't read the bloody document. I don't know what was written on it. If you lot dreamed up the whole thing to catch me out, you must bloody well know!'

And suddenly he realised he had needled them in some way. Without further explanation, the interview came to a close a few minutes later.

It was only a couple of days after that, when he had been taken to the place in Essex and they finally gave him an old copy of *The Times* to read, that Daniel understood. Milton Lithgow had been shot and killed on November twenty-seventh; their apparently bogus document had turned into another accurate prophecy. Daniel's first instinct was relief he had given nothing away. This must have been the information that reached them with the arrival of the new man on the twenty-eighth. They must have been shitting themselves, he thought, when they heard that news. This time, he had saved himself by the skin of his teeth. But as the facts sank in, it dawned on him he must now be closely implicated in Lithgow's murder.

CHAPTER 14

The northern shoot was miraculously back on course. After six hours at the police station in Belfast, Perdita had been released. The RUC Special Branch had evidently satisfied themselves that she had played no part in the kidnap of Lithgow, a matter in which she had a sense that perhaps higher authorities—some branch of the security services, she guessed—had dismissed her role in the whole thing. She was so thankful for this that she hadn't stopped to wonder how they might have known, one way or the other. Had they made the connection with her initial warning to Lithgow, she would surely have been linked to the murder. How, otherwise, could the IRA have known the date? (So how *did* they, she wondered, since it hadn't come from her?) Anyway, for the moment, she was free to leave. By late afternoon, she had rejoined the crew. Over the next couple of days, they picked up the interview and sequences she had missed, and had made it to Larne for the final day's shoot at a textile conference with Frazer. Perdita had needed to put their relationship back on a professional footing before the interview, and had invited him for a drink, meanly using the crew as chaperones.

But now the accumulated stresses of the past week were catching up with her. Still traumatised from Lithgow's death, she slipped quietly to her room after dinner and locked the door. She had carried throughout the shoot Chris's small Sony digital video camera in the hope there might be something worthy of filming without the crew—*fat chance of that*, she thought glumly, as she unloaded her bag. Then she switched on the television, kicked off her shoes and climbed under the duvet.

She had not intended to fall asleep fully dressed but, when she came to, the television was blank and humming and the room icy cold. Perdita shivered and sat up, rubbing her eyes. A shaft of light fell across one corner of the carpet from the corridor outside, though it took her a moment to realise that this and the cold draught were coming from the door, which stood half-open. Then she understood that she was not alone in the room.

She took a breath to cry out but, before she could do so, a voice said, 'Hush, Perdita. Don't speak. And don't be frightened.' McGrail crossed swiftly to the door and closed it. Then he leaned down to switch on the bedside lamp. The dim light illuminated his face as he turned to look at her. She drew away from him.

'What the hell are you doing here?' Fear hardened her voice.

'I didn't want to give you a fright.'

'Of course you gave me a fright! How on earth did you get in?'

'A key,' he said modestly, holding it up. The chambermaid in Belfast and now McGrail himself. These people were Houdinis.

'You've no business here. Go away.' Her voice was shaking now.

'I have come to make amends.'

'I don't want your amends! You killed Lithgow,' she accused him. 'You nearly got me killed, too.'

'I did not kill him. I intervened as soon as I heard you were caught up in it. That was an appalling blunder.'

His weasel words infuriated her all the more: hadn't he used the dissident republicans to do his dirty work? 'I know exactly what part you played!' she said shortly.

'No, you don't.' His voice was serious. 'But I've never misled you, Perdita. You saw it after Keady. I do what I have to do. It's not your world.'

'Yeah, well we should go back to our own worlds and stay there,' she told him. She pulled the duvet around her and turned away from him.

'But how can I do that?' He flung his arms wide. 'When here's the heaven-sent opportunity to deliver on the promise I made you. I want you to come with me.'

'I'm not interested in your promise. I'm going nowhere. I'm asleep now!'

'You're all asleep!' he said fiercely, kneeling on the floor beside her. 'Wake up, Perdita. I can show you things you will never see again.'

'Oh, I've seen far too much already,' she assured him.

'Not of Frazer, you haven't. Come on now, I promised you that.'

'What about him?' She was listening, in spite of herself.

'Put on some warm clothes,' he told her. 'I'll explain as we go.'

She said, 'The police gave me a very hard time in Belfast. I was lucky not to be taken to Castlereagh.' It was he who had warned her about the interrogation centre and she used its name deliberately.

'But in the end, you were let go, were you not?'

'I was held for hours. It wasn't nothing!'

She had half turned back towards him and he gave her an apologetic smile. 'This is me,' he murmured. 'Trying to say sorry.' She was acutely conscious of his hands folded on the sheet. 'You need to know the truth about Frazer, don't you? You have an instinct about him, but you can't take my word. Now you can see it for yourself.'

'How?' She was still suspicious.

'Three hours. No more. I promise to return you safely. There will be no blood, no killing. No one will know you were there with me.'

'Why is it so important to you?' she asked.

He gazed down at her. He seemed about to give her one answer and then changed his mind. 'Because that is how we will win the war,' he said.

Perdita closed her eyes. Her body ached for sleep. But he was right: whichever film she was making, she did need to know the facts about Frazer. She sat up and climbed slowly off the bed on the opposite side from him.

'I'll be just out by the fire exit,' he said at once. 'Hurry. We mustn't be seen. Oh, and be sure to bring this with you.' He touched the DV camera lying on the table.

They seemed to have been driving for hours along roads with hills to the left of them and sea somewhere to the right. McGrail was at the wheel of the production's hire car. Perdita had preferred it: to take their own car gave a semblance of this being simply part of the research. Despite the warmth of the heater, she wrapped her scarf high around her ears and sank herself in her own thoughts. The man beside her was a murderer. That she voluntarily had dealings with him was barely permissible in terms of her professional interest in the story, but the story itself, probably unfathomable like most things in this strange country, was unlikely to see the light of day. So she told herself she had come with him purely for reasons of compliance, as she had justified it to Jeremy. If one of her major contributors had a secret, she needed to know what it was—not least, because she was still smarting from McGrail's earlier warning that she was in danger of making a fool of the production and herself.

But it was more than that. Perdita looked into her heart and did not like what she saw: for all his dark history, and that of his cause, she felt herself drawn against her better judgement into McGrail's magnetic field. This was not supposed to happen.

'Are you falling asleep on me?' he asked.

'I'm thinking.'

'What is it you're thinking?'

'Never mind.'

'You're thinking, what am I doing driving through the

night once again with this evil IRA man.'

'I am not,' she protested, a little too fiercely.

He laughed softly.

'In fact, I'm glad to meet you again,' she told him, pulling herself properly back into the present, 'because I've been doing my homework, you see, as you instructed. And I have questions.'

He inclined his head towards her. 'I'm delighted to hear it,' he said. 'Ask away!'

'First of all, the bomb at Keady... you seem to be saying that some part of the British secret services was behind it?' She was groping for the connections she had read about in Dublin, and the conclusions she had drawn from them. '... with informers operating within the breakaway factions of the IRA to sabotage the peace process?' She turned to him for confirmation. 'And—knowing about Keady in advance—someone in one of those services invented the memo... to trap Daniel... in order to undermine the minister, Blakemore, and wreck the peace?'

McGrail nodded. 'You *have* been doing your homework. Yes, something like that. Your man's document the other week was the proof of it for me.'

To Perdita, it still sounded so unlikely that even in this wild country she found it hard to believe.

They drove in silence for a few minutes. Then, 'So?' he urged her.

'I'm sorry?' She was lost in thought.

'Next question!'

The next question was more difficult. 'You're saying Lithgow was part of all that; he was against the peace, too?'

she began. 'So, if that branch of the security services was behind Daniel's memo... why Lithgow? Weren't they on the same side? The date he died...' she broke off, trying to frame it without leading him.

'What of it?' His voice was harsher.

'Was there a reason for him to die on that particular day?'

'You tell me.' He cast her a sidelong glance.

'You knew about the date,' she said. 'Didn't you?'

His silence confirmed her suspicion.

'It was the date against Lithgow's name in the second document, the one you were asking me about and I wouldn't tell you.' She didn't dare look at him. She stared out at the shadowy hills. 'How did the IRA come by that date, Joe?'

He didn't reply at once. Then he said, 'Well, you've just told me yourself: there's an alliance between dissident republicans and a part of the British—'

'No,' she broke in. 'No. That doesn't apply this time. You see, I had warned Lithgow about the threat. I went to see him ten days earlier. God knows, I didn't want to because it blew Daniel's cover, but I had no choice: Lithgow's life was in danger.' She threw McGrail an anxious glance. 'He more or less forced me to meet him on the twenty-seventh and, when I arrived, he told me he had checked out the information... with whoever, you know, he would do that with.' She hesitated, casting McGrail another look to see how he was taking it. 'You're saying he was in league with these anti-peace people in the security services, so I guess with them, and his Special Branch man, and the rest of it...' She paused.

McGrail said nothing, his eyes on the road as he drove.

'And, well, he told me,' Perdita continued. 'He said...

He said he had it on good authority there had been no second memo. No threat at all. And of course I couldn't tell him that I had actually seen the memo; that I had the information it contained. Because he was quite certain it didn't exist. And then, what happened, happened...' Her voice tailed off. 'And I wondered, if Lithgow's security people didn't know about it, how the dissidents—or you, in the end—came by that date, Joe?' she finished in a rush.

McGrail was frowning. They drove in silence for a few moments and then he said, 'I have tried never to lie to you, Perdita. But sometimes, you must understand, there are questions I can't answer. There's nothing more I can say.' She could see it was so, from the tone of his voice and the set of his profile in the moonlight. But she was thinking, *you have lied to me: you tried to pretend just now it was the same situation as the Keady bomb. You lied to throw me off the scent!* She was disappointed in him—and shocked that she should care. A deep unease settled over her. They travelled without speaking after that.

'Where are we going?' she enquired eventually.

'To the coast.'

'Will Frazer be there?'

'He will.'

She felt the weight of the Sony on her knee. The model was familiar to her and although she doubted there would be any call to use it, its possibilities gave a legitimate purpose to this insane journey. She groped for one of the new batteries she had brought with her.

After a further couple more miles, McGrail slowed as a single signpost started out of the darkness. She could not read the name. He swung the car onto a track and they bumped through ruts and puddles in the unkempt road, passing first one low croft upon their right and then another. The path began to snake downhill. Perdita shook herself awake and opened the window an inch or two to let in the smell of mud and salt and tar. McGrail turned down the headlights and they edged slowly along, the road now running straighter, close to a great white swath of beach beyond a screen of reeds. Then, abruptly, he swung the car off the track and into a summer car park, deserted now. 'From here, we walk,' he told her.

Perdita, glad the journey was over, closed the window and shut the car door as quietly as she could. They set off briskly along a wide path and after covering a few hundred yards in silence she found she had shaken off the sense that it was all wrong being here with him at night, the very inversion of a country walk. It was work; that was all. And after the horrors of recent days, it was a relief not to be alone.

'How're you doing?' he asked.

'I'm fine.' She was wide-awake now, expectant.

'We're almost there.'

They had reached a tiny harbour edged by buildings; there was an inn, shuttered and dark, with a larger annexe in a modern style, a family hostel perhaps, beside it. In the light from two or three streetlamps she could make out cottages and a boathouse with a ramp descending to the water. The boats lay still, cradled by a sea wall. The road itself curled round and upward, widening into a square at the top with more cottages and a small shop on the landward side; on the sea side, a sheer drop to the quay. McGrail turned to her, laying his forefinger on his lip, and led the way into the shadow of the land. They climbed up the steeply curving road and arrived at the square. Although the village was dark, deserted, from somewhere beneath came a glow of light and a murmur of voices. McGrail led her the long way round in the shadows, skirting the square to the far corner, from which a narrow path with a handrail struck off along the cliff-edge. They crept along it in single file, flattening their bodies to the land side. After about fifty yards, McGrail dropped to his knees and leaned across the path so as to peer over the edge. Perdita did likewise. Directly beneath them, not forty feet below, a boat surprisingly large for the harbour was being unloaded by three or four figures in dark jackets, working by the light of hurricane lamps. The scene was so like the tales of smugglers she had read as a child that Perdita at first could barely take it seriously. But in place of the brandy barrels of fiction, the cargo was composed of long, low boxes and wooden crates. Suddenly McGrail touched her elbow and directed her attention to a figure stationed between the boat and the corner of the quay exposed to public view: it was immobile, but Perdita could just catch, reflected in a stray beam from the lamps, the glint of an automatic weapon.

Lifting the camera from her bag, she felt her way to the controls, focused through the viewfinder and pressed the zoom. The definition was surprisingly good; even in the lamplight she could make out a blotch of letters and figures stencilled on each crate, although she could not read them. She filmed for a couple of minutes, the lanterns swinging slightly from their hooks as the men moved from shore to ship to take up their next load. Beyond the occasional word, they worked in silence. The presence of the armed guard was useful but circumstantial. Besides, he was standing too much in the shadows for the camera to pick him up. Thoughts darting ahead, Perdita could see this was all very well but the whole scene amounted to nothing unless she could determine the contents of those crates. And Frazer, as she had suspected, was nowhere to be seen.

McGrail noted her difficulty with light on the guard. When she closed off the camera and moved back into the shadows, he touched her sleeve and pointed further along the cliff path, indicating that they should continue. Clearly, he knew the place well. They made their way silently on into the darkness, Perdita clutching the handrail for guidance. The quay lights, such as they had been, were now obscured by a bend in the cliff. She heard a stirring of the wind in the clumps of spiky vegetation above them. Something caught at a thread in her jeans and she imagined the grey spines of sea holly. All of a sudden, the angle of the handrail dipped. 'Steps,' whispered McGrail, close ahead of her. They descended first one flight and then, doubling back on themselves, a second, ending at a narrow concrete walkway that bordered a rocky beach beyond the quay. McGrail began to move back along this lower path which, she saw, would bring them out at the quay itself so that they would have to pass the boat at close quarters in order to escape. For a moment she faltered. They would have to walk within a few feet of the armed guard.

'We can't walk right past them,' she breathed.

He stopped and turned to her, speaking softly into her ear. 'We don't have to. The path broadens round this next bend. You can film from the level. You may get some light on your man. Keep to the cliff-side. There's more steps up to another raised path. We pass him that way. Have you the camera ready?'

He was standing close to her. She nodded.

'You're doing fine.' His fingers brushed her shoulder as he turned away. They continued onward around the cliff bend, to find the breeze had stiffened, setting the halyards clacking gently against the metal masts of the sailing boats. The men appeared to have stopped work and Perdita feared for a moment that they might have finished, but in fact they were on the ship's deck, clustered together. Perdita and McGrail, with an eye in the direction of the guard, stole as close as they could to the edge of the shadows, some five metres from the unloaded cargo. The bobbing light from the hurricane lamps sent splintered beams over the seaward side, illuminating the numbers and hieroglyphics that identified each crate. Perdita filmed what she could, but she feared that, on the end of the zoom, the lens would still not have been steady enough to read the information. McGrail held out his hand for the camera. She shook her head but he ignored this; clasped her hand holding the camera in both of his and indicated that she should show him the operating button. This was no place for an argument. Perdita guided his finger to the button, pressed the camera into his hands and shrank back towards the safety of the cliff-face. She saw McGrail lie flat on the quay, levering himself around the pile of crates in a kind of crab motion until he was happy with the angle. She watched for what seemed an eternity as he steadily filmed each of half a dozen cases, twisting onto his stomach at last to crawl back into the shadows. He handed her the camera, taking care to switch it off first. Perdita ejected the battery, felt in her pocket for a new one and clicked it into place. Her fingers were shaking, but McGrail's, as he returned the camera, had been steady. When she was ready, he indicated that they should move on.

They had gone no more than a dozen paces when the knot of men erupted without warning and two of them loomed up at the end of the gang-plank which ran at right-angles to the quay. Perdita froze. Was one of them Frazer? She stopped to watch them. Backlit by the rocking lamp, their features were downturned in shadow. Then, as if she had willed it, the man in front swung slowly round towards them, his eyes focused past them toward the guard at the mouth of the quay. Perdita was transfixed. Beyond the fear of discovery was a crawling terror that was entirely new. McGrail was right: this was a chance she would never get again. The man was not Frazer, but she *knew him.* She had seen him before. *Where?* For a moment she swayed dizzily over the path, grasping at the memory. Then she raised the camera, focused on the man's face and shot. McGrail had walked ahead a few paces, but he now returned and took her arm, urging her on. She turned in annoyance and alarm but, after pulling out for a steady wide shot of the man on the deck, and then wider still, of the entire scene, followed McGrail, the metallic echo from the halyards deadening any sound of their escape. The guard in front of them, she could see, had his back to the boat and was gazing out towards the sleeping hamlet. McGrail's foolhardy filming of the crates had been unobserved. She knew it had also been invaluable and her annoyance with him receded. Within a few more yards, his steadying hand warned her they were at the next flight of steps. Perdita climbed, not daring to look back.

They were now less than twenty feet from the guard and their walkway, designed for access to the quay during rough weather, Perdita guessed, ran less than two metres above his head. He had simply to turn towards them and shift his eyeline and he would see them, face to face. As they approached, McGrail slowed his pace and flattened himself against the wall. The moment had come to film the guard. Once again, McGrail reached for the camera. But Perdita resisted. This was supposed to be her job. She set the camera running and knelt on the path, eased forward. She fancied she could hear the electronic purr of it, as if the camera were a jet plane that at any moment would attract her subject's attention. She could see him over the parapet. She was visible now, over the parapet, filming the guard with the weapon, the light from the quay falling on both of them, then panning back from the guard to the boat so as to relate one to the other. As she filmed, she saw nothing but the frame through the viewfinder, the guard, the boat and the cargo. It wasn't real, only television. If the guard would only turn and look up, she could get a shot of his face. Perhaps he was British, too, and identifiable—for she knew the man on the boat was a Brit. For a moment longer she filmed, exposed to full view, willing him to face her. Then she forced herself to come to her senses, sank back, trembling uncontrollably, crouched in the safe shadows by the cliff-wall, the camera still whirring. McGrail knelt beside her, reached for the camera and switched it off. His hand found hers and held it firmly, his lips to her ear. 'Brilliant. Now, come on.' He raised her to her feet.

She was still shaking. He kept hold of her hand as they made their way onward, taking care not to dislodge the smallest pebble. Eventually the path turned up a slope and led them out to the road at a point midway in its curve down from the upper square. There, they both stopped and gazed triumphantly at each other, eyes shining, their breath coming in gasps. Perdita cradled the camera in her arms, but McGrail leaned towards her to whisper, 'We still have to pass the guard. We have to walk down the slope and across to the beach side.'

She eased the camera back into her bag and looked at him in alarm. 'There must be another way round.'

'There is not. Unless you care to swim.'

'We can't do it. He'll see us.'

'He evidently didn't see us coming. We'll be all right.'

Perdita was still uncertain. 'I suppose he won't be looking to stop us, will he?' she said, but without conviction. No one went walking at that hour. She wondered whether to tell McGrail she had recognised the man on the boat.

They had barely started down the road when a sound alerted them both; footsteps rounding the corner; the tread of boots, more than one person; low voices. Without a moment's hesitation, McGrail took her in his arms, turning them both into the deep shadow of the seaward bank. He kissed her, shielding her face with his hand to disguise her profile.

She gasped, raised her hands to his face, to his hair, to complete the camouflage. They kissed with passion, with conviction, absolved of all responsibility for a moment and in the absolute certainty that it was the only thing to be done.

But the boots came nearer, juddered on the grit at the side of the road, stopped. 'Where are yous headed?' came a gruff voice.

McGrail pressed Perdita's head gently to his chest and spoke into her hair. 'Jesus, man. If it isn't obvious.'

'Leave it,' said the second man to the first in an undertone.

'Isn't it a bit late for that sort of thing?' persisted the

first speaker. Terror gripped Perdita. She felt McGrail's arms tighten to support her as he said, 'Come on, Mister. It's never too late for this sort of thing.'

'You should be in yer beds,' grunted the man, without any apparent irony.

'And that's exactly where we're headed,' said McGrail. 'Come along, Maura.' They turned away from the men and began walking slowly down the hill. 'Don't rush,' he whispered into her hair. Before the next bend he stopped and kissed her again. 'We'd not want them thinking we were putting on an act now.' He smiled, casting a wary eye in the direction of the two men. 'They're watching. We should give them their money's-worth.'

Continuing down the road after a few moments, they saw to their relief that the guard had left his post. But Perdita now noted out of the corner of her eye a silver van with its rear doors open, drawn up at a point close to where he had been standing. It had not been there before. In the split second of seeing it, she knew whose van it was. Without breaking her stride, she recognised it as a van they had filmed being loaded by Frazer's men earlier that day. Now it seemed to be waiting for the cargo. Frazer and the Brit. Who *were* these people? *What the hell was going on?*

Perdita knew she must film that van. Breaking away from McGrail, she took out the camera and had snatched a single wobbly shot when they both heard footsteps coming back down the street behind them. McGrail caught her arm and they hurried away as fast as any courting couple decently could, the camera awkward and heavy in her other hand. As they turned a corner past the last house, he grabbed the camera from her and the loose bag, and they broke into a run along the path that led from the quay back towards the place where they had left their car. The footsteps—just one set now—quickened on the road behind them until McGrail, without warning, suddenly swept her off the path and down towards the beach, into the shelter of a sand-dune. 'Let him go,' he muttered.

They knelt in the sand and rough grass, not touching now. As McGrail stowed the camera back into its bag, Perdita's mind was grappling with what they had seen and done. And suddenly it came to her—the identity of the man she had recognised on the deck. She caught her breath sharply.

He turned to her. 'What is it?'

'The man on the boat,' she told him. 'The one you didn't want me to film... It was a civil servant, a colleague of Daniel's at the MOD.'

'I didn't *not* want you to film! It was time to go, that's all.'

But Perdita was groping for the man's name. Vernon something—the man who had caught her leaving Daniel's flat after his release from police custody. 'How can it be?' she asked. 'A British civil servant shifting some kind of cargo on an Irish boat?'

McGrail seemed pleased. 'Come on,' he said. 'We're not out of this yet. Think about it later.'

He pulled her to her feet and they scrambled back up to the main path, Perdita kicking the sand off her boots. In this way, they returned to the car, Perdita carrying the camera once more. The car park lay in a hollow and only at the last moment did they realise a second vehicle had joined theirs: a low black Porsche, parked alongside. McGrail paused, glancing around him, then cautiously they approached their car. They had almost reached it when the Porsche's headlights blazed on. It must have been Frazer on the road by the quay; and now he was waiting for them.

'Stay calm,' McGrail murmured. 'It'll be okay.' His hand touched her forearm for a moment. Then he moved away into the shadows.

She was grateful for his words, although she could not believe them, and forced herself to wait quietly as Frazer jumped out of the Porsche, triumph lighting his face. A low laugh bubbled from him as he came towards her.

'Well, well now. Just imagine!' Frazer's eyes darted over her. Next came his hands, frisking her. In one swift movement, before she understood what he was doing, he had removed the camera bag. Perdita recoiled, out of his grasp. 'Prim Miss Film Director—"Don't sleep with the contributors!".' He mimicked her words at their dinner. 'Taking a little relaxation by the shore. And a delightful night for it.'

Perdita said nothing. As if remembering she was not alone, Frazer glanced around. He found himself face to face with McGrail.

'Give it back, Frazer.'

For a second, Frazer's composure faltered as he evidently recognised her companion for the first time. 'This is indeed an extraordinary meeting,' he said, his smile broadening as his voice hardened. 'I must admit, Perdita, I had not thought you to be so intimate with the IRA.'

'She is no more intimate with the IRA than she is intimate with you,' snapped McGrail. 'Give her the bag now.' From the look of resignation on Frazer's face, Perdita realised that McGrail, whom she had been embracing just minutes before, was armed. Well, she should have known. She heard a metallic click.

Frazer heard it too. He handed the camera to Perdita and raised his hands in a gesture of surrender masquerading as a shrug. 'You're very hot in defence of our British friend here, if I may say so,' he remarked to McGrail. He took a few steps back as he said it until he was up against his car.

McGrail moved out of the shadows towards them, the gun trained steadily on Frazer. 'Why don't you tell her what you're doing here at the dead of night?' he suggested.

'Sure, aren't I taking the sea air, just the same as yourselves?'

Perdita could not but admire his coolness at gunpoint.

'Come on, Frazer. You're not at your wee knitting show now.' Next moment, McGrail had covered the distance between them and leaned in to him, pinning Frazer back against the Porsche with the pistol at his throat, while with his free hand he felt deftly under Frazer's left arm, removing a weapon, which he handed to Perdita. She took it unwillingly, holding the vile thing at arm's length. Then McGrail released Frazer, taking care never to lose concentration on his own firearm, which he now held steadily at Frazer's chest.

Frazer shook himself free and ignored McGrail. 'How would your editor react, do you suppose, were I to tell him you were seen late at night in the arms of a senior member of the IRA?' he asked.

'I think he might survive it, if he understood the reason,' she said. Her own sang-froid impressed her.

Frazer laughed. 'My God, you're even more gullible than I thought you were.'

Perdita took a step back. For all his talk, he had probably guessed what they had filmed at the quay. 'Time to go,' she told McGrail.

'Get in the car,' he instructed. He felt in his pocket and gave her the keys. She turned and walked round to their own car, resisting an impulse to throw away the pistol. She climbed in, started the engine and pulled around Frazer's Porsche to the mouth of the car park, pointing away from the village. But glancing back in the mirror, she saw McGrail had spreadeagled Frazer against the side of the Porsche once more. Perdita watched, her heart in her mouth. *Come on, Joe. That's enough.* For a wild moment she thought he might be going to shoot him. Anything was possible. McGrail went through Frazer's pockets and removed his car keys. 'You can take a ride home with your comrades,' he told him. Then, holding the weapon two-handed, as if in order for no mistake to be made, he backed away and rejoined Perdita. 'Go!' he said as he jumped in. The command was unnecessary. Perdita drove as swiftly down the long, straight track as its surface would allow.

She was trying to stay calm on the journey back, hands tight on the steering wheel to keep them from shaking now the immediate danger had passed. 'Wish I'd got a proper shot of the van,' she said. Her voice was not quite steady.

McGrail wound down the window and hurled Frazer's keys into the marsh. 'Van's the least of your problems,' he muttered.

They travelled in silence. Now they had extricated themselves from Frazer, she could feel the gulf between them once more. Well, so it was. 'Will the markings on the crates give us the evidence?' she asked after a while, more to break the silence than anything.

'I'm certain they will. It was arms, all right.'

'We got the film, anyway,' she said. 'We did well! Didn't we?'

'At a price.'

She thought he was going to say more, but another oppressive silence fell. She was thinking that there was nothing on film to connect Frazer directly with the cargo. Aloud, she said, 'What's the problem, Joe?'

'You know the problem!' He shook his head in disbelief. 'I must be going soft.' The anger in his voice was directed at no one but himself. 'So, Frazer has his revenge,' he added.

She could see it all too well. Frazer was in possession of information about them, almost as damaging in its own way as theirs about him. 'He can't do anything,' she told him. 'He would have to reveal his own connection, his own presence.'

'Don't you believe it. He's a very devious man and he has friends in the media in Britain. He will do you damage if he wants to.'

'But I'd tell the truth!' she countered. 'I'd say it was to avoid detection.'

'No one in the British press will believe that,' he said. 'Will they, Perdita? Frazer knows they won't. I have done you harm tonight. I'm sincerely sorry for it.'

'Joe,' she insisted, 'we had no choice!'

He looked at her for a moment. Then his face broke into a grin. 'No more we did,' he agreed.

His fingers found the back of her neck and massaged the knots at the top of her spine as she drove. She remembered their first encounter; during the kidnap, when they were stopped by the army at the roadblock in South Armagh, he had gripped her with an iron hold disguised as a caress. How far she had travelled with him since then. Well, this would be their journey's end.

The winter sky was lightening as she dropped him at the edge of town.

'When d'you leave?' he asked her.

'Today.' Each felt suddenly awkward, knowing it would be too dangerous to meet again, and there would be no reason. He had given her the story she needed.

'I'm glad of it,' he said softly. 'Watch yourself. At home, mind, as well as here.' He touched her cheek briefly. Then he was gone.

Perdita knew there was one more thing she had to do. Blinking away the soreness behind her eyes, she headed back out of town to a place where she had noticed the road crossed a river. She parked on the bridge and reached under the seat for Frazer's gun. Holding it gingerly, she wrapped the pistol in the de-misting cloth from the glove compartment, got out of the car and peered over the bridge in the chill early light for a suitable place to drop it. The dark water sucked the weapon down. As she drove towards the hotel she felt, for the first time since Lithgow's murder, the fog starting to lift. If the boxes checked out, then Frazer must be dealing in illicit arms. She thought about the evidence in the camera: she didn't have Frazer, but she had his van, the Brit, the cargo and the knowledge Frazer was there. She was back on the story, on home territory, where she belonged.

CHAPTER 15

February 1998

It might not have been a prison in the usual sense, but to Perdita it certainly looked like one. From the railway station a minicab drove her out into the dreary afternoon, a fusion of grey sky and glum landscape. At the gates she climbed reluctantly from the taxi into a drizzle, groping in her pocket for her talisman: the visiting order for Daniel. It had taken weeks to obtain. First, she had been blocked by the edict that no request would be entertained without an invitation from the prisoner. As far as she knew, Daniel still held her responsible for betraying him to her ex-husband and the press, but after tracking down his sister Mary via an interview with her in *The Mail on Sunday*, Perdita persuaded her to ask him, and was delighted when Daniel wrote, inviting her for a visit. Even then, there was a further delay—for 'processing'. The permit reached her already crumpled in its thin manila envelope. The date was inconvenient, but it would have to do. It was already February; the edit of her film was almost finished; and Daniel had been in solitary confinement for over two months.

Perdita was admitted into a low red-brick reception centre by a soldier in uniform. Her bag was searched and her money counted, and she was instructed to leave her possessions in a locker (at the owner's risk) once she had removed some small change and her cigarettes.

'I didn't bring him cigarettes. I brought him a book.'

The soldier scrutinised the book suspiciously. 'The rule is two magazines,' he grumbled. He placed the book in a tray on the counter.

Her work had occasionally taken her into prisons, but something was different about this place: the silence. She wondered what crimes were punished here, but the only two that came to mind were homosexuality in the armed forces and treason. Poor Daniel would probably be indicted for both. When she entered the waiting room it was empty except for one man. He was sprawled on a plastic sofa reading a newspaper with his back to the door. Something about the folds at his neck alerted her. Perdita caught her breath. She could not believe the bureaucracy capable of such a gaffe. It was her ex-husband.

Hugh turned towards her. In the split second of noting the lack of surprise on his face, she understood that far from being accidental their timing had been engineered.

'Perdita.' He did not smile.

For a few moments she was speechless. Then she asked,

'Is this your doing?'

He gave a short laugh. 'Oh, come on. Even *The Sunday Times* doesn't have that much influence!'

Perdita looked around for the surveillance cameras. There were three: the whole room was covered. Despondency welled up in her. She walked to the furthest corner, unbuttoned her coat and threw herself into a chair. Since her belongings had been locked away, she had nothing to read. There was so much she needed to ask and to explain to Daniel, so much to clear up. Even allowing for the visit to be bugged she had spent some time thinking through what she could and could not say. With Hugh present, their meeting would be pointless.

'So what are you doing here?' he asked. 'I thought you didn't know our friend.' He did not bother to disguise the sneer.

'Thanks to you I feel I owe him an explanation, whether I know him or not.'

'Oh, come on, Perdita. Everyone knows what happened.'

'*I* don't know what happened,' she retorted. 'Somebody ratted on Daniel Booth. Who was it, Hugh?'

Hugh regarded her smugly. 'Tell me,' he said, ignoring the question. 'You know a few things I don't understand. The death of that Unionist MP, for instance.'

Lithgow. Perdita sat up. 'Did you know him?' she asked.

'Met him,' replied Hugh, evasively. 'Talked to him shortly before he died, as a matter of fact. For the Blakemore profile.'

'Why?'

Hugh sighed. 'You're writing a piece on the new Northern Ireland minister. You do a trawl of the old Unionist hands, obviously.' He shrugged. 'How did *you* get involved with him?'

'Oh, I didn't really know him,' she said. 'Just spoke to

him for research.'

'For the film about Irish linen,' he observed nastily.

'Yes, Hugh. The film about Irish linen.' She jumped up from her chair and went to look out of the window.

Hugh said, 'He had quite a penchant for younger women, I believe.' She could sense him watching her. 'He was having an intimate late-night supper with you on the night he died, I'm told.'

She turned back into the room, disconcerted. 'And you know this—how, exactly?'

Again, he ignored the question. 'So tiresome of the IRA to spoil your evening.'

She said nothing.

'Well, aren't you going to tell me about your brush with terrorism?' he asked.

'There's nothing to tell, Hugh, and I didn't come here to talk to you. I came to see Daniel.' She scowled up at the camera and tapped her watch.

'Well, well. You are jumpy.'

Perdita turned back to the window, deep in thought. This bringing them here on the same day must be deliberate. 'Hugh,' she said suddenly, 'can I have a look at your VO?'

'My what?' He glanced up from the rugby report. 'Sorry, Perdita. I'm not as familiar with the jargon as you are. What are we talking about?'

She crossed the room and stood in front of him, holding out the visiting order from her pocket. He examined it briefly before handing it back to her. 'I don't need one of those,' he said. 'They just told me to pop along.'

'Who?' she asked. 'Who said, "pop along"?'

He flapped a hand in the direction of the prison interior. 'This place. The authorities.'

'Have you had security clearance?'

'I dunno. Shouldn't think so. I just said when I wanted to come and the office fixed it with someone or other.'

That must be it: he could fast-track the system but they still needed to ask Daniel. 'I had the permission,' she explained. 'You didn't. But they think it's okay because we're related.'

'*I* had the permission,' he corrected her.

'From Daniel. Did *Daniel* say you could come?'

'They're asking him now,' said Hugh complacently.

She stared at him for a moment. 'Well, if you're still on the case, Hugh, will you ask your friendly spooks who presumably "authorised" you to come here today, *who* invented those documents and set Daniel up in the first place? And I don't care if those bloody cameras up there hear me say it.'

Hugh's eyes had started to bulge. 'Are you accusing *me* of somehow being an agent in all this? My God, you're even more cracked than I thought you were! I mean, I know it may seem preposterous to you, but I am a very well-respected, senior member of the British press.'

'Precisely!' She rounded on him. 'And you still don't get it, do you? With Blakemore gone, the hawks are having a field day in Northern Ireland—thanks in part to you!'

An officer entered the waiting room. 'Mr Williams?'

Hugh stood up, ready to leave.

'I'm sorry, Sir. Mr Booth says he doesn't want to see you, Sir.'

Hugh was stunned. 'But I'm with my former wife here.'

So it *had* been deliberate. Perdita marvelled at

270

his shamelessness.

'Mr Booth will see Mrs Williams, that is, Ms Burn,' the guard confirmed. 'But he doesn't want any other visitors.'

Perdita walked to the door, her expression neutral.

'If you'd like to follow me, Ma'am,' the guard said.

'Think about it,' she told Hugh as she left the room.

To Daniel, every day was the same. He inhabited a room, rather than a cell, but in every other respect he might as well have been in prison. His barred window looked out onto a yard where other detainees exercised in groups, although Daniel was invariably taken out there alone. On the far side of the exercise yard there were further low red-brick buildings, similar to his own block, and between the buildings he caught glimpses of bare trees and a wall. Beyond that, he could see nothing.

He had been allowed to order two newspapers and had chosen *The Guardian* and *The Mail on Sunday* because the *Mail* had taken the trouble to interview his sister. It was uncharacteristic of Mary to have talked to them. He wondered if The Homophobe was aware of it, or whether she'd defied him, and reflected gratefully that ordinary families reacted in extraordinary ways when injustice entered their lives. But for that interview, he felt he might have been forgotten and he wrote to Mary and thanked her, hoping his letter wouldn't get her into trouble with her husband. The *Mail* piece had been followed by a sprinkling of short reports in the broadsheets, and most notably by *The Guardian*'s authoritative security correspondent. It was his occasional articles that kept Daniel better informed than anything he was told officially. He had

had one meeting with a lawyer from the organisation that Perdita had suggested and was grateful when they agreed to take on his case. But since his initial charge under the serious but unspecific Section 2 of the Official Secrets Act had been replaced by a charge of theft of the documents, he had made no court appearances as a civilian prisoner on remand would have done, and his solicitor's enquiries to the MOD went unanswered.

His initial plan had been to pass the time by reading all the books he had never got around to, starting with the classics: Dostoyevsky, Elizabeth Gaskell, Henry James, James Joyce. His friends responded to this by keeping an eye on reality, delivering lighter fare alongside. The books took weeks to pass the censor; he imagined off-duty guards detailed to read them nodding off every couple of pages. Ben mischievously sent in *Boyz* magazine and the *Pink Paper*, which were regularly handed to him a week late without comment. But as the weeks passed, Daniel began to lose his appetite for reading. His concentration disintegrated. *Boyz* depressed him because it made him think of the olden days. He tried turning to thrillers but found he had no patience with them, real life being more disturbing than anything they could dream up. He attempted to keep a diary but there was nothing to say. He wrote letters to his friends, but even their loyal correspondence, though keenly anticipated and joyfully received, seemed irrelevant to his present existence.

Daniel knew enough about the effects of solitary confinement to understand that he was becoming disoriented and depressed. In the first few weeks he struggled against it, telling his sister in the weekly, monitored phone conversation that he was merely 'bored'. He supposed they were gathering information for his trial, but in all the weeks of incarceration there had been no further questioning of any kind. Since there was no impending court case, there had been no further lawyers' visits, either. The inquiry into Blakemore was presumably grinding ahead in some room deep inside Whitehall, but all mention of it had dropped from the news. Apart from *The Guardian* references, the only two events to give him any sense of purpose were a question in the House of Commons by his MP and a follow-up article about the irregular human rights issues raised by his case, which he was so thankful to read that he started to compose a letter to the newspaper. But by lunchtime he had lost heart. What was the point? The people here would never let him send what he had written. He shoved the notepad angrily into a drawer to get it out of his sight.

It was in this frame of mind that Perdita found him. Their meeting took place not in the usual grim public space but in a room that was large and carpeted: it looked like the prison boardroom. Daniel, who had been agitated at the prospect of speaking to someone face to face, read all too clearly the fleeting shock in Perdita's eyes when he was first brought in. What was she seeing, he wondered, that he couldn't see for himself? The business with Hugh's attempt to muscle in on the visit unexpectedly eased an encounter that could have been awkward on both sides. All the same, their conversation started gingerly. Perdita asked him about life inside; he about life 'out there', attempting to show an interest he didn't actually feel.

'Do you get many visitors?' she enquired. The set-up of

the place seemed so odd. 'You mentioned your partner, Alex? Is he able—?'

Daniel shook his head. 'Sadly not.' He hesitated. 'Guess I'm… I'm just not very good at talking about him in the past tense, am I?' He gave her one of his apologetic smiles. 'It was AIDS, of course. Rather unoriginal.'

'Oh Daniel, I'm so sorry.' She had suspected they had split up, but not that Alex had died.

He shook his head. 'It's a while ago now. Just months before they found the new therapy in '96.'

They talked a little about Alex, or Daniel did. To his surprise, it was a relief to put some of the sadness into words and Perdita was a good listener. Before long, however, they found their way into the subject that had brought them together, each taking care not to mention their own part in the matter of leaked documents; and to consider, before speaking, what every topic of conversation might reveal. They discussed who might have told Hugh about Daniel's former connection to Blakemore and Perdita wondered aloud if it might possibly have come via Milton Lithgow, since Hugh had just acknowledged talking to him for the Blakemore profile.

'Lithgow…' Daniel mused, thinking back to his interrogation. 'Why does everyone ask me about him?' He told her of his interrogators' sudden change of heart on the second document.

Perdita could not discuss the business of Lithgow's death with the prison officer in the room but, reassured that he had retreated to the doorway, she told Daniel that he might have been framed by elements within the intelligence services that wanted to sabotage the peace by getting rid of the Northern

Ireland minister. It was pure McGrail, of course, but she didn't say that.

She expected him to be as incredulous as she had been, but Daniel sat listening intently. She could see her words were making sense and realised that, since his second arrest, his perspective had altered radically.

He thought for a while, and then said, 'Those bastards don't give a damn about me or my life. We preach to other countries about our precious democracy.' His voice was low but fierce. 'We go on about our human rights record and our world-beating justice system, and all the while we're breaking the rules and deceiving our own people.'

Perdita tried to explain that none of it would have been personal: he was just a means to an end. 'My guess,' she said, 'is that once they've achieved whatever it is they want with Blakemore, they'll quietly drop this theft charge against you.'

Daniel gave her a strange look. 'Oh really? What makes you think they'll stop there? I tell you, Perdita, I've done a lot of thinking in here and what you're saying comes as no surprise at all.' He told her about the case of an army information officer in Belfast back in the 1970s, who was kicked out of the service, ostensibly for leaking information to a journalist, but in reality—it had come out years later—for refusing to take part in a secret service dirty tricks campaign against the Labour government of the time.

'And they hadn't finished with him,' Daniel went on. 'To shut him up, because he knew other awkward truths about stuff in Northern Ireland, he was then put on trial for the manslaughter of someone he knew and spent six years in prison.' He thought for a moment. 'Have you heard of the

Kincora boys' home?'

Perdita, startled, replied that she had. This was back to what she had read in Dublin, and what McGrail had told her about Lithgow.

'Well, they ruined this officer's life, Perdita, for refusing to keep his mouth shut about what was going on there. I never used to believe that story, but I now realise they can—and will—do anything that suits them. It doesn't seem to make any difference which party's in power: maybe ministers don't even *know* what's being done in the government's name.'

She was alarmed to hear him speak like this, but it was not a subject for discussion here. 'Nothing like that is going to happen to you, though,' she promised him.

'Oh, no? Well, don't bank on it.' His voice had started to rise. 'They can get rid of me just like that, if they want to.'

Perdita thought how little she actually knew about Daniel. Was he paranoid, she wondered, a conspiracy theorist? Or was it perfectly understandable that someone who had been through interrogation and solitary confinement, as he had, might be driven to such views? What he needed was the care of a trusted friend, of an Alex, or the friend he had mentioned, Michael—not someone like her who shared with him this one episode and nothing more. Yet their shared experience had drawn them together across the boundary between journalist and source, forming a bond that brought affection as well as responsibilities.

Regretting her misjudgement of his state of mind, she touched him lightly on the arm. 'Daniel, you were the one with faith in the system,' she suggested gently. 'Come on. This is England. They'd be too muddle-headed to do anything really terrible!'

Daniel drew back. 'You don't believe me, do you?'

She looked at him in dismay. 'It isn't that. You just need to get out of this horrible place. Everything will be fine. I'm certain it will.'

He leaned forward, gazing at her steadily. He dropped his voice again. He was calm now. 'Promise me something,' he said.

She wondered what was coming. He took both her hands in his and spoke so softly she could barely hear. 'I love my country, you see,' he explained. 'And I feel, well, I suppose it's *despair* at what it's turning into... If anything happens to me, Perdita, I want you to promise you'll clear my name. Will you?'

Was he thinking of suicide? 'Daniel,' she said urgently, 'I'll help however I can, but the most important thing is to get out of here and, one day, tell everyone what's happened to you. The best way to make a stand and to clear your name is to do it yourself!'

He nodded. 'Of course it is. But if I can't... if I'm not able to?'

She stared at him, puzzled. But his request was so heartfelt it required a serious response. 'I promise,' she said.

*

The editor switched on the overhead light and Jeremy Jordan leaned back, pushing his fingers through his short blond hair. Perdita re-ordered her script and waited. She was always nervous at the end of a viewing. But when at last she looked up, Jeremy was smiling.

'After all that,' he said. 'After all the fuss. It's fine. It has what Boston wants: excellent local colour, a few cultural insights, nothing too heavy.' He consulted his notes. 'Your man Frazer's good value. Was he the one you had concerns about?'

'Yes. I—'

'Well, you shouldn't have. He gives a terrific interview.'

'Different sort of concerns, really. I'd like to show you something.' She took from her briefcase a VHS tape and crossed to the video machine in a corner of the edit suite. John the editor, taking his cue, went off to organise tea.

'What happened to the civil servant?' Jeremy asked. 'The one Hugh Williams dropped in the shit with that article.'

'He's in custody. I went to see him a couple of days ago, as a matter of fact.'

'God. Have they been holding him all this time?'

Perdita fed the tape into the machine and pressed the rewind button. She wanted to ease Jeremy into this part of the story gently. The fact he had liked the film at the first viewing was good news and bad news. It put her in credit, but it meant Jeremy might be less amenable to the changes she was about to propose. 'Daniel's in a prison out in Essex that I didn't know existed,' Perdita said. 'It's a military correctional centre. They seem to be treating him as a military prisoner because he worked for the MOD, which is pretty irregular because he's a civilian. And they've got him in solitary confinement.'

Jeremy had turned towards her. 'What's he supposed to have done?'

'He was arrested under the Official Secrets Act, but they've dropped that now and charged him with theft—theft of the documents, that is. As you know, he was originally supposed to have leaked them to me. But no one has ever asked me about them and since they haven't been published, it's not certain there's an offence.' Choosing her words with care, she continued, 'As I've told you before, the man in the film, Frazer, the man you like, may be connected in some way. My greatest concern about him is that all the evangelical stuff about equal rights and the spirit of a new Ireland is a front.'

Jeremy was sceptical. 'Are you sure you're not just prejudiced?'

'Well, after the last day of filming I went to a place on the East Coast. There was a shipment of something being unloaded—this is the dead of night: all pretty illicit. Frazer was there.'

'What are you saying?'

'The word is, he's involved in running arms to loyalist paramilitaries. That's where his real money comes from. He's a figurehead in Northern Ireland. If he's up to this illegal stuff, it puts a completely different—*Come on!* We need to know for our film!' she added hurriedly, as Jeremy started to object.

'Makes no sense!' He held up a restraining hand. 'If this Frazer is a model industrialist, he must be in favour of peace.'

'Not if he's making money out of the war,' Perdita reasoned. 'And not if the end of the war eventually means an end to Protestant power in the North.'

Jeremy was unconvinced. 'But from what he says in your film, he's embracing peace. He's delighted those watchtowers are being dismantled on the border. He's shaping it. He *is* the future.'

'That's the trouble,' she agreed. 'That's exactly why the

film bothers me.'

'But what are you going to do about it? You go haring off into the night and watch some bloody smuggling operation— how did you know it was smuggling, for God's sake, and how did you know it was arms?'

'I had the markings on the crates authenticated,' she said, trying to keep her voice steady. 'Barret Light Fifty heavy calibre sniping rifles. Made in the US. Ammunition.'

Jeremy was staring at her. 'What are you talking about? You found a friendly arms dealer and took him down with you?'

Perdita said, 'I filmed it.' She indicated the VHS.

'You have *pictures* of the arms being unloaded?' He was staring at her in disbelief, but she could see the cogs in his brain beginning to turn.

'I don't have film of Frazer there,' she said hastily. 'But he was in it all right. I saw him there—and he saw me. We— we spoke. Oh, I also got a shot of a man on the boat who's a British civil servant. MOD.'

'You have *film? Here?*'

'D'you want to see? It won't take long.'

'Where's the master?' asked Jeremy swiftly.

'It's completely secure,' she said. It was locked in the production company safe.

'Does he know you have this film?'

'He will have guessed. He found the camera.'

'Secret filming.' Jeremy pulled a face. 'Unauthorised from here... okay, let's look at this stuff.'

*

A couple of days after he had seen Perdita, Daniel received another visit. Unlike the arrival of Hugh, about which he had at least been consulted, this visitor was sprung on him. Lunch was over dismally early, as usual; he had not in his ten weeks' imprisonment adjusted to eating the main meal of the day at eleven-thirty in the morning. The boredom of the afternoon had settled on him with its habitual torpor, when suddenly a key slammed into the heavy lock of his door and a guard walked in. It was an unscheduled occurrence at this hour, when most of the military personnel were starting their own lunch break. Daniel, who had flung himself onto the bed, sat up, suppressing a wholly irrational annoyance at being disturbed.

'Visitor for you,' announced the guard.

'Are you sure?' Daniel asked. He had been permitted only two visits, each preceded by the most enormous fuss.

'Look sharp,' the guard said.

Daniel stood up a little unsteadily. He went to the locker, picked up a comb and ran it through his hair. There was no mirror. He would like to have washed his face but the wash-room was some way away and he was suddenly consumed with curiosity. Could it be his lawyer? An MP? Someone else to help him? For a crazy instant it crossed Daniel's mind that the visitor might even be Clive Blakemore. As they walked down the corridor, he wished he had put on a jacket.

But it was none of these people. Daniel could scarcely suppress his disappointment when the man turned to greet him. It was Vernon Potts, his unfriendly colleague from the press office.

'How are you?' asked Daniel incuriously as they shook hands.

They discussed this and that for a while. Daniel was asking himself what the hell was his colleague doing there, when Vernon said, 'Still, you won't be in here much longer, will you?'

Daniel was suddenly alert. 'I don't know. You tell *me*.'

'From what I hear,' said Vernon. 'They've got nothing on you. People are starting to ask questions. In Parliament. In the press. You're becoming an embarrassment.'

'What people?'

'You know. You must have read about it. Don't you get the papers?'

'There's been a bit. Nothing to write home about.'

'Nah,' said Vernon. 'It's the PQs. You know how it gets to them. Goes into Hansard. Picked up all over the place. The Americans don't like it. Nor do the Europeans.'

'We don't give a stuff about the Europeans, do we?'

'We do now,' Vernon assured him. 'You don't know what those New Labour boys are up to. It's all "ethical foreign policy" these days. We need to be squeaky clean.'

'Some hope,' said Daniel wistfully.

'I don't know about any of this, of course. Not my province,' Vernon went on. 'But it's my view the French, for instance, wouldn't take your peccadilloes too seriously.'

Daniel looked down at his hands. They were shaking. 'There were no peccadilloes,' he said. He was starting to understand why Vernon had been sent.

'So, who d'you reckon passed you the documents?' Vernon asked.

Daniel said, 'I think they came from somewhere in the security services.' He was watching Vernon carefully. He wanted to test out Perdita's theory. 'I think I was collateral damage in a dirty tricks campaign.'

Vernon did a double-take. 'No kidding! Do those boys still get up to that kind of stuff?'

'Six months ago, I'd never have believed it,' Daniel said quietly. 'But I do now. They needed a security risk to get at Blakemore, didn't they? Nothing too direct. Nothing he could refute. They thought we'd had a relationship. So they framed me.'

'Christ.' Vernon stretched and yawned. 'Wallace territory.'

'Well, yes,' said Daniel. Wallace was the information officer he had mentioned to Perdita. 'Something like that.'

'Blimey!' Vernon stood up and wandered over to the window. Neither spoke for a moment or two. Then Vernon, his back to Daniel, remarked casually, 'Wallace went public, didn't he? What d'you reckon *you'd* do?'

'Oh, God.' Daniel massaged his temples and thought about it. 'You're jumping ahead a bit,' he said. 'I just need to get out of here.' Then he sat up straighter, staring defiantly at Vernon's back. 'But don't think I'm going to sit on my hands and let them get away with it!' As soon as he recognised it, he understood that this was what he had been feeling all along. It wasn't depression that had him in its grip. It was anger.

Three days later, as Vernon had predicted, Daniel was released from custody. He was placed for a few days' observation in a hospital psychiatric wing. Whatever the evidence against him, the theft charge was dropped.

CHAPTER 16

Perdita, Jeremy, and one of the broadcaster's lawyers were clustered around the Avid. Perdita had been able to verify, from the single shot she had grabbed, that the van at the quay was indeed Fraser's, but there was no evidence of the cargo being loaded into it.

'We will, of course, be offering him a right of reply,' she told them.

'You most certainly will,' said Walter Cusp, the lawyer, with feeling. 'Okay... let's start with Frazer, then. What kind of a reputation does he have to defend?'

Perdita gave a summary of Frazer's status and his many achievements.

'Is he fairly articulate, would you say?'

'As you see, he's a persuasive and charismatic speaker,' she answered, looking Cusp straight in the eye. She glanced down at her hands and saw a line of red indentations where the nails of her right hand had been pressing into her left. Ever since their night at the quay she had grown in certainty that Frazer would at some point reveal her apparent relationship with McGrail. It would not sound good in public.

Cusp thought for a moment. 'Did you say you were with someone else? Could they give a statement about Frazer's involvement?'

Perdita drained the cold dregs from her mug of tea. 'The person with me was the same person who had told me the shipment was coming in. He has to stay off the record.'

'He's some kind of terrorist, I suppose? No credibility at all,' said the lawyer.

Perdita nodded slowly.

Jeremy cursed under his breath. 'Don't you think, Perdita, it was a little naive of you not to have told me about this earlier?'

'It's a dirty war,' she reasoned. 'You don't get your tip-offs from the vicar's wife.'

Jeremy groaned. 'I talked it through with Boston. The Americans are amenable to a political element in the film. They'll put it out on *Frontline* if it's good enough. But they've no time for the IRA.' He jumped to his feet and paced around the room for a few seconds. 'Bloody good story, though, Walter! Isn't there some way we can run it?'

'Not without more than this,' said the lawyer drily.

Jeremy resumed his pacing. Then he turned back to them. 'Okay, here's what you do, then. You go back to Belfast. You put it to Frazer on camera that he is involved with arms smuggling. He will, of course, deny it—which we shall have to use. But you're also filming with a secret camera that stays on throughout. The man's a public figure: we can surely argue public interest, Walter, can't we?'

Cusp began to object, but Jeremy cut across him. 'If they actually met there, which I understand they did?'—glancing at Perdita for confirmation—'He's more likely to at least acknowledge the fact, once he thinks he's not being recorded.'

Perdita started to feel very nervous. This would require a cooler head than hers, and Jeremy didn't yet know what Frazer had against her. She was relieved to see the lawyer shake his head.

'ITC regs., Jeremy. Broadcasting an admission to a crime—'

But Jeremy had scented blood. 'Secretly filmed evidence is admissible in court, though, isn't it? So we could film, but not for broadcast. We could allege his involvement and when he threatens to sue, we can tell him what we've got. Can't we, Walter?'

Walter Cusp looked at him bleakly. 'I'd not be happy. We'll have to see what Perdita comes back with and take a view.'

*

Daniel was transported home from the hospital in a minicab and left on the doorstep of his flat. Remembering the trauma of his last homecoming with Perdita after the police raid, he had telephoned Michael in Clapham who was there to meet him, with the cat. Daniel's release had been strictly low profile and to his great relief there were no reporters. It was Michael who pushed open the front door, still not properly repaired from Daniel's first arrest, and gathered up the mail strewn over the doormat and into the hall. It was Michael, too, who sorted through the stinking contents of the fridge and unpacked the carriers he had brought with him from Selfridge's food hall: a modest celebration, he told Daniel. Michael cooked while Lalibela made a thorough inspection of the premises. She ignored Daniel for the first half-hour and then leapt without ceremony into his arms and placed a sandy paw tentatively on his chin. Daniel leaned back in his chair, feeling briefly at peace.

'I think you should come and stay with us for a few days,' Michael said when they had finished eating. Daniel accepted gratefully: he felt he badly needed to be among friends.

'I want to spend one night here, though,' he said. 'Just to sort out this lot,' nodding at the stack of letters, 'and, er, you know, break the wicked spell...' He tried to smile and realised how odd it felt. The smile failed to convince Michael, who left a short while later looking concerned, having persuaded Daniel to join them in Clapham next day when he and Ben came home from work.

Buoyed by this thought, Daniel strayed around the flat after Michael had left, touching his books, examining familiar objects. *It will be all right*, he told himself. At length, unpacking his few things and setting out the anti-depressants prescribed by the hospital psychiatrist, he ran a bath and went to bed, exhausted.

At four o'clock next morning he was awake, wide awake on the instant, listening, fretting. Would they come for him again? No one had contacted him from the Ministry to talk about his future and he wondered if there was a letter waiting among the pile of post that would tell him if there was any future left for him in the Civil Service. Well, he thought defiantly, he'd had it with the Civil Service, though he did wonder about his pay, his mortgage payments. The thought of the mess concealed within the bank statements filled him with apprehension. He forced himself to lie still and listen to the radio to distract his thoughts, but after an hour or so he could bear it no longer. Gently disengaging his ankles from beneath the small circle that was Lalibela in her habitual sleeping place at the bottom of the bed, he pushed back the covers and swung his feet to the floor. She raised her head and looked at him: *what are we doing now?* But noting she was not required to take part, curled tighter, paws over her eyes.

Daniel switched on the heating and filled the kettle. He stood in the kitchen drinking tea. Through the open door he could see the heap of envelopes, where Michael had piled them at one end of the table. His stomach knotted; he felt he had no strength in his legs to approach them. At last, with an effort of will, he began to sift through them, picking up each letter unsteadily. The bank statements he quickly located and placed to one side. They could wait. There was something else he sought. Was it this one? ...this? His eye fell on a slim, Ministry envelope, the name neatly printed: 'Mr D. Booth' and his home address. Daniel ripped it open. With a cry, he sank to the floor and crouched there, rocking. He didn't need to read it all. He knew the signs. There was no mistake, no displaced room number. It was a third document and it was meant for no one but him. One name. A village in North Yorkshire: 'Burn.' The date was today.

Her answer machine was on. He left his name, trying to keep the panic from his voice, but there was something about the wording of the message, the quantity of pips, that told him she must be away. It was still too early to call the number she had given him for the cutting room. He forced himself to shower and dress. He even attempted to eat. At eight-forty-five he picked up the phone.

'Yes?' barked a voice.

'Oh, hello. I wondered. Is it possible to speak to Perdita Burn, please?'

'Who?'

'Ms Burn. Perdita.'

'Never 'eard of her.'

'I—I was given this number. She was cutting a film.'

'Hang on.' A hand was placed roughly over the mouth-piece. He could hear a muffled conversation. 'I'm told she finished on Friday. This is just edit suites, mate. Try the production company.'

'I don't know which one it is.'

'Nothing I can do, I'm afraid,' said the voice, catching Daniel's note of desperation. 'We're all freelance in this business.'

Daniel was almost sobbing as he put the phone down. He paced around the living room racking his brain for other numbers he might have had for her in the past. They had known so little about each other. The only one he could remember was some hotel in Belfast. She had given it to him for emergencies long before Christmas, the day she brought him home. What was the point? She wouldn't be there now. He forced himself to go through the rest of his mail in the hope of some communication from her. Yes! He lifted the envelope with her writing on it. He almost kissed it. Inside, a card: one of the Auerbach landscapes of Primrose Hill. *'Welcome home, dear Daniel, and many congratulations. I'm sorry I can't be there with you. We'll speak very soon. I'll call.'* She had signed her name with three kisses. He peered at the postmark: Hounslow. She could have sent it from Heathrow. Daniel hurled the envelope onto the floor. She was making it so bloody easy for them! He hurried into his bedroom. The number in Northern Ireland. It was a long shot but he must do something. She had no inkling of the danger she was walking into. He rummaged furiously through his wallet, his pockets. They had deliberately kept no record of each other's existence, but this number was an exception because it was so impersonal and because he had felt he might need it. Where the hell had he put it? He knelt on the bed trying to recall what he had worn that day. There was nothing in the pocket of his jacket. Nothing in his jeans. No, wait a minute, he hadn't been wearing jeans when he was arrested. He started to go through the pockets of his other trousers—not his work suit, of course: he hadn't worn that. Fumbling through back pockets and side pockets, whimpering with the urgency of it, wondering how thorough the police search had been, wondering—oh God, it hadn't occurred to him last night—whether there might have been further searches during his second imprisonment. And suddenly he found it, balled-up, caught in the side-pocket lining of his navy trousers. He remembered now. It was the other half of the bus ticket on which he had scrawled Lithgow's name.

'I was wondering...' He was stammering, his words falling over each other. 'Have you by any chance a Ms Burn staying there?'

'Ms Burn from England, is it?' The young woman, calm and friendly, switched him to hold for a few moments. Then she said, 'Dónal says she went out. You just missed her, I'm afraid.'

'You mean, she *is* staying there?'

'Oh, to be sure.'

Daniel could scarcely believe his luck. 'That's wonderful,' he said. His eyes filled with tears of relief. 'And she'll be coming back later?'

'I believe so.' The young woman sounded amused. 'Just one second. Dónal! Ms Burn didn't check out, did she?' There was a muffled conversation. 'She'll be here tonight,' the receptionist confirmed at last.

'Listen,' cried Daniel. 'Listen. Do you have any more rooms?'

'We do tonight.'

'Please can you reserve me one? I'm coming. I'm coming over.'

'What name is it, Sir?'

'Booth... Daniel Booth.' Oh Heavens, he wondered, should he have used a false name? Too late now.

The receptionist gave him the name and address of the hotel. 'Will I let her know you're on your way, Mr Booth, or is it to be a wee surprise?'

'No, no. Tell her.' In his agitation he had forgotten to say it. 'Tell her it's urgent. I have to see her.'

Daniel grabbed his passport and an overnight bag and shook out a large bowl of cat biscuits for Lalibela, who was still curled up on the bed. He touched her head gently in farewell, and received a deep sigh in response: I'll be home again tomorrow, he promised her, as if to reassure them both.

*

One of Perdita's objectives on returning to Belfast was to find Francie, whom she had not seen since the night of Lithgow's murder. By now, it would be apparent that in return for his saving her life, she had not identified him to the police. It was a good basis, she decided, for a working relationship and Perdita needed someone she could trust. The seriousness of the allegations against Frazer had persuaded her bosses in London to grant permission for secret filming, and now her task was to set up a hidden camera in Frazer's office. If McGrail was right when he first introduced Francie as an expert in such things, Francie would do very well.

She hesitated as to how she should contact him: knowing what sticklers they were for protocol, it ought to be through Sinn Féin. But she had no time to go and petition the advice centre. Instead, she made for the place where Francie had first, quite literally, picked her up: the taxi office across the road from the restaurant where she had dined with Frazer.

An elderly man sat behind the office desk. On the wall behind his head hung a small statue, '*Our Lady of Lourdes*', it said, the halo sparkling with tiny flashing lights. 'That'd be Francie Hagan, more than likely, he said when she told him the name. 'He's away now.'

'Away?'

The man passed a hand over the folds of his face. 'He doesn't work here no more. But he came to us because his auntie is my wife's cousin. May Smith. You'll find her in Snowdrop Street. I don't rightly remember the number but she painted her front door the most atrocious shade of red.' He laughed. 'Old May. Flower-pot red. It's the only one. You can say I sent you.'

Amongst the friendly people of West Belfast, the hunt proved extraordinarily easy. May Smith was out, but a neighbour sent Perdita to the bakery in Ballymurphy where she worked. Francie was staying at his daddy's by the mountain, Slieve Gullion, down near the border, May told her. There had been some forestry work—his daddy was a forester—but she had heard Francie was away to Dublin—today? Tomorrow, was it? Perdita might just catch him if she hurried.

'Is there a telephone?' Perdita asked.

No phone, May told her. Not at his daddy's, tucked away in the wilds as it was. Then Perdita remembered the mobile on which they had called McGrail, the night of Lithgow's murder. Did Francie have his mobile? she asked May.

'Of course he does. How could I have forgotten?' May reprimanded herself with a tap on the forehead. 'They all have them now, I suppose, but it was the talk of the entire family when he got it. I expect he needs it for his work.'

'He certainly does,' Peredita agreed. May could not give her the number but after more enquiries and phone calls Perdita was told to leave a message at the bar of Paddy McCann's in Dromintee. She suspected the mobile number was being withheld, quite reasonably, until they had checked her out. Returning to the hotel, she left her number at McCann's and sat down to wait. It sounded like a long-shot but she knew by now that, in this country, haphazard arrangements paid off, and her supposition was confirmed when Francie called within half an hour. He said that if she wanted to see him, she must drive down to Newry where he would meet her. He gave her his mobile number and said they could go together to his father's. By this time, she had received news of Daniel's imminent arrival and tried to call back and put him off for a day. No answer: he must already have left for the airport. (What on earth was he coming for, anyway? What could be so urgent?) She asked Francie for directions to the house. These she copied into a note for Daniel, which she gave to the receptionist. Then she threw some clothes into a bag and left.

*

As the tube trundled through West London it occurred to Daniel that he might not be permitted to leave the country. No one had discussed it with him. He was also acutely aware that if he were still being watched, to race off to Belfast the day after his release was about the most unwise thing he could possibly do. Well, it was no use worrying about that: Lithgow had died on the appointed day, and now Perdita's life was in imminent danger. He had got them both into this mess; he must get her out.

But when, several hours later, he walked into the Wellington Lodge Hotel and introduced himself, the receptionist gazed at him in dismay. 'Oh, Mr Booth, such a terrible thing. Ms Burn's gone. She said she had to leave, sudden like. She'll not be back until tomorrow.'

Daniel was horrified. 'Did you tell her I was coming?'

The receptionist nodded vigorously. 'I gave her your

message and we tried to call you. She said to tell you she was really sorry, but she had no choice. Oh, she left you a note, though. Let's see. Where is it now?' She rummaged around on the desk among piles of faxes. The sense of dread that had receded since he had managed to track her down, washed over Daniel anew. He watched her anxiously.

'Here it is!' said the receptionist at last. She handed him a folded sheet of hotel writing paper.

Daniel read and re-read the note. There was a house name in Irish at a place beyond Newry. That must be down near the border. The directions sounded complicated and it was already after two o'clock. In the aftermath of his release, and in his general state of apprehension, driving into that wild country was the last thing he wanted to do. The sensible course would be to wait until tomorrow. But the date on the memo was today.

'I can get you a hire car,' the young woman said helpfully, seeing his indecision. 'They got here really quickly for the other gentleman.'

'What gentleman?' Daniel asked.

'Oh,' she blushed. 'I did this daft thing, you see. A gentleman came in earlier asking for Ms Burn. I thought it must be you. I was that excited, I gave him the note before I even enquired, and it wasn't you at all!'

'Who was it?' asked Daniel, alarmed.

'Well, that's just the thing. I didn't find out because when he read the note, he was that keen to see her he asked me to call him a car and he rushed straight off. She's a popular person, that Ms Burn, I told Dónal, with all these gentlemen chasing after her!'

That decided it. 'I'll have to go as well,' Daniel said.

'There you are. What did I tell you? Why don't you sit yourself down, Mr Booth, and Dónal will get you a cup of tea while you're waiting. You look as though you could do with a rest, after your flight an'all. Would you care for a wee sandwich now? There'll not be a lot down there and it's going to freeze tonight.'

By the time Daniel left the motorway and headed South, the temperature was already dropping and crimson streamers of cloud flared in the sky. The sunset light warmed the browns and intensified the fertile greens of the countryside around him. Starved of colour in his prison cell, the beauty of it gave him a sudden sense of joy. Life would be happy again, he told himself. No more Civil Service: they would move to Suffolk, him and the cat, and he would find a job somewhere; maybe run his own bookshop after a while. He still had half his life ahead of him, might even meet someone to share it… With the whole dismal business behind him, everything would come right. Doing this good thing for Perdita would be the start of it. He prayed he would be in time.

On he drove, Perdita's list of towns and villages propped against the dashboard. Newry. Camlough. Lislea. 'If you reach Forkhill,' the note said, 'you've gone too far.' The problem, he realised, was that it had been written not from knowledge of the road but from someone else's directions. There were no landmarks. His spirits faded with the light. Suddenly, around a sharp corner, his headlights caught a hand-painted sign glaring in the dusk: waist-high white Celtic script against a black background: *IRA*. This was a foreign country; the landscape had deceived him. Daniel was struggling now to keep in check the incipient panic, fearing the identity of the stranger on the road whose pursuit of Perdita had a clear start on his own.

He thought of the space at the end of his passport: *next of kin*. It had been Alex's name in the old one. When he'd renewed it, he ought to have put his sister, but couldn't face doing that. Tomorrow, he would move on; but for this last night that space still belonged to Alex. He had given to Michael, worried and disapproving, the Belfast telephone number, and that was all.

'You're in no state to do this,' Michael had warned.

'I'm afraid it can't be helped,' Daniel said. He couldn't explain any of it on the telephone. No one knew he was here. No one knew why. The space at the end of his passport was empty. No one would be contacted. He must reach Perdita. He must warn her. Then at least he would have achieved something worthwhile.

By now, he ought to be getting close. The directions said he was to look for signs to a caravan site at the edge of the forest park. The road closed in around him, a plantation on either side. Up ahead, he saw a small signpost of the kind that in England denoted picnic spots. He followed it. The road wound among the trees, upward. After a while he came to a passing place and stopped. What the hell was this? No caravan would ever get up here: he must have missed it. He opened the window and looked out, hoping it would be wide enough to turn. Not wide enough. He picked up Perdita's note again and reread it. The letters jostled and fell over each other. Her handwriting was clear as a rule; she must have been anxious or written it in a hurry. Then suddenly it occurred to him that perhaps this was not Perdita's note: what if it were the stranger's, to throw him off the scent? Terror engulfed him. *Must get back*, he thought.

Must turn round. He threw the car into gear. It was bigger than anything he was used to but at least it had power steering. He pulled over hard to the right. The car slewed at right-angles across the track, its nose overhanging a drainage ditch, its rear bumper inches from the white trunk of a birch. *Gently,* Daniel told himself. *Don't panic.* He moved the unfamiliar gear into reverse and let out the clutch. The car jumped back, grazing the tree and stalling. The crunch of it in the forest night seemed unnaturally loud. Daniel breathed deeply. He re-started the engine. Inch by inch he pulled the car's nose around, the front wheels spinning on mud and frosty leaf mould but always— just—holding on. Eventually, he completed one-hundred-and-eighty degrees and started gingerly back down the steep track, his one thought to return to some kind of civilisation. He opened the window again, gulping at the freezing air and hearing the sound of the engine bounced off the trees and thrown back at him like a fleet of cars across the mountain. Was that all it was—an echo? He held his breath to listen. Or was he being followed? Who was behind him? Who in front? And where was he to go now? If this note had indeed been substituted by the stranger, he ought to be anywhere but here. If the note were Perdita's, on the other hand, he must follow its directions. He must try and save her. He was tormented by the possibility that it was already too late.

Suddenly he saw ahead of him on a bend an opening leading to a clearing in the trees. It defied any caravan to enter from the upward slope, but facing down, as Daniel now was, the entrance was wide and straight. Daniel plunged through. To the left stood a small house, set back at the edge of the forest and invisible from the road. He read its faded name in the headlights. He had found it.

He was about to jump out of the car when he realised he was not alone in the clearing. Drawn up in the far corner, away from the house, dark and apparently empty, stood a second car. His headlights caught a flash of chrome. Around the side of the house he could detect the metal angles of further vehicles and maybe farm machinery. The car backed neatly up in the clearing was not, he sensed, a country car. Daniel's elation evaporated. He saw himself paralysed, foolish; his headlights blazing out news of his arrival. Who waited in the darkness? He took a deep breath. First, he must prepare for escape. Swinging his own car round, he parked facing the entrance, forcing himself as he did so to consider the options. The simplest explanation, and the most attractive, was that the car in the corner of the clearing was Perdita's and that she was in the house: the instructions had been genuine; he was among friends. If the note were a fake, Perdita could be miles away, meeting her fate in another wild place. Then again, she might still be on her way, her killer waiting for her here, not fifty feet away. Her killer might have mistaken his arrival for hers... As if on cue, Daniel heard another car slowly approaching in low gear up the hill. If this were not Perdita, it might be someone who could help him. He launched himself out of the driving seat and began to run towards it.

'Daniel Booth!'

The most unlikely sound of his own name stopped him short in his tracks. He whirled around and saw a figure in the shadows.

'Hello?' called Daniel.

The approaching car had turned into the clearing, lighting

up the scene, but the owner of the voice seemed to be skirting him, keeping to the trees. 'Are you Daniel Booth?' it repeated.

It was an English voice. So that must be all right, then. 'Yes, that's me!' Daniel answered, his own voice brimming with relief. 'Who are you? How did you know I'd be here?'

The figure didn't answer.

'I'm looking for Perdita,' Daniel called out again. 'Do you know Perdita? It's urgent.'

Suddenly a shout from the side of the house: 'Get down, Daniel! It's you he's after!' An Irish voice this time.

The newly arrived car had stopped now. Daniel, reeling, stumbling, saw Perdita in the driver's seat. She was safe. He had found her. It was when he tried to run to her, to warn her, he realised he must have been hit. How peculiar, when he had heard no gunshot. He had heard no shot and therefore it must be all right. It was a nightmare. He knew it was a nightmare because of having to drive so slowly out there on the road just now. He couldn't run, but he could shout. 'Perdita!' he screamed at the top of his voice. She was peering through the windscreen at him. He heard a rasping whisper. Not his voice. Perdita was out of the car now, and someone else with her. Her face was a mask of horror. What was wrong? Had she been shot, too? She was crying out his name but he couldn't answer. He wanted to save her, otherwise what was the point of all this? 'They're after you!' he gasped. He was so cold. If only he could keep still. She was holding him, her arms incapable of containing the convulsions of his body.

'Not me,' she wept. 'Oh Daniel, it's *you*, not me.' Francie, the passenger in Perdita's car, had drawn his weapon and stepped between her and the gunman. Perdita held Daniel tight. 'You were right all along,' she whispered. 'And I didn't believe you.' She was still holding him when McGrail reached them.

CHAPTER 17

Later that night, McGrail drove Perdita to a house in the Mourne mountains. She felt like a fugitive.

'I must stay with Daniel,' she had said.

But McGrail had been adamant. 'I will give you half an hour and then Francie must call the police. We can't delay longer. The body—'

'Then I must speak to the police,' Perdita insisted.

'You must not!' Francie retorted.

'It will be said that Daniel was a traitor. I promised to protect his name.' They had searched Daniel's pockets and found the third document. Comprehending the urgency of it, Perdita had wept again. 'He had come to save me and I sent him straight to his death.'

McGrail was leaning against the mantelpiece, as if to distance himself from the discussion. Now his voice was stern.

'Had Daniel waited for you in Belfast, Perdita, they would have shot him when he walked down the street. They would have shot him in his room. But they would have shot him. Daniel's time had come. The document is proof. They used your name as a decoy. It was the one thing that would get him out of London.'

'Speaking to the RUC will not ensure the truth is told about Daniel,' said Francie quietly. 'Quite the reverse, I'd say.'

She turned to him. 'But then they'll do *you* for it!'

'They will not,' Francie said. He looked over at McGrail.

'The firearm that killed Daniel,' McGrail explained, 'would not have been available to anyone here.' Immediately after the shooting, he had slipped away in the direction of the killer, returning without explanation twenty minutes later.

Perdita mistrusted the sense of information withheld. 'What's the point of bringing him here if they don't want to pass it off as a sectarian killing?' she demanded.

'They wouldn't have cared about that,' answered McGrail. 'They just will have wanted him away from London. They knew you were returning to Ireland, of course, so that was ideal for them. For Daniel to go to Ireland suggests a treacherous intent, but they'll probably say it was suicide. You mentioned he'd been sent to a psychiatric hospital before his release? That will have laid the trail.'

This was the last thing she wanted to hear. It was what Daniel himself had predicted when she visited him in the detention centre, and she had dismissed the suggestion. 'Are you saying they released him from custody in order that he should die?' she asked fiercely. 'That's nonsense, surely!'

McGrail shrugged. 'There's no way of knowing. But look

at the circumstances. It was not a random death. The man who called out to him knew Daniel's name. He had an English accent.'

Perdita absorbed this, groping for the truth of it.

'That was the terrible thing,' McGrail went on. 'When I heard Daniel's car I went outside, thinking it was you. The killer must have been waiting, but it wasn't till he called out to Daniel that I realised he was there—and why. I should have had him covered, but the bloody Brit was all in the shadows. I should have hit him first, and I couldn't.' He sounded surprisingly emotional.

'Come on,' said Francie softly. 'We're wasting time. I will tell the RUC you were expected here tonight, Perdita, but you never showed up.'

'Why can't I stay?' she implored them. She didn't want to go with McGrail.

McGrail moved away from the fire. He stood before her and spoke firmly. 'There's the body in the woods of the man who shot him. He's no ID on him but they'll get word soon enough he's a Brit. You have to be out of here. I have to be out of here.'

'What about Francie?'

'Sure, Francie lives here—and they'll know he's not up to it.' McGrail's face burst into a grin as he clapped his comrade on the back. 'Your man in the woods was shot with his own weapon.'

Perdita didn't understand.

'Joe might as well have left his signature on the body,' Francie explained. 'That's why yous both have to be away. Now.'

The temperature had dropped sharply by the time they reached the mountains. When McGrail parked Perdita's hire car, its wheels crunched on ice. They entered the house in silence, Perdita still deep in shock. The place was unlived-in, chilled through, but neat and scrubbed. She crouched shivering beside McGrail as he lit a fire, building a pyramid of twigs and dried bark. He moved around the place briskly, inspecting the cupboard for supplies, spreading clean sheets and blankets on a clothes airer over the fireplace, warming soup, boiling a large kettle. Was it prison that made him so orderly? There was a military precision about it that reminded her of her father. She found it comforting.

Perdita wondered to whom the place belonged. He treated it as if it were his own home and she imagined his former clandestine life being littered with such places, remote, Spartan, functional; and he arriving by night, staying as long as necessary, moving on. She had heard him rummaging around in the kitchen as he waited for the soup to heat on the Calor gas ring. Now he returned to her carrying thick socks and a fresh pack of coffee.

He threw the socks into her lap. 'Put those on,' he told her. 'Warm them first.' He lifted an old-fashioned coffee-grinder with a rotary handle from the dresser and carried it over. 'Then you can grind the coffee. That'll warm you up.' He bent down to give it to her and she took it mutely. He rested his hand for a moment on her shoulder. Then he was away again, arranging oatcakes on a griddle near the fire. For all the strangeness of being in this remote place alone with him, her thoughts were with Daniel. She was still shivering, but she listened to McGrail, her eyes anxious, and did as she was told. After they had eaten she went to the kitchen to make coffee. When she returned, he had taken the cushions from the sofa and two armchairs and laid them on the floor in front of the fire, covered with the bedclothes from the airer. Pillows had appeared and a bottle of vodka. 'The bedrooms are a fridge,' he announced. 'We're better here,' adding in a matter-of-fact tone with his eyes concentrated on the embers, 'We'll need to sleep in all our clothes as it is.' He banked up the fire with bricks of turf that she had never seen before, though she recognised the bittersweet smell.

All night he held her to keep the demons out. She lay staring at the glowing peat, her body convulsed by shudders and bouts of weeping, then dozed in snatches, clasping his arms to her for fear they slip away. Waking, she would stare into the fire again and feel the life ebb from Daniel's poor body. Daniel had foreseen his death and she had dismissed his fears. Guilt gnawed at her. Now his prediction had come true in the most incriminating circumstances for him, and she had made him a promise. How was she to clear his name? She lay adrift on a raft of nightmares. Once she cried out. McGrail stirred in his sleep and his arms tightened around her. Eventually, she slept again herself, restless and full of dreams. She awoke thinking of the stiff body of Daniel's murderer shot in the forest with his own gun. 'He was shot,' McGrail had said; not, 'I shot him.' She had noticed this construction before, the distancing from responsibility. McGrail had shot him, whoever he was, and Perdita was glad. Before dawn she slept again and this time did not dream.

When she finally woke, she lay still, contemplating her

situation, fearing that as soon as she moved, the truce of the night would give way to awkwardness. McGrail lit the fire and brought her coffee, which she accepted silently, noting a watchful expression in his eyes as he briefly sought hers before looking away. She padded to the window and caught her breath. The house was set in a wide valley dotted with barns and small farms; beyond them lay pale, bare mountains interleaved with mist. Sheep tugged at tufts of grass around the garden fence, their fleece backlit by the horizontal sun. Everything—the grass, the shrubs planted for shelter and the sloping field beyond—gleamed with a late frost, each rose-hip and gorse spine mirrored in white ice.

'We should stay here today,' he told her. 'I'm going for food.'

'I'll come!'

He shook his head. 'I'm known. They'll think nothing of it. If you're with me the mountain will be talking. The whole of Bessbrook barracks will be here in a trice to save you from the IRA. You wouldn't want that now, would you?' She shook her head. The British had killed Daniel.

When he had gone, she ventured to the bathroom. The back boiler had heated enough water for a meagre bath. She stepped into it as a fog of steam swirled about her in the chill room, but the water was good. She dried her hair in front of the fire, put on clean clothes from the overnight bag she had brought from Belfast, and walked out into the bright, crisp morning where, eyes narrowed in the sunshine, she examined herself sternly.

Since Hugh's departure she had come to understand that her life in London had a predictability that suited her very well; a selfish, self-indulgent life she imagined might continue quite happily alone. But Lithgow's murder and Daniel's death had broken her defences. Grief had made her long suddenly for intimacy, for someone to take care of, who would take care of her—everything she thought she had successfully walled off. And here she was, holed-up in a house in the mountains with a man she barely knew, a man who killed. She was not in a fit state of mind to navigate such dangerous ground.

He was gone almost two hours, returning with food, newspapers, batteries for the radio. As they prepared the meal together, she could feel him watching her. She tried to insulate herself against his concern for her and the care with which he performed each task. She resisted the inflections of his voice and rarely turned her face to him lest it reveal her feelings.

He made no enquiry of her silence but sat reading the newspapers while the food cooked. They ate sitting on the floor in front of the hearth. He had baked potatoes at the edge of the grate and they sucked at the butter on the burnt, ashy skins. 'Being here with you reminds me of my time in London,' he announced happily. 'It was a good time.'

She frowned. As far as she knew, his trips to London had been to plant bombs.

He caught her look and said in a low voice, 'Perdita, there is more to my life than that.'

More to his life. If he had a good time in London, then, it was because of Caitlín O'Connor; green miniskirt abandoned in Cricklewood. 'I don't want to hear about London,' she cut in.

He misunderstood, of course. 'My God, I thought we'd got beyond that, you and I! Is that all I am to you still: a terrorist?'

He threw down the word like a gauntlet; the cold edge to his voice a lifeline to her drowning principles.

She clutched at it. 'What else should you be to me?' She forced herself to look him coldly in the eye.

'Jesus!' He took up a turf and fairly hurled it onto the fire, releasing a cascade of sparks. Perdita flinched. When he turned back to her his eyes were sparking, too. 'What do I have to do for you? Immolate myself? Purge through fire? Atone by clutching at some wee rock in the ocean for a hundred years licking up salt crusts? *What?*'

'Nothing,' she said. 'You've made your choices. Of course you don't have to justify yourself. As long as you don't delude me.'

'When have I ever misled you about anything? Have you *ever* thought I'm pretending to be someone I'm not?'

She shook her head. 'I don't know,' she replied. 'You might be so cunning that I don't suspect.'

He let out a hiss of vexation. 'And what about you? Are you some holy deity that I have to propitiate? Because I'll tell you this, Perdita Burn, I've been watching you and I've reached a conclusion that I want you to consider. I mean this now: listen carefully to what I'm saying. If it was *you* back there in 1972, and your people were lying outside the Rossville Flats ripped to pieces by the Paras, I think *you'd* have been the one with the bomb at the barracks.'

'I'd *what?*' She twisted away and gathered the plates noisily together, scraping the potato skins into the fire where they sizzled and spat.

'*You* would have done it,' he insisted. 'In similar circumstances you would have done the same as me.'

'Oh, please!' Her voice was dry with contempt. 'Besides, what's it to you *what* I'd have done?'

He stared at her for a moment. 'It's not me deluding you,' he told her. 'It's you deluding yourself if you won't face up to the glaring truth of it.'

She thought he was still talking about her politics, but when she raised her eyes to his face, she saw it was not that at all.

Seeing that she understood his meaning, he held her gaze defiantly. Beyond the exasperation, she caught an expression in his eyes. Anger? A question hung in the air. No, not anger. She looked away in confusion.

It was at that moment there came a knock at the door.

It was Francie. They had both lost sight of the time, but the meeting was by appointment; the subject, deferred by Daniel's death, was filming Frazer the next day. Although neither Perdita nor McGrail betrayed by a word or gesture what had just taken place, Perdita could sense Francie notice the tension between them. McGrail was businesslike but reticent; Perdita distracted. She made tea and sat beside them at the table, her hands clasped in her lap, her eyes on Francie's face, although she was barely in the room with them at all. McGrail would bring her firmly back with questions, since the decisions to be made were chiefly hers. She answered succinctly, looking all the while at Francie, never at McGrail. But Francie seemed to catch the avoidance. She recognised his discomfort as he watched them both, very likely wishing to be anywhere but here.

From London, she had arranged with Frazer by telephone to interview him at the Mill, implying her editor's enthusiasm with the footage they had already shot, but saying there were further questions requiring his response. It had been a delicate conversation, their last encounter lying unspoken between them. She was puzzled, and uneasy, that he was agreeing to see her at all.

Francie would pose as sound recordist. Chris the cameraman, who was already booked to fly over for the shoot, would be fully informed about everything except Francie's true identity. Francie asked about the layout of the room, the prevalence of bookshelves and files.

'I have a suggestion,' McGrail said. He left the room and went out to the car, returning almost immediately with a folded plan. To her surprise, Perdita saw it was an architect's drawing of Frazer's office. How on earth had he come by that? McGrail ran his forefinger along the curved wall that mirrored the bow window Perdita had so much admired on her first visit there. 'The mill-owner's office,' he told Francie, 'was traditionally constructed against the wall of the chimney.'

'That's right,' Perdita confirmed.

'What you may not have known,' said McGrail, 'is that a stairway for maintenance of the flue runs two-thirds of the way up the chimney on the inside, until it gets too narrow towards the top. You can reach the stairwell at the bottom through a maintenance store at ground level.'

'Locked?' Francie asked.

'It will be taken care of,' replied McGrail. 'Now. Originally, of course, there was no vent between the office and the flue. But when Frazer installed the modern heating system he broke through several vents for ducted air. And something else was discovered.'

Perdita noted his careful use of the passive tense again. She had no idea when he could have recced the place himself. She found it odd.

'...Remember priest-holes in the Cromwellian era? Well, Frazer's installed himself an access point right through the wall to that staircase. He can leave his office through the chimney. There's a secret door. He can leave the building if he wants, and his secretary think him still there. He can steal away and back again with the perfect alibi. Or he can receive unofficial visitors. I propose to pass the interview listening behind that door.'

They both stared at him.

'I think that's a terrible idea,' said Francie. 'What the hell for, anyways?'

'I'm not missing out on the fun!' McGrail protested. 'Our man knows that Perdita has unwelcome information about him. It could be a trap. I might even come in useful.'

'You'd come in useful like a hole in the head,' Francie told him. 'You'd be a liability, known to him as you are.'

Watching Francie's face, Perdita realised he had misread the signs and thought they were lovers; he believed McGrail's judgement was clouded. She felt responsible. 'Don't,' she begged McGrail. 'Please don't.'

Still looking at Francie, he replied, 'Frazer will have no idea I'm there.' They were all silent for a few moments, Francie holding McGrail's gaze. 'Well,' said McGrail soberly, 'we'll discuss it later.'

They talked about the secret filming equipment. Francie had brought a couple of lenses to show Perdita, the most useful operated from a tiny fixed camera that could be hidden in a box file or over a picture; a second could be concealed in Perdita's lapel. 'That one's not brilliant,' Francie explained. 'You tend to get a lot of shots of chins and shoulders, particularly since you told me he's taller than you, but if you angle it right it works fine; it's actually more powerful than the other one. There's a third kind that's a better angle.' He beamed at her. 'But the camera is located in the bridge of a pair of heavy spectacles. Frazer might smell a rat if you turned up in those!' They decided to go for the fixed camera, with the lapel for back-up, and position the camera in one of the heating vents in the chimney wall, at a point where it could be easily retrieved from the far side afterwards.

'It's certainly the best angle for me,' Francie said.

Perdita made more tea and he told them about Daniel. 'They took him to Belfast for a post mortem, and there'll be an inquest in due course, but I bet they hush it up as much as possible. It's too early for the papers: just a wee paragraph today.' He showed them the *Belfast Telegraph*, which announced that the body of a man had been discovered in the Slieve Gullion Forest Park. There was no mention of how he had died and no mention of the second body, the man who killed him.

Perdita shook her head in disbelief. 'It's a huge story when it eventually breaks.'

'If,' corrected McGrail.

'They can't hush it up indefinitely,' she said.

'Wait and see.'

The sun was starting to dip behind the mountains and the small thaws of the morning were halfway to freezing again when Francie left soon after. 'See yous tomorrow,' he called.

She shivered. The thought of tomorrow lay like lead upon

her heart. 'Come on!' she said to McGrail. 'We've time to get some air!'

They were climbing to the summit of the hill behind the cottage, their breath in clouds, boots stamping through the semi-frozen mud, when she asked, 'Did you come here with your wife?'

He turned to her in surprise. 'Why, no. What makes you think that?'

She shrugged. 'You said your life was all on the run. I wondered.'

She thought he might be angry, but he laughed. 'I may have exaggerated somewhat. There was a time, in the South, when we lived in a terrace, just like other couples. I was sent out for nappies.'

'I thought you were in jail.'

'Not all of the time.'

They climbed in silence. Above them, the calls of seagulls fell in descending scales.

'Where's your son now?' she ventured.

'In Dublin, with his auntie, his mummy's sister. They grew up almost in the same house for a while, Fionn and her kids.'

She said nothing but he seemed to sense her regret, and added, 'It's better that way. I want him to be educated, not moving around. Above all, I don't want him mixed up in politics. He had enough of it when Caitlín died.'

Emboldened by his willingness to talk, she asked, 'I wondered... why she did what she did? Go back to active service. All that.'

He stopped. His face hardened. 'It was Cait's way of coping,' he told her.

'But you had just come out of jail! You could have been a real family for once.'

'How could we?' His voice was torn from him by the freshening wind. 'How could we do that when she was waiting to die?'

Perdita was startled. There were tears in his eyes, though whether from the cold or from the memory she couldn't determine.

'Cait had breast cancer. There was chemotherapy, but she knew it would be back. For a while it seemed to paralyse her spirit. But she wanted to go out fighting—literally. To do something useful. She said, better that she do this than some wee girl with a future. She promised she would come home to us well before the end.' He gazed out at the setting sun, remembering. 'But it didn't work out like that, did it? She was arrested; her final months wasted in jail in Germany where we couldn't even visit her. That's why she made a break for it. It was a crazy thing to do but, for her, the stakes were worth it. She was trying to get home to us, you see. She was trying to keep her word.' The seagulls had flown away to the west. 'I loved her very much,' he finished simply.

She put her arm around him and they walked on companionably until, turning a corner, she suddenly saw the sea, grey and rose, away beyond them.

He said, picking up the explanation from the point he had left it, 'That's why I do what I do. Everything I do now, I do for peace. It is the only thing that matters to me, Perdita, that my child should not have to do what I have done. That his generation should not waste their lives on all this. I've explained it to him. I think he understands. He's a brilliant wee boy. I see him whenever I'm in Dublin, but I don't want to contaminate him.'

'You'll not contaminate him!' she cried. 'He needs you, Joe.'

'I've told him,' McGrail continued. 'When he's old enough, he can make his own choice. I want him to be free.'

'The war's over,' she said. 'Why can't you just go home now?'

He was silent for a while. 'The war *is* over. But the peace has a way to go. I hope,' he added softly, 'that no one will know what I've had to do. That peace will hold, and there will be an end of it.'

She didn't understand: everyone knew what he had done. His young son must know. There would be no shame in that; to them he was a freedom fighter, a republican hero.

Dusk was falling now as they found the path back down the mountain. They quickened their steps and walked in silence, until she skidded on a patch of scree and he caught her, holding her tight.

'Perdita.' The way he spoke her name with the 'r' in it.

She looked up at him. They were standing on the edge of a valley, the little stone house somewhere beneath, out of sight.

He took a breath to speak, but didn't. He laughed ruefully. 'Can't say it,' he told her.

'What?'

'I—Jesus, when was I ever lost for words? Okay, here's a poem for it, then—from the Perdita Burn Irish song collection, of all things. And me being so rude about your taste!' He recited softly: 'I could never go with you, no matter how I wanted to. D'you understand, Perdita?'

In truth she didn't, but she knew he was right. 'Nor I with you,' she said.

He nodded. 'Though I *did* want to. Very much.'

'So why not, Joe?'

'I hope you never find out,' he said. That line again. 'But if you do, you will thank me.'

She thought, what is it with these terrorists and their damn scruples? 'So, tell me now and I can be grateful to your face!' she challenged him.

'If I told you now, I would have to kill you,' he said solemnly.

And laughing, they continued back down the path.

It was past six in the evening when they left the house and crossed the border to Dundalk. Here they were to part. The memory of her previous visit to the railway station at the end of her first encounter with McGrail, combined with a new sense of foreboding. She gladly took refuge in the driving as a diversion for her overflowing thoughts. Caitlín O'Connor, she thought sternly, would not have betrayed herself at a time like this. McGrail, too, appeared preoccupied. Lower down the mountain the thaw had held; the road was wet and full of stinking trucks that hurtled past them, drenching the windscreen in oily spray. They drove in silence.

The nearer place to drop him would have been Newry, but he had considered that too dangerous. After the shooting yesterday, they must not be spotted together in the North. From Dundalk he would take the train to Belfast and make his own way out to Frazer's mill—for, predictably, his wishes had prevailed. He would be there, he said, to guard her although, if all went well, she wouldn't see him. As the time approached, she had been feeling increasingly anxious about this encounter with Frazer, wondering what tricks he would pull to turn it to his own advantage. So, despite her opposition to it, she was thankful for McGrail's protection and determined to get the disclosures she needed, knowing him to be a witness.

About the future, they hadn't spoken. Perdita knew they would never meet again. She pushed the subject away.

Before they dropped down towards Dundalk, he told her to turn off the main road and directed her through a labyrinth of lanes. 'Stop here,' he instructed at a field gate and when she did so, glancing at him enquiringly, he said, 'I'll just disappear when we reach the station. This is where we say goodbye.'

She turned to him. He took her in his arms as comprehensively as the steering wheel would allow, kissing her with such tenderness that tears rose to her eyes in spite of her resolution.

'Don't,' he murmured. 'Don't cry.' He looked at her. There were tears in his eyes, too. They laughed at each other. 'This has been the sweetest day,' he said. 'Whatever happens, will you think well of me, in this respect at least?'

'What do you mean?' She was reminded of their earlier conversation.

He shook his head. 'I want you to know that this was real.'

She watched him. He seemed to be holding some kind of private debate in his head. 'It is real,' she assured him. She saw that it was.

'Time to go,' he said at last.

'Yes.'

Neither moved. At length she said, 'Okay.' She broke from him, groped for her seat-belt, started the engine and moved back into the lane. The clouds had lifted and a full moon slanted over the fields, lighting the blades of winter wheat.

'From here,' he said, twisting in his seat, 'you can see four counties.'

'Rubbish!' Laughing through her tears she broke the countryside into a thousand prisms.

'You can so!' he insisted. 'Two in the North and two in the South.'

'Don't try and justify yourself to *me*.'

'Oh, it's far too late for that,' he said quietly. They continued in silence to the outskirts of town, his fingers tangled in her hair.

Perdita drove back towards Belfast feeling deeply confused. First, she was forced to acknowledge that had their lives been different, if history had been otherwise, she and McGrail might have loved each other. But even as she pondered this, the sweet regret that it could never be was tinged with disquiet. She started to ask herself what exactly had happened over the past twenty-four hours. What was McGrail even *doing* at Francie's? Well, of course, in the republican way (as she was learning to understand it), he would have been informed there was to be filming, and would have made it his business. What did he have on Frazer that the man so obsessed him? Or— Perdita frowned—what might Frazer have on *him*?

Then, after Daniel's death, she could see that McGrail needed to disappear from the scene of the murdered killer, if this mad claim about his trademark assassination technique were true. But there was no reason why *she* should not have stayed. After all, she was in possession of the third document to prove that Daniel had come to this remote place to warn her of the threat to her life. Why had she not been more assertive? She had allowed McGrail to stifle her own conscience, and it was not a good feeling. At the first test of her promise to clear Daniel's name, she had abjectly failed.

And as she drove through the night her unease deepened. It was almost, in retrospect, as if she were being preserved, *groomed*—the word made her recoil—to finish the business with Frazer; spirited away in order not to be caught up with the police and deflected from this main purpose, as though it were McGrail's objective, not hers. Was that why he wanted to be present tomorrow, to see it through? Perhaps she was getting things out of proportion. But as she reached Belfast, she found herself repeating, as if it were a mantra, *we are not lovers. We never were. We never shall be.* And she knew that one day she would be thankful for that.

CHAPTER 18

On Friday morning, Perdita drove out to the airport where she was to meet Chris, the cameraman. His flight had made good time and they had a few hours' grace before they needed to be at the mill. They were to pick up Francie in Belfast.

'Perdita, you look pale,' Chris observed sharply.

'You'll look pale,' she grinned at him, 'when I tell you what we're here to do.'

He continued to watch her, his eyes narrowing. 'There's something different about you. What is it? What have you been up to?'

'Cutting the film.'

'Oh yeah?' He was appraising her critically.

She opened the window a touch. 'If you must know,' she confided, 'the most notable thing to happen to me in the past week is that a friend of mine has been murdered. And I was there.'

'Again!' His tone changed completely.

'It has a bearing on what we do today, so I'm going to tell you about it.'

'Perdita, I'm sorry. I'd no idea.'

Ahead, she could see the turning she was looking for, a bar and shopping complex dumped apparently in the middle of nowhere on the airport road. Over two large cups of coffee she at last told him what he had been longing to know: the story behind the story of the film and how she had come to take it on.

'Hang on.' Chris interrupted her at the same point Jeremy had. 'You say some spook in the secret services is sending the memos... in order to discredit the minister... by means of the leaky civil servant?'

She nodded. 'Something like that.'

'So how come they bump off Lithgow—one of the very people they're presumably trying to protect?'

'They didn't kill Lithgow,' she said. This was the trickiest part. 'Something must have gone wrong. The IRA got on to it somehow and did the job anyway.' Now that she was away from him, she regretted once again that she hadn't pressed McGrail on this.

As she told him about her night at the quayside after their last day of filming, Chris looked increasingly concerned. 'It all sounds pretty far-fetched to me. Frazer doesn't come over like a terrorist at all—and certainly not a Protestant paramilitary. Quite the reverse. And besides, if Frazer knows you know this stuff about him, how can he possibly grant you another interview?' he asked.

Chris's scepticism was not helping Perdita's nerves. 'Well, he obviously has a right of reply,' she pointed out. 'He must think it will look more incriminating if he doesn't use it.'

'It could be an ambush, Perdita. You're asking me, and an unknown Irish sound recordist, to stick our heads in the crocodile's jaw. It's not on.'

Was he going to pull out? It was on the tip of her tongue to tell him about the protection of McGrail on the secret staircase, but instinct told her that news of her collaboration with the republicans would only make matters worse. She saw herself through his eyes all too clearly: a naive woman, way out of her depth, dragged into bandit country. She could no longer remember where it had begun; at the army roadblock on that first night, perhaps, or at the Felons Club, or seeing Daniel demoralised in his sinister prison? Too late to turn back now. 'Chris,' she said. 'I'm really sorry not to have put you in the picture before. I simply couldn't do it on the telephone.'

She watched him, holding her breath, waiting for his decision.

'Not much choice, really, have I?' he said gruffly. 'The only interesting part of the shoot, that quayside, and you didn't take me with you!' He patted her arm. 'I always thought you had guts, Perdita. A bit daft, mind. But plucky.'

She smiled at him gratefully. 'Right,' she said. 'Here's what we have to do…'

They reached the mill at one-thirty. Perdita was relieved to find Frazer was not expected for another hour. Chris, Francie and Perdita were shown into the magnificent office by the young woman from Twinbrook, Sinéad Brennan. Was there a moment of recognition between Sinéad and Francie? Perdita had not foreseen this possibility. Francie looked away. But Sinéad chattered excitedly about cameras, greeting Perdita as if she were an old friend, and went to make coffee.

Chris took in his surroundings with approval. 'He certainly knows how to look after himself,' he observed.

'Beautiful, isn't it,' said Perdita, but she threw him a warning look. They had agreed there would be no discussion of what they were about to do, on the expectation that the room might be bugged.

Francie unpacked the secret camera and microphone and located one of the air vents high up on the chimney wall. 'How's that there for you, Chris?' he asked, pointing at the vent. 'Position okay for you, is it?'

'Should be fine,' Chris said. Then, to Perdita, 'How about if we half-close the shutter here and sit him in front of that?'

The set-up complete, they drank their coffee and waited for Frazer. Perdita nervously scanned her questions, re-ordering, memorising, noting key words on a fresh page of her notebook. Held at bay by the tumultuous events of the past week, the full implication of what they were about to do now assailed her. She looked over at the others: Chris calmly chatting to Francie about Liverpool's chances in the cup; Francie stretching, grinning. What the hell was she getting them into? She jumped up from the sofa where she had been sitting in for Frazer so that Chris could light the shot, and began to prowl along the chimney wall, struggling to calm herself, her mind on McGrail, looking for signs of the secret door. She could see nothing: stripped back to the bricks, the wall was solid, its only ornament the line of expanded prints of the original mill, exterior and interior. The picture beneath the air-vent, to which Francie had taped the camera cable, was the one exception. It was the portrait of a nineteenth century gentleman, perhaps the founder of the mill, and sat oddly with the others, being narrower and deeper and hanging too low on the wall. It was the only feature of the room that was aesthetically out of place, which puzzled her. Leaning close to the edge of it, Perdita now saw that its position and dimensions exactly mirrored the lintel of a door. Dropping to her knees she traced with her outstretched arms a line running vertically. from the bottom of the picture on either side to the floor. The exposed wall in between, now she felt it, was not brick at all but some kind of synthetic moulding, shaped and matched with such skill that only by feel could one tell the difference. Without speaking, Perdita turned to Francie and beckoned him over. The position of the vent relative to the secret door had not been evident in the plans. As it was, if McGrail were to burst through the door for any reason he would, literally and figuratively, blow the camera. Francie understood on the instant. He pointed to the camera and tapped Perdita's lapel. She nodded, praying they had time to make the change. Francie's fingers moved deftly, undoing his careful handiwork. He retrieved the camera from the vent and bundled it into its container, pulling the other, even smaller, camera from a zipped pocket at the back. Perdita stood still, holding her breath, while he wired this new camera to the upper pocket of her jacket, looping the spare cable neatly out of sight and running a feed from the body and its battery to the tiny lens out through her buttonhole. But how to conceal it? They searched frantically around.

Chris, who had been keeping watch on the yard below, asked, 'What kind of car does he drive?'

Perdita joined him at the window. Frazer's Porsche was manoeuvring into the managing director's parking space. No time. 'He's here,' she said. Francie flew across the room. He snapped two freesia heads from a large vase on the coffee table and pinned them to Perdita's buttonhole, nimbly concealing the lens while somehow maintaining a clear eyeline.

'You've done this before,' she said to him, intrigued.

'Indeed I have,' he replied. The sound was easier. He placed a tiny clip-mic at her throat inside her collar, handing her the cable to drop down inside her shirt, and the radio battery, which he switched on, to tuck into her waistband under the jacket. Perdita's fingers trembled at the buttons. They could hear voices, a conversation in the lobby between Frazer and Sinéad. Francie was calm as he pinned a second feed to the inside of her jacket; this was for the camera control and ran into the left-hand pocket of her skirt. *Come on,* she prayed. *Come on.* He had thankfully shown her how to operate it back at the cottage. 'You're doin' great,' he whispered. She attempted to smile. Footsteps came swinging up the corridor towards the office. Francie stepped back, his eyes twinkling. Perdita gazed over at the secret door. Was McGrail in place on the other side? *Give me strength,* she willed.

Frazer strode into the office, glanced around with evident disapproval at the disruption and slung his briefcase onto a chair.

'All right, Perdita,' he said by way of greeting. 'What do you want? I've not long.'

'If you come and sit down, Mr Frazer, we'll talk about

it.' She indicated the sofa, which they had positioned in the window, and sat herself in his office chair, obliging him to take the interview seat.

He did so with reluctance. 'Do you always rearrange the furniture?'

'Almost always,' said Chris amiably.

'I'd rather be behind my desk,' Frazer said.

'You would?' Perdita smiled. 'And look like every other man in a suit interviewed in his office? I assure you this will come over much better.'

'What have you got in your viewfinder?' Frazer asked. Chris stood aside and allowed him to look. 'I don't trust you, you see,' he resumed, walking to the window and throwing himself on the sofa again. The note of menace in his voice was unmistakable. Perdita caught Chris's look of surprise. This was not the man they had interviewed before.

Francie approached with Frazer's microphone. Frazer scowled at him. 'Who are you?' he asked bluntly. 'You weren't here last time.'

Before Francie could answer, Perdita cut in, 'I'm sorry, Mr Frazer, I failed to introduce you: Billy Campbell, the sound recordist.'

'Hello there, Sir,' muttered Francie. Perdita guessed it was not the first time he had been forced to impersonate a unionist.

'You're from here!' Frazer said, catching the Belfast inflection. 'Why?'

'For a one-day shoot, it doesn't pay to fly across an English sound man,' Perdita interposed.

Frazer grunted. 'All right. Let's get on with it. If you were doing your job properly you would have covered this last time.'

Her hand in her pocket, Perdita pressed the remote control to activate the secret camera and moved to the seat set up for her beside Chris, angling herself to the position which, she fervently hoped, would focus the lens at her lapel onto Frazer's face. All she needed was an admission that he had been present at the quay on the night of the shipment. Just enough to link him to the illicit arms. 'As I said on the phone,' she began carefully, 'there are some fresh issues we need to discuss. Before we start, I'd just like to run through them with you.'

'You said you wanted to ask some follow-up questions on "other aspects of my work", I think.'

'I was referring, of course, to our meeting during the night after the previous interview.'

Frazer's face froze. 'What are you talking about?'

The handling of the next few questions was crucial. If he denied point-blank he was there, she would have no case. 'Mr Frazer, you don't deny, do you, that you saw me near the quay that night?' She forced herself to hold his gaze. Once he acknowledged that, she could pass on to the principal allegation.

He was staring at her with open hostility. 'This is monstrous. You have come here under false pretences. If you had given me any inkling of the subject, I would not have let you within fifty miles of here.'

'You must have known what I was talking about.' Perdita held her ground. 'So I wonder why the subject disturbs you so much.'

'I have nothing to say.' His eyes were ice.

'What's your problem, Mr Frazer? You saw me that night.

I've come for your account of events.'

'It's none of your business and nothing to do with the subject of your film.'

'So, you do acknowledge you were there?'

'No comment.'

'I must take that to mean you don't deny it.'

'This is unspeakable. Do you not hear what I'm saying?'

'Okay, in that case let's not waste time arguing about it,' Perdita said equably. She would have to put the arms dealing allegation to him straight, in the officially-filmed interview. 'Let's just do the interview and we'll get out of your way.' She was still confident she would be able to catch him later when the formal filming was over.

'There will be no interview,' he snarled. 'Now get out.'

Perdita wasn't having that. 'You saw me on the quayside and you saw my camera. You were armed. You must have known when I made this appointment that I would be asking about that night.'

'Out.'

'You have been accused of illicit arms dealing, Mr Frazer. I've come here to give you the opportunity to refute that charge.'

Frazer jumped up from the sofa and strode to his desk. 'Get McCluskey,' he barked into the intercom. 'I want the film crew off my property. Now.'

Chris darted her a look. Perdita nodded. The crew began to dismantle the lights and pack the gear. Perdita, thankful for the last-minute change of strategy on the secret camera, turned it off and waited. Within a couple of minutes three security guards had arrived in the room to escort them. Perdita took a deep breath. 'I think we ought to talk, Mr Frazer.'

'Oh, don't think I'm letting *you* go. You're staying here.'

Chris, who was packing the camera box, looked up sharply.

'That's fine,' Perdita said. Behind Frazer's back, Chris shook his head vehemently. 'You go on into town,' Perdita told him. 'I'll meet you at my hotel. I'll be back before you have to leave for the airport.' She was relieved not to be thrown out too, telling herself she had nothing to fear with McGrail positioned behind the door just a few feet away. The laborious packing continued in silence. Frazer stood staring out of the window, hands behind his back, flexing his fingers as she had seen him standing before. Chris and Francie eventually trooped out, each flanked by a security guard. There were no goodbyes.

Perdita looked at Frazer as they went and caught him watching with a faint smile. In a flash, she realised he had never intended to give the interview. He simply wanted her there: on his territory, on his terms, alone. She switched the camera back on.

'You are a stupid little fool, Perdita,' he said. 'I had to get them out of the way. You wouldn't have wanted them to hear what I'm going to say to you.'

She was determined to retain the initiative. 'You're the loser, Mr Frazer. I came for a denial. Whatever your business with arms, I hardly expected you to put your hands up to it on national television.' Speaking for the hidden camera, she added, 'You can't deny you were there that night and that arms were being illegally unloaded into your van.'

'Does it not occur you,' he responded, 'that I might have

been there for a legitimate reason? That shipment was no more mine than yours. You had been taken there for a purpose. You had been used for a purpose. You still are being used: you are the pathetic dupe of terrorists—and worse.'

'That's nonsense,' Perdita told him.

Frazer tipped back his linen-covered desk chair. This was clearly where he felt most at ease. 'Let me ask you a question,' he said. 'When your friend, the little civil servant, received his second document, the one with poor Lithgow's name on it, did you show it to the IRA?'

Perdita was wary at the change of tack. 'I didn't see that document,' she replied. 'As I explained to Milton Lithgow, I was told of its contents. I passed them to him, to warn him. Not to the IRA.'

'Precisely so. Yet you had consulted them about the first memo, had you not?'

'*Consulted?* Hardly! Can we stick to the point, please?' She could not see where this line was taking them. She didn't like it. 'We're talking about your involvement in a shipment of arms.'

'This *is* the point,' he insisted.

'You're changing the subject, Mr Frazer!'

'Listen!' He smashed the flat of his hand down on the desk, making Perdita jump. 'We will come to it directly. Answer the question!'

Perdita struggled to keep her voice steady. 'I had informed Sinn Féin of the existence of the first memo because it appeared to indicate some kind of trickery,' she said. 'I was trying to find out where the document had come from.'

Frazer leaned forward. 'From the moment McGrail discovered that you had been leaked that document, he decided to use you, Perdita. Have you never asked yourself how the writer knew the dates of forthcoming IRA atrocities? And, in particular, how McGrail and his terrorists knew that Lithgow's name, and the date of his projected death, was on the second?'

She scowled at him. It was the question of the second document she had wanted McGrail to answer; the question they all wanted to know and he had ducked. 'McGrail did not use me,' she said. 'He had no reason to *use* me for anything.'

'Oh, really?' Frazer laughed. 'Let's talk about something else. Let's talk about Joseph McGrail's wife, the lovely Caitlín O'Connor. I don't want to distress you, Perdita, but he loved her very much, you know.'

'Just get to the point, Mr Frazer.' Perdita could not begin to guess what McGrail's wife had to do with any of it. So far, Frazer had clarified nothing. All the same, she was intrigued to hear what he had to say.

Frazer explained that another branch of the intelligence services had become involved in the story of Daniel's memos: as she might know, he said, parts of the service had been instrumental in back-channel negotiations within the peace process over many years. They could see their painstaking work unravelling if the removal of the minister, Blakemore, became permanent because of some trumped-up security breach involving an ex-lover. So they decided to put a stop to it.

He had lost her. If the second document was supposed to do that, how could the murder of a British politician possibly further the cause of peace?

Frazer was preening himself on the apparent extent

of his knowledge in the face of her ignorance. 'Oh, on the contrary,' he drawled. 'I'd say it was a great success for them. The immense political fallout from Lithgow's death destroyed some—' he hesitated, his cold eyes narrowed, 'some delicate structures here in the North that had been built up over a long time. And in London, I'm told that document exposed the plot against Blakemore for exactly what it was: a crude piece of black propaganda. They will have been more than satisfied with a result like that.'

'It caused the death of an innocent man,' she reminded him, '—an elected MP. Are you telling me that's how British intelligence operates?' But even as she said this, she knew that someone had seen Daniel as expendable, too.

He shrugged. 'Well, of course, as far as poor Lithgow is concerned it was just collateral damage for them—but at the same time it removed a major obstacle to their precious peace process. A satisfactory outcome for them; less so for him, perhaps.'

She had heard this opinion of Lithgow before. It fitted eerily with McGrail's. 'And you know all this about the secret services *how*, exactly?' she asked him warily.

'Oh, very suspicious, I'm sure!' he sneered. 'You'll have *me* tied up in it next! Perdita, in this close-knit little community we have over here in the North, people know each other and people talk. Those of us who move in the public eye,' he savoured this fact for a moment, '…have security men to watch over us. Security men need to make it their business to know what other branches of the service are up to. After Lithgow's death, his security man was for the high-jump for not finding out. My man got the whole story.'

'But…' Even had it been remotely credible, Perdita knew first-hand that Lithgow's murder was nothing to do with the security services. 'Dissident republicans killed Lithgow,' she pointed out.

Frazer leaned forward. 'The question you have to ask yourself,' he said, 'is who were they killing Lithgow *for?*' The pale eyes burned into her. 'Think about it. Your man, Joseph McGrail, loved his wife very much, did he not?'

Perdita hesitated. Why did he keep coming back to this?

'…Loved his wife Caítlin O'Connor, who was diagnosed with terminal cancer while he was still in prison. Joe McGrail was desperate to be with her.' He paused for effect. 'And suddenly—just like that—Joe McGrail, terrorist, murderer, republican hero, was released.'

'What are you saying?' she asked. She had always assumed McGrail had left prison under the government's early release scheme after the ceasefire.

As if reading her mind, Frazer said, 'Early. Much too early. Now, how could that be, Perdita?'

The scheme allowed for release once half of a prisoner's life sentence had been served. But she had to admit that with his escape and re-arrest she had never worked out how long McGrail had actually spent in jail. She suddenly felt unsure.

He continued softly, 'A mere six years for bombings in which servicemen were injured and three people died?'

'You're saying the Brits did some kind of deal with him? That's absurd!' She was incredulous.

Frazer shrugged. 'Too short a sentence, Perdita. Unprecedented. Unheard of.'

'You're saying they *turned* him?' There was a ringing

in her ears. She thought of McGrail behind the secret door, listening to this accusation. 'If any senior republican defected, surely the—the leadership would realise?' she added lamely.

'Oh, really?' He leered at her. 'Well, clearly you have a more intimate knowledge of senior republicans than I. I merely point out to you that McGrail loved his wife very much. Everyone has his price.'

'You have no evidence!'

'Sure I have evidence,' he contradicted her. 'You tell me you had not shown the memo with Lithgow's name on it to the IRA. How, then, did the IRA know that Lithgow was to die on November twenty-seventh? Acting on information from Joseph McGrail, their agent, the intelligence officers would have created a second memo on which they wrote Lithgow's name. Then McGrail made it happen. Oh—no doubt he took care to ensure his men knew the reason for it. With the war officially at an end, he would have needed to pass it off as a dissident act, but he would still have had to justify it to his own side. It will have tied him in knots that they bungled it and caught you up in it, too. Am I right?' He was watching her shrewdly.

She forced herself not to react. Frazer was in his element now. 'McGrail had you exactly where he wanted you,' he went on. 'He next used you to smear me—it was to have been a public denunciation on television. It was to have ruined my reputation and my business on both sides of the Atlantic. Valuable to the peace process *and* to the IRA. And he probably got to go to bed with you into the bargain.'

Perdita felt very cold. She said slowly, 'Why would any faction on the British side want your downfall? Don't you represent the peace dividend, the future?'

Frazer regarded her contemptuously. 'As I have been telling you ever since we met, Perdita, you are way out of your depth here.'

She pushed on, 'Well, if McGrail is working for the British to discredit you, that can only be because you oppose the peace process, just as Lithgow did. You can't have it both ways, Mr Frazer.'

'Can't I?' He smiled unpleasantly. 'You won't be suggesting that in your film, of course. You haven't the proof.'

Fighting to keep her voice steady, she dragged Frazer back to the main issue. 'Your van was at the quay that night. It was a smuggling operation. It was arms. You were there.'

'A routine check with the RUC Special Branch will reassure you that I was there with their full knowledge. The arms are safely in their custody. You can check with HQ.'

Perdita took a deep breath. If this was a bluff, Frazer made it sound pretty darned authentic. She hesitated. 'Prove it,' she demanded.

'My God!' His eyes drilled into her for a moment. Then he rounded the desk, turned the phone towards her and punched out an apparently familiar number, handing the receiver to her as he finished. 'Go ahead, then. Ask them.'

Perdita took the handset uncertainly, forcing herself to hold his angry gaze. There was a catch, of course. She was acutely conscious of the English civil servant, Daniel's colleague, she had recognised on the deck. Vernon Potts could have been working with the police. She had to admit Frazer had given her a more plausible explanation than the alternative of collusion between one of the security services and loyalist paramilitaries. The phone rang and rang at the other end. Her eyes still on Frazer's, she hung up. She needed time. If he was innocent, what was Frazer doing at the quay? Something didn't fit.

'Why would you, a well-known Belfast businessman, be working with the RUC?' she asked. 'Why would you need to be at the quay at all?'

He spread his arms wide. 'My dear Perdita, that's for you to find out. Until you do, you can't report a word against me. And I warn you, very seriously, not to try. My lawyers will be recording your film. Your career won't survive it.'

'Is that a threat?' she asked, startled at his lack of subtlety.

'Let's just call it advice.'

Perdita suddenly thought of Daniel; of the interests that would dispose of Daniel but protect a man like this. 'No,' she said firmly. 'I'm afraid that's not how it works. You see, the filmed evidence of the arms shipment has already been seen by my editor. It's with *our* lawyers. I need proof of your innocence that will satisfy them if I'm to drop it.' She was bluffing: the burden of proof was on her. The only evidence that could help her would be a denial by the police that Frazer was working with them; without it, the allegations against him could not be transmitted. She had to gamble on Frazer not yet knowing that. 'So how do I check it out, Mr Frazer? They're hardly going to talk to me about special operations.'

He stared at her coldly. 'You will be told.'

'When?'

He shrugged. 'Monday. Tuesday.'

'I have to return to London on Monday. I have to finish the film on Tuesday. I need proof this weekend if I'm to take it out,' she repeated.

He jumped up and went to the window, standing with his back to her. 'All right then.' She could hear his suppressed fury. 'Where are you staying?'

Should she say? Well, he would probably know in any case and she needed that proof. After a moment's hesitation, she told him.

'So. You will be shown the proof.' He turned back from the window and came towards her, standing oppressively close. 'Frankly, Perdita, I hadn't thought you so dumb that I would have to spell it out. You must know I have only to call two or three newspaper editors with the information of what *you* were up to at the quay that night. I'm sure Hugh Williams, for one, will be delighted to run the story.'

Perdita stepped back. She had known this would happen; it was just a question of when. She had planned to argue that this would only verify his own presence, but he had already disposed of that.

'...With a known terrorist.' Frazer was relishing it. 'I believe the technical term is *shagging*, is it not?'

'I was *not*,' she retorted, anger welling up inside her again.

'Oh, really? Looked pretty much like it to me.'

Perdita said tersely, 'There aren't many ways to justify loitering around a jetty at three o'clock on a winter morning.' She glowered at him. She had not forgiven him for assaulting her after their dinner. 'Which way would *you* have chosen, Mr Frazer?'

'The British press will lap it up, Perdita,' he smirked. 'A glowing example of the ploys used by a female TV producer to get her hands on a good story. Literally. Front page headline in *The Guardian*,' he continued. 'I can see all those liberal friends of yours reading it over their muesli. I can see your daughter Daisy reading it at—where is she now?—15 Back Hyde Park Terrace, Leeds?'

'You bastard!' said Perdita softly. Forcing herself to meet his gaze, she suddenly saw staring back at her the pale eyes of a killer. He would do it. She could believe him capable.

Frazer shrugged. 'Perhaps you should have thought of that beforehand.'

For a moment she was winded, her mind a total blank and all too well aware the camera was still running. Well, she had his admission, for what it was worth. Her hand in her pocket, she hastily switched off the tape. 'If—if Joseph McGrail works for the British, as you claim,' she managed to say, moving away from Frazer and raising her voice for McGrail's benefit, 'then whether or not I was having an affair with him is no story at all.' She hoped it would not be obvious to either of them that she didn't for a moment believe this.

Frazer laughed softly. 'To save your skin you will have to tell the world that your lover—'

'He is not my lover!'

'…that your lover is not a terrorist but a British spy. And his people will execute him as a traitor to republicanism. Which is it to be, Mrs Burn: your honour, or his life?'

Perdita was shaking. She walked to the door. With a last gasp of bravado she managed to say, 'Tell the press what you like, Mr Frazer. Of the three of us, your treachery is by far the greatest.' But she could hear the tremor in her voice as she said it, and she knew the two men listening would hear it also.

Chapter 19

All the way back to Belfast, Perdita attempted to order her thoughts. McGrail must have heard Frazer's allegations against him. It was logical, of course, that he had not revealed his presence at the mill. The only reason to do that would have been a threat to her. There had been no physical threat. McGrail would contact her later and explain that Frazer had been talking nonsense. Of this, she was sure.

No physical threat to *her*, but what about Daisy? The fact Frazer had taken the trouble to find out Daisy's address filled Perdita with terror.

Hugh was still at the office when she called him; Friday was always his latest night. She came straight to the point. 'Hugh, Daisy's in danger. You must please go and get her. Bring her back to London.'

'I beg your pardon?'

'Someone delivered a threat against her an hour ago.'

'What are you talking about? How d'you know?'

'I'm sorry. It's just really scared me.'

'An actual threat? "I'm going to harm your daughter"?'

'No, of course not. But he knows where she lives. He was trying to stop me doing something.'

'If you think he's serious, you go and get her.'

'I can't. I'm in Belfast.'

There was a beat while Hugh took this in. 'Those terrorist friends of yours?'

'An eminently respectable unionist.'

'Then you're imagining it.'

'Hugh, I mean it. They've got her address in Leeds.'

'They're spooking you, Perdita.' Perdita didn't respond. It was the habit of many years spent with this stubborn man. He had to reach the decision himself. She heard Hugh sigh heavily. 'All right, what's it about?'

'I have... information on this person. Very damaging information. I could use it. He's trying to stop me.'

'If he's trying to stop you, he won't touch Daisy until he knows he's failed.'

Perdita pressed the fingers of her right hand to her aching temples. 'You don't take chances with your own daughter, Hugh.'

'Keep your hair on,' he said. 'I'll go tomorrow afternoon. Hang on—' he broke off to consult the schedule on his computer screen. 'Bloody inconvenient,' he grumbled. 'Be clear about this, I shall tell her it's all your fault.'

'Tell her what you like,' said Perdita wearily. 'Just go early, please, and get her home. And don't let her out of your sight. You have Monday off, don't you? I'll be back Monday evening.'

'You've got your priorities sorted out then.'

'Believe me. I have no alternative.'

'I expect an exclusive on this if it's any good. Which I doubt,' he added.

Perdita replaced the phone on the bedside table and leaned back against the thin pillows. Her head was throbbing with anger against Hugh, and guilt that it was not she who would be flying to Daisy's rescue. Still, it would be a good thing for all of them if Hugh did something for his daughter, for once. He was probably right that Frazer would not move against Daisy yet.

After waving off Chris to the airport, wishing in her heart that she could leave too, Perdita felt deeply alone. She sat in front of the television worrying about Daisy, wondering about the RUC Special Branch. She was already regretting the pointless challenge to Frazer that would keep her in this wretched city over the weekend. As she had told him, she was not due back in the cutting room until Tuesday and, despite the material she had filmed that afternoon, there would be little to do. They had preserved the original cut on optical disk and all that remained was to reinstate it. The material from the quayside would be worthless if the RUC confirmed Frazer's claim, and she had little doubt that they would. His implied admission that he opposed the peace process; his oblique threat to Daisy; none of it was explicit enough to be usable.

She thought back to the film she had shot that afternoon: there must be something she could do. An idea began to take shape. Chris had left her the DV camera for emergencies; the tapes were compatible. Carefully unrolling the pair of socks in which she had concealed the footage from the secret lapel camera, she slotted the cassette into the DV and rewound the tape in vision. Through the viewfinder in black and white, Frazer hurled down the telephone receiver and backed around his desk. That was it. Perdita pressed stop. Then, frame by frame, she advanced the film. Frazer jerked up from his chair with an air of Buster Keaton, hopped around the desk, turned the phone towards her and dialled. Perdita froze the frame, fetched her notebook and pencil and squinted at the tiny screen. Zero, clearly, then one. Was it eight or seven? Eight; it preceded a diagonal move to four. Then across to six. Where was that? A British code, or Northern Irish. She reached for the hotel telephone directory: the code was Lisburn, probably some central Special Branch number. Well, then, she would call them and have done with it. She peered into the viewfinder again, noting down each remaining digit. Then she dialled the number. After the second ring, a man answered.

'Security.'

'Hello,' Perdita began, feeling foolish. 'Is that Special Branch?'

'What?'

'I'm—I'm sorry,' she stammered. 'I was given this number but I don't know what it is. I understood it might be the police. Is it?'

'This is Security. The warehouse is closed now.'

'Am I speaking to the RUC? Special Branch?'

'You have the wrong number, ma'am. There's no police here. We're security. You've come through to the night-security office at the warehouse.'

'Warehouse?'

'The Ulster Linen warehouse. There's no one here. May I suggest you call Frazer Linens on Monday and ask them? Wait 'til I give you the number now.'

Perdita waited. She wrote down the familiar number, her heart singing, thanked the man and rang off. So Frazer hadn't been calling the police! And if he was bluffing about the RUC, was he bluffing about McGrail? More than ever, she needed to speak to McGrail. In a superstitious recreation of the night they had driven to the quay, Perdita left her door unbolted and attempted to go to sleep.

But no midnight caller disturbed her. No chambermaid came with a message. As she lay, wide-awake, her tumbling thoughts turned to Daniel. She had an undertaking to Daniel she could not fulfil. He was discredited. Even if she were able to tell the entire story of Frazer, there would be no proof, and no place in her film, for the exoneration of Daniel. Guilt sat heavily alongside her other failures and anxieties, but she fell eventually into an unquiet sleep, waking only once when a guest in the next room made a late arrival. The fumbling of a key in the lock of the hollow door sounded unnervingly close. From the top of the television, the strident red digits of the hotel clock blazed out the time: 02.57. For a moment she was wide-awake. The lamp on her bedside table trembled slightly as the new guest moved around. She remembered the neighbouring room had a connecting door to her own; that was probably why the noise was so loud. This explanation reassured her and she fell asleep again.

The next time she started awake it was early Saturday morning. Perdita sat up, the unaccustomed Belfast weekend settling uneasily around her shoulders. She gazed out at the silent street, trying to ignore the sense of foreboding. Venturing downstairs for breakfast she found the hotel deserted. The staff seemed to be giving her odd looks.

'Never seen you here on a weekend before, Mrs Burn.'

She pulled a face. 'Lots of work to do.'

'Well, it's quiet here. That's one thing can be said for it. You're our only guest.'

'Not quite, am I? There's someone in the room next to me.'

'No, ma'am. No one.' The receptionist was amused.

'But I heard—I thought—' Perdita broke off uncertainly.

'Oh sure. We all hear things. Your ears play tricks in this old place at night, don't they? Not to worry, Mrs Burn. The ghosts are quite friendly.'

Perdita stayed in her room all morning attempting to work on the script, while hoping for Frazer's 'proof' to arrive or for McGrail to contact her. The day was miserable, a throwback to mid-winter, and by lunchtime she could no longer bear to sit and wait. Leaving instructions with the receptionist to take messages, she set out for the Sinn Féin office.

'Yes?'

'I need to get a message to Joseph McGrail. It's urgent.' She gave them her name.

'Wait there.'

It was humiliating to have to stand at the gate, but she knew no other way to make contact. As a journalist, she told herself, she must put it to him. Beyond that, was an intense need to know who he was, what he had done and to what extent he had used her.

At last, a different voice. 'Mr McGrail's away just now.'

The euphemism, so expected, caused a small explosion in her brain. She looked up, searching for the security camera. 'I'm—I'm a journalist.' She addressed the lens above her head. 'I have had a very serious allegation made to me about him. I need his response urgently.' Was he there? Was he watching her at this moment?

There was a short silence. Then the voice spoke again. 'Do you want to tell me what it is?'

'I can't. It's confidential.'

'Then it's probably bullshit.'

'I don't know,' she said, her eyes searching the camera as if to find him on the other side. 'I don't know. Will you tell him to contact me when he returns? I shall be at the Wellington Lodge Hotel.'

'That there may be difficult.'

Perdita stared into the camera. 'Just tell him, please,' she said.

She turned and walked away.

The afternoon faded and there was still no word. For the third time since returning from West Belfast, Perdita called Hugh's mobile: he must have reached Leeds by now. As before, it went straight to voicemail. Perdita told herself fiercely to keep calm. There had been no actual threat, *and yet Frazer knew where Daisy lived.* She could tell she was starting to get unhinged. *Forget it!* urged a voice inside her. *Just leave.* If she hurried, she would still make the last shuttle home to London. But she couldn't bring herself to go. Quitting was something you didn't do. She sighed. The dreaded upbringing: *seeing things through.* Appointments must be kept, even with those who wished you ill. Besides, returning early to England wouldn't help Daisy. It would not resolve the question of Frazer for the film, let alone of McGrail.

He might not even have been listening behind the secret door and heard the allegations against him, so he wouldn't realise how important it was to explain. But he had been very determined to be there. The more Perdita thought about it, the more she had to concede that Frazer might just be right about McGrail working for the British. Why, McGrail had told her himself that his wife had cancer. For her sake, and for the sake of their child, didn't it make some kind of sense to get out of jail in order to be with them, no matter how high the price? He didn't even have to compromise all of his ideals: as an agent for British intelligence, he could still work for peace against those who were trying to sabotage it, just as he had told her on the hillside.

Perdita jumped up from the table where she had been sitting and started to pace around the room. Then might this not also explain Cait's late return to the struggle?—Cait, perhaps the purer republican of the two, comprehending that her husband's release had come at a terrible cost? Her anger and revulsion. Her moral dilemma: if she denounced him, their small son would be left an orphan. Faced with that, the only honourable compromise for someone like her might well be to return to active service, despite her illness, even despite the little boy—but she would never have intended to get herself captured, locked-up for precious months. Perdita began to understand it: Cait could simply have needed to atone for her husband's treachery.

And gradually her vision cleared to reveal the true state of affairs. It must have been as Frazer had told her. The first and third documents would have been sent from the same source—hadn't Daniel himself told her that, back in the 1970s, parts of the intelligence service had a history of dirty tricks like that? But the second document could have come from somewhere else—which explained why Lithgow's security contacts had no knowledge of it. By showing McGrail the first, even with some of its information redacted, hadn't she herself given him the template for the second? How could she have been so blinded by him not to realise before? When she asked McGrail on their way to the quay how the dissident republicans could have known the date on that document, the date of Lithgow's death, he could not answer her. He had probably written it himself.

Then yesterday, when Frazer spelled out the choices that confronted her about McGrail, had she not challenged him to go to the press? Wouldn't this have implied to McGrail that she would do nothing to stop the disclosure of his true identity? Quite apart from being a news story, it would put herself in the clear and McGrail's vital cover would be blown. As far as he knew, she had every rotten word of Frazer's accusation on film, and would be returning with it to London. The idea that she could have wanted him to come and explain to her—had actually informed Sinn Féin she was still in town and left her door unbolted in the hope that he would—turned her blood to ice.

Everything I do now, I do for peace, he had told her. Like bumping off Lithgow, perhaps? On whose orders had he authorised that particular act of harmony? *I hope no one will know what I've had to do.* Now it was all too clear what he meant. Far from seeking to protect her, his only course would be to silence her. The threat from Frazer was nothing in comparison to the threat from McGrail. Perdita launched herself across the room to double-lock and bolt her bedroom door. As darkness fell, she was half out of her mind.

At eleven-thirty pm she made what she resolved would be the last call to Hugh. Still no answer. As she replaced the receiver and got into bed, a faint vibration from an unidentified source set the lamp juddering on the bedside table again. She listened, wondering what had caused it this time. After a few seconds it stopped. She forced herself to relax, but even as she did so the silence seemed to be ruffled by a *something*. Not a cough. Not a creak of bedsprings. She fancied she heard breathing. Impossible. She held her own breath. *Close to her.* But now all she could hear was the silence and the clock of a Protestant church on the Lisburn Road, tolling midnight.

She didn't know what woke her but was instantly aware of the faint shaking, once again, of the lamp close beside her pillow. No sound beyond to explain it. No truck thumping down the distant Malone Road. She imagined the hotel's ancient floorboards interconnected from room to room, an insomniac pacing the night away somewhere down the corridor. Except that the hotel was empty. There it was again, nothing more than a reverberation of the cheap ceramic lamp base on a sheet of glass. But as Perdita's ears sharpened there came a second noise: a key in the lock. No fumbling: a single turn, precise and efficient. Thank God tonight her door was bolted. No one with a pass-key would be able to enter.

But this was not the door leading out into the corridor. This was the interconnecting door with the adjacent room, the room where she fancied she had heard breathing. Acting without thought, she shot out of bed on the far side and shrank behind the inadequate bulk of a small armchair. The door opened with a slight squeak of hinges. A half-light from the room beyond backlit a shadow in the doorway. It moved soundlessly toward her bed. The man she had searched for and now most dreaded. The man with the keys. The man whose networks gave him access to every room in Belfast. It could only be McGrail. She heard a click. At any moment he would discover the bed to be empty, would turn and find her. There was nowhere to take cover. To reach either the pass door or the bathroom she would have to cross in front of him. And the door to the corridor was bolted.

She imagined rather than saw the figure bend over the bed, extend its arm; and then straighten and turn. She imagined the soft muzzle of the firearm sweeping the room, as if to seek the heat of a human body. She heard him move, the slight creak of the sleeve of a leather jacket. She imagined the warm jersey, enclosing the stone-cold heart within. *If I told you that, I would have to kill you.* Now she had found out, she must die.

'Perdita!' It was a whisper. The way it sounded the silent 'r' in her name. How she feared it now. She crouched, sweating in the cold night, exposed behind the small armchair, her hands clasping her knees like a spellbound child. But in her anxiety she had not realised she was leaning against the chair-back for support, which now shifted minutely, just enough to alert him. With a couple of strides he had rounded the bed. She could imagine the gun, held in his two hands in order for no mistake to be made—just as she had seen him at the quay with Frazer—arms outstretched, the elbows stiff. And then it seemed a double shadow, and at last the shot. There was only the chair between them. As he lurched towards her she felt the gobbets of thick blood slap onto her cheek. She felt its warm stickiness start to ooze through her nightdress. She wondered where he had hit her, amazed she felt no pain, though she dimly recalled hearing that one did not, and faintly, beyond these sensations, she was aware of a commotion at the door, feet hurrying. Someone was coming, then. Thank God for that.

Hours later it seemed (though she knew it was probably minutes) she regained consciousness with surprise. She was alive. No one had come. The room, the entire, empty hotel, was silent again. Crawling, whimpering, too horrified to turn on the light, she dragged herself out into the corridor.

CHAPTER 20

April 1998

Perdita and Jeremy Jordan were attending a reception for the passing of a major bilateral treaty in the Northern Irish peace process. It was being called The Good Friday Agreement and had been signed in Belfast earlier that month. Unofficially, the party was also to celebrate the reinstatement of Clive Blakemore. It had not been Perdita's idea to go.

*

'Come on, I absolutely insist!' Jeremy had said when he first managed to rustle up an invitation. 'My God, it's your story.'

'It's Daniel's life,' she corrected. 'I've nothing to celebrate.'

'Oh, lighten up, Perdita! Nothing's going to bring poor Daniel back.'

That was the problem: he was right. They had reached an uneasy truce these past days. It didn't mean they actually liked each other, but it was a working relationship.

'Listen, you're a celeb,' he told her. 'Let's enjoy it, for goodness' sake. The US transmission got huge ratings.' He rummaged on his desk.

'You told me,' she reminded him. 'Is that huge? You never know with North America.'

She had been summoned to see him that afternoon to talk about her next project. WGBH, it appeared, were so pleased with *Ireland's Dirty Linen*, which had just gone out in the prestigious *Frontline* strand on PBS, that they were keen for her to make another documentary on an Irish theme. Jeremy had suggested an observational film about exorcist priests. Perdita had other ideas: she arrived with a list, none of them anywhere near Ireland.

'Perdita,' his brow furrowed. 'They're terrific, some of these. But where are the pictures in...'—his eye ran down the list—'phone hacking?'

She promised to go and think of ideas with pictures, got up to leave and was halfway to the door when he said, 'Hang on a sec. I almost forgot this.' He rummaged in his desk drawer for a moment and brought out a bulky box. 'Present from the Network Centre,' he told her, holding it out rather awkwardly. 'Services rendered and all that. Office thought it was time we dragged you into the twentieth century.'

Perdita took the box gingerly, glancing down at the picture on its shiny surface. It was a neat bluebottle-coloured Nokia mobile phone.

'And write that date in your diary,' Jeremy instructed. 'Tuesday: six o'clock. I don't trust you. I shall send a car.'

*

Perdita gazed around at the other guests, speculating as to who they might be. She wondered whether Daniel would have been invited had he been alive. No. No public reinstatement for *him*. She wondered whether the secret services were present. Did they go to parties? So often when a film went out it fell into the ether, respectfully reviewed in a couple of broadsheets and then respectfully forgotten. She was so accustomed to this that the response to *Dirty Linen* had come as a total surprise. Even here, people were proffering congratulations when she reluctantly explained who she was; success on the back of other people's tragedy. *Not my own work at all*, Perdita wanted to say. She felt a complete fraud.

'I wouldn't have had the guts,' Clive Blakemore's wife told her.

Perdita remembered Sarah Blakemore's performance on television after Hugh's article first appeared. 'Oh yes you would,' she said. 'You sailed through the ordeal with your husband. I couldn't have done that.'

The minister's wife shrugged. She looked older than she had on the TV news. 'Oh, that. You just have to get on with that. That's being a political wife. I believed in him. I needed to be there... but to film that smuggling operation: you must have taken such a risk!' She shuddered.

'It's only television,' Perdita said. 'I didn't have to do it.

You had no choice.'

'It was a horrible few months,' Sarah admitted. 'But now Clive's in the clear, he's determined to nail them. Secretary of State has been brilliant throughout—as you can imagine. She's incandescent about the whole thing; calling for an ISC inquiry. I think they'll get one. Well—' She pulled a face. 'It won't be public, of course—that particular committee is all secret. But they do report directly to the Prime Minister, and there's a PMQ lined up that will hopefully force it into the public domain.'

This was interesting. 'I hope the inquiry will cover the civil servant who was framed,' Perdita said.

Mrs Blakemore nodded. 'Oh yes, it must. That poor man! Clive only vaguely remembered him, you know; wasn't even sure which one of the gay rights group he actually was. Their so-called affair—the whole thing—was invented. That's why it's so outrageous.'

Daniel denied, then. Or was Sarah simply speaking to her as a lawyer to a journalist? Who knew what really went on in the private lives of public figures? Whichever it was, some secrets didn't need to be told.

But others must be.

'...Clive was so upset about that,' Mrs Blakemore was saying. 'They must have literally driven the poor fellow to suicide.'

'Not suicide,' said Perdita quickly. 'They shot him.'

The minister's wife recoiled. '*Shot* him?' She frowned. 'No, no, you're wrong about that. He drove his car off the road, poor chap. They had to hoick it off the side of a mountain. We were told by... by—Oh, well, by someone who would definitely have known. In fact,' she broke off for a moment, 'I could swear Clive saw the inquest report. I'm certain he did.'

'It was murder, Mrs Blakemore. I was there.'

Sarah Blakemore looked at her, aghast. 'By terrorists, then? Are—are you sure? Why didn't they tell…?'

'You might call them terrorists,' Perdita said. 'Depends on your point of view. But if there's an inquiry, the Committee needs to hear from an eye witness; it sounds as if they're getting into a muddle.'

'We're talking about the civil servant at the MOD who was leaking documents?'

'We are. And if your husband's angry now, he'll be even angrier when he hears what really happened.' Perdita gave her a bright smile. It wouldn't do to sound like a mad person. This was a party, after all.

'Oh… Oh. And you were actually with him? There was no mistake?'

'The killer called out Daniel's name before he shot him. He had an English accent. Daniel died in my arms.'

Sarah blinked at her for a moment, then she recollected herself and glanced urgently around the room. 'You must tell Clive this yourself,' she said briskly. 'Where's he got to?' She took Perdita's arm and guided her past a pillar. 'Oh bother. He's over there with the Irish Ambassador! They particularly needed to speak. I can't interrupt them.'

Perdita handed her a business card. 'Please give him this later, then. It's so important. I'm the only person who really knows what happened. I need to appear before that committee, if I'm allowed to—or do they only take evidence from their own?'

Mrs Blakemore took the card and scrutinised it as if she suddenly doubted everything in her world. She gave Perdita the direct line to her husband's office. 'I'll tell him not to let them fob you off,' she promised.

Perdita was about to move away when Sarah said, 'My goodness, weren't you there when Ian Frazer was shot, too?'

Perdita attempted to smile. 'You make me sound like the angel of death! But yes, I believe that one *was* a—a terrorist shooting.'

'It must have been petrifying!'

'It was,' Perdita admitted. 'I was lucky to get out alive.'

'We met Mr Frazer, you know,' Sarah Blakemore told her. 'People are extraordinary, aren't they, the way they can lead double lives? I'd never have had him down as an arms smuggler. He was charming. Perfectly charming.'

'Yes,' Perdita agreed. 'He was.'

*

Quite apart from the horror she herself had suffered on that terrible night in Belfast, Frazer's death continued to obsess her. The Irish pronunciation of her name played through her head: the whispering voice she had taken for McGrail, must have been Frazer. Armed and apparently on the point of firing, Frazer had himself been gunned down in front of her. She had read everything about it she could lay hands on, but the reports were infuriatingly short on detail. Who was the second killer in her room that night? She knew, because she had been told, that the commotion she dimly recalled at the door before losing consciousness must have been not help arriving but the killer's departure. So how was he or she able to vanish into thin air unseen by the night porter at the desk downstairs? For the first few nightmare hours, the prime suspect for Frazer's murder had been Perdita herself, but ballistics experts and scene of crime officers had ruled her out almost immediately for reasons she was too stunned to question. She told the police of her suspicions that someone had been sleeping next door (was that Frazer, she wondered, awaiting his moment?) but the records showed no booking had been made for the room; it had been empty all week. Cleaning staff testified the bed was unslept in, a fact Perdita knew to be untrue: on Friday night someone had unquestionably moved in. The officers shook their heads and told her she must have dreamt it.

As time passed and she had to acknowledge that Frazer had come to her room that night to kill her, the assumption followed that he had been lying about his innocence, lying about Special Branch monitoring the smuggling operation. So, what of his theory about McGrail working for the British? She had abandoned the notion that she would ever get to the bottom of that, although it certainly would explain the origin of Daniel's second document. Whatever the truth, she'd been forced to accept that McGrail had manipulated her almost from their first meeting, a fact of which she felt deeply ashamed. But faced with the allegation that he had betrayed his cause, she still found it hard to believe. She recalled the reverence in the eyes of his fellow republicans after the quiz. How would they, and his comrade Francie, have reacted had they known? It still made chilling sense to her that his wife, Caítlin, had realised and sacrificed herself. Small wonder McGrail's eyes filled with tears at her memory. Well, it was pointless to speculate. No one would ever tell her. Their night and day in the Mourne mountains haunted her. His parting words, 'This was real', perplexed her. And, earlier, 'I will try never to lie to you, but sometimes I can't answer the question.'

*

Banishing the unwelcome refrain from her thoughts, Perdita went in search of a new drink and suddenly found herself standing beside her former husband. Hugh had not spoken to her since her return from Ireland—and, since the UK transmission, she could understand why. Immediately following the death of Ian Frazer, his had been the most fulsome of the obituaries to appear in the British and Irish press. The Irish, in particular, had pulled their punches, but *The Sunday Times* piece had been such a eulogy that the evidence of his duplicity in Perdita's film, transmitted shortly afterwards, had made Hugh look a complete idiot. She wondered at his being here now; she couldn't imagine him best friends with the Blakemores. But Hugh was a senior political writer. Hugh must be invited everywhere. That was journalism. That was politics. He would support Blakemore in future, all right.

'I would have phoned that Saturday,' he said, sloshing red wine into her glass as though they were already in the middle of a conversation. 'But you never gave me the number.'

'I called you right through the evening. Why did you leave your phone off?'

'I was probably driving. And your number didn't come up.'

'Daisy had it.'

'I took Daisy to that little pub out beyond Holmfirth, actually. Very pretty it was, too. I had a chap to go and see in Manchester, so we stayed over till the Monday. We had a lovely weekend.'

Perdita already knew this from Daisy, of course. She threw him a sardonic look. He must be feeling guilty. 'That's good,' she said.

'Anyway,' he went on, 'obviously by Sunday the danger had passed.'

Perdita shrugged dismissively. She didn't want to talk about *that*.

But Hugh did. 'Of course,' he pointed out. 'You couldn't have used a foot of that material if Frazer hadn't been bumped off, could you?'

Good old Hugh. Ever quick to undermine a chum's success. She grinned at him mischievously. 'You make it sound as if I arranged his assassination.'

He took a large swallow of wine, regarding her over the glass as if to say that was precisely his meaning. 'Jolly useful, all the same. You must have been over the moon when it happened.'

'Not exactly,' she said.

*

...Every detail of Frazer's death and its aftermath had continued to reel through her head. The story was still breaking on the Monday when the RUC allowed her to fly back to London and she made the edgy transition from traumatised witness and suspect to TV viewer. Blakemore, newly exonerated, had been interviewed on Channel 4 News, his voice modulated to tragedy. 'Mr Frazer's shocking death is a blow to all those who worked for prosperity and equal opportunities in Northern Ireland.' Blakemore can't have known the truth when he said that, Perdita decided. Could he? 'This callous terrorist act must not be permitted to blight the progress that can at last be made towards peace...' he had continued. Progress indeed. With Lithgow gone and Frazer himself gone, with Blakemore back in office, the path was becoming clearer every day. The last message on Perdita's machine on the night she got back to London had been from Jeremy.

'Call me as soon as you get home! This changes everything.'

Perdita had felt a sense of panic. She left it until the following morning. 'Jeremy, we can't alter it. The online's booked for Thursday.'

'Cancel it. I've been speaking to the execs. We'll have to delay transmission anyway: a decent interval after the death. We have time to re-cut.'

'You said WGBH liked it as it was!'

'They'll like it even better when we lift the lid on loyalist hypocrisy. Boston: heartland of the Irish in exile? This will be a big story for them.'

Desperately, Perdita hoped the ITV executives would find some compliance issue with the film, withhold permission to transmit the secret footage and take it back to that bland corporate for the linen industry they had been so keen to commission in the first place. She even contemplated going to see her old ally Nick and telling him exactly what had happened, but when she tried to think through what had happened, she wasn't sure. And Nick himself had been no help when he, Jeremy and the lawyer viewed the re-cut film a week later.

'As you know, Perdita, you can't libel the dead,' Walter Cusp told her at the end of the viewing. 'You may not think that's fair, but it's the law. Were Frazer to be alive, I couldn't advise you that the material is without risk. But he's not alive.' He shrugged. 'The interview you got with him on that last day links him to the arms shipment. As long as it wasn't an operation set up by the RUC, as he claimed, you're in the clear. Wait for your official statement from them. Send me a transcript of what they say. If it's okay, and you get the go-ahead from upstairs, you're free to use what you like.'

This was her last chance to tell them there and then about McGrail. What would they all have said if she'd admitted she'd fallen, in every sense, for the republican line? Or was it a British intelligence line? The fact was, she didn't know, so she said nothing.

When they got up to leave the edit suite, Nick grumbled, 'Trust you to turn it into a political tale, huh? Should have known!' He gave her a hug. 'Nice work, kid.'

Within two days, the RUC confirmed there had been no operation: they had not been working with Ian Frazer. To allow for viewing tapes, trailers, publicity, *Ireland's Dirty Linen* was scheduled for broadcast four weeks later.

Frequently when a film went out, the production team would congregate in somebody's house to watch it on transmission, just a couple of bottles of wine and a cheery debrief. Not this time. She had watched the UK transmission through her fingers, hunched up on the sofa alone, barely able to look at the screen. Whose propaganda it was she had no idea, but she had sent it out into the world and was mortified. Yet was it propaganda, since it was actually true? The following day, and the day after the film was broadcast in Ireland on RTÉ, she prepared herself for the phone call, the scornful email denouncing her. It had never arrived.

*

Perdita and Hugh passed to safer subjects and discussed Daisy, who was getting high marks in her course work. It was amazing, Perdita thought to herself, how men like Hugh always bounced back. He seemed as unabashed as ever; perhaps he had even lost a little weight around his chins.

They were joined by a man in slightly short grey flannel trousers. 'Thought I might run into you here, Hugh,' he said.

'Vernon,' Hugh greeted him. Perdita thought she detected an air of caution. 'Perdita, may I introduce Vernon Potts? Vernon, this is Perdita Burn.'

Perdita smiled at him, thinking to herself that Vernon would never know how close he had come to having his cover blown, whatever that was.

*

'Who's this chap?' asked Cusp, reaching over to freeze the frame on Vernon's face.

'His day job is press officer for the MOD,' she had said.

Jeremy's eyebrows shot up. 'How d'you know that?'

'He was a colleague of Daniel's,' she told them. 'I met

him briefly. But on this occasion he seems to be working for someone else. Frazer? MI5, would you say?'

'You don't know that.'

'You're right. I'm guessing.'

'Never mind who he is: do we have a release form?' asked Cusp.

'Hardly,' Perdita murmured.

'You'll have to lose him then,' Cusp decreed. 'He's too heavily featured, and the shots are incriminating, obviously. You'd have to blur him, at the very least.'

In the end, it was easier to remove Vernon from the film.

*

Perdita wondered now if Vernon Potts recognised her from their brief encounter on the stairs outside Daniel's flat. She realised he must at least have known who she was: there was no flicker of surprise as they shook hands and he said, 'Oh yes. That film... Hugh—' He turned away from her abruptly. 'I got the report you were after. It's pretty interesting, as a matter of fact.'

'Vernon's my mole in Whitehall,' Hugh informed Perdita.

Potts explained with a small frown, 'All perfectly legit., you understand. I'm a press officer. Just moved to the Northern Ireland Office.'

She looked at him, weighing the risks. What the hell? It was all over now. 'We've met before, haven't we?' she said.

There was a second's hesitation before he acknowledged, 'Daniel Booth's flat, yes. The man you claimed not to know.' The words came out with an undisguised sneer.

'Oh, I never said that,' she told him. 'We had met. That was why the allegation appeared to hold water.'

'You must feel bad about his death.' Potts was watching her closely. 'Poor fellow. It really got to him. He was in a terrible way by the end. Didn't think of himself as a traitor, you see.'

'Well, he wasn't a traitor, was he?' Perdita said quietly.

'I saw him at the MCTC, the place where he was being held, as a matter of fact,' Potts went on.

Perdita and Hugh exchanged glances. Hugh was furious. 'How d'you manage that?' he asked. 'They wouldn't let me near him.'

Potts shrugged. 'Well, I was an old colleague. An old friend. I think they could see what sort of state he was getting into and realised he needed a bit of contact with the outside world.'

This was curious. 'When I saw him,' Perdita said, 'he complained that they wouldn't let his friends visit. He had plenty of close friends, you know.' She didn't care if this sounded rude.

If he caught the snub, Vernon ignored it. 'They sent him to hospital before he went home. Psychiatric wing,' he added pointedly. 'I could tell which way it was going. Poor Daniel. I must confess, it came as no surprise when he took his own life—though God only knows what he was up to in Northern Ireland.'

Perdita was about to put him straight on the suicide, as she had the minister's wife, when McGrail's words flashed into her head: 'They will probably say it was suicide… it will have been arranged.' It occurred to her Vernon had quite possibly arranged it. So she said nothing.

Hugh had lost interest in Daniel. 'Vernon,' he said. 'Tell me about this report.'

'Well,' Potts began, apparently glad to change the subject. 'It's quite intriguing...'

Perdita began to move away. 'Don't go.' Hugh detained her with a hand on her arm. 'You were there, after all. It's about how your friend Frazer came to a sticky end.'

Perdita recoiled from the adjective, but she turned to Vernon eagerly. How unlike Hugh to share some information with her, voluntarily. She wondered why he was interested.

'...Whoever shot him had keys to the hotel,' Vernon was saying. 'Manager says he personally bolted and double-locked the service door before going off duty at nine. Still double-locked after the murder, but unbolted. Killer must've let himself out. Got clean away.'

'What about the night porter?' Perdita asked. He must have been given a hard time.'

'Worked there thirty years,' Potts said. 'Also, he's an Orange Lodge member. Lives in Sandy Row. Hardly likely to have it in for Frazer.'

'Well, someone let Frazer in. He had no business to be there, any more than the murderer.'

'That's what they concluded,' Potts agreed. 'Porter denied it, of course.'

Hugh asked, 'Any clues from the body about who shot him?'

Vernon shrugged. 'Whoever did it, knew what he was up to. One shot.' He put a finger, childlike, to his temple. 'Right up close. No prints on the gun.'

'I didn't even know there was a struggle,' Perdita heard herself say. 'For a few hours they thought it could be me. I started to wonder if they were right.'

'Nah,' Vernon said. 'Professional job. Blood hit you in all the wrong places, anyway.'

'Was that it?' Perdita's voice was not quite steady.

'Maybe it was suicide?' Hugh suggested hurriedly.

'Forensics ruled that out. Angle of entry.'

Perdita had to support herself with a hand on the edge of the drinks table. 'How did the killer know Frazer was going to be at the hotel?' she asked. 'None of his staff could have known, could they? He'd apparently come to kill me, after all!'

'They arrested one of his typists, a young girl. SDLP family, but her sister's a terrorist.'

'Sinéad Brennan?' Perdita said. 'Oh God, she wasn't implicated, was she?'

'They held her overnight but they could get nothing out of her.' Vernon grunted. 'Frazer's only got himself to blame, silly bugger. That's what you get for practising equal opportunities with a bunch of Micks.'

Perdita put down her glass. It was time to go. She turned to Vernon. 'Well, we'll never know who shot him, will we?' she said coldly. 'But whoever it was, saved my life.'

She was about to say more, but he broke in, 'That's where you're wrong. Of course they know.'

Perdita and Hugh stared at him.

'You media lot are all the same,' Vernon rushed on. 'You all congratulate yourselves that you're the ones who uncover the facts. I tell you, there are people who get extremely pissed-off with it.'

Hugh's eyes narrowed. 'What people?' he asked.

Perdita had a pretty good idea.

'They'd been on to Frazer for months,' Vernon said. 'They knew the whole bloody lot. Far more than was in your film.'

'The British *knew* Frazer was involved with terrorism?' Perdita felt a surge of relief.

'The Brits. Special Branch. That's what I mean. We never get the credit.'

She wondered if 'we' was a slip of the tongue. 'They might have got some credit if they weren't so damn secretive,' she argued. 'All I had from the RUC was denials.'

'Maybe you weren't asking the right questions,' Hugh said, with a return to his usual venom.

Perdita ignored him. She was staring intently at Vernon. 'Are you saying the *British* killed Frazer?' She thought of Vernon at the quayside. Maybe the boat was a sting—a sting to catch Frazer.

'Of course not!' Vernon glared at Perdita contemptuously. Then his face broke unexpectedly into a grin. 'Who needs the Brits to do it when the Micks'll do it for them?'

'Everyone assumed it was the Provos,' Hugh agreed.

But that wasn't quite Vernon's meaning. Perdita couldn't believe what he was telling them. He must be drunk. 'Is this what you call a... joint initiative?' she asked tentatively.

For a split second, Vernon said nothing. Then he turned to Hugh. 'Wait, this is the best part. The killer must have been a Paddy. Frazer was shot with his own weapon!'

The floor started to revolve under Perdita's feet.

'Killer forgot his?' Hugh crowed. 'I mean, thick or *what?*'

'Only in Ireland, I tell you!'

Hugh and Vernon dissolved into brays of laughter. When they had recovered, Perdita said to Vernon, 'I'll tell you what Daniel Booth was doing in Northern Ireland. He had received a third document, you see, another death threat. It had my name on it. He had come to warn me. *That's* the story you should be writing, Hugh.'

She watched the effect of her words. The smirk had dropped off Vernon's face. He regarded her, cold-eyed. With a smile at them both she walked away, across the room, out into the arched hallway with its hanging loops of telexes from the Press Association. The machines were silent now; everyone had left the office. She retrieved her jacket from the rack and stepped through the cool lobby into the dusk outside. The smell of early mowing from St James's Park mingled with exhaust fumes in the first promise of summer. It might just come out all right, she told herself through her tears. Thanks to that creep Vernon Potts she might even get over it, in the end. As a bid to clear Daniel's name it had been feeble, but she needed to keep her testimony safe for the inquiry. Although the mysterious Intelligence and Security Committee sat in secret, its members were elected MPs; her words would be placed on the record and sooner or later the truth would get out. She wondered wryly whether some idealistic civil servant might even leak it…

Besides, she had retained her own small pieces of evidence: the original copy of the first document predicting the Keady bombing; the second, forecasting Lithgow's death, which she and Michael had retrieved from the Guide to Wiltshire, second edition, in Daniel's flat. (She smiled to herself: Vernon Potts and his mates would have an interesting time explaining that one.) And the third, the memo with her name on it found in Daniel's pocket after he died, still in the incriminating envelope addressed to him by name at home. It was the third document that conclusively proved the trap had been personal. From her conversation with Blakemore's wife just now, she was suddenly thankful McGrail had steered her away from the police that night: had she handed the memo to them as evidence, it would surely have vanished.

As she walked away through the mild evening, she turned over what else she had just learnt. McGrail had evidently heard every word of their interview at the mill. He had understood what she had not: that Frazer would come for her. While she had gone looking for him at Sinn Féin, it must have been McGrail who had been waiting for Frazer all along, inches from her hotel bed. She had no illusions. He would probably have been acting on orders. But his safest course would have been to kill her as well as Frazer. He had had the perfect opportunity and had chosen to save her life. And he had restored other things to her, of course. First, by shooting Frazer he had given her the means to broadcast her film—the film he had set her up to make; a publicity coup for the peace process to be seen throughout the US, UK and Ireland. But it was the second thing that mattered most to Perdita: that he trusted her with the knowledge of his double life, if he had one; his own deadly secret, he knew she would never tell.

By the time she reached home, she felt a dawning calm. Perhaps she would be able to move ahead now, put some of this behind her. Already, within a few days of the transmission, things had started slipping back into place. She had lost the sense of being watched and even the sinister telephone calls from her own answer-machine had finally petered out. As she passed the mail boxes in the lobby, she trailed her hand, from habit, over the front of her pigeonhole and felt the sharp edge of a postcard. It must have arrived in the second delivery. She took it absently upstairs, unlocked the flat door and flung off her jacket. A small sandy cat hurtled down the hallway and cast itself at her feet in greeting. Perdita scooped Lalibela into her arms, speaking to her softly, and carried her into the study to listen to her messages; the comforting ritual of a life not quite alone.

It was only later, after supper and the TV news, she caught sight of the postcard lying forgotten on the hall table. Just her name and address—she had never given him that—in stylish handwriting. There was no message, of course, because there was nothing to say. She felt her heart beating as she made out the postmark: *Cleveland, Ohio. Visit The Great Lakes.* He must have seen the *Frontline* version, just ten days ago. Jeremy's co-production had its uses. Perdita steeled herself to light a candle and carry card and candle carefully to the sink, where she held one to the other. But as it started to burn, she realised it was not a postcard of the Great Lakes he had sent her. She turned it over. Curling and fading, it was a picture of the Mountains of Mourne.

GLOSSARY

An Garda Síochána — Ireland's national police and security service.

An Phoblacht — Republican News, the Sinn Féin newspaper.

AP — Assistant producer.

Craic — 20th century Irish, adapted from Scots 'crack': 'a good time'.

DoP — Director of Photography (cameraman).

DTI — Department of Trade and Industry (UK government).

Green Cross — Funds provided by a republican charity, the Green Cross, to enable families to visit convicted IRA prisoners in British jails.

ISC — The House of Commons Intelligence and Security Committee.

L.T. — Loose talk [republican abbreviation].

MCTC — Military Corrective Training Centre, Colchester, Essex.

MI5 — The British Security Service.

MI6/SIS — Secret Intelligence Service, the British overseas intelligence service.

MOD — Ministry of Defence (British government).

NIO — Northern Ireland Office (of the British government).

OSA — Official Secrets Act.

PBS — Public Broadcasting Service (US).

PMQs — Prime Minister's Questions (House of Commons).

PQs — Parliamentary Questions (House of Commons).

Provo — Member of the Provisional IRA.

RSPB — The Royal Society for the Protection of Birds.

RTÉ — Raidió Teilifís Éireann, Irish public service broadcaster.

RUC — Royal Ulster Constabulary, the name of the Northern Irish police force, until it changed to the Police Service of Northern Ireland (PSNI) in 2001.

SDLP — Social Democratic and Labour Party, a social-democratic Irish nationalist political party in Northern Ireland.

Sinn Féin — An Irish republican and democratic socialist political party, active across the North and the Republic of Ireland.

Sticky (n) — Member of the Official IRA.

TA — Territorial Army: a UK volunteer force to provide a reserve of trained military personnel for emergencies.

Tiocfaidh ár lá — Republican motto: 'Our Day Will Come.'

WGBH — Major US public TV and radio network based in Boston. (Literally, Western Great Blue Hill, after its transmitter.)

Young Militants — Title given to the youth wing of the Ulster Defence Association (made illegal, 1992).

ACKNOWLEDGEMENTS

There are several books on the Irish Troubles which I have found invaluable for the background and context of this book—in particular, *Who Framed Colin Wallace* by Paul Foot (Macmillan, 1989) and *The Kincora Scandal,* by Chris Moore (Marino Books, 1996). However, my story is entirely a work of fiction and its characters bear no resemblance to anyone living or dead.

I'm very grateful to Christy Moore, Dónal Lunny and Silverstream Music for permission to quote from Dónal and Christy's song, *Time Has Come.* A big thank you to all the friends, relations and members of the notMorley writing group who kindly read earlier drafts and gave me helpful comments; and particularly to Eric Lane, my editor; Barbara Mitchell for her careful re-reading; and Pat and John Gray for putting up with my questions and correcting my blunders in the geography and idiom of the North. Any surviving blunders are my own.

Recommended Reading

If you have enjoyed *Border Lines* you should read Ros Franey's first novel *Cry Baby*.

If you like novels about The Troubles and the sectarian strife in Northern Ireland you should read the novels of Pat Gray:

The Political Map of the Heart
Dirty Old Tricks
The Redemption Cut

If you like novels set in Ireland by Irish authors you should read the three novels by Eoghan Smith:

The Failing Heart
A Provincial Death
A Mind of Winter

and

Jabberwock by Dara Kavanagh
Le Fanu's Angel by Brian Keogh

and the short story collection:

Take Six: Six Irish Women Writers edited by Tanya Farrelly

If you like thrillers which are very different and with an edge about them, read:

The Mysteries of Algiers by Robert Irwin
God's Dog by Diego Marani
Naples Noir: La Strada degli Americani by Giuseppe Miale di Mauro

For further information about Dedalus' titles please visit our website
www.dedalusbooks.com
or email info@dedalusbooks.com for a catalogue.

Dirty Old Tricks by Pat Gray

A chilling noir novel set in the Belfast of the Troubles in which Pat Gray introduces us to the flawed but dogged and honourable policeman McCann.

'Belfast in 1975 provides a gloomy backdrop for this murder mystery, which opens with RUC officer Michael McCann lying awake, half-expecting to be kidnapped and killed, setting the tone for the discovery of fifteen-year-old Protestant schoolgirl Elizabeth McCabe, murdered and dumped in a Catholic area. It's a grim enough crime as it is, but the constant presence of armoured cars and automatic weapons adds a further layer of bleakness to the oppressive mood. Even the routine business of door-to-door enquiries becomes a military operation with the potential to escalate into violence. McCann has to consider the possibility that the paramilitaries have sunk low enough to sanction tit-for-tat schoolgirl murders, and it's "not easy to detect clues, in a hard country where men never cried". Creepily compelling, Gray's fourth novel probes deeply into darkness, weaving an atmosphere of tension and distrust that permeates every part of McCann's investigation, including his relationships with colleagues. It's masterfully done, but chilling and hard-hitting stuff.'

Alastair Mabbott in *The Herald*

£9.99 ISBN 978 1 912868 26 1 270p B. Format

The Redemption Cut by Pat Gray

Belfast, 1976. The city is rife with rackets. Paramilitary gangs, the British Army, Police and Intelligence struggle for control. Will McCann be able to redeem himself by solving the case that haunts him? Will those above him allow him to do so? Pat Gray's second Inspector McCann mystery goes to the heart of the moral darkness that was Ulster's troubles. It is a worthy sequel to *Dirty Old Tricks*.

'Gray tells a very enjoyable story and shows up the entrenched attitudes, the bad behaviour on all sides (you go climbing up on the moral high ground because there's none of that left says one criminal to McCann and, when asked, "Aren't people meant to be innocent until proven guilty?" he responds, "Not here they're not." It's safer to assume everyone is up to something till you've proof of the opposite.) Fortunately, McCann has more or less been proved wrong.'

John Alvey in The Modern Novel

£9.99 ISBN 978 1 912868 66 7 260p B. Format

The Political Map of the Heart by Pat Gray

A tale of doomed love, set against the backdrop of Ireland's Troubles. Brutally pessimistic and agonisingly romantic, Pat Gray's novel recaptures the spirit of a lost Ireland. It follows the fortunes of an English family, stranded in the apparent backwater of Ulster at the end of the Second World War. Bernard, the flawed and eccentric father, who was injured in the war, Eileen his wife, and their three children, are all torn apart as the troubles engulf them.

'Absolutely wonderful! There's a strange tension about it, almost like a melodrama. Beautiful, the way it links the history of Ireland with the troubles in the family. I loved it.'

Lynn Barber in *The Sunday Times*

'This convincing and evocative novel may lack the terrors of involvement and love across the sectarian divide, none the less, it explores the universal confusions and complexities of adolescence from an original perspective.'

C. L. Dallat in *The Times Literary Supplement*

'Pat's teenage romance with the lovely Elaine is tenderly related, their innocent relationship at odds with violence around them. With understated compassion, Gray shows a family torn apart and a love tainted by political divisions. His novel is blissfully free of sentimentality and endless rain that plagues so much Irish fiction.'

Lisa Allardice in *The Independent on Sunday*

£7.99   ISBN 978 1 873982 54 9   196p   B. Format

The Failing Heart by Eoghan Smith

'Brilliant! Dark and atmospheric. It's a compulsive account of how it feels to be tortured and mired in anxiety.'

Sue Leonard in *The Irish Examiner*

'Reading *The Failing Heart* is like taking a trip; part escape into another consciousness, part suffocating delusion. The story — or rather the scaffolding upon which Smith displays elegant philosophical architecture — follows a young scholar whose mother has just died. Estranged from his father after stealing his money, hounded by the ominous figure of his landlord, and oppressed with images of his ex-lover's impending labour, he wanders into an existential purgatory. "All these open mouths, living or dead, they never shut up." Death is everywhere, through the needs and revulsions of the body, its smells, secretions, drives. The narrative circles in on itself in an ever-decreasing gyre, examining ancient and modern ideas about existence, subjecting philosophical scholarship itself to a sardonic inquiry using its own tools of scrutiny. The writing is self-aware and wry, with rare flashes of humour amid a claustrophobic search for meaning and desire to confess. Time expands and contracts; it is unclear what is real, what is internalised: at the end of this brief novel there is the sensation of having witnessed the dark dream of a stranger.' *The Irish Times*

'I was exhausted after each chapter, drained and spent but I devoured every single word of this truly exquisite debut.'

Dymphna Nugent in *The Waterford Star & News*

£9.99   ISBN 978 1 910213 91 9   152p   B. Format